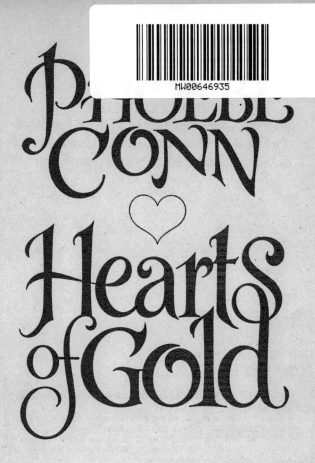

PHOEBE CONN

♡

Hearts of Gold

POPULAR LIBRARY

An Imprint of Warner Books, Inc.

A Warner Communications Company

DEDICATION

Hearts of Gold is dedicated to WLB, the founder of the Lady B Bar B Land and Cattle Company in grateful acknowledgment of his invaluable contribution.

Popular Library® and the fanciful P design are registered trademarks of Warner Books, Inc.

Cover illustration by Don Case

Popular Library books are published by
Warner Books, Inc.
666 Fifth Avenue
New York, N.Y. 10103

 A Warner Communications Company

Printed in the United States of America

First Printing: October, 1988

10 9 8 7 6 5 4 3 2 1

HEARTS OF GOLD

Is it no more than chance
    that drew us together?

Is it no more than shared danger
    that makes us close?

Is it no more than passion
    that binds our hearts?

Or is it our destiny,
    my dear friend, and love?

I

March 1849

Lyse raised her delicate hand to shield her eyes from the harsh rays of the morning sun and swore in disgust at the buzzards circling slowly overhead. The slender girl despised the winged ghouls. Their vile passion for carrion turned her stomach, and as she moved about her father's ranch doing her morning chores she did her best to ignore the sickening images their presence called to mind.

Unmindful of the young woman's scorn, the birds gradually tightened their pattern and began a graceful descent. They had a tasty meal in sight and as the sun rose higher in the sky the gnawing hunger in their bellies drove them lower still. It was not yet time to sloop down and light upon the carcass, but it would be soon. Soon! they called to one another with excited cries. Soon!

As long as the buzzards were in the sky, Lyse knew their prey still clung to life with a tenacity she had to admire. While their stock was all accounted for, as the morning wore on she found herself plagued with uncomfortable feelings of guilt for growing up on an isolated ranch; animals were the only friends she had ever had. She hated to think some poor creature would soon provide the heartless scavengers' noon meal. Finally, she could no longer bear the thought of the buzzards' razor-sharp beaks and wicked talons ripping the flesh from the bones of some skinny old burro or other wretched animal mere seconds after it had drawn its last breath. She so detested the evil birds that in a sudden burst of inspiration she decided she had nothing better to do that morning than to deprive them of a meal.

Before taking any action on that plan, the lithe blonde cast an apprehensive glance over her shoulder at the house. Her father had gotten drunk again last night. Lyse knew he would call her a damn fool, if not far worse, for caring about the fate of the buzzards' hapless prey when she had more work to do than she could ever finish. Since he would be unlikely to leave his bed before noon, she would just keep her rescue mission, like all her private thoughts, to herself. She helped herself to her father's rifle, then saddled one of the mares. Taking along a shovel to bury whatever beast she found if it could not be saved, she rode in the direction the birds' lazy, circular path of flight clearly marked.

The day was a warm one for early spring and sweat had dampened her faded cotton blouse and begun to trickle down her back by the time she reached the top of the rise to the west of their house. She wiped her sweating palms on her coarse woolen pants, disgusted with herself for forgetting her gloves. From this vantage point she could see what the birds were after and since the horse was still on its feet, she was glad she had made the effort to save him. She spurred her mount and swiftly crossed the low-lying plain to reach him. It wasn't until after she had leapt from her mare's back that she saw the buzzards, while undoubtedly eyeing the chestnut horse, were after a man lying a few yards away. The right shoulder of his shirt was stained with the blood that had seeped into the dirt beneath him and if he weren't already dead, she knew he soon would be.

Frightened by her grisly discovery, Lyse again scanned the barren terrain with an anxious glance. She then felt very foolish for being scared, for if the man who had fired the shot had wanted to make certain his victim was dead, he had had plenty of time to do so before she arrived on the scene. Though it was always wise to be alert for danger, the still-ness of the prairie was unbroken except for the cry of the buzzards that had grown louder as they saw a prime source of food clearly threatened. Picking up a rock, Lyse hurled it into the air. It sailed across the sky but was too low to strike any of the bloodthirsty birds. They scattered only momentarily before again taking up their slow, swirling death watch.

Lyse sighed unhappily as she gathered her courage and approached the wounded stranger. Rescuing a lame burro was one thing, coming to a young man's aid quite another. Men meant only one thing to her: trouble and lots of it. Even if this man were dead, he still meant the worst kind of trouble. He was too well built for her to be able to lift him across his horse's back, so she would have to go home and get the buckboard to take his body into town. He might be wanted, so she might get a reward but it probably wouldn't be very much or the man who had shot him would have claimed it. Most likely, he was just some drifter who had insulted one man too many and she would be stuck paying for his burial. That kind of charity was something she could ill afford.

"Mister?" she called to him as she prodded his hip with the scuffed toe of her worn boot. "If you're dead, I'll bury you right here. You'd be too damn much trouble to cart into town and trouble is the one thing I don't need more of."

The man lay sprawled facedown in the new spring grass that had only just begun to sprout and he made no response to Lyse's informal funeral plans. Flies buzzed around his head and lit upon his bloody shirt, as eager as the buzzards for a taste of him.

"Señor?" Lyse tried this time, for the man had black hair and the beginnings of a black beard and she thought he might be Mexican. Still, there was not even a moan in reply. Disappointed, she walked back to her mare and pulled her canteen off the saddle horn. After taking a long swallow of the cool spring water it contained, she took the time to wipe her chin with a careless swipe before walking back and kneeling at the stranger's side.

"Nice hat," she complimented sincerely as she set the broad-brimmed black hat aside. She took a moment to observe the rest of the wounded man's clothing and found him surprisingly well dressed for a near corpse. Scolding herself that his attire was of no consequence for the moment, she felt for a pulse in his throat. When she found a faint but steady beat, she shook her head sadly.

"I might have beat the buzzards to you, but I'll be damned if I know what to do with you now." Before she could withdraw her hand, the man suddenly came to life. He grabbed her wrist with his left hand and with a savage lunge tried to pull himself up into a sitting position. All he succeeded in doing, however, was knocking Lyse off balance. The water from her open canteen splashed in his face before the battered container struck him a sharp blow on the chin. When with a mournful cry he released her, Lyse scrambled to her feet and backed away.

Her heart still pounding with the awful fright he'd just given her, she screwed the cap back on the canteen and slung the worn strap over her shoulder. She waited to see what the injured man's next move would be but he did no more than remain flat on his back where he had fallen. Not wanting a repeat of that scare, she dashed back to her mare for the rifle. When she approached his side this time, she was far more cautious.

"You're trespassing on my land," she threatened convincingly. "I'll give you to the count of ten to get up and go, or I'll step aside and let the buzzards pick your bones clean. Take your choice, but hurry up about it. I'm too busy to spend much time out here chatting with you."

Buck Warren managed to open one badly bloodshot eye. Blinded by the sun, he could make out only the slender silhouette of what he mistook for a reed-thin boy. "At least help me get into the shade where I can die in peace," he responded in an insolent drawl.

The stranger wore a Colt revolver strapped to his left hip. Not wanting to take any more chances with him, Lyse waited for him to again close his eyes, then she walked around him slowly, reached down, and yanked the pearl-handled gun from his holster. It was difficult to judge his height with him lying at her feet, but he looked quite tall. He might be six feet two, or three, she judged silently, and easily close to two hundred pounds. "There's no way I could lift you," she declared sullenly. "You'll have to die where you lay."

An eerie sense that he was no longer alone had awakened Buck from his pain-racked dreams, but he had hoped anyone passing by would prove friendly and he was badly disappointed that wasn't the case. "Look," he offered in a voice so hoarse with thirst it resembled a croak. "I've got money to pay for your help."

With a perverse sense of delight, Lyse found she was actually enjoying tormenting the injured man. "That so? Then all I have to do is finish you off and take it."

"Please—" was all Buck could manage to gasp before he passed out. He had been reaching out to Lyse and his hand fell limply across the toe of her right boot. The gold ring on his little finger was crusted with blood but clearly worth whatever it would cost her to tend him.

"Oh, if this don't beat all," Lyse swore under her breath. She looked up, half expecting to see the buzzards diving for her but they had flown no lower. She was ashamed of herself for taunting the man because clearly he was in a bad way. The ride into town in the back of the buckboard would probably kill him, she thought angrily, knowing she had no way to dump him on the doctor's doorstep.

"As if I didn't have enough to do," she complained bitterly. She knew there was no point in even trying to move the man because she couldn't lift her pa when he had passed out and this fellow was a bigger man than him.

If he wanted to die in the shade, she would have to bring it to him, and convinced he lacked the strength to spring for her again, she placed both her rifle and his revolver several feet away. She then gathered the scrub brush that grew nearby and fashioned a crude lean-to. That chore swiftly completed, she brushed off her hands and turned her attentions to the dark-haired stranger. This time expecting the worst from him, she drew her knife from her belt before kneeling at his side. When he gave no sign of being aware of her presence she cut away the bloody portion of his shirt so she could take a look at his wound.

Finding the bullet had drilled a neat hole clear through his right shoulder just below the collarbone, she sat back on her heels to consider her next move. The stranger had been shot in the back by a cowardly assailant who had left him for dead. What manner of man was he to deserve that? Because she could now see his face, which was pale even under his deep tan, she studied his features closely, thinking if evil showed in men's faces, it didn't in his.

She wondered if women found him handsome. After a moment's reflection she decided they probably did. He appeared to be in his late twenties. His brows were as black as his hair, his lashes long and thick with a slight upward curl. His nose was straight and not too wide. His upper lip had the inviting curved shape of a bow while the lower had an insolent fullness. There was a slight dimple in his chin that might have looked boyish in some men, but even while he was unconscious his jaw held a determined tilt that dispelled all hint of youthful weakness.

"You're a pretty one, all right," Lyse mused thoughtfully, thinking a handsome stranger the worst kind. Though he was dark, from the familiar sound of his accent she could tell he was an American rather than a Mexican. Not that his nationality would have mattered to her. Her family had lived in Texas long enough to have been Mexican citizens themselves at one time.

Staring at the unconscious man wasn't getting either of them anywhere, Lyse's conscience informed her. She had no experience treating gunshot wounds, but since his appeared to have stopped bleeding of its own accord, or perhaps simply because he was nearly out of blood, she thought she could get by with just bandaging his shoulder tightly for the moment. For that chore she would need some clean fabric.

The chestnut gelding shied away as she approached him, but Lyse spoke to him in so soothing a voice he was soon standing quietly while she searched through the stranger's saddlebags for something to use for bandages. Finding a clean white cotton shirt, she slit the hem with her knife, then ripped the back into strips. When she returned to her patient's side, she knelt down and cut away the rest of his stained shirt. As a precaution, she left the knife close at hand as she began to bandage the gruesome wound. Though it would pain her to stab a man already half-dead, she vowed to do it before she would allow herself to come to any harm at his hands.

The injured man's broad chest was covered with a thick mat of coarse black curls, but Lyse wasted no more time admiring his looks. He moaned when she had to lift him slightly to secure the bandage with a long strip that encircled his chest. Alarmed, Lyse drew back for a moment because she didn't like having to come so close to him even though he was in desperate need of her help. When he remained quiet, she tied the ends of the final strip in a firm knot at the center of his chest. Hoping she had the wound so tightly bound he would not start bleeding again, she dampened the clean sleeve of his discarded shirt and wiped the man's face lightly. "Mister?" she coaxed. "Can you wake up for a minute? We need to decide what do to with you."

Buck was slow to respond, but finally the cool water Lyse dripped upon his face brought him around and he managed to open his eyes. They were a rich, warm brown, but their golden flecks were dulled by pain as he tried to speak. "You didn't leave me," he whispered in a hoarse rasp. He tried to smile but was only partly successful, and that effort was totally wasted on Lyse. When she offered him a drink from her canteen he gulped it down so eagerly she finally had to pull it away.

"Hey, not so much. There's no reason for you to get all excited about my being here," Lyse warned him as she lay the canteen out of his reach. "You're still in a heap of trouble."

Buck tried to sit up, but the agonizing pain that shot through his shoulder instantly changed his mind. Lyse had bandaged him so securely he could barely draw a breath, which only added to his discomfort. "Damn!" he swore angrily. "Help me get up. I've got to get to Galveston."

Not about to let a stranger order her about the way her pa did, Lyse ignored his demand. "Well mister, unless you expect a miracle, you aren't going to get there any time soon." She picked up his hat and waved it above him slowly to discourage the flies from the smell of his blood, and gradually the annoying insects flew away.

"I'd be lucky to get you back to my house without opening up that wound again and I don't think you can spare any more blood. Since my pa is even less charitable to strangers than I am, you're probably better off here than trying to reach the house anyway."

Buck still could not see Lyse's face clearly because her hat was pulled down low to shade her face. The battered sombrero also completely covered the wild mop of blond hair that would have given away her sex. He saw only a skinny kid, who though reluctant, seemed to be the only source of help he had. He felt sick to his stomach but stubbornly resisted the wave of nausea that threatened to wash over him. He hated being so helpless; it was the worst feeling he had ever known but he would not let sickness compound his wretchedness. "I'm afraid you're right," he admitted grudgingly. "Besides, the fewer people I meet the better." He then began to vent his frustration with language so colorful Lyse blushed deeply, for not even her pa used words that foul in front of her.

"If you'll just calm down a minute and tell me why you have to get to Galveston," Lyse offered in a more kindly tone, "there might be a way for me to help you." If there was some money in it for her, she didn't add, but she didn't run errands for anybody for free.

Buck laughed out loud at the thought of turning over to a skinny kid the job he had set out to do. When his deep laugh erupted into a hacking cough, Lyse had to lift him into a sitting position and give him another drink from her canteen to help him catch his breath. That frightened her as much as him. "I thought that shot was too high to have pierced your lung. Maybe I was wrong."

"You're a right cheerful son of a bitch, aren't you?" Buck closed his eyes again as he tried to take a breath deep enough to clear his head. "There's no way you can help me with what I have to do but go and unsaddle my horse. I can prop myself up on my saddle. That ought to help me some."

His words were spoken as a command, not a request, and though Lyse instantly rebelled, she didn't want to spend the day holding him in her arms and eased him back down flat on his back. "There, you all right?" Though she thought him ungrateful, if not downright rude, she was beginning to feel a sense of responsibility for the poor soul and though that annoyed her, she couldn't overcome it.

"Yeah, I'll live another few minutes. Now get me my saddle."

"Yes, sir," Lyse responded flippantly. "Can I get you anything else while I'm up?"

Buck risked opening one eye to look up at the kid. He would have laughed at that question had he not been afraid of the consequences. "Yeah, my saddlebags. I've got some food in them," he answered instead.

Lyse walked off without replying. She unsaddled the horse and because there was a branch of the Oyster Creek nearby, she led him to it to drink while she filled the stranger's canteen. When she took the horse back to the patch of newly sprouted grass where he had been grazing, the well-mannered gelding stood quietly as she bent down and tied his forelegs together with the leather hobbles she had found in the saddlebags. He was a fine animal and as she removed his bridle she gave his neck an affectionate pat before moving away. She then lugged the heavy saddle back to Buck, dropped it next to his head, and made a second trip to carry the leather pouches and bedroll that had been slung over the horse's rump. She unrolled the blanket, then knelt down and helped Buck shift himself into a position where he could recline comfortably against the saddle then stood up and moved away. She was too smart a girl to stay close to any man for long, even a badly injured one.

"My pa would skin me alive if he found me out here with you, so I hope you're not too weak to stay by yourself. I've got to go home now, but I'll come back later and check on you. Here's your canteen. I'll fill it for you again when I come back. Try to drink all the water you can." As she picked up her rifle, she handed him back his Colt but if he wondered why she had put it aside he didn't ask.

Buck nodded. With food and water handy, he was confident he would survive the day. "Do me another favor, kid. If your dad doesn't like strangers, don't tell him about me. Is that a deal? You help me for a couple of days until I get back on my feet, and I'll make it worth your while."

Lyse frowned pensively; she needed money desperately, but taking it for helping a half-dead man just wasn't right. "You in trouble with the law?" she finally had the presence of mind to ask.

"Not yet," Buck assured her, his words meant as a joke.

He was disappointed, however, that his youthful companion did not understand them.

"Well look. I've got to go," Lyse insisted more for her own benefit than his. "I'll come back around sundown."

"Hey, what's your name, kid?" Buck called out as she started walking away.

"Lyse," she tossed over her shoulder before mounting her mare.

Misunderstanding, Buck attempted a feeble wave. "So long, Lee, see you later."

Lyse hesitated a moment, wondering if she ought to correct him, but she just shrugged her shoulders and let it go because it didn't matter what the man called her. He would be up and gone by the end of the week and she would be unlikely to see him again. She returned his wave and fearing she had been gone too long, she hurried home at a full gallop, but her father had already been out looking for her. He swung open the door to greet her.

"Just where in the devil have you been, missy?" he shouted in a hoarse challenge. "You expect me to go hungry while you wander off daydreaming all day?"

Disappointed to find him in so black a mood, although she knew she should have anticipated it, Lyse slipped by him and entered the house. "I'll have dinner ready in a minute, Pa. All I have to do is heat it up."

"That takes wood, don't it?" he reminded her sarcastically. "I don't recall hearing you chopping none this morning."

"There's wood, Pa," Lyse assured him. She had already filled the stove that morning and in only a moment she had the fire lit and the iron kettle of chicken soup simmering. There was leftover cornbread and she warmed that and carried it over to the scarred wooden table her father had made before she had been born.

Frank Selby eyed his daughter suspiciously as she removed her hat and shook out her hair. The fair tresses were uncombed and tumbled down her back in wild disarray but their pale yellow sheen reminded him too much of her mother. "How many times do I have to tell you to wear a scarf when you cook? You think I like fishing your hair out of my soup?" he scolded crossly. "You spend more time with the horses than minding the house and it sure as hell looks it. Didn't your ma teach you nothing before she run off?"

"Let's leave Ma out of this," Lyse pleaded under her breath, knowing only too well what was coming. Predictably, her father's anger erupted with full force.

"Women!" he spit out the word with clear contempt. "Ain't a one of you worth more than five minutes of a man's time."

Lyse blushed as she placed their bowls of steaming soup on the table because she knew exactly what her father expected a woman to do for him in that five minutes. She sat down and concentrated upon eating the flavorful soup while her father continued to complain about the inadequacies of women in general and his scatterbrained daughter in particular. Occasionally she would steal a glance at him and wonder why her mother had married such a mean-spirited man. It was no wonder he spent so much of his time drinking, for he was so nasty an individual he had few friends.

She saved every penny she could from what he gave her to buy staples for the kitchen but he was so miserly she hadn't accumulated nearly enough to strike out on her own. That was her dream. Her mother had been a beautiful woman who had left with the help of an adoring lover, but she had only to look in the mirror to know she would never be popular with men. If only her mother had loved her enough to take her along, Lyse mused wistfully. How could she have left her there with the man whose foul temper and constant complaints had driven her away? Maybe her pa was right: Women were no damn good, but Lyse sure wasn't impressed with the male sex either.

Buck had been alone for no more than five minutes when he got sick to his stomach. He could barely lean over to retch but somehow he managed to accomplish it. He lay back then, so weak he doubted he could make it until his newfound friend returned. He had thought his mission a simple one: to find Arvin Corbett and put an end to the spineless weasel's miserable life. The problem was, he had been chasing the bastard ever since the day Arvin's jealousy had cost five good men their lives. One of them had been David Bailey, the best friend Buck could ever hope to have and he had vowed to make Arvin pay dearly for that. A court-martial at the close of the Mexican War would have been too good for the filthy swine but Arvin had deserted before charges could be brought against him. Now Buck wanted him dead. He considered meting out that punishment his responsibility since Arvin had set out to get him killed rather than David and the others.

"Lying bastard," he muttered to himself, using his hatred to gather the strength he would need to survive. "I'm going to kill that rotten son of a bitch if it's the last thing I ever do." As he felt the nausea welling up in his throat again, he had the fleeting thought he just might die without ever making good on that vow. Arvin would have killed six of them then, and he wasn't about to let the smooth-talking snake get away with that.

Lyse paid scant attention as her father rambled on about her laziness. Hell, she cursed silently, he did so little she was the one running the ranch. She wasn't a bit lazy either. She just didn't wait on him hand and foot the way he mistakenly thought she should; that was what created all their problems. He wanted to be treated like a king, though he sure didn't treat her like a princess.

"I have to go into town. What kind of thread was it you said you needed, black or white?"

"Both," Lyse replied, hoping he would remember at least one. "Some extra buttons too, please."

Frank stretched as he rose to his feet. "I might be home late, but I expect supper to be ready when I get here all the same."

"Yes, Pa." Lyse tried to smile as she looked up at him, but it was difficult. Her father was slight of build, his features pinched as tight as his purse strings. His unruly thatch of light brown hair always hung down in his pale blue eyes because he seldom stopped at the barbershop to have it cut. He wore his clothes until they fell apart in the wash, then he blamed her for not doing the laundry right. All in all, he was a miserable excuse for a man and Lyse relished the peace and quiet she would enjoy while he was gone.

This wasn't the day her father usually went into town, but after he had left she found his last bottle of whiskey empty and knew why he had been in such a rush to go. She could remember her mother's fights with him about his drinking and for a while after she had left home he had been sober. It had been for a few months at least, but that restraint had come too late and hadn't lasted long. He had slipped back into his old habits: neglecting the ranch and drinking himself into a stupor nearly every night. Had she liked the man she might have felt sorry for him, but she had never seen anything in his character to admire.

Because her father's absence would provide her with the best chance to sneak back to check on the wounded man, Lyse hurriedly washed their dishes and gathered up what food she could spare to take along. She chose another horse this time, a bay gelding she sometimes rode, and made even better time than she had that morning. The buzzards were gone. She hoped they had had to fly a long way away to find a dead creature for their ghoulish feast, but as she walked toward the stranger she wondered if the birds wouldn't soon be back.

"Mister," she called to him in a frightened whisper. "You all right?"

The sound of Lyse's voice woke him, and Buck turned her way. He was too exhausted to wave or smile, but he was overjoyed to see her again. He had lapsed in and out of consciousness worrying the father might be the one to come back in Lee's place. In Buck's pitiful condition, he knew he couldn't even lift his Colt, let alone aim and fire it. Someone could come, steal everything he had, including his horse, and leave him for dead. "Hey Lee," he replied weakly, far more glad to see her than he wanted her to know.

Lyse had brought the rifle again, just in case he had more energy than she thought, but clearly he couldn't do her any harm so she left it in the scabbard on her saddle. She refilled his canteen, then stood uneasily by his side. "I brought you a couple of slices of ham, and some cornbread. I'm sorry, but it's all I can spare."

Buck nodded, then remained motionless when he instantly became dizzy. "Thanks. I figure if I'm not dead yet, I'll make it."

Lyse had to lean closer to hear him as he mumbled something about relieving himself. When she realized he expected her to help him, she blushed deeply. "I don't think you ought to try and stand up," she cautioned him nervously.

"I'd rather try that than wet my pants," Buck replied impatiently. "Come on, give me a hand."

Lyse looked around, trying to find an alternative, but the two geldings simply stared at her and she couldn't think how to use their strength rather than hers to hoist the injured man to his feet. "I don't even know your name," she blurted out in a breathless rush.

"I'm William Warren, but my friends call me Buck. Right now you're the best friend I've got, Lee."

When he held out his left hand, Lyse laid the neatly wrapped package of food beside his saddle and walked around him. She couldn't recall ever being so badly embarrassed. She knew she wasn't a pretty woman, but she didn't understand why Buck was treating her so casually. Since she was the only person there, however, what choice did he have? Reluctantly, she took his hand, but continued to hold back.

"I don't think I'm strong enough to pull you up. Maybe if I get behind you and push I could do it, though," she suggested helpfully.

"I don't care how we do this, Lee, but we have to do it now!" Buck let fly with another string of colorful curses as he waited for her to rearrange the brush lean-to and step behind him. "I shouldn't have drunk all that water but I hoped it would keep my temperature down."

"You have a fever?" Alarmed, Lyse leaned down to touch his forehead, but he wasn't overly warm. "You're fine," she assured him. With the saddle in the way, she had difficulty reaching him and it took considerable maneuvering to bring him into a sitting position so she could step between him and the cumbersome saddle.

Kneeling on one knee, she slipped her right arm around his waist to get a firm hold on him, then encouraged him to help her all he could. "You just try to stand up as you normally do, and I'll give you a push. That ought to work."

"Yeah, let's give it a try." Gritting his teeth, Buck attempted to move with his usual grace but he was so dizzy and weak he staggered rather than rose to his feet. With Lyse's help, after several false starts he managed to haul himself upright, but he didn't think he could stay that way long. Swaying slightly, he grabbed her arm and pulled her around by his side where he could lean on her for support. "Come with me," he ordered gruffly. "Let's try to make it to the bushes over there. That looks like a good place for a privy, doesn't it?"

"Perfect," Lyse agreed, although she was near collapse herself from the burden of his weight. She wrapped both arms around his slim waist and managed to propel him where he wished to go, but his next order mortified her completely.

"Dammit, Lee, I can't get my belt undone or my pants unbuttoned with one hand. You'll have to do it and be quick about it!" Buck shouted in her ear.

Lyse knew she would never, ever be more embarrassed than she was by that demand, but once she had removed his gun belt and unbuttoned his fly, Buck waved her aside. Hoping he would think she was merely respecting his privacy rather than filled with shame, Lyse stepped behind him and took hold of his waist to make certain he didn't fall. Whenever she felt him begin to tilt one way or the other she would shove him to the opposite side and she managed to keep him on a fairly even keel until he finished.

"Just fasten my belt and get me back to my saddle," Buck ordered faintly. "You can button up my pants after I lie down."

"Good plan," Lyse instantly agreed, wanting to end her ordeal as swiftly as possible. He turned to wrap his left arm around her shoulder and did his best to walk back to the spot where he had been resting. Unfortunately, his best wasn't quite good enough. They were within one step of the saddle when his knees buckled, and unable to hold him upright, Lyse fell to the ground with him. Her old hat flew from her head and they ended up in a tangled heap of arms, legs, and long, silky blond hair.

With the wind knocked out of him, Buck lay groaning in the dirt, certain the fall had killed him and he was just too stubborn to die. When he realized Lyse was trying to yank the ends of her waist-length hair out from under his left shoulder he was so shocked he started to shriek. "Jesus Christ! Why didn't you tell me you were a girl!" He was now more embarrassed than she had been.

That the man hadn't known she was female appalled Lyse all the more. When she finally got it free, she flipped her hair out of her eyes and sitting back on her heels she stared at Buck as though he were some sort of loathsome bug. "Just what did you think I was?" she asked accusingly.

Buck lay where he had fallen, mesmerized by the angry sparks that had turned his companion's bright sapphire blue eyes to a menacing purple. She was quite slender, and her features so delicate her remarkably expressive eyes appeared enormous. There was no way to describe her but as a disheveled mess, and yet she was easily the most beautiful woman he had ever seen.

"Forgive me," he began apologetically, "but I never saw you clearly. The sun was too bright, and with your hat, I—" He gave up then as she rose to her feet and walked away. She swung herself up into her saddle and without a backward glance rode away, leaving him feeling even more wretchedly alone than he had the first time she had gone away.

II

March 1849

*F*or the second time that day, Buck found himself face-down in the dirt. It was not a circumstance he enjoyed either. Physically, he had never felt worse and it was infuriating to be unable to think of any way to get himself feeling better fast enough to catch up with Arvin. He had been within an hour of overtaking the double-crossing coward when he had been shot. How that good-for-nothing skunk had managed to circle around and get behind him he didn't know, but it wasn't something he would let happen again.

His only comfort was the knowledge that Arvin must surely believe him dead. The bastard would go about his business in Galveston never dreaming Buck Warren was still on his trail. He had already begun to grow a beard, and he wasn't above dressing any way he had to to disguise his identity. He had changed horses once and he would do it again so Arvin would not recognize him by his mount. He had plenty of plans for carrying out his mission, but unfortunately, he could implement none of them while he was too weak to stand.

Plotting Arvin's demise was a fascinating activity, and it helped to pass the time while Buck recovered from the lingering effects of his fall. Luckily, he had landed on his left side, rather than his right, so he had not reopened his wound. When he finally felt strong enough to crawl, he had only one good arm to help him and it took all the determination he could summon to cover the few feet that separated him from his saddle. It then took him more than fifteen minutes to turn over on his back and get comfortable. When he saw his gun belt where Lyse had dropped it he groaned loudly, for it lay just out of his reach. Since he couldn't afford to lie there both helpless and unarmed, he had to work himself over to it, and drag it back with him when he returned to his saddle.

Exhausted, he eyed the package Lyse had brought and wondered if he could keep down enough food to gain some strength. Deciding he had nothing to lose, he unwrapped the small parcel with shaking hands. When the first few crumbs of cornbread didn't immediately bring on another bout of retching, he chanced taking a larger bite. To his amazement, it was the finest piece of cornbread he had ever had the pleasure of eating: light, but moist and filled with flavor. As he alternated bits of the delightfully sweet cornbread with tiny bites of ham he wondered if Lee had baked it herself.

"She sure is a strange one," he mumbled between bites. Why any woman who went around dressed like a boy would be insulted when she was mistaken for one he couldn't understand. As the savory ham and remarkably flavorful cornbread worked their magic on his stomach, Buck's mood grew more mellow and he began to wonder if perhaps Lee had no choice about her garb. Neither of his sisters would have been caught dead in her getup, but maybe the girl's family was so poor they had no money to spend on her clothes.

He hadn't gotten a really good look at her until just before she had left, but then he had noted her frayed sombrero, old clothes, and well-worn boots. She had been a sorry sight he had mistaken for a carelessly dressed boy. Now he knew she was probably a girl who had been made to work like a boy all her life. That brought a real twinge of regret, for he would never have knowingly hurt her feelings and clearly he had or she would not have run off without saying good-bye. When he got well enough to ride, he decided to try to find her house. It had to be fairly close and as he saw things, she had saved his life even if she hadn't been all that gracious about it. He chuckled, then winced, angry with himself for forgetting how badly it hurt to laugh.

Not wanting to eat so much he would make himself sick, Buck set aside the remainder of the ham and cornbread for later. Cutting across the prairie to make better time than Arvin, rather than staying on the road, had seemed like a good idea at the time. Now he knew he had been extremely foolish. It was his own damn fault he was stuck out in the middle of nowhere too weak to ride, and he would just have to make the best of it until he felt well enough to be on his way. He grabbed his hat, plunked it down over his eyes, and went to sleep thinking if he did have the good fortune to wake up, he could not possibly be in any worse straits than he was already.

Lyse was far too proud to cry over a stranger's mistaken impression of her. What did his opinion matter anyway? she asked herself repeatedly. It took a bit of effort to become totally indifferent to the young man, but by the time she had arrived home, she had shut out all thought of Buck Warren. She finished the rest of her chores, then brought in the old wooden bathtub and placed it by the stove. It leaked badly, but she ignored the mess it made and always mopped the floor afterward without complaint, thinking the ancient tub merely saved her the trouble of lugging water twice.

It was impossible to soak for long in a tub that so closely resembled a sieve, so she bathed and hurriedly washed her hair. Since Lyse was fond of horses, she didn't mind smelling like them by the end of the day, but she never went to bed still reeking of the odor of the barnyard. Her father often accused her of wasting water, but she ignored his complaints and had more than once pointed out he could use a bath far more often than he bothered to take one. Such insolence usually got her a painful slap across the face at the very least, but she didn't care. Just because her father chose to live like a pig didn't mean she had to live that way too.

Wrapped in a thin towel, Lyse mopped up the mess left by the tub, then went to her room to see what clean clothes she had. She had been too small to wear the few dresses her mother had left behind, but that hadn't mattered because her father had burned them along with every last stitch of feminine apparel left in the house. He had even taken the ribbons Lyse had worn in her hair and cast them into the fire. She didn't have a single thing that had belonged to her mother, but Lyse remembered her well.

Millicent Selby had been petite and graceful, not tall and awkward like her only daughter. Her hair had also been blond, but naturally curly rather than hopelessly straight as Lyse's was. They had just the small mirror her father used for shaving, but when she peered into it, Lyse saw only a faint resemblance to her lovely mother. She had always suspected that her mother had been ashamed of having such a homely daughter. It was no surprise she had abandoned her child at her first opportunity.

Depressed by the sadness of that thought, Lyse ceased to dwell on her mother's motives for deserting her. The woman was gone and she would never see her again. Trouble was, while Lyse had been terribly hurt at being left behind, she didn't blame her mother one bit for leaving home. No, on the contrary, she merely envied the pretty woman her escape.

Sorting through her meager wardrobe, Lyse pulled on a blouse whose bright stripes had faded to soft pastel lines, and another pair of worn pants. She didn't own a dress, or skirt, or even any feminine undergarments. She sank down on the side of her bed then, as with a sudden flash of insight she realized it probably hadn't been Buck Warren's fault he had thought her a boy. The poor man was badly hurt. Why should he have paid her any mind when he was in pain?

Lyse had been deeply insulted, but now she was overcome with remorse for not having accepted Buck's apology for his mistake. Her already downcast mood blackened. She combed out her hair with long, slow strokes and wondered if she dared go back to check on Buck the next day. After a few moments' reflection, she realized she was too curious not to pay him another visit. Men didn't get shot in the back riding across their range every day. She wanted to know exactly why he had suffered that misfortune.

When Frank Selby came home, he noticed Lyse had tied her hair at her nape with a piece of yarn and immediately grabbed for it. "No need for you to go prettying yourself up for me, missy," he remarked scornfully as he shoved the bit of blue yarn into his pocket. "Here's your thread, but the buttons cost too much."

As her hair spilled about her shoulders, Lyse brushed it aside. "Thanks for remembering the thread, but I wasn't trying to do anything but keep my hair out of my eyes. I know it would take a damn sight more than a piece of yarn to make me look pretty."

"That's the first sensible thing you've said all day. Now where's my supper?" Frank sat down at the table, opened the bottle of whiskey he had bought at the Capital Saloon, and took a long drink before he began to eye Lyse with a suspicious glance. The girl was seventeen, and he considered that a dangerous age. Her mother had been no more than seventeen herself when her father had forced him to marry her. The way Millicent always told it, she had been forced to marry him. Little slut, he mouthed silently. He was glad she was gone. "Hurry up, missy. You're so damn slow I could eat whatever you're fixing for breakfast."

"The food is already on your plate, Pa." Lyse carried their supper to the table and pretended she was dining alone where she didn't have to listen to her father's angry ramblings about the troubles she caused him.

When Buck heard the sounds of a horse approaching, he drew his Colt. He had already discovered if he propped the barrel on his thigh, he could aim it well enough to shoot with what he hoped would be something close to his usual accuracy. When he recognized Lyse, he slid the weapon back into the holster that lay at his side. He looked up at the sun, and deciding it must be past noon, greeted her warmly. "Good afternoon, Lee. I'm glad you came back. I was afraid you wouldn't."

"I'd not leave you to starve," Lyse called out as she swung down from her horse's back. She had ridden a pinto mare that day, thinking it would be wise for her to work her way through all their stock as she paid him visits. It wouldn't do for her pa to think she had gotten attached to one mount. Whenever that had happened in the past, he had scolded her for making pets of his horses, and paying no need to her protests, he had sold the animal. Convinced he didn't want her to have anything to love, she had soon learned to give her favorites treats when he wasn't watching and to show them no special treatment when he was.

"That wasn't what I meant," Buck replied crossly, hurt by her flippant response to his greeting. "I was hoping for the pleasure of your company rather than more of that delicious cornbread. If you brought some with you, though, I'll sure be happy to eat it."

Lyse walked over to him, but remained out of his reach. "You must be feeling a whole lot better if you've gotten so bored you missed me. Or was it this?" She tossed him two more neatly wrapped pieces of cornbread and ham and tried not to laugh when he had difficulty catching them.

Buck made a clumsy grab for the package but set it aside, preferring to give his attention to her. Lyse had worn her hair in a single plait that day. The end brushed her waist and as he looked up at her, he wondered if she had chosen that hairstyle to make certain he was more respectful of her from now on. "You have such beautiful hair," he complimented her sincerely. "Why did you have it hidden under your hat yesterday?"

"My hair is as straight as straw," Lyse responded defensively. "No one in his right mind would call it beautiful."

Buck raised his hand to his forehead. "Still no sign of a fever, so I can't use that as an excuse. No, I stand by what I said. You do have beautiful hair. Besides, a woman isn't supposed to argue with a man when he pays her a compliment."

"Is that a fact? Just what is she supposed to do?" Lyse inquired with scant interest because she doubted she would ever have much need of his advice.

Enjoying their game, Buck smiled, broadly displaying teeth that were a near dazzling white against his dark beard. "She says," he began in an exaggerated imitation of a feminine voice, "'Why thank you, sir.' Then if she is smart, she will pay him a compliment in return."

Lyse nodded, then dug the toe of her boot in the dirt as

she tried to come up with a compliment he would want to hear. "What if she can't think of one?" she finally asked.

"Well then, she just smiles so prettily the man won't remember if she said anything or not." Buck was surprised to find that Lyse appeared to be taking his teasing comments so seriously. Apparently she wasn't used to flirting with men or she would have recognized his remarks for the game of words they were. "Come sit down next to me, that way I won't have to look up at the sun while we talk."

Lyse looked around, making certain his camp was still safe from whomever had shot him, before she leaned down and picked up his canteen. "I'll fill this first. That ham will make you thirsty."

Buck turned his head to watch her walk away, wondering if everyone found her so difficult to get to know. Not that he would have much time to get to know her, but most women fawned all over him and she sure couldn't be accused of that. Must be the beard, he mused silently, although he had always thought he looked quite handsome when he grew one.

After Lyse had taken the horse to the creek, she returned with Buck's canteen but she was still hesitant to sit down with him. "I brought along some clean cloth to change your bandage. Are you up to trying that?"

"No," Buck refused emphatically. "Let's just leave my shoulder alone for a few more days. I don't want to start it bleeding again."

Though that sounded sensible, Lyse didn't think she had done all that good a job on her first attempt and was anxious to replace his bandage with one she hoped would be better. If he didn't want her to try, though, she wouldn't argue with him about it. "Are you feeling well enough to take care of yourself now or will you need me to, well, to help you out again like yesterday?"

Buck shook his head. "I can crawl over to the privy on my own. It took half the morning, but it gave me something to do."

Lyse was glad to hear he wouldn't need her help, and even more relieved when she noticed he had managed to button his pants on his own. "That's good. Maybe you won't be stuck here too much longer then. Was the man who shot you trying to keep you from reaching Galveston?" she inquired impulsively.

Buck looked up at her a long moment, uncertain whether or not he wanted to respond to that question. Finally he decided that because she had come to his rescue, she deserved the truth. "Sit down, Lee. Since you saved my life, I figure I owe you quite a bit, at the very least, an explanation." Not that he planned to go into much detail, but Buck wasn't ashamed to tell the tale.

Because she feared he would keep badgering her until she finally gave in and sat down, Lyse sank down by his side but she took care to remain out of his reach. Getting comfortable in a cross-legged pose, she removed her hat to use as a fan as the day was another unseasonably warm one. She looked him directly in the eye and nodded. "Well go ahead. Let's hear it. I haven't got all day."

Buck had had a long while to wonder if his first impression of her had been wrong. After all, he had lost a lot of blood and he had gotten only a fleeting glimpse of her. He had thought perhaps he had only imagined her as being pretty. Now that they were close again, he noted the astonishing length of her thick fringe of eyelashes and swallowed hard to force his thoughts into the direction he wanted them to take. Yet his glance refused to follow his brain's insistent command. He found her eyes as vivid a blue as the bluebonnets that blanketed the Texas plain each spring, and her features were precisely as delicate and well shaped as he had recalled, making any sort of concentration difficult.

"What are you gawking at?" Lyse asked abruptly, thinking she must have crumbs from breakfast stuck to her chin or something equally absurd wrong with her appearance.

"I'm sorry, I didn't mean to stare. It's just that you are far prettier than I had expected you to be, Lee. It's a surprise but a very pleasant one."

"Cut the lies, Buck," Lyse ordered gruffly. "I know I am frightfully plain. Oh yeah, one other thing. My name's Alyssa. My mother thought if she gave me a lady's name, I'd act like one, but she was wrong. Everyone calls me Lyse, not Lee. It didn't seem to matter what you called me yesterday, so I didn't bother to correct you. I guess I should have."

Buck frowned, unable to understand why so pretty a young woman would consider herself plain or talk about herself in so derogatory a manner. "You aren't serious, are you?" he finally asked.

"Of course. Lyse fits me better than Alyssa. I'm just not an Alyssa."

Buck combed his hair out of his eyes with his fingers, amazed she had difficulty understanding him. "No, I meant about being plain. You aren't in the least bit plain. How could you think that you are?"

Lyse raised her eyes toward the heavens, thinking Buck daft. "I've got hair that's straighter than string, eyes that are too big for my face, a figure you mistook for a boy's. If that's not plain, I don't know what is."

"Now just wait a minute. I'll grant that you are a mite on the slender side, but you've got hair like spun silk and eyes a man could drown in. You're a beauty, Lyse. A real beauty."

Lyse rose to her feet and started to back away. "I can see I'll never get the truth out of you, so there's no point in my hanging around. I'll bring you more cornbread tomorrow."

"You come back here!" Buck insisted loudly. "No one calls me a liar and gets away with it!"

Lyse just laughed at what she imagined was a feigned show of righteous indignation. "You're a liar, Buck Warren, and not even a good one. Adios." She laughed almost all the way home and found herself smiling again each time she recalled his description of her. "Crazy fool," she said to herself with a laugh, but when she rode out to see him the next day he certainly wasn't laughing.

Buck eyed Lyse with a cynical glance as she tossed him another portion of cornbread and ham. Each of her gifts of food had been wrapped in a sheet of the *San Felipe Telegraph and Texas Register* and though the news was old, it had provided him with something to read.

"Sit down," he commanded sharply. When she reached for his canteen instead, he had to lean over to grab the strap with his left hand, but he managed to wrench it from her hand. "That can wait. Now sit down like I told you to and listen without interrupting me if you can."

Though she barely knew Buck Warren, his caustic manner was so different from what she had seen of him before, she was reluctant to stay longer than it would take to fill his canteen. "I don't see that we've got anything to discuss," she replied from where she stood.

Buck swiftly discarded the thought of drawing his Colt on her because he didn't trust her not to overpower him and finish him off with his own gun. "Just take my word for it. We've plenty to talk about. Now sit down!"

"You've no reason to yell at me," Lyse complained as she began to back away.

With little to occupy his mind, Buck had been nursing his anger with her for twenty-four hours, and he was furious now. "Either you sit down and let me do the talking, or don't bother to come back!" he shouted in an even louder tone.

Lyse turned her back on him. She led his horse down to the creek and waited while he drank his fill. It was a pretty spot, but the beauty of the scenery didn't improve her mood. Fortunately, by the time she returned to her horse, Buck's mood had improved.

"Lyse, I'm sorry," he called out with a sheepish grin. "My shoulder hurts like hell, and I'm not used to anyone calling me a liar. Now please sit down here with me and I promise not to yell at you again."

It was her curiosity that made Lyse approach him, but as on the previous day, she dared not sit too close. "I'm all ears," she remarked rather sarcastically, but Buck pretended not to notice.

"What do you know about the Mexican War?" he asked to introduce his topic.

Lyse thought his question strange but had a ready answer. "President Polk started it as an excuse to take more land from Mexico. What else is there to know?"

Buck nodded. "There are some who say that. I was talking about the war itself, though, not its cause."

"What has the Mexican War got to do with anything?" Lyse complained with a shrug. "It ended a year ago."

"Yes, I know that," Buck countered impatiently, then he

had to pause a moment to catch his breath. He had barely enough energy to breathe, and not nearly enough to argue. Because he had made the effort to begin, he forced himself to continue. "I'm from Dallas, and when the war began, my best friend and I enlisted in the army. We were with General Winfield Scott's troops. There were five thousand of us. We landed in Vera Cruz and marched the three hundred miles to Mexico City. Santa Ana had thirteen thousand men he thought could stop us."

"As I recall, he failed," Lyse said as she picked up a rock and began to trace a lazy pattern of circles in the dirt while she hoped Buck would soon get to his point.

"You've a good memory. We routed his troops at Cerro Gordo and after that, there were only scattered guerrilla bands to worry about as we made our way to the capital."

When he fell silent, Lyse looked up, wondering why he had paused. "I knew I should have gotten that water for you first. You want a drink?"

"No, thank you." Buck tried to clench the fingers of his right hand, but his arm was too weak to provide an adequate response. The attempt at exercise, however, helped to focus his mind on something other than his memories while he spoke. "There was a man from Austin in my company who resented every order I gave. Now I think he was simply jealous that I had been made an officer while he hadn't. Arvin was constantly trying to take credit for other men's acts of bravery. Sometimes he actually got away with it, so it wasn't until later that I discovered what a craven coward he really was. One day I sent him ahead to scout for us, but he lied when he reported the way was clear. We walked right into a guerrilla ambush while Arvin was safe in the rear. I lost my best friend and four others before I could give the order to pull back.

"I would have court-martialed the snake, but he deserted before the day was out. He had wanted me dead, you see, not the others. When he saw I'd escaped harm, he knew I'd not rest until he was punished for what he'd done. When the war ended, I found it impossible to track him through Mexico, but on my way home I stopped in Austin and offered a large reward for information should Arvin Corbett ever return there. Two weeks ago I got word that he had, but by the time I reached his door he had discovered I was looking for him and had fled for Galveston. I started out after him and you know the rest."

Lyse nodded thoughtfully. "If he's on his way to Galveston, he must be planning on taking a ship. From what I hear, everyone who can get the money together is on his way to the gold fields in California. You prepared to follow him that far?"

That was a question Buck hadn't stopped to consider. "I'd hoped to stop him long before he set his foot on board a ship," he confided. "If I can't, well, then I'll go to California if need be. Or anywhere else that bastard tries to hide. I owe it to the men whose lives he sacrificed so needlessly."

Lyse looked at the wounded man with new interest and respect. His cause, as he explained it, was a just one and she couldn't fault him for it. "What you need is an accomplice," she suggested in a conspiratorial whisper. "Someone who can get information on this Arvin person without arousing his suspicions. Someone who can watch your back so he doesn't get another chance to put you in your grave."

Shocked by this suggestion, Buck regarded Lyse with a skeptically raised brow, then shook his head. "While I see this as a question of honor, there are others who might view it differently and call me a cold-blooded murderer. I can't take the chance of involving anyone else."

"You may have no choice," Lyse advised truthfully. "Until you recover your strength you're no better than a sitting duck. If Arvin is still in Galveston when you get into town, you must know he'll try to kill you before you can kill him. At least he'll have to try, won't he?"

"He'll fail," Buck insisted stubbornly. "Besides," he argued as he surveyed the barren countryside. "Where am I going to find an 'accomplice,' as you call it out here?"

Lyse tried to hide her smile but failed. She had an enchanting smile that revealed a charming dimple in each cheek. "My help won't come cheap, but I'm available."

Buck stared at the delicate blonde with mouth agape. "I got shot in the shoulder, not the head, Lyse. I know better than to drag a woman into this."

"Hell, I can pass for a boy easily enough. You know that."

"That is beside the point," Buck replied sternly. "I wouldn't involve a boy in this either. Obviously Arvin is a dangerous man and I can't risk losing any more friends. Now go fill my canteen. All this talk about revenge has made me thirsty."

"Yes, boss," Lyse replied with a giggle as she reached for the canteen. It was a crazy idea, she would readily admit that, but the money she would earn helping Buck find Arvin might be all she would need to strike out on her own. "Lord knows, pa won't miss me," she whispered to herself as she strode down to the creek.

By the time she returned to his side, Buck had realized that though absurd, her offer had a certain charm. "You mentioned your pa. Wouldn't he and your mother object to your going to Galveston with a man?"

Lyse again sat down at a respectful distance from Buck's side. "My ma left home five years ago and I've got no reason to stick around either. I've saved all the money I can the last couple of years, but I don't have nearly enough yet. Working for you would help me earn it."

Buck was amazed by that revelation, as all the young women he knew stayed home until they were married. None would blithely volunteer to track down Arvin either. "Well, where is it you plan to go?"

"I was thinking of Houston, but Galveston will do. Maybe I'll go to California if what they say about gold being so easy to find is true."

"I'm sure it isn't," Buck replied brusquely, "but women can't just go wandering from town to town, Lee. I mean Lyse," he hastened to correct himself.

"Afraid I'll get shot in the back?" the feisty blonde asked snidely.

"No!" Buck argued. "It's just that, well, a lady has to be careful of her reputation."

Lyse laughed at that warning. "Yesterday you didn't realize I was female. Now you're telling me to act like a lady?"

"Yes," Buck assured her, although he had to admit she had a point: A woman usually had to look like a lady as well as behave like one. "It wouldn't hurt you to act like a lady for a change."

Lyse sent a significant glance roving over his bare chest and the crude bandage wound around his right shoulder before she replied. "Ladies don't go out riding to see what the buzzards are after either, so I'd say you're damn lucky I'm not a lady or you'd be nothing but a pile of bones by now."

"Is that what brought you out here, buzzards?" In spite of himself, Buck shivered at the thought of being eaten by the hideous birds.

"Sure was." Lyse picked up the rock she had laid aside and again began to draw circles in the dirt. "You said yourself I saved your life and I think you owe me something, Mr. Warren. A little cash to give me a start in the world shouldn't be too much to ask."

Buck stared at the young woman, thinking she had a far more practical streak than his sisters could ever hope to have, and yet he considered what she asked hopelessly impractical. "How old are you, Lyse?"

"Seventeen," she replied proudly. "That's plenty old enough to be on my own. How old are you?"

"Twenty-eight," Buck responded with a slow smile.

"Well, maybe someday you'll learn how to take care of yourself too." Lyse rose to her feet and brushed the dust off the seat of her pants. "I'll try and bring you something different to eat when I come out tomorrow. I can't promise anything, though."

"Hey, I can take care of myself," Buck protested readily, ignoring her comment on food to focus on what he considered another blatant insult.

"Oh yeah? Then you go hunting tomorrow, and I'll come by in the afternoon for the barbecue."

With a lilting giggle she was gone, but it took Buck a long while to get over his anger at her playful teasing. He wasn't an incompetent fool, but he reluctantly had to admit he sure must look like one to her. He decided he wouldn't mind having an accomplice, but what he'd need was a man who could back him up, not a smart-mouthed girl with eyes so big and blue he couldn't wait to see her again.

March 1849

*B*uck took Lyse's teasing suggestion that he go hunting as a serious challenge. Never in all his life had he met so exasperating a female, but he would be damned if he would let her get the better of him. Though there was no way he could hunt game, he did have a fishing line in his saddlebags. Leaning against his horse, he managed to make it down to the creek. Because he had nothing better to do, he didn't care if it took him the whole day to catch a fish; he was determined to do it. When Lyse arrived that afternoon, he proudly told her where she might find the large-mouthed black bass he had caught.

"You went fishing?" the dismayed blonde exclaimed. "All by yourself?"

"More or less," Buck replied with a wide grin.

"Just what do you mean, 'more or less'?" Lyse pressed him to explain.

"I took my horse along. There's more grass growing along the streambed than there is here."

Lyse nodded, knowing the horse did need more room to graze. She had brought along some of the chicken and dumplings she had served her father at noon. Because it was one of her favorite meals, she was disappointed to find that Buck wanted to eat something else. She held the towel-wrapped bowl awkwardly as she tried to decide what to do. It had been difficult enough to sneak out of the house with hot food, but sneaking it back in would be twice as hard. Food was too precious a commodity in her home, however, to simply throw away.

Because Lyse didn't seem half so thrilled about the fish as he was, Buck wondered what was wrong. Being a perceptive man, he made an accurate guess. "It will take awhile to fry the fish over a fire. If you brought along something else for me to eat, I'll sure be happy to eat it first."

With that offer solving her problem, Lyse naturally agreed. "Sure. Here you are." Grateful the man seemed hungry, she handed him the chicken and dumplings then went down to the creek to find the bass. There were three nice ones, and she picked up the line Buck had threaded through their gills and brought them back to his campsite.

"I haven't had time to go fishing in a long time. These ought to be good."

Buck looked up as he swallowed the last bite of dumpling. "You are one hell of a good cook, Lyse. I've never had dumplings nearly so delicious as these. How do you make them so light?"

Lyse merely shrugged. Her father never paid her any compliments on the meals she served him, so she thought Buck was just trying to be polite. "They're nothing special," she argued as she began to gather up wood for a fire. "If my pa sees any smoke, we'll be the ones who end up getting cooked rather than these bass."

Buck finished the last drop of chicken gravy in the bowl, licked the spoon clean, then wrapped it and the empty bowl in the towel she had brought. After he had set them aside, he regarded her with a curious gaze. "You make the man sound like an ogre. Is it only strangers he dislikes, or everyone?"

Lyse was too busy starting the fire to respond for a moment, but when she did she spoke the truth. "That man doesn't like anyone, including himself."

"That can't make your life very pleasant," Buck mused thoughtfully, beginning to understand why Lyse was so anxious to leave home.

"It isn't," the distracted blonde assured him.

Most young women Buck knew talked excessively, and especially so when the topic was themselves. Lyse certainly didn't fall into that category, though. When she had the fish sizzling in the frying pan she had taken from his gear, he motioned for her to come close. "Come here a minute. I want to show you something."

Lyse took only one step closer. "Show me from here," she replied suspiciously.

Buck just smiled at her reluctance to join him and opened his hand to reveal a small, horned lizard. "Found me a pet. I haven't caught one of these little guys since I was a kid. You ever catch one?"

"Sure. I used to catch horny toads all the time when I was little." Lyse relaxed then, relieved to find the young man wasn't trying to lure her to his side in order to play some rude trick on her. When he held out his hand and offered her a chance to hold the small spiny creature, she came right over to him and scooped it off his palm. She rubbed the spot between the two small bumps on the lizard's head that passed for horns and laughed when it closed its eyes in apparent rapturous contentment.

"Maybe we can find him a bug or two so he won't feel left out when we eat."

"Naw," Buck argued, "let him find his own dinner." When Lyse turned away to check the fish, he took the horny toad back and set him down on his thigh. He had a plate and fork in his saddlebags, but she had to return to the creek to wash the bowl and spoon so she would have a dish for her fish. When she handed him his plate, he put the horny toad down on the dirt and watched him dash for cover on his short legs. "So long, pal," he called after him before turning his attention to his food.

The fish was as delicious as everything else Lyse had brought him. "I'm surprised a pretty girl who can cook so well as you isn't married. What's the matter with the men around here?"

That question made Lyse laugh out loud, but she still thought he was teasing her about being pretty. "I don't think there's anything wrong with the men, but the last thing I need is a husband. I told you I want to be on my own. I don't want to have to answer to any man. Lord, no," she said, and shivered in disgust.

Her hair was tied at her nape with a leather thong that day. Even though she had again worn the old hat, her pretty blond hair hung free to her waist and caught the sunlight with each turn of her head. Buck thought her both attractive and smart, but she had what he considered very peculiar ideas about being independent. He couldn't help but wonder where she had gotten them. "Your mother's gone, you said?"

"Yeah, but I don't see that that's any business of yours," Lyse replied flippantly.

Stung by that unexpected rebuke, Buck ate the remainder of his portion of the bass in silence. Lyse was a fine cook, but she was so difficult to get along with he decided the men living nearby were probably smarter than he'd thought if they left her alone. When he set his plate aside, he stretched lazily, looking forward to taking a nap. "I'm almost well enough to go, Lyse," he announced suddenly. "Maybe not tomorrow, but I bet I can leave the next day."

"So soon?" Lyse tried to ask with casual indifference. Having someone to talk with was something new for her, and though their conversations never ran smoothly she didn't want him to know how much she had looked forward to seeing him that day.

"Yes. I've already lost four days. I can't afford to waste many more."

"You can't even stand up yet, Buck. You're not wasting time. You're trying to get over being shot," she scolded, hoping he didn't consider talking with her a waste of his time. "There's no point in your catching up with Arvin while you're too weak to do anything about it."

Buck nodded, conceding that point, but he thought she was only partly correct. "I have to get to Galveston, Lyse. Once there, I can find out what Arvin's up to and take him in my own time. I'm left-handed," he pointed out with a rakish grin. "I can still shoot as well as I ever did."

"Were you ever any good?" Lyse inquired with a skeptically arched brow.

"Oh, hell yes!" Buck claimed proudly. "I'm damn good."

Lyse knew he didn't want to take her with him, but she had thought of little else since she had suggested it and tried again to persuade him to her point of view. "You could leave for Galveston in a couple of days if I went with you. Then while you rest up in a hotel room, I could look for Arvin. That makes a lot more sense than for you to go limping around the town looking for him yourself."

"I do not limp!" Buck denied crossly. They sat staring at each other for a long while, but he stubbornly refused to give in and accept her help. "I'll give you a generous reward for saving my life, Lyse, but I won't take you with me. Now don't ask me about it again. That subject is closed."

Disregarding that order despite the severity of his frown, Lyse continued. "If you're ashamed to be seen with me, don't give it another thought. I'll find a boardinghouse, so we won't be staying in the same place. I'll ask around, find out where Arvin's staying, then let you know. I can be, oh, what's the word, discreet? Yeah, I can be discreet. Besides, when I find Arvin, you'll need a second."

"A second?" Buck gasped in dismay, astonished she felt qualified to act as his.

"Sure," Lyse insisted, not understanding his question. "You plan to call Arvin out, don't you? Or did you just figure on gunning him down in the street?"

"It will be a fair fight," Buck assured her. "I'm not ashamed to be seen with you either, Lyse, although you could do with some new clothes, but I told you this is dangerous and I'll not involve you in it. I just won't do it."

Lyse got up and carried their dishes down to the creek to wash. When she came back, she picked up the towel to dry her hands as she told him good-bye. "Just think about it some. As I see it, I'm already involved up to my neck in your troubles. I ought to be the one to say whether or not I'll go to Galveston, not you."

That was really more than Buck could take sitting down, and he struggled to his feet where he was pleased to find he towered over her by nearly a foot. The last time they had been standing together he had been in too much pain to notice her size. She was tall for a woman, but he was a very tall man. "Now just you look here," he began, but she interrupted him.

"Christ almighty, look at you," Lyse exclaimed as her glance swept over him. "Just how tall are you?"

"I'm six feet four, which has nothing to do with anything!" Buck had to concentrate to remain upright, but he managed to do it.

"Oh, no, of course not. You're just so damn tall all you have to do is go out on the street for Arvin to spot you and we already know he doesn't care for fair fights. You'll have to take me with you, Buck. You've got no choice at all."

As she turned away, Buck reached out to catch her arm, then he had to grab her in a frantic clutch to keep from falling. Nearly crushed in his arms, Lyse struggled to get free until she realized they would both land in the dirt again if she didn't hold still. Her face pressed firmly against his bare chest, she broke into wild peals of laughter. "You plan to hug Arvin to death, Buck?"

As she looked up at him her hat fell from her head and he could see her face clearly. A light tan graced her flawless complexion and her dimples were so charming Buck couldn't recall why they were arguing. Lyse was a very pretty girl, despite having an obnoxious streak a mile wide, and without a second thought he bent his head and kissed her soundly.

Whether it was that impulsive gesture in itself, or the remarkable softness of his lips that stunned her, Lyse would never know. Rather than enjoying Buck's affectionate kiss, however, she was terrified by it. The instant he began to draw away she fled his arms. She paused only long enough to pick up her bowl and spoon before running for her horse, her heart pounding in her ears as the same sudden wave of panic she had experienced when she had found him swept through her. For the first time in years the one place she wanted to be was home, and she couldn't wait to get there.

Buck swayed slightly, but he remained upright as he watched Lyse and her horse fade to no more than a faint blur in the distance. What a hellion she was, but in the instant their lips had touched he had felt a heady current of excitement that had left him craving more. He laughed then, certain she had never been kissed before, but he promised himself it wouldn't be the last time it happened. He wouldn't take her to Galveston, but that didn't mean he wouldn't stop by to see her on his way back home.

Lyse spent one of the most miserable nights of her life, tossing and turning, as she tried to decide what she should do about Buck Warren. She even debated the wisdom of letting him go on his way without telling him good-bye because trying to convince him to take her to Galveston had been no easier than talking to a brick wall. It seemed unlikely she could change his mind when he was so anxious to leave, so what was the point in going out to see him again? Now that he could get down to the creek on his own and fish, he didn't need her help any longer to survive. She didn't want him thinking she was hanging around just to collect the money he had offered her either.

As for his kiss, that had only complicated the issue unnecessarily. She knew women could get whatever they wanted from men if they paid for it with their flesh, but that was one thing she would never do. It wasn't simply a matter of pride either. She wanted to be free, and having a man dependent upon her kisses, if not hungry for far more, wasn't any kind of freedom that she could see. She punched her pillow down repeatedly with punishing blows, but it was nearly dawn before she finally fell asleep and she had answered none of the perplexing questions that were troubling her.

When Lyse awakened late, she didn't feel rested but she had to scramble out of bed and hurry to make up for lost time as she began her chores. As she worked to clean out the stalls in the barn she forced all thought of Buck Warren from her mind, but her head soon began to ache with that effort. Before he had come into her life, leaving home had been merely a dream. That he might make it come true sooner than she had had any right to hope had forced her to admit how desperately she wanted to go. Damn it all! she swore silently. She wanted to leave for Galveston when he did, so why did he have to be so dead set against it?

The day had dawned warm and clear, but by ten o'clock the sky had begun to fill with the ominous black clouds that meant a norther was on its way. Knowing the cold, sharp wind driving the clouds across the sky would soon bring torrential rains, Lyse found herself presented with still another dilemma, for she feared Buck would be unable to reach higher ground on his own. The concern for his safety now paramount, she set aside her complaints about his stubbornness. She made certain the horses were all safe, then headed out over the plain to see what she could do for Buck. Because she had no time to waste, she had saddled the stallion. Her father's pride and joy, the big red horse responded readily to the lightness of her touch and carried her with an effortless ease that rivaled the chill north wind for speed.

Buck had recognized the signs of the coming storm as readily as Lyse. Knowing he was too close to the creek should flash flooding occur, he had gathered up his belongings. When he tried to saddle his horse, however, he had found he just couldn't do it. He could lift the heavy saddle in his left hand, but then he couldn't swing it up into place without falling over backward. He didn't need to suffer that indignity more than once to know he would have to ride his mount bareback and leave the saddle behind. Finding a place to stand proved to be his next problem when he found he couldn't draw himself up on the horse's back with one hand either.

Thoroughly frustrated, his mood as black as the menacing clouds drawing near, he saw a rider approaching and drew his Colt. He hoped it would again prove to be Lyse rather than someone who would cause him more grief than he already had. The horse fooled him at first, for unlike the others she had ridden this beast was huge. He came flying across the plain, his hooves echoing with the deep rumble of thunder, and when Buck could at last make out the rider he realized that not only could Lyse cook like an angel, but also she could ride like the devil himself. When she drew the stallion to a shuddering halt and leapt from his back, Buck twirled his Colt as he replaced it in his holster, his mood suddenly remarkably good.

"How much you want for that horse?" he asked immediately.

"Thor is my pa's horse and he isn't for sale," Lyse replied breathlessly as she saw he was already making preparations to leave. "We've no time to waste. I'll saddle your horse, but do you think you can ride?"

"That all depends on how far I have to go," Buck responded with a ready grin. "Are you taking me home to meet your pa?"

"Good heavens, no!" Lyse declared as she went over to his chestnut gelding. She smoothed out the saddle blanket, then hoisted Buck's saddle up on the horse's back and hastily fastened the cinch. She tied the bedroll on the back, then slid his saddlebags into place. "There, let's see if we can get you out of here."

Buck tried not to look too clumsy as he swung himself up into the saddle, but he was grateful Lyse had been standing close should he need a helpful boost. "Just where is it you're taking me then?" he asked as he took a firm grip upon his mount's reins.

"It isn't far. There's an old house that's been abandoned for as long as I can remember. I used to go there sometimes to think. It isn't much, but at least you won't get washed away in the storm there." She looked around to make certain he had left nothing behind, then ran to Thor. "You just follow me."

Lyse set what she hoped would be a comfortable pace, but Buck soon called out to her. She drew Thor to a halt and waited for him to catch up with her. "What's wrong?" she asked the moment he reached her side, for he was so pale she was afraid he was about to faint. He was wearing his hat, but still had no shirt on, and he looked thoroughly forlorn.

"I can't make it, Lyse. It hurts too much to ride."

"I sure can't leave you here, Buck. There's too much chance this land will all be flooded. Do you think you could stand to ride double with me? That way you could lean on me and I think it would help. It isn't much farther, really it isn't."

"I'm no coward," Buck insisted, "but—"

"But nothing. If you're hurting bad, you shouldn't be ashamed to admit it." Lyse slid down from Thor's back, then helped Buck dismount. She managed to get him up on Thor's back but not without wearing herself out in the process. By the time she mounted the stallion, she was again out of breath and certain she would never beat the storm home.

"Your horse will follow us. Just hang on to me as tightly as you can," she ordered as she nudged Thor's flanks with her heels, but Buck wrapped himself around her waist with so desperate a clutch she could scarcely breathe. If that weren't bad enough, rather than clinging to her waist, his left hand kept wandering upward until he was firmly cupping her right breast. Had the need for speed not been vital, she would have shoved him from Thor's back and made him walk. Since she dared not do that, she tried simply to ignore the warmth of his touch through her worn blouse until the abandoned adobe house came into view. She then laced her fingers in his and forced his hand down to a more respectful resting place.

Buck had been telling the truth. The rocking motion of his horse had jostled him so badly he had been in awful pain, but once seated behind Lyse, he found that anguish subsiding to the point where he could focus his attention upon her. His thumb had first brushed the smooth swell of her breast quite by accident. She was so slender a young woman he had not expected her to be well endowed. Her ill-fitting shirts certainly didn't indicate much in the way of womanly curves, so he had been downright amazed to find that she had them. He had no excuse for what he had done after he had made that delightful discovery other than the fact it was far more pleasant to think about how pretty she was rather than how badly his shoulder and arm ached. When Lyse took his hand and pulled it away, however, he knew he was in for it.

Rather than assist Buck so he could dismount easily, when they reached the house Lyse walked off and left him to fend for himself. The door had long ago fallen from its hinges, and the sod roof had fallen in at the back of the small, square building, but for the most part it would provide a safe place to wait out the storm. She searched the interior to make certain no snakes had taken up residence there, then went back outside.

"There's a shed round back where your horse will be out

of the rain." She unsaddled the gelding and heaved the heavy saddle, bedroll, and saddlebags through the open doorway. "Go on and make yourself at home," she called out to Buck. "Sorry, but I can't stay for tea."

Buck thought he was getting off surprisingly light considering the liberties he had taken on the ride, but he couldn't help noticing Lyse's deep blush. Hoping she was too embarrassed to scold him for being so forward, he ducked his head and entered the deserted dwelling. He pulled his saddle well inside, but he hoped he wouldn't be stuck there for long because he preferred the open prairie to such cramped living quarters. When Lyse came back to the door, she waved then turned away. "Hey! Come back here!" Buck called out after her.

"Yes, what is it?" Lyse asked as she adjusted her gloves, but she didn't dare look up at him. She thought what he deserved was a good smack across the face, but she knew his health was too poor to permit her to give free rein to her temper.

"I appreciate your bringing me here, but I wouldn't have embarrassed you if you had taken me home," Buck promised sincerely.

Lyse responded with an impatient toss of her head. "Lordy, you don't understand a thing, do you? It isn't you I'm ashamed of, Buck." When he reached out to touch her arm as she turned away, she refused to delay her return home a moment longer. "Just let me go before I leave you in worse shape than when I found you," she threatened angrily, for she had expected him to apologize for the way he had pawed her rather than to criticize her father's hospitality. It had upset her badly that he hadn't made any attempt to ask her forgiveness. There was a difference between being poor and being cheap, but clearly he didn't know it.

"Oh, Lyse, you don't really want to hurt me, do you?" Buck knew he was pushing his luck, but for some reason he couldn't resist doing it. She wasn't always easy to like, but he did like her and he wanted her to like him in return.

Large raindrops began to thud into the dirt at her feet and having no way to reply to Buck's teasing question, Lyse left it unanswered as she hurried to Thor. Before she could swing herself up into the stallion's saddle, however, Buck reached her side. He grabbed the saddle horn so he wouldn't fall as he flashed what he hoped still looked like a charming grin. "Be careful on your way home," he offered politely. "I'll wait until you come back to leave. After all, I promised you a reward for saving my life and I want you to have it."

Lyse had no time to demand he hand over the money immediately, but before she could place the toe of her boot in the stirrup, Buck moved to block her way. "Does the rain always make you so damn amorous?" she complained as she tried to shove him aside.

"Every last time," Buck admitted with a low chuckle. He couldn't help himself now, he wanted to kiss her good-bye too badly. Her eyes glittered with the fiery sparkle of diamonds as she glared at him, but he didn't care. He liked women with spirit and she had plenty. "Give me a kiss, Lyse, and I'll let you be on your way."

With a coy slyness, Lyse reached up to take his hand from the saddle horn as though she wished merely to hold it in a warm clasp as she granted his request. She watched as his smile filled his face with a deep glow of satisfaction. Then without a hint of her intentions, she gave him a savage shove to the midsection that sent him reeling backward and left him seated in the dirt.

"Maybe that will teach you to keep your hands to yourself, Mr. Warren. Don't make the mistake of trying to kiss me again 'cause it will only get you far worse the next time. I offered to help you find the man you're after, but I sure didn't volunteer to be your whore!" Considering that the farewell he deserved, she leapt upon Thor's back, and with all the speed the powerful horse possessed she sprinted away toward home.

Because he had already landed in the dirt once that day, and was sure he had the bruises to prove it, Buck began to swear with the foulest words he knew. "The little minx!" he finally muttered darkly as he hauled himself to his feet. The rain was falling hard now and as furious with himself as he was with Lyse, he hurried into the house where he would at least be dry if not warm or happy.

* * *

Frank Selby stood at his front window sipping whiskey-laced coffee as he waited for his daughter to return home. When he saw her ride Thor into the barn he was tempted to go have it out with her there, but seeing no sense in getting himself wet, he decided to bide his time and wait for her to come to him. He had suspected she was up to something for a long time and he was certain he had finally caught her at it. As soon as she stepped across the threshold, he began to shout at her.

"I thought you knew better than to ride Thor without my permission!" he began in an accusing snarl. "Any fool could see it was going to rain. That's no time to be out riding, and especially not on our best horse. He gets hit by lightning and this ranch would be out of business quick."

Lyse leaned back against the door. Water was pouring off her clothes and making a large puddle on the floor, but she had known her father would be furious with her for riding Thor when she had taken him. She had thought helping Buck worth that risk, but now she was certain it hadn't been.

That her father cared more about his horse than her was plain, for clearly he wasn't in the least bit concerned about what might have happened to her. If she had been struck by lightning a dozen times, he probably would not have noticed. She had learned as a child it did no good to argue with her father when he was angry. The best thing to do was just to let him rant and rave until he ran out of steam and she tried to prepare herself for a long wait.

"Ain't you got nothing to say for yourself, missy?" Frank screamed as he stepped close.

"No, sir," Lyse responded softly, trying not to antagonize him any further. She had known he would be angry about Thor, but that would be nothing compared to his fury should he find out where she had been.

As though he could read her thoughts, Frank tossed out another question in an insulting tone. "Where did you meet him?"

"Meet who?" Lyse tried to ask innocently, but her heart leapt to her throat as she wondered if he had followed her.

"The man you've been sneaking off to meet." Frank reached into his pocket to withdraw the handkerchief she used to hold her savings. "Where did you get this money, missy? You been out whoring just like your ma?"

Lyse's eyes widened in horror as he swung the small bundle close to her face. "It's taken me years and years to save that money, Pa. I sure didn't get it from men. Don't be silly."

"You take me for a fool?" Frank laughed at her efforts to wrench the handkerchief from his grasp. "Oh, no you don't, missy. This money is mine now."

"It is not!" Lyse screamed defiantly. "It's mine! I told you I saved it." That money was her life savings. It represented her freedom and she wasn't about to let him take it away. "You had no right to search my things. You give that back to me!"

"I'll give it to you!" Frank laughed as he drew back his hand and belted her across the face with it. The silver coins were heavy and the blow left her dazed, but Lyse wouldn't give in. She staggered back against the door, staring at the angry man in front of her as though she had never really seen him before. She was certain the horny toad Buck had caught had more character than this pitiful individual. How could such a loathsome human being possibly be her father?

In that instant, she realized something she had always known in her heart: If her mother was half the tramp he liked to call her, then it was more than likely he wasn't her father. Inspired by the possibility they might not be even remotely related, she lunged for him, determined to get back the money she had worked so hard to save. Frank responded by hitting her another staggering blow with the coins. When that didn't stop her he used his fists, but she didn't give in until she was so badly battered she fell to the floor and no longer had the strength to rise.

"Missy?" Frank bent down beside her but when he touched her hair his fingers came away sticky with blood. "Missy!" he shouted as he shook her shoulder, but she didn't stir. Terrified that he had killed her, Frank dropped the makeshift bag of coins in front of her. He got out the bottle of whiskey he had bought on his last trip into town and poured one drink after another until he was too drunk to care how badly he had mistreated the delicately built girl.

When she came to, Lyse saw the handkerchief full of coins and pulled it close to her chest. Suspecting a trick, she tensed, expecting the man she had called pa to kick her senseless, but he had passed out and sat slumped in his chair. Lyse swallowed to force the taste of blood from her mouth, but it took several minutes before she felt strong enough to get to her feet. She went into her room, and too weak to pull off her wet clothes, she fell asleep still wearing them.

It rained all that day and most of the next, but Lyse refused to come out of her room. Frank knocked on her door repeatedly and begged her to forgive him for hitting her, but she knew his next swallow of whiskey would drown his remorse. When she heard his snore that night, she gathered up the few things she owned, placed them in the middle of the bed, and wrapped them with the thin spread. With her belongings rolled up tightly under her arm, she left the house for the last time and walked through the muddy yard to the barn.

Thor turned in his stall and tossed his head, but she walked on past him and chose a pinto mare instead. She was still so sore it took her half an hour to saddle the horse rather than a few minutes, but she knew there was no rush. Frank would be unlikely to awaken before dawn, and if he found her gone she doubted he would try and follow to bring her back.

The moon lit her way as she rode toward the old ranch house. Her whole body ached from the beating she had taken and she gained a grudging respect for what Buck had suffered when he had tried to ride. That still didn't excuse his behavior, however. When she reached the house where she had left him, she went first to the rear to leave her mare with his horse. Then she walked around to the front and knocked politely on the doorjamb because there was no door.

"Buck?" she called out in a hoarse whisper. Her lips were still so swollen she wasn't certain he would recognize her voice. "It's Lyse."

Buck had spent so much time resting he was no longer tired, but though the lateness of the hour surprised him, he couldn't hide his delight at finding Lyse at his door. He rose to meet her, but she walked past him and using her bundle of belongings as a pillow, she stretched out on the rough plank floor. "We can talk in the morning. I'm going to Galveston when you do. That doesn't mean we are going together, though. That ought to make you happy."

"Lyse?" Buck could tell something was wrong, he just couldn't tell what. He wasn't about to go to sleep, however, without finding out what it was. He had matches in his saddlebags, and kneeling by her side he lit one. She blew it out quickly, but not before he had seen enough of her face to make him sick. "Dear God in heaven, Lyse. Who did this to you?"

"It doesn't matter, Buck. Just let me go to sleep."

"No! You tell me who it was this instant!" Buck reached for her wrist with his left hand and pulled her up beside him. "Did your pa do this to you for riding his horse?"

"That was one of his complaints," Lyse admitted hesitantly. "He found the money I'd saved and—" She couldn't bring herself to say what he had called her and tried to change the subject. "It doesn't matter, Buck. I've left home and I'm never going back."

Buck could not recall ever being so angry. Lyse had tried his patience on more than one occasion, but he would never have hit her. He hadn't wanted to involve her in his troubles, but he eagerly jumped right into the middle of hers. "All right, Lyse. You can come with me to Galveston. I've been tall so long it didn't occur to me Arvin would recognize me from my height alone. I could use a discreet detective if you still want the job."

"I need the money," Lyse admitted frankly. "I've decided to go on to California and I've heard the passage is expensive."

"California! You get beat up at home, and you want to chance going all the way to California?" he asked with an incredulous gasp.

"Yeah, I figure I got nothing to lose. I'm real tired, Buck. Can we argue about it in the morning?"

That request was stated with so wistful a sigh, Buck moved his bedroll next to her and lay back down. "Sure, there will be plenty of time to talk tomorrow." He lay awake as he listened to the soft rhythm of her breathing as she fell asleep. The rain had stopped and he could see the stars through the open doorway. The night had seemed like a peaceful one until she had appeared, but his anger kept him from enjoying any sense of calm. He would take Lyse to Galveston as he had promised, but he vowed he would teach her father some badly needed manners first.

IV

March 1849

*B*uck awakened with a start, alarmed to find himself again alone in the run-down adobe until he saw Lyse had left her bundle of possessions where she had dropped it. He relaxed then, knowing she could not have gone far. The slice of sky visible through the open doorway was a dreary gray. The lingering threat of rain made the morning air heavy with moisture and he shivered as he sat up, disappointed the day looked so bleak. He was hungry, but for the moment satisfied only his thirst by tilting his canteen far back to finish what water was left, confident Lyse would know where to find more.

Not content with his own company when he knew he still had a lot to settle with the continually perplexing blonde who had to be somewhere nearby, Buck struggled to his feet. He stretched as best he could to shake off the stiffness of the night, taking care not to put any strain on his right shoulder. He raked his fingers through his hair and across his new beard hoping he didn't look nearly as bad as he felt. Though still somewhat shaky, he had spent more than enough time resting on the uncompromising hardness of the small dwelling's warped plank floor. Craving both exercise and fresh air, he headed outside.

Awake before dawn, Lyse had let the horses out to graze. She sat hugging her knees as she watched them contentedly eating their fill of spring grass while her stomach complained loudly of neglect. Though she felt pangs of hunger, the thought of food sickened her and she had made no effort to prepare any breakfast. When she heard Buck call her name she turned away, too ashamed of her appearance to face him.

"We need to talk, Lyse," Buck called out as he approached the shy young woman. When the sound of his voice made her cringe he stopped several feet away. "Hey, I don't look all that handsome myself this morning. You don't need to hide from me."

"I'm not hiding," Lyse denied untruthfully as she pulled her hat down so low it nearly covered her eyes.

Her huddled pose contradicted her words, but Buck could not forget the brief glimpse of her face he had gotten during the night. He didn't need to see her clearly to know she could not possibly look much better now. "I don't think there is anything lower than a man who'll hit a woman. Please tell me what happened. I promise not to get any more angry than I am already." She was seated on a board that had fallen off the side of the horses' shed. Taking care to keep his distance, he leaned back against the ramshackle structure to take some of the weight off his legs.

"I told you all there is to tell last night," Lyse insisted stubbornly. "I'm riding to Galveston with you when you feel up to it. We'll find Arvin and then I'll be on my way to California. My plans are all made."

Buck took a deep breath and let it out slowly in an effort to tame the anger he didn't want to direct at her. "That's not the part I want to hear, Lyse. Tell me exactly what happened with your pa."

Lyse shook her head. "He's not my pa anymore. I've heard of folks disowning their kids. Well, I've disowned him. He no longer has a daughter and I don't have a pa. It's as simple as that. When do you think you'll feel up to riding?"

Buck's eyes narrowed as he studied the rigid curve of Lyse's spine, thinking she was holding on to her knees so tightly she would roll like a ball if he gave her a nudge. With an admirable bravado, she was trying to pretend she didn't care about what had happened to her, but it was plain to him that she had suffered a great deal—and not just physically —because of it. She was extremely embarrassed about the way she looked, and disowning her father, if such a thing were possible, obviously hadn't made her any less ashamed of the brutal way he had treated her.

How could any father beat his own child the way Lyse's had beaten her? he wondered. For that matter, why had the man convinced her she was plain when she was so extraordinarily pretty? It wasn't just being on his feet that sickened Buck then, but the natural progression of his thoughts. "I wouldn't think it was your fault," he began with a forced calm. "I wouldn't yell, or swear at you if you told me you'd been raped, Lyse. Is that what really happened? Is that what the bastard really did?"

Lyse was so shocked by that question she turned around to look at Buck, her mouth agape, then just as quickly she turned back toward the horses. "The man's my pa, Buck. Or at least he was," she mumbled, too embarrassed by his shocking question to say more.

Buck swallowed hard, for truly she did look worse than he had remembered. Her right eye was not only black and blue but also swollen shut. Her cheek was cut, and her lower lip was split and badly swollen. The villain who had been her father had given her a thorough beating Buck did not intend to forgive or forget. Buck Warren had always looked out for his friends, and he considered Lyse a close one after what she had done for him. Trying again, he lowered his voice to an enticing whisper. "Just tell me the truth, Lyse. Whether he was your pa or not, did he do it? Did he beat you up and then rape you?"

"NO!" Lyse screamed this time, mortified he had not let the matter drop. "It doesn't matter what he did. Just forget it," she pleaded with him, on the verge of tears.

"It matters to me," Buck assured her. "I want to start for Galveston as soon as we've had breakfast, but I want to stop by your ranch first. There's something I'd like to say to your pa."

Completely mystified by his words, Lyse forgot her cuts and bruises for the moment and again turned to face him.

"Why would you want to get mixed up in my troubles, Buck? That's just plain crazy."

The dark-eyed young man tried to smile, although it was difficult while he was looking at her badly battered face. She was so fair he knew she would have been bruised had she only been slapped, but clearly her father had beaten her with his fists to cause such terrible damage. He let his imagination play out that scene in his mind, and could barely control the fury of his temper as he replied to her question. "Let's just say I'm making your troubles mine for today. What is it your pa raises on his ranch, cattle or horses?"

"Horses, but that's the last place I'm going."

"You don't have to come with me. Just show me where your place is and I'll go by myself." Buck folded his arms across his chest, trying to find a comfortable pose to strike later so her father wouldn't know he had been wounded. He wanted to look not only mean as hell, but also strong enough to back up his words. "I'm going, Lyse. Whether you give me the directions or not, I'm going to pay your daddy a call. It hasn't rained since you arrived last night. I'll bet I can just follow your tracks if you don't want to ride along with me."

Lyse leapt to her feet, certain Buck would never have a worse idea. "Look, I've left home. I don't want to ever go back. What's the sense in making trouble for yourself with my pa? He's nothing to you," she argued persuasively as she walked toward him. It was plain to her that now that he was well enough to get up and walk around, she wasn't going to find getting along with him nearly so easy.

Buck raked his left thumbnail along his chin, deciding to shave off his beard as soon as they reached Galveston. "You're right, the man means nothing to me. Less than nothing in fact, so let's not argue about him. Let's have something to eat instead. I've still a little of the ham left, and some jerky."

"I'm not hungry," Lyse murmured as she ran her tongue over her front teeth. They still felt a little loose and that fright had taken away her appetite. All she needed was to lose a tooth or two. Then she would be downright ugly rather than merely plain. "I'm not hungry," she insisted as she looked down at the muddy toes of her boots.

Buck reached out to tilt her face up to his with his finger-tips. "If we are going to be partners for the time being, Lyse, we'll have to trust each other. That means being truthful."

Lyse jerked her head away. "I just don't feel like eating. That's not a lie."

It wasn't Lyse's defiance that fascinated him, it was the challenge of breaking through the wall of toughness she continually hid behind. Buck was used to people taking his word as law, to being trusted. He was a long way from home now, though, and Lyse clearly trusted no one. He came from an affectionate family where everyone hugged and kissed often. Lyse couldn't abide being touched and after what she had been through, he couldn't blame her. She was definitely a challenge in every possible way, but he certainly didn't feel up to taking her on that day.

"I've two younger sisters, Lyse. After I've dealt with Arvin, maybe you'd like to come home with me to Dallas and meet them. My family is all very nice and they'd make you feel at home," Buck offered with a friendly smile.

Lyse had never been invited anywhere, and couldn't imagine what would possess Buck to ask her to visit his family. Unless he had done it out of pity. Deciding that must be his reason, she turned him down cold. "I'm too old to be adopted. Don't want another family anyway. Besides, I'm going to California just as soon as I have the money to pay for my passage." She stole a glimpse at Buck through her lashes and was shocked by the sorrow that had suddenly filled his expression.

"Look, I'm sorry if I hurt your feelings. I didn't mean to insult you either. I'm sure your family are all real nice people and it was kind of you to ask me to your home when I can't ask you to mine, but I'm going to California, not Dallas," she stated again.

"I bet you don't weigh a hundred pounds," Buck mused aloud.

"What's that got to do with anything? They charge people by the pound for the voyage to California?" Lyse found it difficult to argue when she didn't want to face him, couldn't face him the way she looked, which she was certain was hideous.

Lyse had a strange way of questioning his motives that made Buck take a second look at them himself, but he just laughed at her now. "What I meant was, your size is deceptive. You're so slender you look like the fragile type, but you've got a heart harder than steel. Don't worry about how much it costs to go to California. I promised to give you a reward for helping me and I'll see you get there if that's where you really want to go."

"'Course that's where I want to go!" Lyse protested loudly. "How many times do I have to say that?" Her whole body ached and she was so ashamed of what her pa had done to her she didn't ever want to go home again, and Buck thought she was made of steel? Hell, the man had no sense at all. "You fix whatever you want for breakfast, I'll saddle the horses." She turned away, disgusted she had been unable to convince him to forget about meeting her pa.

"Wait a minute," Buck called out after her. "I'll need some water to clean up and you'll have to help me get this bandage off so I can put on a shirt. I want to be properly dressed when I pay your daddy a call."

"All right, I'll help you," Lyse reluctantly agreed, but not for the reason he assumed. She was sure removing the bandage from his shoulder wouldn't be easy and if he fainted, he wouldn't be paying anyone any calls, which would suit her just fine. "Better eat while I fetch the water. We'll need plenty to soak off the last layers of your bandage."

"That sounds like fun," Buck joked bravely.

"It will be," Lyse assured him, but the task proved to be not nearly so disagreeable as she had feared.

"I don't know whether Arvin's aim is poor, or whether he had forgotten I'm left-handed," Buck commented slyly as Lyse used her knife to cut away the strips of shirt she had used to bind his shoulder. He was seated in the adobe's doorway where she would have plenty of light to work.

"It's his aim," Lyse replied with an easy confidence. "He must have been going for the middle of your back, aiming for your heart. What I don't understand is why he rode off without first making sure you were dead. That was just plain stupid."

"Lyse!" Buck cried out in mock anguish. "Were the man not so incredibly dumb, I'd be dead. Maybe that doesn't bother you, but it sure as hell bothers me."

Lyse stepped back slightly as she pulled away the strips that had encircled his chest. She had gotten used to seeing him without a shirt. The skin of his back and chest glowed with the same healthy tan that graced his features and she knew he must have gone without a shirt often. He had a muscular build, so clearly he was used to physical labor, but as she studied his appearance the fact that he was a very handsome young man failed to move her. Emotionally, she was simply too numb to notice.

Sorry she had again insulted him unintentionally, Lyse ruffled his thick, black hair as though he were a small child. "Don't take on so, Buck. Just 'cause I called Arvin stupid doesn't mean I want to see you dead."

Though that wasn't the greatest compliment a woman had ever paid him, Buck knew it was high praise coming from Lyse. "Well, thank you. I'm touched to learn you have such tender feelings for me," he teased playfully.

"I didn't say that!" The man was impossible in Lyse's opinion, and she forced herself to concentrate on removing the layers of fabric she had used to stem the flow of his blood instead of on his teasing banter. "This is stuck fast, Buck. I planned to wet it down before I tried peeling it off, but do you want me to go ahead? After all, you're the one who's going to be screaming, not me."

Not pleased by that prediction, Buck ran his left hand over the blood-encrusted squares of material on either side of the wound in his right shoulder and shook his head. "Warm water will work a lot better than cold. Let's wait until we get to Galveston. There's some soap in my saddlebags, just help me clean up and we'll let it go at that."

"Just what do you expect me to do, Buck, bathe you like a baby?" Lyse shook her head, not about to agree to that.

Buck took the precaution of rising slowly to his feet before he replied, wisely using the time to reconsider his request. "I'm sorry. You're a young lady and a pretty one. I shouldn't have asked you to take on so personal a chore. Just find the soap for me and I'll take care of myself as best I can."

For some reason, that politely worded apology made Lyse feel worse than his original request had. "Oh, what the hell, Buck. That's no worse than some of the other things you've had me do."

Buck knew exactly to what she was referring and had to laugh. "Come on, I said I was sorry I didn't realize you were a girl. Aren't you ever going to forgive me for that?"

"Nope," Lyse replied truthfully. "But I figure the least I can do is help you wash up since you asked so nicely. If we are going to be partners, that is."

She hurried inside to hunt for the soap before he could reply. Buck made no effort to hide his smile when she returned, but he did not smile for long. She sat him down again on the front step and with the same lively enthusiasm a mother would give to bathing a naughty eight-year-old boy, she poured cold water over his head and began to shampoo his hair.

Buck had no idea what he was getting himself into, but he had not expected Lyse to bathe him the same way he was certain she must be used to bathing a horse. It wasn't so much that she was rough, it was just that she was so damn thorough. She started with his hair, then taking care not to disturb the still-healing wound in his shoulder she worked her way down his back to his waist. She then stepped around in front of him to scrub his chest and arms. When she was finally satisfied he was clean, and used the last of the cold water to rinse the soap bubbles from his hair and body, Buck's once bronze skin held a decidedly pink glow.

When she handed him the small towel he had had in his gear, Buck was more relieved than grateful. "Christ almighty, Lyse. You're not supposed to scrub a man like you would a floor!"

"Did I get soap in your eyes?" Lyse asked sweetly.

"No, that's the one place you missed."

"No, it's not. You left your pants on."

Buck stopped drying his hair abruptly to regard her with a malevolent stare. "You want me to take them off?" he asked snidely, daring her to say yes. Lyse didn't respond as she picked up the two empty canteens and started off at a brisk walk to refill them. Buck realized instantly he had just made a serious mistake. Lyse was so damn touchy she couldn't take the least bit of criticism, while at the same time he knew he could tell her from dawn to dusk that she was pretty and he would not make the slightest impression on her. Though her moods were maddeningly predictable, she still baffled him completely. Clearly she had regarded his remark about his pants as the sarcastic insult he had meant it to be, so why he wasn't pleased with himself he didn't know.

Buck had not been certain Lyse's tracks would still be visible when he had boasted he would follow them, but luckily they were. She was riding along behind him, making conversation impossible, which he thought was probably smart, because neither of them was in a good mood. He had once compared her independence to his sisters' sheltered up-bringing, but to distract himself from the discomfort of the ride he began to draw a comparison of an entirely different sort.

He had vowed to get Arvin not only to avenge David Bailey's death, but also in a noble attempt to ease Constance Thorn's inconsolable grief over the loss of her fiancé. Both he and David had courted the vibrant brunette, but she had quickly let them know David was her choice. When he had returned home alone at the close of the war, Buck had hoped Constance would turn to him for comfort because the affection he felt for her hadn't cooled. Unfortunately, that had failed to happen; Constance's lingering despair over the loss of her first love was as dark as the mourning attire she still wore. Whenever he went to see her, she had talked of nothing but how dearly she had loved David. She still wept when she spoke his name and swore she had no future without the man she would always adore. Nothing he had said or done to lift her spirits had had the slightest effect upon the despondency of her mood.

It was not that Buck was unsympathetic to Constance's plight. It was tragic. She had lost the man she had planned to wed, but damn it all, he had lost his best friend and she had never once shown him any sympathy. Now he was riding across the prairie with another young woman who was equally unwilling to share anything of herself, and he couldn't help but wonder how he could have had the misfortune to meet two such impossible females.

Then Buck remembered that it was Lyse who had found him. Rather than leave a badly wounded stranger to die alone she had stayed to care for him and in the following week had done all she could to help him survive. Maybe Lyse wasn't nearly so hard-hearted as she seemed. Both amused and encouraged by that possibility, he turned back and waved to her.

Lost in her own thoughts, Lyse didn't notice Buck's friendly gesture. She was preparing a mental list of things she would need to take to California because from what she had heard, common items like shovels and picks cost a fortune there. She wasn't afraid of hard work, and she wanted to be able to get to the gold fields without having any delay caused by a lack of tools. She didn't want to waste a minute of her time once she reached California. The gold couldn't last forever and she wanted to be certain she got her share.

Buck drew his horse to a halt on the rise and waited for Lyse to reach his side. "That's your ranch in the valley below, isn't it?"

"Yeah, but I still think this is a damn fool thing for you to do," she responded darkly.

"Do you have any hired hands? I don't want to confront the wrong man."

"My pa's too cheap to hire anyone to help out with the work. Now that I'm gone, maybe he'll finally learn there's too much to do alone."

Buck touched the brim of his hat in a farewell salute. "I plan to do my best to see he learns a valuable lesson this morning. It should only take a few minutes. You just stay here and watch me." He turned away then and rode his horse down the path that led across the floor of the valley to the front of the ranch house. He slid off the gelding's back, and wrapped his reins loosely around the rail that ran the length of the adobe house which looked little better than the one they had just left. Because all of Lyse's clothes had been old and worn, it didn't surprise him that her home wasn't the showplace his was. "Anyone home?" he called out in a friendly tone. Rather than a reply coming from the house, Frank called to him from the barn.

Buck turned around, leaned back against the hitching post, and hooked the thumb of his nearly useless right arm in his belt. "Good morning. I'm looking for good brood mares. I heard you might have some to sell."

Frank had been attending to Lyse's chores and paused to wipe the sweat from his brow. The day was still overcast and cool, but he wasn't used to such hard work and hoped his fool daughter would come home soon. "I've got some mighty fine mares, but they don't come cheap," he advised his visitor. Because the man was neatly groomed and well dressed, Frank decided he could probably afford his price. "Name's Frank Selby. Hope you don't mind if I don't offer my hand, but I've been working in the barn and I'm none too clean."

Because Buck was not able to shake hands anyway, he naturally accepted Frank's apology. "I'm Buck Warren," he stated proudly, wanting Frank to remember his name. "I own a fine stallion, but I need a couple more mares."

"I understand. I got a beauty in the barn. Let me bring her out and we'll start with her."

"Fine." As soon as the man had turned away, Buck looked up toward the bluff, but he saw no sign of Lyse. For all he knew she had continued on toward Galveston, but he was confident he could overtake her because he didn't plan to spend long with her father.

In a matter of minutes Frank returned with a sleek mare whose bright red color exactly matched her sire's. She had good conformation and a sweet disposition, which he took care to point out as he began a rambling narrative of her virtues.

Buck paid no attention to the man's sales pitch but nodded thoughtfully as though he were while studying instead Frank's manner and expressions. He soon showed himself to be a crude fellow, and clearly had little schooling. It struck Buck as remarkable he had produced so bright and lively a daughter when he lacked those characteristics himself. That

Lyse looked nothing like Frank was also a surprise, but he thought perhaps she resembled her mother.

Stepping over to the mare, he ran his left hand over her back lightly. "Yes, she is a beauty. Fine mares ought to be treated like women, don't you agree, Mr. Selby? They need plenty of love and attention, but a very light hand. I caught a man abusing a mare once. I can assure you he'll not make that same mistake ever again. Were I ever to catch a man abusing a woman, why, I can't promise he'd survive longer than ten minutes."

Frank gripped the rope encircling the mare's neck more tightly, beginning to suspect his visitor had not really come to buy horses after all. Though he was certain Lyse had been involved with a man, he was positive it couldn't be this one. This fellow was too well dressed and good looking to care anything about the likes of her. Still, his comments about abuse worried him. "I give my animals the best of care," he announced proudly. "There's not a one that's ever felt the sting of a whip."

"That a fact?" Buck walked around the red mare, apparently studying her closely. He then returned to the hitching post and casually leaned back against it. "You run this place by yourself, Mr. Selby?"

Frank never carried a gun unless he planned to go hunting, but he began to wish he also had a forty-five strapped to his hip. His visitor looked like he could use his weapon, however, and Frank had never been much of a shot. "You come here to buy mares or to conduct a census, Mr. Warren?"

Buck was surprised to find the man had a sense of humor. It seemed out of character until he realized Frank Selby couldn't possibly have much in the way of character. With a disarming grin, he confessed he had lied. "I came here to do just one thing, Frank."

Frank was standing between Buck and the mare, so he had no way to jump back to avoid Buck's first blow, which he hadn't seen coming. The vicious left hook caught him on the chin. He dropped to the dirt where he sat stunned, blood dripping from between his lips from the deep gash he'd bitten in his tongue. He stared up at Buck, his vision too blurred to clearly make out his assailant's expression, but the fire in his dark eyes was unmistakable. "Hey," Frank began weakly, but before he could finish his sentence Buck leaned down, grabbed him by the collar, and with one hand hauled him to his feet. He propped him against the mare then hit him again, this time breaking his nose. Frank's knees buckled, but before he slipped to the ground Buck cracked three of his ribs with a powerful left jab.

Frightened by her owner's grunts and groans, the mare bolted away but Frank still clung to her rope so tightly she dragged him right along with her. Dazed, his face covered with blood, he went bouncing along on the seat of his pants as the horse trotted back to the barn. It struck Buck as a comical sight, but he had not come there to have a good laugh. He followed Frank through the barn doors and when the mare reached her stall, he untied the rope to free her. He then knelt down and pried the other end from Frank's trembling hands.

Waving the rope, Buck cast a significant glance up at the rafters. "I ought to string you up in your own barn, Selby. You know why too, don't you?"

His watery blue eyes filled with terror, Frank bobbed his head up and down quickly but that didn't satisfy Buck. He rose to his feet and continued to toy with the rope.

"I want to hear it in your own words, you miserable coward. Why did you hit your daughter? Why?"

Frank brought his hands to his face but that only increased his pain and he dropped them to his lap. When he saw his fingers were covered with blood from his shattered nose he started to shake. "You don't know nothing! Nothing, you hear. The little slut's just like her ma. She'll turn out a whore too and I got every right to beat her. I got that right!"

Had Buck been able to fashion a noose with one hand, he would have hanged Frank Selby then and there. Because he couldn't do that, he yanked him to his feet. "You hate her mother so you treated your own daughter as though she were trash? How did you treat your wife? Did you slap her around too?" Buck struck Frank across the face with the back of his hand and when he fell again he left him where he lay.

"You're worse than stupid, Selby. You're a pitiful excuse

for a man." To emphasize his point, Buck gave him a savage kick in the groin. Frank passed out then, but Buck found a bucket, filled it with ice cold water from the horse trough at the side of the barn, and poured it over his head.

Certain he was now being drowned, Frank shook himself awake, then tried to crawl away. Buck leaned down to grab his ankle and pulled him right back. "We aren't finished yet, Selby. I want to make certain you understand why we had this little conversation."

Frank raised his arms to protect his face, certain he was going to be hit again. "I know! I know!" he screamed.

"Why?" Buck prompted him.

Frank was in so much pain he would admit anything now. "'Cause I hit Lyse," he sobbed in a tear-choked whine.

"That's only part of it," Buck began as he drew back his foot, meaning to kick him again. "I doubt you've ever been a father to her. Instead, you lied to her and made her think she was plain. You made her work like a slave. I ought to kill you for that, Selby, and slowly."

Frank fainted again as the toe of Buck's boot found its mark. Buck drew his knife then, intending to leave the fallen man with an unforgettable reminder of his visit, but Lyse suddenly appeared out of nowhere and grabbed hold of his arm.

Quickly taking in Frank's bruised and bloody face, she shuddered. "Lordy, if there's ever another war, I want you on my side. Come on, let's get out of here. You've hurt him bad enough already. If I'd wanted him dead, I would have killed him myself."

Buck glanced down at the young woman who was tugging on his arm, still so angry he didn't really see her for a moment. Finally, he took a deep breath to clear his head and not wanting to cut Frank in front of her, he put his knife away. "I think I made my point, Lyse. Hell, even if I didn't he'll never forget meeting Buck Warren, and he'll think twice before hitting another woman."

"You introduced yourself?" Lyse clearly thought Buck a worse fool than her pa, or the man she had always called her pa, had been. Releasing her hold on him, she walked out of the barn and mounted the pinto mare she had left tethered just outside.

Buck followed, then stopped to give her knee an affectionate pat, his grin a rakish one as he explained his reasons. "There's no way your pa can report the beating I gave him to a sheriff, Lyse, without admitting what he did to you. There was no danger at all in giving him my name, but it will keep what I did and why in his mind forever. Believe me, it will."

Lyse nodded, thinking she understood. "You mean like knowing Arvin Corbett's name? It will give him a real person to hate?"

"That's right. You're not only pretty, Miss Selby, you're bright too."

As he started across the yard to his horse, Lyse called out after him. "How many men you got tracking you, Buck?"

Buck swung himself up on his gelding's back and eased his pace so they would ride side by side as they left her ranch. "No more than half a dozen. Does that frighten you?" he asked with a teasing chuckle.

Not understanding his joke, Lyse straightened her shoulders proudly. "I can take care of myself if we meet up with any of them."

While her bruised and swollen face made that boast seem preposterous, Buck nevertheless believed her. "Good. You just keep an eye on my back and I'll watch yours."

"Sure, Buck. That's what partners are for." Pulling her hat down even lower to shade her eyes from the bright sunlight that had just broken through the clouds, Lyse turned her mare toward the road that led to Galveston. With the first hint of a smile lifting the corners of her swollen lips, she again let her mind fill with vivid dreams of the riches she would find in California.

V
—

March 1849

B^{*y passing*} Houston, it took Lyse and Buck two days to reach the busy port at the eastern end of Galveston Island. Located two miles off the Texas coast, the city of Galveston was made bright not only by an abundance of lush oleander and bougainvillaea blossoms but also by its colorful past. The Spaniard Cabeza de Vaca, the first European to explore the interior of Texas, was shipwrecked on the island in 1528. The city was the stronghold of the pirate Jean LaFitte from 1817 until 1821 when he was ordered to leave by the government of the United States and wisely chose to go. The presence of LaFitte and his band of rowdy followers attracted scores of European soldiers of fortune, privateers, adventurers, and the women of easy virtue who provided amusement in the bawdy saloons and gambling halls.

Despite its notorious reputation as a pirate's den, Galveston was designated as a port by the legislatures of Coahuila and Texas in 1825, and during the 1830s the city finally began to attract law-abiding residents who were interested in legitimate commerce rather than piracy. In 1836, during the fight for independence from Mexico, it served briefly as the capital of the Republic of Texas. By 1849, Galveston was a thriving commercial port, exporting not only cotton, sulfur, and grain but also swarms of men eager to make their way to the gold fields of California by the swift Panama route.

To get the best price, Buck had helped Lyse sell her horse and saddle before crossing to the island. As he led her up the steps of Galveston's finest hotel, she was still clutching the money tightly. In her mind, pirates still roamed the streets and lurked behind every corner waiting for an unsuspecting citizen to rob, and she wanted to take no chances on losing what little money she had. "I can't afford to stay here," she argued in a hoarse whisper, but he did not release his firm hold upon her arm.

"Nonsense," Buck replied just as emphatically. "You'll be working for me the next few days, so I'll cover your expenses."

"But—" Lyse got no further in their debate than she had when she had tried to convince him not to visit her father. Buck shot her so fierce a glance, she dared not dispute his word any further and create a scene in public. Within the first hours of their journey, she had found she much preferred Buck's company when he had been wounded and flat on his back to that of the arrogant dictator he had swiftly proved himself to be. Since he had recovered the strength to force things to go his way in addition to making that demand verbally, she had grown increasingly glad their partnership would be a brief one.

As they approached the desk, she tugged on the brim of her hat to shade her eyes, hoping the desk clerk would not notice the bruises that had faded only slightly and now decorated her right eye and cheek with pale lavender shadows. At least her lips were no longer swollen, but she was ashamed of the dust that covered her well-worn clothes and she wished Buck would have allowed her to go her own way before the hotel's manager insisted she did.

Buck had boarded his mount at a livery stable on the mainland and had carried his saddlebags slung over his left shoulder. As he reached the desk, he let them slide to the floor before taking the pen that lay by the register. "I'm supposed to meet a friend here. His name is Arvin Corbett. Has he already checked in?"

"I'm sorry, sir, but we have no one by that name registered here."

Buck flashed a disarming grin as though Arvin's whereabouts mattered very little to him. "I'm sure he'll turn up soon. As for us, Miss Selby and I will each require one of your best rooms. They must be adjoining, of course."

The desk clerk on duty was James Peters, a slightly built man in his late thirties. He caught the unmistakable ring of authority in Buck's voice, and needed only a glimpse at the solid gold ring on his hand to have no doubts the tall stranger could pay for whatever he ordered. It was the reference to a Miss Selby that puzzled him, however, for there was no lady in sight.

"I can promise you will be pleased with our accommodations, sir. If Miss Selby is waiting outside in a carriage, I will send a porter to attend to her luggage."

Though Buck was clearly dumbfounded by that question, Lyse was not. Looking up, she fixed the clerk with an evil stare and announced proudly, "I am Miss Selby, you dolt, and I have everything I own right here."

Though the hotel was a popular one and Peters had seen a broad cross section of humanity as guests, his mouth fell agape as he noted Lyse was an extremely attractive if a very poorly dressed and badly battered young woman. He immediately tried to make up for his error but found it impossible to kindle a glow of sympathetic understanding in her vivid blue eyes. "My apologies, Miss Selby. I thought you were, well—" Because he could scarcely admit he had mistaken her for a teenage boy, he grew even more flustered. "Obviously I had no idea who you were. Please forgive me."

Buck turned away in a futile attempt to hide the broad grin he couldn't suppress, but he had to admit Lyse still looked more like a disheveled youth than a young woman. Because he knew that wasn't her fault, he grew ashamed of himself for finding humor in an incident that had surely embarrassed her. He quickly turned back and with his customary confidence seized control of the situation.

"Miss Selby's carriage overturned, her luggage spilled open, and her traveling clothes were ruined. I had hoped you would be gentleman enough not to comment upon her appearance until she had time to bathe and dress in more suitable attire, but—"

After turning the register to ascertain their latest guest's name, Peters interrupted what he was afraid was about to become an announcement the unusual couple would seek lodgings elsewhere. He simply could not allow that to happen as it would damage the reputation of the hotel, and if they complained to the manager it might lead to his dismissal. "Forgive me, Mr. Warren, Miss Selby, I beg you. That momentary lapse in manners will not reoccur. I'll have a porter show you to your rooms immediately. You'll want to order baths, of course, and perhaps request a physician to attend to Miss Selby?"

Because that was precisely why he had mentioned the nonexistent accident, Buck was quick to agree. "Yes, if you can recommend a competent doctor who would be willing to come see her this afternoon, I would be very grateful."

Readily understanding there would be a generous tip for providing such a service, Peters promised to arrange it. Lyse stared first at the overly officious clerk and then up at Buck, certain the last person she needed to see was a doctor. After all, he was the one who had been shot. Was he too proud to ask for medical attention for himself?

"You needn't call a physician for me, Buck. I'm fine, just a little tired is all." Lyse assumed he had lied about a carriage accident to provide an excuse for her bruises and old clothes, but she intended to ask him about it as soon as they were alone. She didn't want him walking around Galveston offering fanciful excuses for the way she looked when she wasn't ashamed of it.

Realizing he should have warned Lyse he didn't want anyone to know he had been hurt, Buck had to resort to another of his darkly menacing stares. "Don't argue with me, Lyse. Just sign the register so we can go up to our rooms." When Lyse hesitated, Buck's heart fell. Instantly suspecting she did not know how to write, he offered to sign for her rather than cause her the additional embarrassment of having to admit such ignorance in front of the clerk. "Don't bother to put down your things, I'll write your name myself to save time."

Lyse was too bright not to understand exactly what Buck thought of her abilities. After quickly balancing her bundle of belongings on her left hip, she picked up the pen before he could. She dipped it into the inkwell and signed her name, Alyssa Selby, with a flourish that would have made Queen Victoria proud. "I've been on my own a long while, Buck. There's no need for you to treat me like an infant."

Reacting to the lively undercurrent of tension between the attractive pair, James Peters raised his brows slightly then discreetly kept out of an exchange that looked to him like it might become a long and noisy argument. He wondered what sort of a report he would receive from the night clerk on these two. Clearly the young woman was not the man's mistress, for what man of means would allow his woman to speak to him in so disrespectful a fashion? Deciding if they were going to fight, he wanted them upstairs in their rooms rather than at the front desk, he summoned a porter. After assigning them to rooms seven and eight, he handed over the two brass keys. "I hope you enjoy your stay. Simply let me know on the morning you wish to leave and I will prepare your bill personally."

Unwillingly, Buck tore his eyes from Lyse's defiant frown to reward the clerk with another smile. "We'll be here a few days. I can't be certain just how many yet. I expect to hear from that physician within the hour."

"I will arrange for him as I promised." As the porter showed Buck and Lyse to the stairs, James Peters pulled out his handkerchief and wiped the rapidly forming beads of perspiration from his brow. He had not only a wife, but also an aged mother to support and he couldn't afford to lose his job. Something about Buck Warren and Alyssa Selby just didn't sit right and after a dozen years as a desk clerk, he knew trouble when he saw it. Hoping it didn't occur on his shift, he sent another porter off to summon the nearest physician.

Lyse was given room seven, while Buck followed the porter through the connecting door into number eight. Located on a front corner, it provided a clear view of the street below and satisfied it would suit his purposes, he gave the elegant furnishings no more than a casual glance before tipping the porter and sending him to fetch a bathtub. When the young man returned to place it in Lyse's room, she called through the still-open doorway between their rooms the instant he left to fetch hot water.

"Buck, you've got to come in here and see this. Why, this tub is big enough for the both of us!" Lyse walked around the gleaming copper tub, her fingers caressing the rim, her words spilling out in an excited rush. She was absolutely fascinated by the tub's generous size and thrilled by the fact that it looked so new it couldn't possibly have any leaks.

Buck came to the doorway and leaned back against the doorjamb. With a sly chuckle he crossed his arms over his chest and agreed with her observation. "Sharing the tub sounds like a lot of fun. I'm game to try it if you are," he teased, hoping to put the feisty blonde in a better mood than she had been downstairs.

Stepping away from the tub, Lyse tossed her hat upon the bed and began to unfasten the leather thong at the end of her single braid. "I might have said the tub would hold us both, but that doesn't mean I'm looking to get in it with you," she denied hotly, appalled by his suggestion. He missed no opportunity to make fun of her and she heartily disliked him for it.

With a wistful sigh, Buck replied regretfully, "Yeah, somehow I knew you wouldn't." When Lyse appeared too embarrassed to reply and began to rummage through her things for her hairbrush, Buck wisely changed the subject. "I should have had the sense to tell you before we reached the hotel that I don't want anyone knowing I need to see a doctor, Lyse. If Arvin finds out I'm here, he's got to believe he just plain missed. I can't let him suspect his shot damn near killed me."

Grateful he had let her foolish comment about the size of the tub drop, Lyse sat down on the edge of the bed and began to draw her brush through her hair. "That makes sense, but Lordy, Buck. How am I supposed to know what you're planning if you don't tell me? I don't want to contradict you every time you speak, but when I don't know what you're talking about half the time it's difficult not to argue."

"I said I was sorry and I am. I just didn't think of how it would sound to ask for a physician until I got here. What do you think of your room? Mine seems comfortable."

Lyse tried to appear nonchalant, but truly the beauty of the room's furnishings nearly overwhelmed her with feelings of inadequacy because the hotel's things were so much finer than what she had grown up with in her home. The bed and dresser were beautifully carved cherry wood rather than rough-hewn pine. The walls were covered in a striped blue silk and the curtains at the window were of the finest lace she had ever seen. The feather bed was as comfortable as sitting upon a cloud. That this was a hotel room rather than a bedroom in the palace of royalty simply amazed her. "It's very nice," she agreed shyly.

Having no clue to her thoughts, Buck continued to give what he thought of as merely one of his sensible suggestions, not realizing she considered his directions highhanded orders. "When the porter comes back with the water, give him a dress to press so you'll have something to wear down to the dining room for dinner."

"A dress?" Lyse asked weakly as she peeked up at him through a silken veil of hair. Her brush almost slipped from her fingers she was so startled, but she managed to get a firm hold on it and kept brushing the trail dust out of her long blond tresses.

Not understanding how she could possibly be confused by so innocent a request, Buck grew impatient. "Yes, a dress. You did bring one with you, didn't you?"

After a painful silence, Lyse reluctantly admitted the truth then made light of it. "No. I didn't have one to bring, but that's no loss. It will be easier for me to move around Galveston in pants than it would be in some frilly gown. I won't need dresses where I'm going either."

Hearing the porter's knock, Buck straightened up. Every time he made an assumption where Lyse was concerned he found himself in the wrong. Why he hadn't learned not to do it, he didn't know but it hadn't even occurred to him she didn't own at least one dress. "I may not be able to escort you downstairs for dinner after I see the doctor anyway. Let's just plan on eating up here tonight and tomorrow I'll see you get some new clothes."

"My clothes are fine," Lyse insisted proudly. "Or at least they will be for working in the gold fields."

Not eager for another round in what had become a contin-
uous stream of arguments, Buck nodded toward the door.
"Answer that," he ordered gruffly. "The sooner you get your
bath over with the sooner I can take mine. We can talk about
adding to your wardrobe later." Before Lyse could respond,
Buck closed the door behind him to give her the privacy to
bathe, but he didn't bother to lock it.

Lyse flipped her hair out of her eyes and let the porter in
with the first of several buckets of hot water. He brought
perfumed soap and the softest towels she had ever had the
pleasure to use. Because Buck hadn't seemed at all impressed with the hotel's many luxuries, Lyse wondered if his
home were as nice. Maybe he had so much money a whis-
per-soft towel was what he usually used to wipe mud off his
boots.

"Must be nice to be so spoiled," she mused softly to herself when the porter had left the room for the last time. She
then hurriedly stripped off her badly soiled shirt and pants,
then her rumpled undergarments and stepped into the over-
size tub.

The soothing warmth of the water was so pleasant, Lyse
nearly dozed off before she remembered Buck was waiting
to use the tub. She sat up then and began to shampoo her
hair, but she had gotten no further than working foamy lather
through her fair tresses when she heard a knock at the door.
Suddenly realizing she had failed to lock it, she hastily
called for Buck.

Buck opened the connecting door as he wiped the last of
the shaving soap from his face. "Yeah, what is it?" he asked
as he lowered the towel. Then he discovered Lyse seated in
the copper tub, looking for all the world like a beautiful
mermaid whose hair was filled with billowing seafoam. The
late afternoon sunlight streaming in the windows gave the
drops of water clinging to her fair skin a golden sparkle.
That sheen lent her remarkably natural beauty a radiance all
its own. Soapy water lapped at the pink tips of her breasts,
but did not hide their lush fullness. Buck was as stunned as
he had been in the instant he had first realized she was a
willowly young woman rather than a painfully thin boy. He

could not recall why he had stepped through the door, but he was exceedingly glad that he had.

Lyse failed to notice Buck's rapt stare she was so surprised by the difference in his appearance. She had judged him good looking with a beard, but now that he was clean-shaven she thought him far more handsome. There was no hint of softness in his features, but instead there was a firm reflection of the toughness of his spirit. His shirt was open, displaying his broad chest, and as her eyes traced the path of the dark curls that tapered to a thin line as they reached his belt buckle, she began to blush. She was horribly embarrassed that he had caught her staring so openly at him, but when her eyes returned to his she found his expression as filled with flustered confusion as her own.

Another insistent knock at her door brought them both rudely back to reality and she whispered excitedly, "That must be the doctor. You'll have to get the door." When Buck started for hers, she grew even more alarmed. "Let him in your room, not mine!" she nearly shrieked.

"Of course," Buck agreed with a slight nod. He turned on his heel and this time, as he strode through the door between their rooms, he slipped her key into his pocket so she could not lock him out even if she wanted to.

Lyse sunk down into the water, mortified that Buck had seen her bathing. Imagining her figure to be no more appealing than a scarecrow's, she was deeply ashamed. She had no idea his impression of her had been one of passion-inspired splendor rather than mere disgust. Tears of embarrassment flooded her eyes as she rinsed out her hair and climbed from the tub. How could she ever face him again? She didn't take the time to appreciate the comforting softness of the towel as she hurriedly patted herself dry. All she knew was that she wanted to be fully dressed the next time she had to face Buck Warren, but she hardly dared hope she had that much courage.

Dressed in clean clothing, which was no more fashionable than the soiled garments she had discarded, Lyse went to her door and peeked out into the hall. After a long wait she saw the porter who had brought her bath reach the landing and she summoned him with a frantic gesture.

"Please empty the tub. Mr. Warren will need hot water, but not for a while yet."

The porter thought the fragile blonde's choice of apparel appalling, but he knew better than to insult her by saying so. "I will take care of it immediately," he replied, doing his best to imitate the way James Peters addressed the hotel's guests. "Should you need any other service, just use the bellpull by the bed."

"The what?" Lyse turned around to look at the bed, but she had no idea what a bellpull looked like.

The porter stepped by her and crossed to the far wall. Pointing to a knotted silk cord hanging beside the bed, he pantomimed the manner in which it was to be used. "When you pull the cord, a bell rings downstairs, and someone will come to see what it is you need."

"Oh yes, of course, the bellpull. I just didn't see it." Lyse was ashamed to think she had called the desk clerk a dolt when clearly she knew less than one of the hotel's porters. When he had emptied the tub and left her room, she paced up and down wondering how Buck was doing with the doctor. She knew she hadn't done a very good job on his shoulder, but at least she had kept him alive and that ought to be worth something even if her methods had been crude. When she heard another knock at her door, she was in no mood to greet callers and approached the door apprehensively.

"Yes?" she asked nervously as she opened the door a scant few inches. When she found a balding young man wearing a threadbare suit and thick glasses regarding her with a curious stare, she had no idea who he might be until he changed his pose and his doctor's bag swung into view.

"Miss Selby? I'm Dr. Malcolm Glover," the young man announced in a strained whisper. "Mr. Warren said I was not to leave the hotel before I examined you. May I come in?"

"I'm not sick," Lyse declared empathetically. "Just tell Buck I'm fine and go."

"No, I'm afraid I can't," Dr. Glover insisted as he nudged his wire-rimmed spectacles, which continually slipped down his nose, back into place. "He said I was to examine you thoroughly."

That was so humiliating a prospect, Lyse slammed the door in the young physician's face and hurriedly locked it. She had never had any illness so serious as to require treatment by a doctor, but she knew she didn't want this man touching her. Just how thorough was a thorough examination anyway? she wondered fretfully. Had he expected her to get undressed and let him do Lord knew what?

When Buck opened the door between their rooms, his chest was bare except for the clean white bandage that now covered his right shoulder. His deep tan had paled several shades, and he looked as miserable as he felt. "I'm not up to playing games with you, Lyse. You took a brutal beating three nights ago and I want Dr. Glover to check you over."

Completely forgetting her dread at their next meeting, Lyse instantly refused his demand. "I'm not some filly you can ask a vet to 'check over,' Buck. I don't want him touching me. I don't want him anywhere near me!"

Buck leaned back against the door, sorry the lovely mermaid he had found in her room earlier had vanished with the last drops of her bathwater. "Excuse us a minute, Dr. Glover," he called over his shoulder.

Stepping into her room, Buck closed the door and lowered his voice to a conspiratorial whisper. "I didn't mean to insult or frighten you, Lyse. What is it you think the doctor expects you to do, take off all your clothes and climb into bed with him?"

Not amused by that provocative question, Lyse's eyes widened in horror. "I'm not taking off my clothes, Buck. Oh, no. I won't!"

"But you don't mind getting into bed with him?" Buck asked with a deep chuckle.

"I won't do that either," Lyse hissed through clenched teeth.

The bright sparkle of tears on the tips of her long lashes warned Buck too late that he had again gone too far. He had also stupidly assumed Lyse would not mind speaking with a physician for a few minutes. "Is it the fact he is a doctor, or the fact he is a man that bothers you?" he asked in a far softer tone. Lyse had spent the last two nights cuddled beside him as she slept. He hadn't felt up to doing more than sleep, but he was sorry now he had wasted the hours he had held her delightfully pliant form in his arms.

Reacting to his more moderate tone, Lyse began to calm down but she wrapped her arms around herself protectively as she shuddered with revulsion. "Look, I wasn't hurt all that bad and I'm fine now. I don't need his say-so to know that. Please just tell him to go on home."

Buck frowned thoughtfully; he had never met a woman who had such an aversion to male company, but from what he had seen of her father he didn't blame her one bit for having such a low opinion of the male sex. "I'm worried about you, Lyse. If I stay with you, and you don't have to remove any of your clothing, will you agree to allow the poor soul to ask you a few questions? Doctors are concerned with helping people, not upsetting them needlessly. Even if you don't trust Dr. Glover, you trust me, don't you?"

He looked so damn sincere, Lyse couldn't bring herself to lie. "Yes, I trust you, but—"

"Come on, this won't take more than five minutes." Buck crossed to her side, took her by the hand and led her back into his room. Once there, he sat down in the easy chair near the corner window and pulled her down upon his knee. "As you can see, Miss Selby is painfully shy, Dr. Glover, but she has promised to answer your questions truthfully."

Embarrassed to be treated like a child when she didn't think her desire for privacy was in the least bit childish, Lyse tried to rise, but Buck clamped his left hand down upon her shoulder and she had no choice but to stay put. She turned her attention to the young physician then and found his blush even deeper than her own. It hadn't occurred to her he would be as embarrassed by this ordeal as she was and she felt a sudden twinge of sympathy for him. "I'm fine," she announced again. "Can't you both see that?"

What Malcolm Glover saw was a young woman, who though clearly underweight and shabbily dressed, was the most exquisitely beautiful blonde he had ever seen. Damp, her hair held only a hint of the silver glow that would shine so brightly when dry, yet he knew then it would be glorious. Her fair skin was flawless, her dark brows and lashes accenting prettily the delicacy of her sweet features. She looked like a finely painted China doll and he envied Buck Warren the ease with which he had drawn her down upon his lap. Suddenly realizing both Buck and Lyse were awaiting his answer with rapidly diminishing patience, he nodded. "Why yes, you do look well, Miss Selby. Just tell me what happened to cause the bruises to your eye."

"I fell," Lyse lied, and immediately Buck's hand tightened upon her shoulder until the pain compelled her to speak the truth. "Or rather, I got into a fight with a man," was all she was willing to admit. When Malcolm shot a fearful glance at Buck, she shook her head. "Not him. It was someone else."

Relieved, Malcolm again pushed his glasses up into place. "Did he knock you unconscious?"

Lyse didn't want to go over the details of the confrontation with her father, but she sensed it would be the fastest way to send the inquisitive doctor on his way. "Yes." She could feel Buck's fingers grow tense upon her shoulder again, but this time his anger wasn't directed at her. "It wasn't for long, though."

"Have you had headaches or problems with your vision since then?"

"No, I'm fine. Why doesn't anyone want to believe that?"

Dr. Glover reached out to take Lyse's hand and was surprised by the calluses on her palm. "Did you get into fights frequently with this man? Did he ever break any bones?"

"No!" Lyse shook her head as she pulled her hand away, wanting the wretched interview over. "Never."

Summoning all his courage, Malcolm Glover tried to couch his next question in more subtle terms. "There are other things a man might do to a woman, indignities he might make her suffer."

Understanding exactly what he meant, Lyse turned to look at Buck, then found him so close their lips were nearly touching. He had kissed her once, and briefly, but she had not forgotten the remarkable softness of his lips. His cheeks were now so smooth she found it difficult to stifle the impulse to reach up and touch his face. Then she remembered what she had wanted to say to him and anger drove such tender thoughts from her mind.

"I told you I wasn't raped. Didn't you believe me?"

Buck raised his brows slightly, not pleased to be forced to respond to so delicate a question in front of a third party. He had told the doctor to be discreet in his inquiries, but he hadn't realized Lyse would know he had prompted them. "I was afraid you were too ashamed to admit the truth, Lyse."

"I don't have to admit anything to you, Buck Warren, not one damn thing. Just try and remember that for a change." Lyse turned back to the young physician whose embarrassment had not lessened. His cheeks were still filled with a bright blush. "Is there anything else you're dying to know?"

Dr. Glover had observed Lyse carefully when she entered the room. She hadn't walked with a limp, nor had she displayed any difficulty when taking her perch upon Buck's knee. She did indeed appear to be in good health. "You are much too slender, Miss Selby. I've told Mr. Warren to stay in bed for the next few days and to eat plenty of nourishing food. The same advice would also be excellent for you."

Buck was tempted to ask Lyse to share his bed as well as his meals, but he knew such a suggestion would send her into a screaming fit and refrained from making it. He gave her a helpful nudge to set her on her feet but remained seated. "Thank you for coming to see us so promptly, doctor, but you mustn't tell a single soul why you came here or what you did. Is that clear?"

Buck had already paid him, and reaching for his bag, Dr. Glover began edging toward the door. "You have my word on it, Mr. Warren. I don't discuss my patients with anyone."

"Good. Thanks again." Buck waited until the doctor had let himself out before he spoke to Lyse. "Ring for the porter, will you? I want a quick bath, then the thickest steak the chef can find. You'll eat here with me. Do you want steak too, or something else?"

Lyse rang for the porter, inordinately pleased that she knew how to do it. She had never eaten in a restaurant, so she didn't have any idea what it was possible to order. "A steak is fine. I'll have whatever you're having."

When Buck leaned his head back against the chair and closed his eyes, Lyse couldn't help but suspect he had been putting up a brave front for her benefit, but clearly he couldn't do it any longer. "Was it bad?" she asked softly.

Buck opened one eye and grinned at her. "I didn't scream once. I hope you aren't disappointed you didn't get to rip that first bandage off me."

Why he thought she would enjoy seeing him suffer Lyse didn't know, but before she could defend herself the porter knocked at the door and she went to let him in. He brought the tub into Buck's room, then left to fetch hot water for his bath.

"I'm sorry if changing the bandage hurt you," Lyse commented shyly. "That's got to be my fault. If only I'd known how to put it on right in the first place—"

"Cut it out, Lyse," Buck interrupted as he pulled himself to his feet. "You'll not hear me complaining about your talents for healing. I'll put up with your attentions over that of buzzards any day."

Lyse went to the connecting door, then hesitated slightly before returning to her room. She thought Buck probably expected her to say something clever, but winning out in a contest with buzzards wasn't her idea of a flattering compliment. "Enjoy your bath," she finally called out cheerfully, but by the time she had shut the door behind her her eyes had already filled with tears.

VI

March 1849

*B*uck slept long past dawn, then awoke painfully aware that the brass key he had been clutching when he fell asleep now lay directly beneath his right shoulder blade. That discomfort was enough to inspire him to roll over, but not enough to provide the motivation for him to get up and order breakfast.

Though his travel-weary body continued to enjoy the soothing warmth of the high feather bed, at the sight of the key his vivid imagination immediately began to torment him anew with the same impossibly distracting images that had kept him awake far into the night. Despite it being enjoyable then, losing himself in such a frivolous pastime now presented a serious problem. Now that they had arrived in Galveston, he wanted to focus his attention upon outwitting Arvin, but try as he might he couldn't suppress the enticing memory of Lyse posed nude in her bath.

She had combed out her hair but left it falling free to her waist when she had joined him for supper. She had looked so delightfully feminine, it had seemed as though he had his mermaid within reach. Yet when he had told her how pretty she looked, she had swiftly brushed his compliment aside, obviously considering it empty flattery rather than the sincere words of praise it truly was. She had consumed the sumptuous meal he had ordered with as much enthusiasm as he, also thinking it a feast after the meager rations they had shared on the trail. She hadn't said much though, despite his best efforts to amuse her. Though she was never talkative, it wasn't like her to be so subdued and he was afraid she hadn't forgiven him for insisting she speak with the doctor.

As he recalled the hours they had spent together the previous evening, it seemed to him the only topic Lyse had shown any interest in discussing had been Arvin Corbett. She had wanted a complete description of the man, but he had been able to provide little in the way of information that would help her identify him. A man in his late twenties, standing five feet nine inches tall with brown hair, brown eyes, and a mustache, Arvin's description fit three quarters of the male population of any town in Texas. There was no way he could provide clues that would permit her to recognize him on sight. There was nothing in the least bit remarkable about Arvin except for his penchant for cold-blooded murder.

It was that gruesome thought that worried him. Despite Lyse's eagerness to help him locate his adversary, Buck still wasn't certain he should involve her in his scheme to trap the man. He would never forgive himself if she were hurt trying to help him and from what he knew of Arvin, the snake wouldn't hesitate to shoot a woman, even a very young and pretty one.

Buck tossed the brass key upon the marble-topped nightstand beside the bed, thinking himself very foolish for having taken it from Lyse's side of their common door. Since she had grown up on a ranch, she would undoubtedly know all there was to know about sex among animals, but clearly she knew nothing about how different the relationship was between a man and a woman. She was most definitely not the type of young woman who would be swept away by passion but she was instead one who would have to be courted with the utmost caution and courtesy. Certain he lacked not only the time for such an endeavor but also the patience, he didn't understand why he couldn't force thoughts of the headstrong blonde to the back of his mind where they belonged. Lyse had provided help when he had needed it desperately, but they would soon part and he wanted it to be without regret for either of them.

His well-chiseled features set in a deep frown, Buck ignored the rising level of noise outside in the street. With a concentrated effort he forced his thoughts into the proper channel, namely extracting revenge from Arvin Corbett, until he heard an insult shrieked in a feminine voice he was sorely afraid he recognized. Rolling off the high bed, he grabbed a shirt to hide the bandage on his shoulder before going to the window. He drew back the curtains and looked down into the street below.

"Damn it all!" he swore under his breath, for he was afraid the hostile crowd milling about below had all the makings of a lynch mob and Lyse was standing right in the middle of it. "How can that woman have stirred up so much trouble this early in the morning?"

Buck needed no more than a few seconds to discover the feisty blonde had taken exception to something a well-dressed young man in a gray suit had said. Apparently oblivious to the rapidly swelling crowd of spectators, they were standing toe to toe, each trying to outshout the other and Buck wasted no time in reaching for his Colt. Taking careful aim, he fired a single shot into the dirt between the hostile young man's heels.

Terrified, Tim MacCormac leapt three feet in the air, then spun around and looked up to see who had fired the shot he was certain had been meant for the middle of his back. When he saw a dark-haired young man with an expression every bit as fierce looking as the smoking weapon he held, he raised his hands and took a step backward, too frightened to turn tail and run.

Lyse sighed dejectedly, knowing Buck would never forgive her for her part in creating such a noisy spectacle. Raising her voice so he could hear her clearly above the rumblings of the crowd, she tried to explain what had happened. "This damn fool bumped into me as I left the hotel. He nearly knocked me down, mind you, then he accused me of picking his pocket. Tell him I'm no thief, Buck. Maybe he'll believe you 'cause he sure as hell doesn't believe me."

Buck rested his left arm on the window ledge as he stared down at the young woman whose haunting beauty had tormented him not only well into the night but also again that morning. With her fair hair hidden beneath her frayed straw hat and her tattered ranch clothes, Lyse again looked like a fourteen-year-old boy. Obviously she expected him to vouch for her character, but as he watched the faces of the bystanders turn up toward him, he hesitated to reply. He knew just how eager she was to get to California and he couldn't help but wonder if she might not have picked the man's pocket. She might have saved his life, but he really didn't know her well enough to swear that she wouldn't yield to such a temptation. Then again, they were partners, and he couldn't leave her screaming her head off in the street.

Gesturing with his Colt, Buck made his demand brief. "Both of you march right back into the hotel. Sit down in the lobby and stay put until I get there. I'll get to the bottom of this quick enough." When Lyse turned to go, but the young man didn't, Buck didn't wait but pulled back the hammer on his pistol with a dramatic flourish. "Unless you want to risk catching my next bullet in your right knee, get a move on!" That threat was enough to send the man scurrying after Lyse, but Buck leaned out to make certain he had entered the hotel before he slammed the window shut. As he hurriedly got dressed, he muttered that all women were trouble and he was beginning to suspect Lyse caused more than her share.

Lyse sat perched primly on the edge of a settee while she waited for Buck to come downstairs. She had hoped to surprise him, to locate Arvin that very morning, and she was disappointed her plan had fallen so far short of her goal. She knew precisely what Buck was going to say to her. He was going to laugh at her for attempting to play detective, then lose his temper completely over the fact that the results had been so disastrous. She clasped and unclasped her hands nervously, ignoring the man at her left who, no happier than she, was fidgeting anxiously with his hat.

Lyse had recognized his kind instantly. The harshness of his speech gave him away as being from the East and, like her, she bet he was on his way to California. From the looks of his well-tailored suit, he definitely wasn't poor, so he would be seeking adventure as much as gold. Well, if it was an adventure he wanted, she was certain it wasn't the kind he was having right then. He was fair haired, and blue eyed. His expensive clothes didn't hide the soft pudginess city folks' builds often had. Though Lyse thought city women might consider him good looking, he looked like an easy mark to her but she had never stolen anything in her life and she wasn't about to start now. When Buck finally appeared on the stairs, she leapt to her feet and rushed to meet him.

Tim MacCormac had been positive the skinny kid coming out of the hotel had taken his money and he had thought it would be a simple matter to shake it out of him. As he watched Buck Warren approach, he wished with all his heart the man had stayed out of the argument he had seemed so eager to settle with a bullet. He had been warned Texas was filled with men who made their living as gunfighters, but he had arrogantly thought himself far too smart to get involved with any. Now he realized that had been a mistake and he feared such dangerous associations were beyond the realm of choice. He rose to his feet, but remained by the settee and waited for Buck and the obnoxious kid to reach him before he told his side of the story.

Buck listened attentively as Lyse repeated her version of what had happened. He then offered his hand to Tim. "Good morning. I'm Buck Warren. Miss Selby and I are partners in a business venture, so naturally it pained me to see her accosted in the street, but I can see you're upset too."

Tim had to crane his neck to look up at Buck. He didn't ever recall meeting any man so tall, nor another man with so determined a gleam in his dark eyes. "This, this person is Miss Selby?" he stuttered as he glanced toward Lyse, noticing for the first time her features were far too delicate to be male.

Buck reached out to encircle Lyse's shoulder with his left arm. He gave her a squeeze and a teasing wink. "You see, darlin', you can't go parading around town dressed like a boy or everyone will mistake you for one."

Since she was most definitely not anybody's "darlin'," and most especially not his, Lyse shook off his embrace. "Stop it, Buck! This fool thinks I stole his money. This is no time for your jokes!"

"I wasn't joking," Buck assured her with a ready grin.

"Now let's hear your side of this, mister. Start with your name." His words were friendly, but he continued to eye Tim with a menacing glance.

"MacCormac. Timothy MacCormac." Tim drew himself up to his full height, but he was no more than five feet ten at best and felt at a terrible disadvantage. He needed to see the sheriff, not some giant who claimed to be a pickpocket's partner!

"All right, Mr. MacCormac, tell me what you think happened." Buck watched Lyse's pained expression out of the corner of his eye as Tim hurriedly explained how he had been robbed.

"I came here to meet with a Captain Randolph about booking passage to Panama on his ship. I had the gold to pay for it in the inside pocket of my coat. As I came through the door, this, well, this girl bumped into me. As soon as I'd stepped over the threshold I reached for my money and found it gone. That's when I turned back and grabbed her. She took my money and I want it returned immediately or I'm going to the sheriff to have her arrested for theft!"

Buck's eyes swept slowly over Lyse's baggy shirt and ill-fitting pants. She had plenty of places to hide a few coins, but he knew better than to suggest she allow Tim MacCormac, or anyone else, to search her. "Just wait a minute," he suggested instead. "Lyse says you're the one who bumped into her." Glancing toward the hotel's entrance, he saw the wide double doors were standing open to permit travelers to come and go with ease. "Come on over here, show me how this happened."

Exasperated, Tim thought Buck was merely stalling, but he followed him over to the open doorway. Lyse slipped right passed him just as she had scooted by him earlier that morning. "I was coming in the middle there, and the girl cut by me on the right on her way out."

Buck nodded thoughtfully. "Did you see who was on your left?"

"On my left? Why no, I told you she bumped into me and—"

Understanding where Buck's questions were leading, Lyse interrupted in an excited rush. "Don't you see, Mr.

MacCormac? Whoever was on your left pushed you into me and while you were distracted, he or she picked your pocket." Certain he would accept her conclusion as fact, she broke into an engaging grin and looked up at Buck, hoping for a nod of approval. Buck, however, was studying Tim's fury-filled expression rather than looking down at her.

"I'm going to send for the sheriff," Tim announced in a threatening whisper. "I don't care whether he searches that slut here or—" Tim got no further with that threat before it was slammed back down his throat. His head flew back with a brutal snap as Buck's fist caught him full in the face. He staggered backward, then reached out to grab the hand of the porter who had come running to break up the fight. With his help he managed to stay on his feet, but he was hurting badly. "I'll have him arrest the both of you!"

Horrified at the mayhem occurring in the hotel lobby, James Peters came out from behind the desk. "Mr. Warren and Miss Selby are guests of this hotel, while you, sir, are not. If you think you have a complaint to make, then take it to the sheriff, but I must insist you leave these premises immediately."

"I'll be back!" Tim pulled out his handkerchief to stem the flow of blood from his nose, but that gesture scarcely marred the drama of his exit.

"Fine, we'll be here." Taking a firm hold on Lyse's arm, Buck kept her by his side as he spoke with Peters. "I appreciate your help, but we need a little more. Can you tell us where to find the nearest shop specializing in women's clothing?"

"But I told you I don't want any new clothes, Buck," Lyse reminded him immediately.

Rather than waste precious time arguing with her, Buck listened carefully as Peters told him where to find a shop called the Rosebud. He then guided a still-squirming Lyse out the door and down the street.

The crowd that had gathered outside the hotel earlier had drifted away when the action had moved inside, but Buck took the precaution of lowering his voice so he would not be overheard by passersby. "Just what were you doing leaving the hotel, Lyse? Dr. Glover said you needed plenty of rest, too, so where were you going?"

First Lyse tried to push away his hand, but when he wouldn't release her, she gave up for the moment and answered his question. "I'd planned to make the rounds of the hotels. If Arvin was here, or still is, his name would be in one of the registers."

"That's true," Buck had to admit grudgingly, "but was that your idea of being discreet? I won't remind you that discreet was your word rather than mine, but I sure as hell thought you knew what it meant. I'd planned to stay out of sight until you found Arvin, but that's impossible now." Before Lyse could utter a single word to defend herself, Buck continued in a hoarse whisper. "Do you have MacCormac's money?"

"What?" Lyse again tried to pull free of his grasp, but he merely exerted more pressure upon her arm and drew her right off her feet until she ceased to struggle.

"Just answer me!" he demanded crossly.

"NO! I'm no thief!" Lyse was absolutely crushed to discover Buck thought so little of her. He had been so charming at supper, she had had to constantly remind herself his flattering attentions couldn't possibly be sincere. When he was so nice it was difficult not to like him, but she was dead set against allowing herself to like him too much. She knew she was lonely, but she sure didn't want him being nice to her out of pity. On the other hand, she had heard her father's crudely worded opinions on why men showed an interest in women so often she couldn't help but be suspicious of Buck's motives. Did he think she knew so little about men, she would be easy?

Lyse raised her chin proudly. She would show him a thing or two. There was a big difference between being innocent and being just plain stupid. Once she had wealth of her own, she wouldn't have to depend on a man for anything. No, sir, she would be free to do as she chose without having to listen to an arrogant man give her endless excuses why things had to be done his way rather than hers.

Buck knew the frankness of his question had offended Lyse, and badly, but he hadn't been able to think of another way to find out what had really happened without asking her right out if she had the money. He had never fought with any woman the way he continually seemed to be with her, and that annoyed the hell out of him because none of their disagreements were his fault. Then with an uncharacteristic burst of remorse, he recalled that when he had wanted her to see the doctor, he had insisted that she trust him. It was no wonder Lyse was hurt when he did not return that trust in full measure. He would apologize for his error, but it would have to be later.

By the time they reached the Rosebud, Buck had his request well thought out. He introduced himself to the proprietress, a tiny white-haired woman by the name of Rose Reynoso, then gave the only story he could. "Miss Selby has lost her luggage. It is imperative that you have her dressed from the skin out as the finest of ladies in less than one hour's time. If you succeed, I'll provide a generous bonus, but if you fail, Miss Selby could well end up in jail. Do you think you can help us?"

After having celebrated more than fifty birthdays, Rose prided herself on being an excellent judge of character. Though she had never heard of Buck Warren, his keen interest in his slender companion's welfare seemed quite genuine. "Am I likely to end up in jail too for helping you?" she asked, a merry twinkle lighting her brown eyes with mischief.

"No. There's no danger to you whatsoever, Señora Reynoso, only to Miss Selby. That's why we haven't a minute to lose." Buck couldn't help but smile because he was certain the little woman would help them even if he hadn't offered a bonus.

Lyse glanced around the crowded shop, taking in the neatly stacked bolts of satin and lace. The sweet fragrance of rose sachet perfumed the air, and surrounded by the many luxuries a true lady would take for granted, she felt totally out of place. "I haven't done anything wrong, Buck. You mustn't make me sound like a criminal."

"I don't intend to. Neither do I want you to look like one. I'm going over to meet the sheriff, and I'll just have to risk running into Arvin on the street. I don't know if I can keep a lawman talking for an hour, but I'll do my best. If I get arrested, you just lay low. Don't try to arrange a jailbreak before midnight." With that teasing farewell, Buck hurried out the door leaving Rose Reynoso giggling while Lyse simply eyed his back with a menacing stare.

"My goodness, but your young man has an unusual sense of humor." Rose smiled invitingly at Lyse as she gestured toward the dressing rooms at the back of her shop.

"He's not my young man and this is no joke," Lyse denied heatedly as she followed the older woman, but after a moment's reflection she decided for once Buck might actually have a good idea. If she looked like a respectable young woman, the sheriff would surely treat her as one. Looking down at her worn clothing, she knew she looked anything but respectable now. She pulled off her hat and began to unbutton her shirt. "I hope you have something that will fit me. It's been so long since I had a new dress, I have no idea what size I wear."

Rose pursed her lips thoughtfully as she pulled her tape measure from her pocket. "You're no bigger than a minute, Miss Selby, and if I'm not mistaken, I have just what you need."

"To look like a lady I'll need a miracle. Can you manage that?" Lyse sat down on a small padded stool to pull off her boots, but she wasn't at all optimistic.

Rose began to sort through the sheer silk lingerie stored in boxes along the wall. She pulled out a lace-covered chemise, pantaloons, and several slips. "We'll start with these." When Lyse made no move to put them on, Rose correctly surmised that she was a very shy young woman and turned her back toward her. "I promise not to turn around while you are putting them on." The tiny woman covered her eyes as she waited.

Despite Rose's thoughtfulness, Lyse continued to hold the garments in a reverent clasp, for she had never touched anything nearly so fine. "I would prefer cotton if you have it, please."

Lowering her hands, Rose peeked over her shoulder. "Ladies wear silk lingerie, dear, and you want to look like a lady, remember."

"But this all looks so expensive."

"That it is, but I think your gentleman friend can afford it."

"He is not my 'gentleman friend' either!" Lyse corrected her sharply, objecting violently to such a description of Buck.

Startled by that unexpectedly hostile response, Rose nonetheless recovered her composure quickly. She was used to dealing with high-strung young women and never allowed their tantrums to upset her for more than a second or two. "Well, whoever Mr. Warren might be, I think he can afford whatever you choose. Now let's hurry so we don't keep him waiting."

"It's not him I'm worried about," Lyse moaned dramatically.

"You needn't worry about the sheriff, sweetheart. I've often heard it said he simply can't resist a pretty blonde," Rose confided with another impish giggle.

With Rose in such high spirits, Lyse found it difficult to remain upset over her predicament. "Well, I guess I could try these things on. My mother had a silk nightgown she used to let me dress up in when I was a little girl."

"Ah, your mother was used to lovely things then?"

Rose was so sympathetic a woman, Lyse saw no reason not to tell her the truth. "Yes, she adored pretty things. The problem was, my father couldn't provide them so she ran off with a man who could."

"Oh, my goodness!" Rose needed a moment to decide what she thought of such behavior, then shrugged philosophically. "I've always thought pretty women have the right to be pampered. If she is as pretty as you, well then, I can't blame her for seeking the company of a man who could please her."

As Lyse stepped into the pantaloons, she asked hesitantly, "Do you really think I'm pretty?"

Completely forgetting her promise, Rose turned around to face Lyse. "Well, of course. Doesn't everyone you meet tell you how pretty you are?"

Lyse waited until she had pulled the slip over her head and adjusted the fit at her waist before she replied. "Some do," she admitted in a rather offhand fashion. "I don't really believe them, though."

Rose put her hands upon her hips as she shook her head. "My, my, I don't know what to say. A woman is expected to be modest, of course, but you'd be a fool not to take advantage of your beauty. Although we've just met, I doubt that you are ever a fool."

Despite the fact that things had gotten out of hand very quickly that morning, Lyse agreed with Rose's assessment. "No, I can't afford to be a fool. I'm on my way to California where I'm going to find enough gold to be set for life," she exclaimed proudly.

"Really?" Rose didn't know what to say to that astonishing announcement. Men were heading for California in droves, but she had yet to hear of another woman making the trip. "Is Mr. Warren bent on striking it rich too?"

"No, but I think he might already be rich so he doesn't need money the way I do," Lyse admitted quite frankly.

"Well, if he has plenty of money as well as good looks, he'll surely make some lucky girl a fine husband. Wouldn't you like it to be you?"

Lyse felt the heat of a bright blush rise in her cheeks and embarrassed by so personal a question, she shook her head. "It's nice clothes I need this morning, not a husband. You said you thought you had something that would fit me. May I see it, please?"

Rose had not meant to embarrass Lyse as she obviously had, and instantly took on a more professional attitude. As owner of a dress shop, she was privy to all sorts of tantalizing gossip and she enjoyed hearing it. She was sorry to learn Lyse might be leaving town before she found out how her story would end. "Yes, I do have something to show you. Sit down and put on these silk stockings, and I will be right back."

As directed, Lyse sank down upon the padded stool. Her impression of a fine lady was a woman with her mother's elegant posture and easy grace and she vowed to model her own behavior after Millicent's until she had gotten herself out of the horrible mess Timothy MacCormac's wild accusation had caused her. Millicent Selby had never for a second doubted that she was a beauty, and straightening her shoulders proudly, Lyse decided she could pretend to have that much self-confidence for a few hours at least, if not for the whole day.

As he returned to the Rosebud, Buck realized dressing Lyse as a lady was only half the battle. Somehow he was going to have to convince her to keep her mouth shut and let him do all the talking. Knowing she would have plenty to say about that request, he frowned as he stepped through the shop's door, but unmindful of his expression Rose Reynoso came rushing from the back to greet him.

"You will be positively thrilled with the change in Miss Selby's appearance, Mr. Warren. She has a lovely figure and with her fair coloring, she can wear so many pretty colors well. She insisted upon taking only one outfit, a gown a customer her size had ordered but then could not afford, but I will be happy to create a more extensive wardrobe for her. Surely so pretty a young woman needs more than one dress."

Buck's visit to the sheriff's office had gone so poorly he was in no mood to discuss ladies' apparel. He paid for Lyse's selections, then dismissed Rose with an impatient nod. "Well, where is she?" Knowing how belligerent Lyse's attitude had been when they had parted, Buck wasn't expecting all that much. When she called his name, in a seductive whisper, he jumped slightly, then catching himself he turned around to face her.

Lyse gave Buck a few seconds for the difference in her appearance to register then she began to laugh. "Why, Mr. Warren, I swear you are the one who could be arrested for looking at me like that."

The exquisite blonde was dressed in a watered silk gown of sky blue. The ruffled neckline brushed her chin, and matching ruffles on the close-fitting sleeves tickled her wrists. Her narrow waist was accented by the gown's tightly fitted bodice that was decorated with tiny pearl buttons. The gathered skirt ended in a deep ruffle that brushed the narrow toes of her new black kid shoes. Though Lyse was fully covered, Buck had never seen any woman's figure so seductively displayed. He had to swallow hard to keep from drooling not only out of appreciation for her beauty, but also out of desire.

Rose had styled Lyse's hair atop her head in a graceful swirl, leaving tendrils that had quickly been curled with a curling iron at her temples. Buck thought the effect far more than merely stunning: It was simply breathtaking. When Rose blocked his line of vision for a moment as she placed a straw bonnet decorated with flowing blue ribbons upon Lyse's crown and tied two of the ribbons beneath her chin in a lavish bow, he drew a much-needed deep breath.

What in God's name was he going to do with Lyse now? he asked himself. It might have taken him half the night to convince himself a romance with Lyse was out of the question, but he knew all hope of maintaining a platonic relationship with her now was lost. He would have to make very short work of Arvin, so he could give his undivided attention to her.

As Lyse pulled on the white kid gloves Rose had provided, she licked her lips as she had often seen her mother do and looked up at Buck through a long sweep of half-closed lashes. "I don't know how long I can continue this ridiculous masquerade, Buck, but if it dumbfounds you, it surely ought to work on the sheriff."

"I, well, I, that is, I," Buck heard himself stuttering like a schoolboy and couldn't believe any woman, let alone a feisty tomboy, had unnerved him so. He had always thought Lyse attractive, but he hadn't dreamed she possessed the poise to change her appearance so completely to that of rare beauty. Clearing his throat, he began again. "You look so beautiful I'm certain you could completely devastate the sheriff. Unfortunately, he's out of town and the deputy he left in charge hasn't the sense God gave a goat."

Concerned with their fate, Rose Reynoso had to interrupt then. "Are you talking about Ernie Hobart?"

"You know him?" Buck asked as he moved toward the door.

"Yes I do, and you needn't worry. He has difficulty enough thinking straight without any distractions. He'll never be able to arrest anybody with Miss Selby in the same room."

Lyse paused briefly to give Rose a hug, then went to Buck's side. "You see, your plan was positively brilliant. You just keep quiet and let me do all the talking and we'll get along fine with the deputy."

Rose saw Buck's glance lift toward the heavens as the attractive twosome left her shop and wondered if Lyse would get her way. She was then so overcome with curiosity about their scheme, she was furious with herself for not asking them to return to tell her if it had been a success.

VII

March 1849

With the talented hand of a fine artist, Rose Reynoso had hidden the remaining traces of the bruises on Lyse's right cheek and eye with an application of a rich skin cream followed with a light dusting of face powder. The cut her father had inflicted was healing nicely and would be no more than a thin line that would eventually fade. Rouge had added the sweetness of an innocent blush to her face and as Buck sat opposite her in the sheriff's office he continued to marvel at how perfectly lovely she looked.

It was not only her appearance he admired, but also the sheer imaginative brilliance of her story. With Lyse telling the tale he had fabricated, she had narrowly escaped death when her carriage had overturned. Two of her favorite horses, a matched pair of bay mares named Sugar and Honey, according to her, had been so badly injured they had had to be destroyed, although she tearfully confessed she had lacked the courage to put them out of their misery herself.

By the time she began describing how she had slipped out of the hotel in cast-off clothing to rush to an appointment with a dressmaker, only to suffer the humiliation of being accused of theft, Buck could readily see that not only the deputy, Ernie Hobart, but also Tim MacCormac believed every word she said. The two men were listening with such rapt attention, the spectacle was almost painful for Buck to observe. On the other hand, he was proud of Lyse for elaborating upon the story he had told at the hotel and wanted her to know it. He was tempted to shout "Bravo!" but had to content himself with no more than a sly wink when she glanced his way.

Lyse looked at each of the three men in turn, trying to appear so innocent she would quite naturally be flustered by Timothy MacCormac's totally unfounded charges. Wisely, she gave the better part of her attention to Hobart, a heavyset man in his late forties who for some inexplicable reason reminded her of her father.

"The Selby ranch raises the finest horses in all of Texas. Surely you must have heard of it, Sheriff." Lyse brought a frilly handkerchief with a deep lace border to her eyes, dabbing at her lashes as she looked toward him. How a woman was supposed to blow her nose on such a useless bit of lace she didn't know, grateful her tears weren't real so she'd have no need to find out.

"I am merely a deputy, Miss Selby," Ernie reminded her, proud that she seemed to think he looked as a sheriff should. In his youth he had had a husky build, but now he was so grossly overweight each time he moved even slightly his oak chair complained with an audible groan. "The name Selby is such a familiar one, I'm certain I must have heard of your ranch."

"Forgive me, Deputy Hobart, if I made a mistake with your title," Lyse begged sweetly, thinking it remarkable he claimed to have heard of her father's ranch when she was certain no one of any consequence ever had. Apparently he wasn't honest enough to admit he had no idea who her people were and she was sure that would work to her advantage.

"I know you must be a very busy man with all you have to do. Frankly, I think Mr. Warren has offered the only possible explanation for Mr. MacCormac's loss: A clever pickpocket caused the disturbance in the hotel doorway to cover his deed. It's a pity neither of us saw who he was. He's the one who should be here answering questions about the crime, not me."

Before Ernie Hobart could comment on Lyse's remarks, Tim MacCormac did. Leaning forward in his chair, he raised his right hand as though he were asking for permission to speak in a schoolroom. He had been astonished to find Miss Selby was so fine a lady when her appearance had been anything but impressive earlier that day. Now he was simply mortified he had added to her recent misfortune. As soon as she had moved through the door, beautifully attired and radiating the composure of a well-bred young lady, he had known he had made a terrible error that had cost him what he was certain was a broken nose. Striving to ignore the painful throbbing that made his whole face ache, he tried to apologize in the most gentlemanly way possible.

"I'm sorry to learn of your accident, Miss Selby, truly I am, and I hope you will forgive me for burdening you with an additional problem this morning. It's clear to me that you couldn't have been the one who stole my money. I'm almost positive there was someone else coming out of the hotel as I entered and I wish I had taken Mr. Warren's questions more seriously when he asked them. Now, well, now I'm afraid I can't recall anything about the man. Nothing about his appearance impressed me."

Relieved, Buck took a deep breath, hoping they would not have any reason to visit the sheriff's office ever again. He was getting hungry, and wanted to return to the hotel for something to eat because he had had no time for breakfast, and he doubted Lyse had had anything to eat either. Offering his hand, he prepared to make a quick exit. "No hard feelings, MacCormac? As I explained, Miss Selby and I are partners and I won't allow anyone to abuse her."

Tim swallowed hard, then felt his stomach lurch when he could discern the salty taste of blood still trickling down the back of his throat from his smashed nose. Returning Buck Warren's icy glance totally unnerved him, but he reluctantly forced himself to shake the taller man's hand. "I understand. I guess I made quite a fool of myself and I got what I deserved."

Grateful to see Tim had bought her fanciful story, Lyse turned again to the deputy. Though she was relieved she was no longer under suspicion, that didn't change the fact that the thief was still at large. "How are you going to go about catching the man who stole Mr. MacCormac's money?" she asked as though she actually believed him capable of apprehending the culprit.

Startled, since he had more experience breaking up fights than solving crimes, Ernie could do little more than shrug, which again released a weary wheeze from his overburdened chair. "Well now, Miss Selby, I don't rightly know what I can do since Mr. MacCormac can't provide a description of the thief."

Reaching out to pat Tim's knee sympathetically, Lyse favored him with an endearing smile. "Perhaps you'll recall more later. This morning must have been as difficult for you as it was for me."

Fascinated by her sapphire blue eyes and their gentle sweep of long lashes, Tim nodded weakly. "Yes, I certainly hope so as I can't afford to lose that money." He watched her begin to rise and leapt to his feet, only to feel so dizzy he had to reach out for the wall to steady himself. "I think I'll go back to my hotel and rest. If I remember anything, anything at all, I'll come back and give you a report, Mr. Hobart."

"Yeah, you do that," Ernie agreed quickly, happy to have the matter resolved for the moment.

After bidding the deputy farewell, Buck took Lyse's arm, but as they reached the street she turned back to ask Tim one final question. "Was that all the money you had?"

"Not quite," Tim admitted sheepishly, still feeling like a stupid fool for having been robbed in broad daylight. "Maybe I can work for my passage to Panama if we can't catch the thief. I'll think of some way out of this mess. I'm just not up to doing it now."

They parted company then as Tim headed in the opposite direction, but Lyse couldn't get his forlorn expression out of her mind and wished they had been able to do something to help him. "He seems so out of place here. Do you think he has the sense to go back home where he belongs?" she asked Buck.

Buck couldn't help but laugh at the unlikelihood of that. "No. Unless I miss my bet, he'll swim to Panama before he'll give up on going to California. Once gold fever gets into a man's blood, he loses whatever common sense he might have had."

Offended by the possibility he might include her in that sweeping generalization, Lyse stopped short and turned toward him. "Do you think me utterly lacking in common sense as well, Buck?"

Exasperated by that reply, Buck took Lyse by the arm to propel her along beside him. "No, of course not, but if you want to talk about the wisdom of your going to California, let's do it while we eat. I damn near bled to death a little over a week ago and if I don't get some food into me soon, I'll—"

"Oh, Buck, I'm sorry," Lyse interrupted contritely. "I've taken up your entire morning and we're no closer to finding Arvin than we were last night. I feel so sorry for MacCormac, but I didn't mean for you to think I cared more about his troubles than I do about yours."

Delighted she had changed the subject so readily, Buck broke into a wide grin. "Well, thank you. We can talk about Arvin while we eat too."

Now that the threat of going to jail had passed, Lyse realized she was also quite hungry. She reached down to lift her skirt above her feet so she could quicken her step. "Dresses are a damn nuisance to walk in, Buck, nothing but a bother."

"You wouldn't say that if you could see how pretty you looked," he confided. Indeed, every man they passed on the busy street had paused in mid-stride to ogle her. Though that annoyed Buck no end, he thought she must be flattered by the attentive glances he knew she couldn't help but see. Because it was undoubtedly a completely new experience for her, he didn't want to spoil it.

"Ha!" Lyse scoffed loudly, not nearly so impressed with her appearance as he seemed to be. As for the stares of the passersby, she thought them a rude lot and ignored them. She waited until they were seated in their hotel's spacious dining room and Buck had again given the order for them both before she made her feelings clear in words.

Lowering her voice to a whisper, Lyse had no idea how seductive she sounded. "I might have been able to give a passable imitation of my mother this morning, Buck, but the minute we are finished eating I'm going back to the Rosebud to pick up my old clothes. In fact, I should probably do that now. This dress is still clean. It doesn't look a bit worn and Rose can give you your money back and sell it to someone else."

"What?" Where Lyse got her ideas, Buck swore he would never understand. "Look, I bought the dress because you needed one. Desperately. It's far too pretty to take back and I won't allow it. I think it's a good idea to go back to the Rosebud, but only to pick up some other things, not to return those you just got."

He sounded so adamant about it, Lyse knew it would be useless to argue. Because he had paid for her new clothes, she supposed whether or not she returned them ought to be his decision. Annoyed that she could not have her own way, she suddenly remembered his remark about gold fever and gave him her opinion on that. "I'm not like the men who are going to California. I don't want to strike it rich. I just want to find enough gold to take care of myself so I don't have to depend on a man to pay for my clothes or anything else."

Because he had heard similar comments from her before, Buck was wise enough to know Lyse firmly believed in what she said even though he thought her daft. "The problem will be with the word, 'enough,' Lyse. It seems no one ever has enough gold to be satisfied."

Raising her chin proudly, Lyse continued to disagree. "I just want to buy some land, and build a little house, not a palace. I'd like to raise horses like I always have, and I won't need a fortune to get started with that."

Buck nodded, having to admit her desires were modest. "Unlike a man, I don't suppose you'll be tempted to squander your money on gambling, wild women, or liquor so you just might make it, Lyse. You just might be able to do it."

"Of course I will," the confident blonde exclaimed proudly.

"What will you call this ranch of yours?" Buck inquired politely with only a hint of a smile playing across his lips. The waiter arrived then with two succulent steaks and though his interest in the meal was keen, Buck continued to ply Lyse with questions about her future home.

Lyse hadn't thought of any name for a ranch, nor had she done any serious planning as Buck's inquiries soon revealed. As with the first steak she had enjoyed there, she had to take small bites and be careful to chew them on her molars. Her front teeth finally seemed more firmly secured in her gums than they had been the morning after her father had hit her and she was relieved to think she would undoubtedly keep them after all. Still, she had to be careful and chew slowly and it was difficult to concentrate upon that task and answer his questions at the same time.

"I thought your version of the carriage incident was positively inspired, by the way. Calling the mares Sugar and Honey was an especially nice touch. That would have sounded ridiculous coming from me, but the names were perfect for a lady's pets. You must remember those names when you get some mares for your ranch."

As happened so frequently when Buck spoke with her, Lyse wasn't certain whether he was serious or not. She was afraid he was mocking her rather than paying compliments, and reacted accordingly. "You must really think me a silly goose, don't you? I just thought a few details would make your story more believable and since it worked, it doesn't matter what I called the dead horses since they didn't exist in the first place. I also know there's a lot involved in running a ranch, but I can handle the work. Hell, I always have."

To have Lyse dressed so beautifully and still talk like her old feisty self kept Buck amused the entire meal. She ate with such delicate gestures, he had finished not only his steak and potatoes but also a thick slice of apple pie before she was through. "No, I don't think you're a silly goose at all. I think you're a remarkable young woman with a lot of courage. I just wish—"

When he paused and looked at her with a warmly appreciative gaze, the attractive artificial blush gracing Lyse's cheeks became vividly real. Though she may have been uncertain about his last remarks, she was positive of his mood now. "I told you dressing up like this was no more than an act, Buck Warren, so get that sappy look off your face right now," she warned in a low hiss. "I may look like a helpless bit of fluff for the moment, but just like you said, I'm harder than steel inside." Lyse recalled being insulted when he had made that comment, but as long as he had said it she intended to get some use out of it.

Actually, she found the liquid warmth of his dark gaze strangely stirring, but Lyse felt merely uncomfortable rather than aroused. Her sudden departure from home had left her already ravaged emotions hopelessly strained and she failed to recognize the easy camaraderie that existed between them as a sign of how swiftly their friendship could develop into something far deeper. Men had always looked at her mother with an openly adoring glance, but she couldn't bear to be stared at in the same way.

"I'm nothing like my mother, Buck, nothing at all," Lyse blurted out suddenly. "She loved to flirt with men. When we went into town it used to take us hours to shop because she would stop and talk with every man who wished her a good day."

Buck frowned slightly, not understanding why Lyse's thoughts ran so swiftly to her mother that day. The one time he had tried to encourage her to talk about the woman, she had told him it was none of his business, so he made no such effort now. Instead, he reached across the table to give her hand a sympathetic pat. "I've met your pa, Lyse, and I think your mother must have been terribly lonely. Don't judge her too harshly for craving the attention of other men."

Lyse nodded slightly, knowing he was right. "I don't, and I never have. All I'm saying is that I'm nothing like her and I don't like being treated as though I were."

"Am I doing that?" Buck asked with a deep chuckle, for he didn't see how he possibly could be.

"Yes, you're flirting with me," Lyse explained too sharply, and when Buck actually winced, she feared perhaps she had made a dreadful mistake. "Or at least I thought you were. Were you?" she asked hesitantly.

Buck leaned back in his chair, thinking himself fortunate to have shared another fine meal with such a uniquely fascinating young woman. She intrigued him enormously, he would readily admit that. But flirting, hell, he didn't ever bother to flirt. "No, I wasn't," he insisted with a straight face. "I don't even know how to flirt."

For an instant, Lyse thought he was serious, then she saw the teasing sparkle in his eyes. "You are not only a flirt, but a liar, Mr. Warren, and we've no more time to waste on such foolishness today. I want to pick up my clothes at the Rosebud and then I'll start looking for Arvin. You're supposed to be taking a nap, aren't you?"

After such a hearty meal, Buck did indeed feel like taking a nap, but only if she shared his bed, which he knew was out of the question. "I'd never be able to sleep, so there's no point in going up to my room. I'll let you look for Arvin, but only if you promise to remain in that dress and make truly discreet inquiries at the hotels while I visit the saloons. If by some chance you find where he's staying, come straight back here. I'll meet you back at our rooms at five and we can report on what we've found then. Under no circumstances are you to approach Arvin and try to speak with him. Is that understood?"

Lyse frowned slightly, but anxious to get started she agreed. "Yes, I understand I'm not to get into another mess like I did this morning, but I'd like to remind you it wasn't my fault. Do you suppose Peters could give me the addresses of all the other hotels? I wouldn't want to miss any."

Before Buck could assure her Peters would provide any service for a generous tip, he caught sight of Timothy MacCormac making his way toward their table. "Oh, Lord, here comes MacCormac. What could he possibly want with us?"

Lyse glanced over her shoulder, and no more pleased to have their plans interrupted than Buck she gave Tim only a tentative smile. He seemed not to notice he had not been welcomed as he grabbed a chair from a vacant table and without waiting for an invitation, sat down between them.

"I've found the man!" Tim began in an excited rush. "He's over at the Queen of Hearts saloon gambling with the money he stole from me!"

Buck looked first at Lyse, whose expression was as blank as his own, before replying to Tim's startling announcement. "Don't you think you should be telling Hobart about this rather than us?"

"I did, but the man is too frightened to act," Tim revealed angrily. "I was hoping I could convince you to help me, though, Mr. Warren." Unmindful of Buck's astonished expression, he paused for a moment to cast a furtive glance around the crowded dining room, then lowered his voice to a conspiratorial whisper. "When I left home, my father gave me a leather pouch filled with gold coins to pay for my passage. It was dark red with a design of interlocking triangles stamped along the top. The man at the Queen of Hearts has one which looks just like it and that can't be due to coincidence."

"And Hobart refused to confront him?" Lyse asked incredulously.

"He said the man would undoubtedly swear he had found it, or won it from someone else. He just told me to keep an eye on him and when the sheriff returns tomorrow, he would question him for me. By tomorrow the man could have gambled away all the money, or thrown away the pouch and there would be no way to prove he's the thief, so I can't afford to wait. I need that money too badly to risk what chance I have of getting it back waiting for the sheriff. Captain Randolph's ship sails day after tomorrow and I want to be on it."

"And for some reason you believe I'm the man to get your money back? Frankly, I'll be damned if I can think of a reason why." Buck had plenty of trouble himself in Galveston without taking on anyone else's. He looked to Lyse for support but as usual, she surprised him.

"I'm as disgusted as you are Hobart won't help you, Tim. I really wish there were some way I could help you myself, but they don't permit women in the saloons here, do they?"

"You stay out of this, Lyse," Buck warned her sharply, amazed to discover she wouldn't march right into the saloon because she obviously thought Tim's cause was just.

Lyse refused to obey his command because she felt he had no right to give it. "Buck, if Tim tries to get that money back by himself he could very easily get shot. Maybe you wouldn't mind, but I sure don't want his murder on my conscience." Hoping that gruesome image would silence Buck for a moment, Lyse turned back to Tim, who at the mention of his possible murder, had begun to regard her with an awestruck gaze. "Where is your home, Tim?" she asked sweetly.

"I'm from Cincinnati, Ohio," he managed to mumble in a hoarse whisper. Then encouraged by the warmth of her smile, he continued. "I worked as an accountant and I was tired of spending all my time managing other men's money. When I heard miners were striking it rich every day in California I wanted a chance to find a fortune too. I took all my savings out of the bank, and my dad gave me what money he could spare. I can't go back home and say I lost the money to pay my way out West and didn't get any farther than Texas. I could never do that."

Tim was so humiliated by that thought he looked ready to cry. There were deep purple shadows beneath his eyes as a result of Buck's blow to his nose and he was again rolling the brim of his hat between his hands. Eager to convince Buck to help him, he tried again to win his support. "I've seen how well you handle yourself, Mr. Warren. I was hoping you wouldn't mind working for me for an hour or two to help me get back my money."

Buck looked across the table at Lyse. "You attract trouble like a magnet. You realize that, don't you, Lyse?"

"I do no such thing!" the elegantly dressed blonde immediately denied. "I just think it's too bad about Tim's money and I'd help him if I could. But he didn't ask me," she pointed out shrewdly.

"Jesus Christ," Buck swore under his breath. "Yeah, I do know how to handle myself, MacCormac, and the secret is in minding my own business, not everybody else's."

"I've offered to pay you," Tim reminded him. "I didn't expect you to help me for free." He looked at Lyse then, still amazed by how greatly her appearance had changed since that morning. Because she was the more sympathetic of the two, he tried smiling broadly at her, but succeeded only in causing his nose another burst of pain that made tears well up in his eyes.

MacCormac was going to start sobbing any second, Buck just knew it. Lyse, on the other hand, was eyeing him with a coolly skeptical glance. She obviously thought he could solve Tim's problem in the time it would take to snap his fingers if he chose to do so. It was wonderful she had so much confidence in him, but he had long ago outgrown the need to show off in front of pretty girls.

"What is it you're offering to pay me to do, MacCormac? You want me to shoot the man who's got your pouch? Is that it?"

Taken aback by the harshness of Buck's tone, Tim had to gather all his courage to respond. "Isn't that how you make your living? You're a gunslinger, aren't you?"

"Hell no!" Buck denied hotly while Lyse began to giggle as though such an assumption were preposterous. "This fool wants me to risk getting killed and you think it's funny?"

"No, it's not in the least bit funny!" Yet Lyse couldn't help herself. She raised her napkin to her lips to stifle the sound of her laughter, but that only infuriated Buck all the more. Finally she took several sips of water and was able to regain her composure. "I apologize to you both. I didn't mean to make light of your problem, Tim, or the danger to you, Buck."

Buck continued to regard her with a dark stare until he was satisfied she wouldn't start laughing again. She was doing well at acting the part of a lady in front of MacCormac, but he was beginning to miss the down-to-earth young woman he truly knew Lyse to be. Because he had asked her to pretend she had the manners to match her dress, he knew he couldn't complain about her behavior and turned his attention back to Tim. Because it looked to him like the only way he could get MacCormac out of his hair was to help him, he took a new tack. "You said the man was gambling with your money. Is he playing poker?"

"Yes." Tim looked a bit sheepish then. "I was headed back to my hotel, and as I passed the Queen of Hearts I decided a drink wouldn't hurt me. When I walked by the poker table nearest the door, I saw one of the players slipping my money pouch into his coat pocket. I just turned on my heel and went straight back to Hobart. You know what happened then."

"Presuming the man's still playing cards, did you get a good look at him?" Buck began to flex the fingers of his right hand, not certain they were strong enough to hold a deck of cards.

"I sure did. He looked about my size, but more wiry. Brown hair and eyes, a thick mustache. He—"

"Let's go," Buck ordered as he rose quickly from his chair.

Understanding the reason behind his sudden desire for haste, Lyse jumped to her feet too. "Do you think it's Arvin?" she asked apprehensively, genuinely alarmed.

Buck shook his head. "That would be too great a coincidence, but I'll go over and take a look at the man."

"You'll both be careful, won't you?" Lyse knew Buck wasn't pleased that she had taken an interest in Tim MacCormac's troubles, but she couldn't help but want to have the real culprit behind bars to completely clear her name.

"Shouldn't we have some sort of plan?" Tim asked nervously as the trio started toward the door.

"You want a plan? All right, I'll give you one." Buck hesitated a brief second then lowered his voice. "You go into the saloon and order a drink at the bar. I'll follow you in, and the first chance I get I'll sit down at the table where the man with your pouch is playing poker. Give me an hour or two, and I'll win back everything you lost. Anything over that, I keep."

"I lost four hundred dollars this morning," Tim informed him. "If you don't win more than that, I'll split what you do win fifty-fifty."

Tim's generosity surprised Buck, but he refused his offer. "No, let's get your money back before we worry about me turning a profit."

As they left the hotel, Lyse had to nearly run to keep up with the two men. "You didn't promise to be careful. I want your promise, Buck."

Buck stopped and turned toward her, exasperated she would make every effort to influence him to help Tim and then demurely ask him to be careful. "I am not going to get into a gunfight, Lyse. I plan to win the money fairly. I'll let the sheriff handle the matter of the theft. Now I want your promise you'll wait for us at the hotel after you've finished the errands we discussed."

Lyse nodded nervously, "Yes, I'll meet you there later." She waited there and watched Buck and Tim walk down the street until they were lost from sight. Then she went back into the hotel to charm James Peters into compiling a list of every place he could name where a man might spend a night or two.

Just as Buck had suspected, the mustachioed poker player wasn't Arvin Corbett, although his description closely matched that of the man he had nearly died tracking. Fortunately, Buck had to wait no more than ten minutes before a man left the table and he could join the game. He bought chips with the same lazy nonchalance he always displayed when he played cards then scooted down in his chair to stretch out his legs and be comfortable. He ordered a beer and prepared to stay as long as necessary to accomplish his purpose. Galveston had a great many saloons, and though the odds were against Arvin strolling into the Queen of Hearts, Buck couldn't help but wish that he would.

When Buck introduced himself to the four other men at the table, the one whose money he had come to take hastily murmured his name was Jack. After playing a few hands, Buck recognized his type: He was a nervous sort who clung to the mistaken notion poker was a game requiring luck rather than steady nerves and skill. He would bet on anything, silently pray for a lucky break, and usually lose. It didn't take much imagination for Buck to figure out why he had picked Tim's pocket when he saw that Jack played so poorly, he seldom won a hand even when he held the best cards.

Jack was down to three hundred dollars when Buck entered the game, and he continued to lose while the pile of chips Buck accumulated steadily grew in height. Two of the original players dropped out, only to be replaced by newcomers eager to get into a high stakes game. Two hours passed, then three slid easily into four. Buck had won fifteen hundred dollars by then, but he continued to play until Jack had lost every cent he had. When the manager of the Queen of Hearts refused to extend him credit, he tried to get a loan from Buck but was instantly refused.

Buck had seen the pouch Tim had described each time

Jack had had to pull it from his pocket to extract more coins for chips. Knowing it was now empty, he glanced toward the bar where Tim had been nursing his third beer for over an hour and motioned for him to join them. Scooping up the chips he had won, he handed them to Tim to hold.

"This is Timothy MacCormac, Jack. Now that you've lost all the money you stole from him this morning, why don't you give him back that red leather pouch? It has a lot of sentimental value."

Though Buck's words were laced with heavy sarcasm, rather than openly threatening, Jack's dark eyes grew wide with terror. He hadn't seen Tim enter the saloon, and even if he had he wouldn't have recognized him because his nose was so badly swollen. Like a cornered rat, Jack panicked and went for his gun. Though he had hoped the man wouldn't be that stupid, Buck had given his chips to Tim so he wouldn't have to be bothered picking them up off the floor should there be a fight. That a cowardly pickpocket had the guts to pull a gun on him surprised him, but he was prepared for that move and countered it swiftly.

Using his left arm and shoulder, Buck flipped the round poker table into the air before Jack's pistol had cleared his holster. Scrambling to escape the airborne table, the hapless man fell over backward in his chair. Before he could bring up his hands to protect himself, the table crashed to the floor, the edge striking him across the throat with the deadly force of a guillotine.

Trying to escape the mayhem, the three other men at the table dived for cover while Tim stood stock-still clutching the chips Buck had won. While confusion reigned all around him, Buck leaned down to lift the heavy table off Jack, but he saw at a glance the man was done for and began to swear the vilest of curses. He had not meant to kill the fool, merely to disarm him and march him over to the jail. Clearly it was too late for that now.

Jack's eyes began to bulge as his frantic gasps pulled no air through his shattered throat to his lungs. His skin lost all color, then took on a deathly blue tinge as he reached out his hand to Buck, imploring him to help him catch his breath. Buck knelt at Jack's side, laced his fingers in his, and gripped his hand tightly as he felt the man's life continue to slip away. His wheezing gasps took on the gurgling sound of a death rattle and in less than a minute from the time he had gone for his gun, Jack was dead.

"Son of a bitch," Buck swore as he rose to his feet. "Turn in those chips, Tim. Looks like we're going to have to have another long talk with Hobart."

As the others in the crowded saloon pressed close for a better look at the dead man, a dark-haired man at the end of the bar stepped into the shadows that led toward the back door. The fight had been over almost before it had begun, but Arvin had gotten a good look at Buck Warren when he had leapt to his feet and though he knew the man couldn't possibly be alive, he was undeniably there and causing trouble like he always had. Arvin was certain ghosts didn't rise from their graves to murder people, but clearly, Buck Warren had. Then as he dashed out the back door in a headlong rush to save his own life, he remembered he hadn't bothered to bury Buck and he realized too late just how great a mistake that had been.

VIII

March 1849

*T*hough there were a great number of witnesses prepared to swear Buck Warren had done no more than overturn a table, Ernie Hobart could not overlook the shocking fact that the bizarre incident at the Queen of Hearts had resulted in a death. No one seemed to know much about the deceased, not even where he had lived much less his last name. Jack had been only one of the countless drifters who spent their time in the saloons of Galveston and he apparently had been without friends or family to mourn his passing. Still, accidental death or not, Hobart couldn't shake the lingering suspicion that there was far more to Buck Warren's story than the tall man had thus far revealed. "Are you positive you hadn't met Jack before today, Warren?"

For the second time that day, Buck found himself seated in the sheriff's office attempting to answer Ernie Hobart's questions diplomatically. Because they were becoming more ridiculous by the minute, that was not an easy task. Thoroughly exasperated, he refused to answer his last one. "Look, you have my written statement to show the sheriff tomorrow and you have the names of a dozen witnesses who'll testify that Jack drew his gun on me. It was an accident the table caught him on the throat, but if you want to call it a killing then you'll have to list it as self-defense because that's all it was."

"You needn't get short-tempered with me, Warren," Ernie

replied curtly, still not satisfied he had done a thorough enough job with his investigation. He was sorry he had not gone to the Queen of Hearts himself when Timothy Mac-Cormac had come for him. Now he couldn't help but wonder if in his absence MacCormac and Warren hadn't planned to kill Jack all along and just made it look like an accident. "There's a big difference between self-defense and cold-blooded murder, and the sheriff will want to make damn sure which one it was before he marks this case closed."

Tim had let Buck do most of the talking, but the mention of murder totally unnerved him. "I have always been a law-abiding citizen. I could no more plot a murder than I could fly." He glanced over at Buck then, thinking his size and dark coloring definitely gave him a sinister appearance. He would not put murder past Buck, but he had seen how Jack had died firsthand and insisted it was an accident. "Jack went for his gun. We all saw that. Even if Buck had drawn his pistol and shot him smack between the eyes, the man's death would still be self-defense. You can make up whatever fairy tale you like, but you're going to have to come to the same conclusion: Buck was merely defending himself and Jack's death was the unfortunate result."

Thinking that summary adequate, Buck rose to his feet. "You know where each of us is staying. If the sheriff wants to question us himself he can send for us."

As Tim MacCormac also rose to his feet, Ernie wished he could think of a reason to arrest them both, just so he could keep tabs on them until the sheriff returned, but he couldn't. "Just stay out of trouble the rest of the time you're here in Galveston, that's all I ask."

Without replying to what he considered an unnecessary request, Buck slammed his hat down on the back of his head and strode out the door with Tim at his heels. It had been one o'clock when they had gone to the Queen of Hearts, past five when Jack had died. Ernie Hobart's idiotic interrogation had wasted nearly two hours and he could well imagine what a state Lyse would be in by the time he got back to the hotel. When Tim stayed right with him, he asked the most obvious question. "Just where is it you're going?"

"Back to your hotel. If Captain Randolph is still there, I'll pay for my passage tonight." Tim was so glad to have his money back, he didn't plan to dwell on the tragedy its recovery had caused and unlike Buck, he was grinning happily. "You said you and Miss Selby were business partners. You plan to be in Galveston long?"

Buck quickened his step, but Tim managed to keep up with him. "No longer than I have to be," he nearly growled. Christ almighty! he thought to himself. He had wanted to take care of Arvin neat and quick. Now, unless he missed his guess, the law would be dogging his every step and if he succeeded in killing Arvin they would be right there to arrest him for murder. Nothing had gone as he had planned it since the day he had heard Arvin had returned to Austin. Not one damn thing!

Tim could see Buck was in a foul mood, but that didn't lessen his desire to see Alyssa Selby again. "Perhaps you and Miss Selby would like to join me for supper?" he asked excitedly as they reached the steps of Buck's hotel.

Buck shot Tim a disgusted glance and shook his head. "No thanks. The last thing I feel like doing is eating." Then realizing by the young man's hurt expression that he had been rude, he offered his hand. "Good luck in California."

"Thank you. I hope I'll have an opportunity to tell Miss Selby good-bye too."

"I'll tell her that," Buck said in parting, but when he reached his room, he found Lyse in no mood to hear polite greetings from Tim.

"Where in the hell have you been?" the vibrant blonde asked accusingly. "You were supposed to meet me here at five and it will soon be eight! Didn't you have any idea how worried I'd be?"

It was obvious to Buck from the tension of her pose and gestures that Lyse had indeed been desperately worried, and he knew when he explained why he was so late she would be more worried still. Tossing his hat upon the dresser, he stretched out across the bed without bothering to remove his boots. It had been another long day and he was so tired he could barely see let alone think up pretty excuses to soothe the temper of a woman so volatile as she.

"I know I'm late and I'm sorry. I'm also so tired I feel sick to my stomach, so I'd appreciate it if you'd just leave me alone for an hour or two."

Lyse was still dressed in the new blue gown and as she rushed to his side her skirt rustled softly at her feet. Afraid he had fallen ill, her anger was instantly forgotten. She sat down upon the edge of the bed and reached out to touch Buck's forehead. When she discovered his skin wasn't overly warm, she lifted her hand to his temple and slipped her fingers through his hair. Shiny and blacker than midnight, it felt as soft as her own and suddenly embarrassed to be fondling him like a pet, she withdrew her hand as she began to apologize.

"I didn't mean to yell at you like that. It was just that I was so worried something dreadful had happened to you. I feel just awful about the trouble I caused this morning, so I kept my promise and stayed here, but I kept imagining the most awful things and—"

Buck took a deep breath and let it out slowly, thinking it was rather nice to be yelled at for so charming a reason. He reached up to catch Lyse's hand and brought it to his lips. Her palm held the faint fragrance of roses from the cream Rose Reynoso had given her and he began to smile. "You sound just like a wife," he commented wryly.

"I do not!" Lyse protested sharply. Sorry she had been fool enough to apologize to the oaf, she tried to yank her hand from his, but rather than release her Buck deftly pulled her down across his chest then wrapped his arms around her waist to hold her fast.

"Yes you do," Buck insisted, and before she could draw a breath to argue, he raised his left hand to her hair, laced his fingers in the handy swirl of curls, and forced her mouth down to his. There was nothing gentle in his kiss this time but the fierce hunger of a man who has all too recently looked upon the face of death. Lost in a haze of desire, he steadily increased the pressure of his lips upon hers, seeking entrance to the delights of what he was certain would be a honey-sweet mouth. It wasn't until a tear splashed upon his cheek that Buck realized she found his affection distasteful rather than wildly exciting. Although deeply disappointed, he relaxed his hold upon her only slightly as he ended his unreturned kiss, but he kept her lying captive in his embrace. With so intriguing a challenge, his right arm didn't pain him at all.

"Lyse," he began, summoning all the patience he possessed. "If you didn't like me you wouldn't care whether I was late or not. When are you going to admit you want us to be more than friends?" Another tear trickled slowly down her face to light upon his cheek, but Lyse was merely staring down at him, her blue eyes bright with the glistening swell of moisture that again threatened to overflow her thick lashes.

Taking the fact that she was neither struggling nor screaming as a good sign, Buck continued to speak in a soothing tone as he plucked the pins from her hair to spill a glorious blond cascade down over her shoulders. "You're so pretty, Lyse, and I've never been much good at keeping my feelings a secret. I want to make love to you, but not if you're going to cry the whole time."

Lyse's heart was pounding so wildly she had difficulty making out Buck's words. She had long ago decided love was a trap she wanted at all costs to avoid, but the rich timbre of Buck's deep voice made his words anything but threatening. It wasn't until he fell silent and began to frown that she found the courage to respond. "You hurt my teeth," she explained in a breathless whisper, choosing to voice her most immediate complaint rather than offer her negative view of love because surely that would set him arguing all night.

Buck knew that had to be the most unusual response any woman had ever given to a man who announced he wished to make love to her. He reminded himself that this was Lyse, however, whose thinking was always unique. At least she hadn't called him any vile names or threatened to castrate him with her own hand, which wouldn't have been unlike her. The fact was, she had beautiful teeth. They were as perfect as a string of pearls, so her complaint made no sense at all to him. "How could I possibly have hurt your teeth, Lyse?" he asked as calmly as he possibly could.

Finally noticing it was her tears that were making his face

wet, Lyse raised a hand to his cheek to wipe them away. "My father hit me in the mouth. It's difficult to eat and—" She started to cry in earnest then because inexplicably, she did want him to kiss her, but she didn't want to lose her front teeth either and it suddenly seemed an impossible choice.

Now her comment made perfect sense and Buck felt like an insensitive ass for not understanding immediately what she had meant. Her lips had been swollen for a couple of days, but he hadn't realized she had been hit so hard her teeth had been knocked loose. No wonder it took her so long to eat; it had to be excruciatingly painful. He cradled her head upon his left shoulder and patted her back gently as she continued to weep.

"Hush, Lyse, it's all right. I wouldn't hurt you for the world. Just stay with me for a little while then we'll order something for dinner that won't cause you a bit of pain."

"You're not angry with me?" Lyse managed to mumble between tear-choked sobs.

"Why should I be angry?" Buck offered with a reassuring chuckle.

Lyse tried to recall his exact words but could not. He had said something about making love. She had said neither yes nor no, but it seemed to make no difference to him that she hadn't answered. Perhaps he hadn't been all that keen on doing it. Still, she was certain when a man kissed a woman he expected a response other than a flood of tears and that thought made her cry all the harder.

Buck stared up at the ceiling, thinking he was unlikely to ever meet another woman like Lyse. She was a headstrong tomboy one minute, and in the next, all soft, sweet woman. She was still lying on top of him, her legs between his and though the abandonment of her pose did nothing to lessen his desire to know more of her than he was certain any man ever had, at the same time he wanted only to hold her in a comforting embrace until she was over her tears. The vague memories of how tenderly she had held him in her arms when she had bandaged his shoulder brought a smile to his lips.

"Hey," he called to her softly. "You're the one who's going to end up feeling sick if you don't dry those tears. You have a lovely smile and I want you to keep it. We'll find a dentist tomorrow who can take care of your teeth. Don't you worry another minute about them."

Lyse couldn't admit that wasn't really her problem now. It had to be the dress, she finally decided. She had looked like a woman for a change and he had treated her like one. The trouble was, she knew only a small part of what her mother had done to charm men, not all of it. She kept reminding herself she and Buck would soon be going their separate ways, so keeping her distance was what she had to do, not seduce him. Still, it felt so nice lying in his arms, she continued to cling to him long after her tears had ceased to dampen his shirt.

When Buck's stomach started to complain of emptiness with loud rumbles, he reached over and yanked the bellpull. "We're on the Gulf, they've got to make a seafood chowder. I'll order that for us."

Not wanting the porter to find her reclining upon Buck's bed, Lyse sat up. "That would be fine, but order what you want for yourself." She didn't dare look at him, she was so embarrassed by the way she had behaved. First she had yelled at him like a shrew, then wept like she had no brains at all. "I won't need to see a dentist. My teeth are getting better by themselves and he'd probably just mess 'em up."

Buck could readily sense by Lyse's downcast mood that something was still wrong, but he sat up and helped her ease off the bed. He knew he had moved too fast and frightened her and that was what he had promised himself not to do. "If you'd rather go downstairs to the dining room, I'll take you there. I'm feeling a lot better than I was half an hour ago."

When Lyse shook her head her hair brushed her cheeks like a shimmering veil. "No, here's fine," she murmured as she crossed his room and entered her own.

Buck stared after her, thoroughly confused, then his face lit up with a cocky grin. She had admitted to being worried about him. Just as he had pointed out that had to mean she cared about him. Trouble was, they would have damn little time to do much about it.

By the time their supper was ready, Buck had cleaned up and changed his shirt. Because Lyse hated the way her face got all red and blotchy when she cried, she had spent the time they were apart trying to remedy that sorry situation with cool water. She still looked a bit flushed, but after braiding her hair in a single plait, she thought she looked presentable enough to share a meal. When Buck knocked upon her door, she suddenly remembered he hadn't told her what had happened that afternoon and she dashed into his room eager to hear it.

The return of Lyse's curiosity struck Buck as a good sign and he smiled as he helped her to her seat at the small table near the corner window. "My story has a ghastly end, so I'd rather wait and tell it after we eat. Tell me what you found out first."

Lyse watched him ladle up what turned out to be a sea-food gumbo and realized she was quite hungry too. As soon as he had filled her bowl she took a spoonful. "This is delicious." She had another mouthful and then wiped her lips on her napkin. "All I found is where Arvin isn't. I tried the hotels near here, then started down toward the docks, but the way I was dressed brought so many stares I gave up and came back here to wait for you. I'll go back in the morning in my old clothes. If I look like a kid out delivering a message, no one will pay me any mind."

Buck frowned slightly as he considered her words. "I'll go with you. I don't want you poking around the docks alone."

"I don't mind. It will give me a chance to find a ship bound for Panama that I can afford. I won't book passage until you've taken care of Arvin, but I'd like to get an idea of how much it will cost and how to go about making the arrangements."

Buck reached for a piece of bread rather than restate his objection to her searching for Arvin on her own. "Let me put it a different way. I don't want to go out alone. I'd rather have your company. Does that make you feel better?"

Though Lyse thought his request strange, she didn't want to be rude and refuse it. "If you think we'd do better to-gether, it's all right with me," she finally agreed. Anxious to hear his report, she finished her gumbo in a hurry then had to wait while he had a second bowl and most of a third. "Well, what happened that was so ghastly?"

Because he hadn't been able to think of a way to soften the shock of what he had done, Buck came right out with it. "I won Tim's money back just like we'd planned, but then I ended up killing the thief."

"You did what?" Lyse stared at Buck in rapt silence as he recounted the afternoon's events in more detail. There wasn't the slightest trace of emotion in either his words or expression. He sounded as though he was talking about a curious incident he had seen happen rather than a death he had been closely involved in himself. That made his story all the more chilling and she couldn't suppress the shudder that shot down her spine and made her cringe in horror. "Oh, how awful, Buck."

Buck waited a moment, expecting questions, accusations, he wasn't sure which, but Lyse simply stared at him. That she would accept such a grisly tale calmly without flying into a tantrum or again dissolving in tears puzzled as well as impressed him. "So, with Hobart so damn nervous, I think I'd better lay low for a couple of days. Not that I'd be looking for trouble if I walked into a saloon, but the news of a death during a fight travels fast and I can promise you there will be plenty of men wanting to prove they are tougher than me. I'd not be able to avoid a fight without looking like a coward either."

"The fights wouldn't be fair either since you've got only one good arm," Lyse pointed out with obvious concern.

"Yeah," Buck admitted reluctantly. "That's a problem too."

Lyse sat back in her chair, her gaze as dark as her handsome companion's. "We've sure had a rotten run of luck, haven't we?"

"We? I'd say I'm the one who's having all the bad luck, Lyse, not you." Buck wadded his napkin into a ball and tossed it upon the table before leaning back in his chair. He looked thoroughly disgusted, but with himself, not her.

Taking offense at his words, Lyse swiftly reminded him he wasn't alone when it came to problems. "Let me refresh your memory. I'm the one who had the fun of finding a man who'd been shot and left for dead. Before I could get you back on your feet, I left home and it sure wasn't with my father's blessing. Then I hadn't been here a day when Tim called me a thief in front of half the town. I'd hardly call that a streak of good luck."

"No," Buck admitted graciously, but he was amused by the colorful way she had described her life since they had met. "I wouldn't either, but all your bad luck comes from being with me, Lyse." He paused for a moment, undecided about going on, but then he realized they had been through too much together to keep any secrets. "There's more to Arvin's story than I told you."

"Like what?" Lyse asked. She leaned forward and propped her elbows on the table, obviously eager to hear it.

Hoping he didn't sound like a lovesick fool, Buck told Lyse about Constance Thorn and how he had hoped to ease her grief by putting Arvin in his grave. When he finished, he found her expression, though one of polite interest, unreadable.

"While I fully intend to make Arvin pay for the grief he's caused her, that's not my main reason for tracking him down. I'm doing it to satisfy my own sense of justice. He's guilty of murder for letting innocent men walk into an ambush in an attempt to settle a personal score with me. I've thought of little else this last year, and now that the coward came so close to killing me with a shot in the back, I'm all the more determined to see him dead."

Buck paused a moment, then broke into a sheepish grin. "I don't plan to lay his filthy carcass at Constance's feet; she'd only faint if I did. I just hope news of Arvin's death will ease her sorrow. Do you think it will?"

When Buck had failed to return to the hotel by five o'clock, or six, or seven, the dread that had filled Lyse's heart had been proof enough her attachment to him had grown far too strong. She had not even dared hope he had any strong feelings for her until he had said he wanted to make love to her. Now it appeared that had only been a passing whim. She had gotten the impression he planned to follow Arvin clear to hell if he had to, but she had not dreamed he had also been trying to impress some stupid girl who hadn't had the brains to fall in love with him rather than his friend in the first place.

"Since you've got your own reasons for wanting Arvin dead, what difference does it make what Constance thinks? Do what you must for your own sake, not hers. You're old enough to know you can't live your life to please others."

"What makes you so smart, Lyse?" Buck asked with a touch of wonder deepening his voice. "It can't be from hanging around that pa of yours."

"I told you, I'm an orphan," she replied flippantly. "I've got no pa." Not wanting to hear any more about Constance or the fool who had once been her father, Lyse rose to her feet. "I think if we get an early start in the morning, we might just catch Arvin still in his bed. As I see it, we've got no time to lose in locating him. He might already have heard about what happened at the Queen of Hearts."

As Lyse moved toward the door that joined their rooms, Buck leapt to his feet to follow her. Before she could slip away, he reached out to catch her hand. "Let's hope not. He won't have changed his ways. He's a loner, so he's not the type who'd hear the latest news. Will seven o'clock be too early for you?"

"No, that's fine." Lyse saw him incline his head as he leaned down, but she made no effort to avoid his kiss. His lips brushed hers only lightly, but whether it was with the gentle caress of a lover possessed of rare tenderness or that of a man who was totally indifferent to her charms, she lacked the experience to tell. When he released her hand, she slipped through the door, completely unaware of how deeply the sorrow reflected in her bright blue gaze had touched him.

By the time Arvin reached the Parker Rooming House where he was staying, he had his plans all made. He had already booked passage on a ship leaving for Panama the next week, but he didn't dare hang around Galveston that long with Buck Warren in town. How the man had escaped his second attempt to put an end to him, Arvin couldn't even begin to understand. He had seen his shot hit Buck in the back, seen him fall from his horse and lie in a still heap.

Damn it all! he swore under his breath. With his own eyes he had seen the bastard lying dead and now here Buck was big as life and from the looks of how easily he had killed poor Jack, he was twice as strong as he had been too.

Arvin raced up the outside staircase of the old building the rooming house occupied then dashed down the dark, narrow hall to his room. He had spent the last year traveling light and needed no more than five minutes to gather up all his belongings. He then went to the room two doors down and pounded excitedly on the door.

"Smitty! You in there, pal?"

John Smith was a stout man in his early thirties. A jovial sort, he liked company and was seldom in his room, but he also had some packing to do that night and came to the door. "Come to tell me good-bye, Arvin? That's right nice of you."

Arvin pushed by the friendly man and shoved the door closed. "This ain't no neighborly call, Smitty. I've got to get out of Galveston quick. I'll trade my ticket on the *Salva Buena* plus a hundred dollars for yours on the *Catarina*. Come on, what do you say? Is it a deal?"

"I'm all set to leave tomorrow," Smitty began to complain. "Hell, Parker's probably got this room rented to somebody else."

"So what if he has? You can have my room," Arvin promised eagerly. "The rent's been paid up until next week too. You've got nothing to lose and stand to come out a hundred bucks ahead. That money will come in handy when you get ready to buy supplies. Come on, Smitty. The *Salva Buena* leaves in a week. What's seven days to you? I got no choice about this and you do."

Smitty swallowed hard, trying to force the acrid taste of fear from his mouth. He and Arvin had gone out drinking together once and it hadn't taken more than that one occasion to convince him to steer clear of the man. Arvin might smile and joke around for a while, but with a couple of drinks under his belt he got just plain mean. As Arvin continued to try and convince him to trade tickets, Smitty could smell the liquor on his breath. When he saw Arvin's hand inching toward the knife at his belt, he realized he was stupidly risking dying over a week's delay, and quickly agreed.

"If you're that desperate, then sure. I'll trade you my ticket for yours but I want to see that hundred bucks first," Smitty bargained cautiously.

Arvin reached into the saddlebags that contained all his gear and pulled out five twenty-dollar gold pieces. "Now you hand over that ticket and you'll have a deal."

Not daring to turn his back on him, Smitty moved over to his bed and picked up his coat. The ticket was in the breast pocket and he pulled it out. "Where's your ticket, Arvin?"

"Why are you so damn suspicious tonight, Smitty? I thought we was friends." Arvin could see the fat man was scared, but he was too distraught over having seen Buck to be in the mood to hurt him just for the fun of it. "Here's the ticket. I'll toss it on the bed. There. Does that make you feel better?"

With all the dignity he could salvage, Smitty exchanged tickets and accepted the money Arvin had promised, but he locked his door the minute Arvin left, and he didn't draw a deep breath until after dawn when he was certain the *Catarina* had already sailed.

Despite being tired, Buck slept no better on his second night in Galveston than he had on his first. He knew, as David Bailey's best friend, he had the right to avenge his death and those of the other men under his command. He also had a very personal score to settle because Arvin had twice come so close to killing him. He had every right to track the putrid deserter down and shoot him point-blank. The thought of watching Arvin beg and plead for his life then twitch and squirm as he died was an immensely satisfying one. Buck kept telling himself killing Arvin would be a service to all humanity, but that didn't silence the voice of his conscience, which insisted seeking revenge was in itself inherently evil. His thoughts in turmoil, he tossed and turned, unable to find a comfortable pose for longer than a minute or two at a time.

Arvin Corbett was no better than vermin. Buck wanted him dead and knew it was up to him to accomplish the deed.

That goal satisfied his outraged sense of justice, but why did all his plans go awry? Why? Because what you are doing is wrong, his conscience continued to whisper. A wrong for a wrong and two wrongs will never make a right.

"Shut up!" Buck finally yelled as he gave up the effort to sleep and sat up in bed. Then embarrassed he might have awakened Lyse, he held his breath, half expecting her to come to his door to look in on him. What could he say to her that would make any sense? There were several excellent reasons for killing Arvin, and only one to turn around and head for home: Murder was a sin. Just plotting murder was in itself a crime, as Deputy Hobart had hinted so strongly.

Buck's head ached with the pain of his dilemma. He couldn't shake the uneasy feeling that his quest to kill Arvin had been doomed from the start. Only his father had understood his need to see the scoundrel punished. His mother had wept, and his sisters had pleaded with him not to risk his life to put an end to a man who would be counted worthless in anyone's eyes. Then there was Constance, he thought sadly. Lovely Constance whose big, brown eyes were always full of tears. Had she even understood where he was going when he had told her good-bye? Had she cared?

"Hell no," Buck whispered to himself. Yet Lyse had been frantic when he had been late for supper. It amazed Buck to think he might have married Constance and been content with her gentle sweetness had he never met Lyse. Now, Constance seemed to him like a beautiful doll, pretty, but lacking the strength of character to survive the first tragedy life had handed her. And look what Lyse had survived! What had Lyse said about a bit of fluff? "That's Constance, all right," he remarked with a chuckle. "Soggy fluff, all wet with tears."

Buck got out of bed then and with a hunter's stealth moved toward the door to Lyse's room. He listened for a moment, but if she were having as great difficulty sleeping as he was, she was being far more quiet about it. He turned the knob and the door swung open easily. Still, he waited, hoping against hope that she would invite him into her bed. After a moment, he could hear the gentle rhythm of her breathing. Unlike him, she was sound asleep. What pretty dreams filled her head? he wondered. Did she dream of California, of the ranch she hoped to own?

Standing in the shadows, Buck was overwhelmed with longing. He wanted Alyssa Selby for his own whether she dressed like a fine lady or a runaway kid. He had gone stalking a killer and found instead a remarkable woman he couldn't bear to let go. He wanted to be with her that night, to be close, to feel her snuggled against him like that first night they had spent together in the abandoned adobe.

Unaware of his presence, Lyse slept on, the excitement of the day having left her spent. When Buck stretched out by her side she didn't feel the feather mattress give slightly, nor did she feel his arm encircle her waist to draw her close. She felt only the comforting warmth of sleep, but it was the promise of love that finally lulled Buck and his troubled conscience to sleep.

IX

March 1849

*L*yse awoke shortly after dawn, and grateful she had no backbreaking chores to do that morning, she stretched lazily. When her elbow struck the solid flesh of Buck's left shoulder, she let out a startled gasp. He was lying on his stomach right beside her, his face turned her way. The strain of the previous day showed clearly in his furrowed brow, but that was no excuse for him to make himself so at home in her bed.

His long underwear covered him from waist to ankle, but his torso was bare. He was snuggled against her, his body providing a comforting warmth. Still, they were no longer sharing a campsite along the trail where huddling together for warmth had been a necessity rather than a matter of choice. Lyse knew the man ought not to be in her room, let alone in her bed, but after her initial shock at finding him there, she felt more curious than upset about the shocking liberty he had taken.

Buck looked completely worn out and she wasn't surprised because he hadn't followed Dr. Glover's orders to get plenty of rest. Well, she chided herself silently, maybe he would have had she not had that awful fight with Tim Mac-Cormac right under his window. The day had been too filled with excitement for either of them to get any rest after that.

Turning on her left side, Lyse propped her head on her hand and continued to study her companion with the same

124

rapt interest she had shown when she had first found him lying in the dirt gravely injured and unconscious. Buck Warren had intrigued her enormously then, but he fascinated her now.

Having had no human playmates while growing up, Lyse had often amused herself by making up fanciful tales. It was a practice she had never given up because it made the dull routine of her days bearable. Now as she watched Buck sleep she tried to imagine what the future held for him. He had impressed her as being far too determined an individual to give up on Arvin Corbett before he had settled the score between them. Surely he couldn't be outsmarted by the spineless weasel again, so he would probably make short work of Arvin and head back home. From the looks of him and what Buck had said, she was certain his family owned a prosperous ranch.

She couldn't help but wonder if Constance Thorn had missed him. Maybe the silly girl had had time to realize she shouldn't have had such little regard for Buck's affection. Lyse was finding it increasingly difficult to ignore her own feelings for him. She didn't understand how Constance could be immune to his charm, especially if her sweetheart had been dead for more than a year. In the two weeks she had known Buck, Lyse had grown closer to him than she had ever been to anyone. It would be heart-wrenching to tell him good-bye, and even worse misery to know he would be returning home to court a woman as indifferent as Constance. He deserved far better and she hoped he would realize that soon.

As for herself, she thought sadly, she had known all along their partnership would be brief. But despite the temporary nature of their friendship, she knew she would remember Buck Warren all her life. Maybe his memory would remind her not to let another man affect her so deeply. Whether it was the lingering sorrow of her mother's desertion, or her father's cruel practice of selling her pets, Lyse had learned quite thoroughly that the price she paid for loving anyone or anything was pain.

Love? Mentally she scoffed at the word. She didn't love Buck. She may have grown too attached to him because of all the trouble they had been through together, but that was a long way from being in love. At least it was in her mind.

With Buck's face only inches from hers, Lyse found such dispassionate thoughts nearly impossible to continue yet it wasn't merely his handsome appearance that appealed to her. When he wasn't being insufferably bossy, she liked everything about him. She had always lavished affection upon her pets when her father wasn't around, but a man, and especially a handsome and bright one, couldn't be considered a pet. She could make that distinction easily enough in her mind, and yet when a sudden impulse to express what she felt for him proved too strong to ignore, Lyse leaned over to brush his lips lightly with a mere whisper of a kiss. His mouth was warm, the sensation very pleasant, but instinctively she knew she ought not to toy with either his feelings or her own. Taking a firm hold on her emotions she turned away, ready to get up, but as she threw back the covers, Buck's left hand shot out to encircle her arm in a firm clasp.

"Don't leave me now when things are just getting interesting," he begged in a lazy drawl.

"You're awake!" Horribly embarrassed, Lyse struggled in a vain attempt to break free of his hold, but when he refused to release her she was forced to remain where she was and lie still. Her worn shift was at least clean, but she felt as though she were stark naked as his glance traveled down her figure in an insolent sweep.

"I wasn't until you kissed me."

"You must have been dreaming," Lyse denied hotly. "I didn't kiss you."

"Yes, you did." A sly smile lifted the corner of Buck's mouth, then spread into a rakish grin. Delighted he had caught her in a flagrant lie, he raised up slightly, then leaned across her and began to nuzzle her throat playfully. Clearly in a teasing mood, he released her arm but kept her pinned beneath him as he kissed her flushed cheeks lightly, then the tip of her upturned nose.

"I have no excuse for being in your bed, ma'am, but since you obviously don't mind, I think I'll stay."

While a bright blush burned her cheeks, Lyse eyed him

with a malevolent stare. "You're wrong. I do mind. It's time we got up and started looking for Arvin. The sooner we deal with him, the sooner I can leave for California."

"That's true enough," Buck agreed, but he again spread light kisses down her throat rather than comply with her wishes.

Lyse tried to get angry with him, but his affection was so delightfully sweet she found it impossible to summon the sort of outrage she knew she should display. It was all she could do to lie still, pretending indifference, rather than to cuddle up against him and put her arms around his neck. He had shaved before supper and the slight growth of his beard merely tickled rather than scratched her fair skin.

"Whether you have any excuse or not, just what the hell are you doing in my bed?" she finally had the presence of mind to ask.

"I'm not in your bed, I'm on it."

"Don't quibble. There's a perfectly good bed in your room. Why aren't you in it?"

Buck leaned back slightly so he could look her in the eye as he gave her question the serious consideration it deserved. "It's not every day that I watch a man die, Lyse. Jack's death was so damn senseless it made me question the wisdom of what I'd set out to do. I didn't like myself much last night, and I guess I just wanted to be close to you again." Because he had already told her he wanted to make love to her, he didn't think he needed to state that another time. "I needed you," he whispered hoarsely instead.

Her father had told her all too often that women only served one useful purpose, and Lyse rebelled instantly at the thought of how Buck must surely have wanted to use her. He had told her he hoped to marry Constance, so what was he doing in her bed? Was she merely a convenient substitute? She positively refused to be that.

"This town must be full of women who are paid to take a man's mind off his troubles. Why didn't you go find one of them?" Already ashamed she had been forced to make such a vile suggestion, Lyse's heart sank as she watched the shock of her question register on Buck's even features. She had been able to think of no other way to protect herself than to make him angry enough so he would leave her alone, but she had not dreamed her words would hurt him.

Buck couldn't believe his ears. He had just told Lyse he had wanted to be with her. He hadn't wanted some woman who could service his physical needs but leave his emotions untouched. How could she even suggest that to him? Did she really care so little for him she wouldn't be jealous of other women? "It wasn't a whore I wanted, Lyse, but a friend," he finally explained in a tightly controlled voice that masked the pain she had so carelessly inflicted on him.

"Well then, if it was friendship you wanted, why didn't you wake me so we could talk?"

"Because I didn't want to argue with you like I knew we would, like we're doing right now." Disgusted he had failed to wrench some words of affection from her, Buck gave her half-open lips a hasty kiss then quickly rolled off the bed. His mood totally serious now, he issued a sharp order as he strode toward the door that linked their rooms.

"I'm leaving the hotel in ten minutes. Get up and get dressed if you want to come with me."

"Yes, sir!" Lyse called out as he slammed the door.

Buck had begun the day in high spirits, but knowing the current blackness of his mood was entirely her fault, Lyse dared not ask why they weren't taking the time to eat breakfast. She washed hurriedly, then pulled on a pair of pants and a faded shirt. She had just brushed out her hair and stuffed it up under her hat when Buck knocked at her door. "Was that ten minutes?"

"It was closer to fifteen, but I'm glad to see you put the extra time to good use." Though she had mentioned wearing her old clothes, Buck was sorry that she had. As they started for the stairs, he couldn't help but bring up the subject of her pitiful wardrobe.

"I want you to get some more dresses from Rose. That way when you strike it rich, you won't have to wait to look your best while some nice clothes are being made. Get a couple of nightgowns too. I won't have you sleeping in that rag you wore last night."

Lyse opened her mouth to argue, then decided he was right. The old shift she slept in was so threadbare it was little more than a rag. "You just stay out of my room at night, then it won't matter what I wear."

Ignoring her obnoxious retort because he felt his overly familiar behavior had undoubtedly caused it, he concentrated his attentions on their task. "Did you bring that list Peters gave you?"

Lyse pulled the carefully folded sheet of paper from her hip pocket. "I've got it right here. We can start where I left off." She frowned slightly, fearing he would not let her do much to help. "I'll go in each place while you wait outside. Then when we find where Arvin is staying, I'll—"

"You'll do nothing but come right out and tell me, Lyse. Is that clear?"

"I think I should look around a bit first, check out the floor plan at least."

"Absolutely not. I don't want you wandering around any hotel where Arvin is a guest. That's just asking for trouble and I won't allow it."

The man was so adamant, Lyse merely shrugged, but she was determined to do what she thought best when the time came to confront Arvin.

When they reached the first of the places she hadn't wanted to visit on her own, Buck pulled open the door, then warned her again. "I'll watch from here. Just ask for Arvin and if he's here you come right back out and get me. Make it short and sweet. Don't hang around to chat with the clerk whether or not Arvin's here."

"No danger of that," Lyse scoffed as she ducked under his arm and entered the inn. In less than thirty seconds she had rejoined him on the street. "No luck there."

With a disgusted shrug, Buck turned away and they continued on down the street. They visited half a dozen places, all leaving Lyse feeling slightly unclean as she walked out and she was glad when it proved to be some distance to the rooming house that was next on the list. The sea breeze was invigorating, but she was so tense she scarcely felt its salt-tinged chill. Her stomach was rumbling noisily, but if Buck heard it, he chose to ignore it. Each time she glanced up at him his frown seemed to have grown deeper and she was sorely tempted to tell him to stop pouting. If he truly loved

Constance, he ought to be faithful to the silly girl rather than climbing into another woman's bed at his first opportunity. The more she thought about that, the madder she got until her expression was as hostile as his.

"Hey, this is it," Buck called out, or Lyse would have walked right by the Parker Rooming House.

She shoved the door open herself, then expecting the same lack of results she had gotten elsewhere, she called to the man seated behind the desk as she approached. "I've got a message for Arvin Corbett. Is he staying here?"

"Number twelve, second floor at the end of the hall," the man replied without glancing up from his newspaper. "I doubt he'll want company this early, though."

"Like I said, I've got an important message for him." Though the clerk still failed to look up, Lyse didn't see how she could go out and get Buck without making him mighty suspicious. Gathering all her courage, she went up the stairs. Sunlight streamed in the window in the top half of the door at the end of the long hallway. Drawn toward the light she went first to make certain the door led to an outside set of stairs. Glad to find it did, she then had to retrace her steps when she discovered room twelve was at the opposite end of the hall. Putting her ear to the door, she listened for a sound indicating the room was occupied, but heard none. Knowing Buck would be angry she had disobeyed him, she hurried back down the stairs and with no more than a jaunty wave to the preoccupied desk clerk, she rushed out to the street.

"Now Buck, don't start yelling at me, just listen," she implored him as she took his arm and started around toward the side of the building.

"What took you so damn long? Is Arvin here?"

"Yes, and if you use the outside stairs, you can come and go without being seen." The enormity of what she was saying hit her then with full force: She was coldly helping Buck plan a murder, but the last thing she felt was cool. "His room is number twelve at the far end of the hall. I can't say whether or not he's in it, though." She hadn't released Buck's arm and she gave him an encouraging squeeze. "Please be careful. If anything happened to you—"

Buck brushed her hand aside. "You needn't worry. I won

back Tim's money yesterday, and a good deal more. It's in an envelope in the hotel safe with your name on it. You'll be able to make your trip to California no matter how this comes out."

Because going to California had been the last thing on her mind, Lyse felt the very same sense of shock and betrayal she had caused him earlier. "That wasn't what I meant!" she denied angrily.

Buck walked past her without bothering to reply, his mind now focused solely on putting an end to Arvin Corbett's miserable life. As he climbed the rickety wooden stairs, he thought with luck he could finish him off in one shot, exit by the side stairs, and lose himself in the crowds near the docks. There would be nothing to tie him to Arvin's murder and as soon as he put Lyse on a ship, he would leave for home. When that thought proved not in the least bit satisfying, he yanked open the door and entered the second floor of the rooming house, wondering if maybe he didn't have the makings of a gunslinger after all.

Smitty had carried his belongings from his room to Arvin's, but he felt horribly uneasy there, as though some trace of the man he had not only disliked but also feared still remained. He had just flung open the window to let in some badly needed fresh air when the door behind him came flying open and a tall man with a murderous gleam in his dark eyes pointed a forty-five at him. Raising his hands, he glanced over his shoulder, wondering if he could possibly survive a leap from the second-floor window.

"Don't shoot!" he cried out in a high-pitched whine. "I've got nothin' to steal!"

Buck stepped back and took another look at the rusted numerals on the door. He had made no mistake, this was room twelve. "Where's Corbett?"

Trembling all over, Smitty dared not lower his hands. Arvin had scared him witless, and if he had fled Galveston to avoid this man, Smitty was positive he didn't want to cross him. Stuttering nervously, he introduced himself and explained how he and Arvin had swapped tickets for the voyage to Panama, but he didn't mention the hundred dollars he had been paid.

"The *Catarina* was to sail at dawn, so Arvin's gone," he concluded.

Buck swore angrily and returned his Colt to his holster with a disgusted shove. "Put down your hands, Mr. Smith, I've no quarrel with you if you're telling the truth. If I find out you're lying to me, though, it will be a different story. Now are you certain Corbett didn't tell you why he was in such a big hurry to sail?"

Smitty lowered his hands and wiped his profusely sweating palms on his pants. "No, sir, he didn't explain, but I can see he had a good reason 'cause he was real upset."

Before Buck could reply, he heard a creak as someone stepped upon a loose board in the hall and suddenly realizing Smitty could be in cahoots with Arvin, he drew his pistol and wheeled around, ready to blast whoever was trying to sneak up on him to kingdom come. When he found Lyse only a few steps away with her knife drawn, he lost his temper completely.

"Are you trying to get yourself killed? I could have shot you just now. I should have been smart enough to bring along a piece of rope to tie you up so you'd stay put since you find it so damn impossible to do what I say!"

Lyse had been far too worried about him to stay at the bottom of the stairs. When she had entered the hallway and seen him standing at the open doorway to room twelve, she had been afraid Arvin had gotten the drop on him and she had wasted no time in coming to his rescue. When she glanced in the room and saw a chubby blond man who couldn't possibly be Arvin, she felt very foolish. Trembling, she took care as she returned her knife to its sheath. "I thought you needed my help. I can see now that you didn't."

Smitty got only a glimpse of what he mistook for a skinny kid before Buck stepped out of the room and slammed the door. He turned around and leaned out the window to take in several deep gulps of air as he tried to force away the terrible fright of the curious stranger's visit. He was convinced Arvin was dangerous, but he thought himself very lucky to have escaped the wrath of the man who was pursuing him. Yes, sir, that was a born killer if he had ever seen one. Certain God must have played a part in his survival, Smitty mumbled a prayer of thanksgiving before wondering what time the nearest saloon opened for business.

Taking Lyse by the arm, Buck nearly lifted her off her feet as he ushered her toward the door. He didn't release her until they reached the bottom of the stairs. Then he strode off, leaving her behind.

"Hey, Buck, wait for me!"

When Lyse caught up with him, Buck let fly with a string of obscenities he would never have used in front of another woman before he bothered to tell her what was wrong. "We're going to find out all we can about a ship called the *Catarina*. We might be able to get a passenger list, but I'll bet Arvin didn't use his real name. He must have seen me, Lyse. That's the only explanation I can think of. He saw me and bolted like a frightened cat."

At least Buck was talking to her even if he hadn't cooled down, but Lyse found she had to take two steps for every one of his to keep up with him, he was in such a hurry. "Where's the *Catarina* bound?" she asked between quick running steps.

"Where do you think? It's on the way to Panama with almost every other ship afloat."

Lyse watched the muscles tense along Buck's jaw and realized he was every bit as furious as when he had beat up her pa. He might have nice clothes, fine manners, and plenty of money, but behind his gentlemanly facade there was a wildness to him that she found most unsettling. Which man was he really—the cultured gentleman who could serve up gumbo without spilling a drop, or a firebrand who spent all his time looking for trouble? The fact that she couldn't answer that question was frightening.

"So what are you gonna do now?"

Buck looked down at her, his dark eyes still ablaze with fury. "I'm going to book us passage on the first ship leaving for Panama. I've no other choice."

Lyse reached out to touch his sleeve as she came to an abrupt halt. The thought Buck might make the trip to California with her was so wildly exciting she could scarcely believe he was serious. "Are you sure you really want to do that?"

It wasn't only the fact that Arvin was gone that had driven Buck into a rage, but also the shocking fact that he had come so close to shooting the shabbily clad young woman who had become as close to him as his shadow. For a reason he couldn't hope to understand, because of Arvin their destinies had become entwined. To give up on trailing Arvin would also be giving up on Lyse, and despite the sorry fact that she gave him damn little in the way of encouragement, he wasn't nearly ready to tell her good-bye. He was wise enough, however, to keep that thought to himself.

"You must have noticed I tend to be a stubborn man, Lyse. When I set my mind on something, I see it through. Maybe I can overtake Arvin in Panama; if not, I'll follow him to the California gold fields if I have to. There's a stench about him that makes him real easy to track. That he'll know I'm coming will work to my advantage too. It will make him too nervous to be careful and the first serious mistake he makes I'll be there to get him."

Lyse didn't doubt Buck could do anything he wanted to do. From what she had seen of him, he thrived on danger, but she couldn't suppress a shiver of dread. "What about your family? Don't they expect you to be home in a few weeks?"

"I'll send them a wire. I'm a grown man, I don't need their permission to travel."

"I know that, it's just that I thought they'd be concerned about you. What about Constance?" Lyse looked down at her worn boots as she spoke her name. "You might be gone several months, and with one sweetheart dead, I bet she'll be beside herself with worry."

With the clarity of a bolt of lightning streaking across the nighttime sky, Buck realized he never should have mentioned the disconsolate young woman to Lyse because his feelings toward her had changed so completely. "I don't give a damn what Constance thinks anymore, Lyse. I'll admit that my pride was hurt when she picked David over me, but whatever I felt for her once is long over. She can wallow in her own unhappiness forever for all I care. She's not going to get another minute of my time."

Lyse's pretty blue eyes grew wide with wonder as she looked up at him. "She isn't?"

"No, she isn't, so you needn't be jealous of her any longer," he assured her with a wide grin.

"I wasn't jealous!"

"No, of course not and you didn't kiss me this morning either, did you?" When the fair blonde's cheeks flushed with a bright blush, Buck congratulated himself on pinpointing her mood so accurately. Lyse might dress like a boy at times, but underneath she was all woman.

Lyse couldn't bear to watch Buck gloat, but it was difficult not to smile with him when she was so overjoyed to hear he no longer cared for Constance. In an effort to salvage at least some of her pride, she quickly reminded him of their purpose.

"Wasn't Tim leaving tomorrow? Maybe there's still room for a couple more passengers on that ship."

Buck nodded thoughtfully. "What if there's only one cabin available? Would you share it with me?"

Without a moment's hesitation, Lyse replied flippantly, "If there's only one cabin left, you can share it with Tim and I'll take his." She put her hands on her hips as she glared up at him. Because she had told him emphatically she wouldn't be his whore, she hoped he would finally get that message.

"I was only teasing you, Lyse." Buck chuckled to himself as he reached out to give her a playful hug. When her slender body stiffened rather than relaxed in his arms, he stepped back at once. "Come on, let's go find the harbor master's office. He'll have information on the ships sailing for Panama and he might have a passenger list for the *Catarina* too."

"Whatever you say." Grateful he had stopped teasing her, Lyse fell in beside him as they continued on down toward the docks. With his usual display of confidence, Buck quickly made a friend of the officer who handled the thriving port's business. Saying he was attempting to locate a man who owed him some money, he got the information he wanted. He scanned the list of names of those who had sailed aboard the *Catarina* and pointed one out to her.

"Arvin traded tickets with this man, John Smith. Since his

name is still here, Arvin might be calling himself Smith for the time being."

"John Smith? Doesn't every town have two or three of those?"

"Probably, but since the *Catarina* has only one, I think it's a safe bet it's Arvin."

"And if it isn't?" Lyse asked hesitantly.

"Well then, I will have provided you with an escort for your trip and that will be enough to make it worthwhile." The words had rolled off his tongue like well-practiced flattery, but Buck was sincere. He had never wanted to see Lyse go to California on her own. First because he had thought it a foolish idea, and now because he cared too much about her to allow her to take such a dangerous risk.

Though the thought that he might be flirting with her crossed her mind, Lyse found his willingness to accompany her very reassuring. She hadn't given a thought to the problems of traveling alone, but she was sure they would have been plenty. "Thank you," she managed to reply, and reluctant to say more she remained silent as he asked the harbor master questions about Captain Randolph's ship.

"The *Spanish Dancer* is part of the Aragon Line. She's a clipper ship no more than a year old, so you needn't fear she's not seaworthy." The officer crossed to the window to point out a sleek three-masted ship moored nearby. "Randolph's a good man, but I've no idea whether or not he's still taking on passengers."

"I met Marc Aragon during the war. He owes me a favor or two. I'll see if I can't collect them from Randolph." After thanking the man for his assistance, Buck held the door for Lyse, but he couldn't help but notice the harbor master's amused smile as he watched the lithe young woman leave his office. Buck had made no excuse for her odd attire, but he hadn't forgotten he wanted to enlarge her wardrobe that very day.

Fascinated by the *Spanish Dancer* because she had never before been on board a ship, Lyse stood at the rail and watched the crew load the last of the clipper's provisions. With a ready show of charm, Buck managed to favorably impress Gregory Randolph, but as she listened to the two men exchange stories about Marc Aragon she couldn't help but wonder if any of what Buck said was true. It seemed to her that he never ran out of convenient lies to help him get what he wanted. Since they had been in Galveston, she had seen him do it with James Peters, Rose Reynoso, Tim Mac-Cormac, Ernie Hobart, and the harbor master. Was he deliberately misleading Randolph about his friendship with Marc Aragon in an effort to book passage on one of his family's ships? She had to admit he certainly sounded like he knew the man, but then whenever he spoke he always sounded convincing.

The captain had a stocky build and though his hair and beard were gray, Lyse doubted he could be forty. As deeply tanned as Buck, the lines around his blue gray eyes made it apparent he laughed often. When he invited them to his cabin to discuss the matter of their passage, Lyse looked around the well-appointed room, hoping the man would offer some sort of refreshments, but unfortunately he didn't.

"I am more accustomed to having a cargo of freight than passengers, but the Aragons know there is a great deal of money to be made with everyone so anxious to get to California and I'm not opposed to helping them get their share. Another man or two will be no problem, but as for Miss Selby, well, I'm concerned about you, my dear."

Before Lyse could point out she was most certainly not his "dear," Buck spoke. "I'll assume full responsibility for her safety, Captain. As I said, her luggage was lost, but this afternoon I plan to replace her wardrobe. No one will dispute the fact she is a lady then, and I'll make certain she's not approached or bothered by your other passengers. She will require a private cabin, of course, but no other special consideration on your part."

That Buck was ashamed of the way she looked was plain from his sidelong glance, but Lyse held her temper and her tongue until he had persuaded the captain that having a lone woman on board would pose no problem. Because Randolph found that a difficult opinion to accept, it took Buck some time to do it. Lyse sat by his side, trying not to fidget nervously. It was all she could do to keep still, but when the captain finally agreed to let them sail on the *Spanish Dancer* and they took their leave, she was astonished to find Buck was upset with her.

As he took her arm to help her down the gangplank, Buck whispered angrily, "I thought I was going to have to talk to that man until midnight to convince him to let you come along. Where was all that charm you poured on Deputy Hobart yesterday? Couldn't you spare a drop or two to help me convince Randolph you'd be no trouble to him?"

Repelled by his confining grasp as well as his insulting words, Lyse pulled free before she replied. "You expect me to be charming when I'm dressed like a stable hand? Don't be ridiculous. I'm not a real lady, and I can't play the part without nice clothes."

"Well you didn't have to wear that awful getup again today," Buck pointed out sharply.

"I did too! Have you forgotten what we set out to do this morning? I was supposed to help you kill Arvin, not prance around like some fancy lady."

As far as Buck was concerned, she had botched that too by not staying at the bottom of the rooming house stairs. "Hush up about that!" he scolded crossly. "Let's just get something to eat and then I'm taking you back to the Rosebud. You need three more dresses at the very least, nightgowns, and whatever else it is you need to act like a lady. I'll have to find myself some more clothes too and luggage to pack up our things. I'll need the money from the hotel safe to pay Randolph. Then I'll go back and sell my horse. That chore alone will take up an hour or two. Come on, we've got no time to waste if we're leaving Galveston tomorrow."

Again Lyse nearly had to run to keep up with Buck. She was too hungry to say she didn't want to eat with him, and she knew if she refused to allow him to buy more clothes he would just go ahead and buy them anyway. Thinking it would be a nice change to spend the afternoon at the Rosebud, she looked back for a last glimpse of the *Spanish Dancer,* dreading the thought of a voyage where she feared Buck would be far too demanding a companion.

X
___

March 1849

When Buck knocked at Lyse's door that night, ready to escort her downstairs for supper, he found her beautifully dressed in a rose silk gown whose exquisite color exactly matched the blush in her cheeks. Another of Rose Reynoso's flattering designs, its feminine rows of ruffles and lace provided the perfect complement to Lyse's fair beauty.

Delighted to find his volatile partner looking like a lady, Buck hoped she would endeavor to act like one. He reached for her hand and tucked it in the crook of his arm as they started for the stairs. "I didn't think anything could be prettier than your blue dress, but I was wrong. Pink is definitely your color. You bought some other things too, didn't you?"

Lyse found the sight of Buck dressed in a suit every bit as appealing as he found her in fine clothes. The dark gray frock coat with matching trousers was brightened by a pearl gray waistcoat and snowy white shirt, but it was his smile that truly dazzled her. Where he had managed to find such well-tailored garments at such short notice she couldn't imagine but afraid it would be considered rude to ask, she didn't raise the question. "You look simply splendid, Buck," she managed to say instead.

"Well, thank you, but you didn't answer my question. I wanted Rose to provide you with everything she could possibly have ready by this afternoon. Tell me what else you bought."

Being a clever woman, Rose had convinced a reluctant Lyse the whims of a gentleman both wealthy and generous should most definitely be indulged. Without revealing that conversation, Lyse provided a brief list. "I got two other dresses, a cashmere shawl, lingerie, and a couple of nightgowns too. The money you left covered everything plus the tip for Rose you wanted her to have."

"Good. I want you to enjoy yourself on the voyage to Panama. Dress up like a lady every single day. The more elegant you look, the more respectful the other passengers will be. Since I gave my word to Randolph you'd cause him no problems, I'll appreciate all the help you can give me."

"I don't deliberately cause you problems," Lyse was quick to deny, but Buck had to wait until they were seated in the dining room to reply.

"I didn't say that you did, so let's not argue about it. Let's just enjoy ourselves tonight and look forward to starting your trip to California tomorrow."

Lyse glanced shyly around the dining room, noting the other patrons were predominantly male. There were a few ladies present, but none as young or as well dressed as she. She felt rather foolish then, for she knew she was far different inside from the sweet, pretty girl her new clothes made her seem. "That's fine with me," she finally agreed, and when Buck ordered a bottle of wine she joined him in toasting their future success, although she feared with his goal that was a bit ghoulish.

"I've never tasted wine before," Lyse confided with a slight grimace. "Does all of it taste so foul as this?"

"Foul?" Buck scoffed, offended. "Actually, this is French and quite good." He tilted his crystal wineglass as he admired the clarity and deep ruby color. "I imagine they have far better wines in France than we ever see here, but this one is really quite good."

Lyse tried another sip, and then another, but her initial opinion didn't change. "It doesn't taste more like dirt than grapes to you?"

"Dirt? Lord, no!" Buck couldn't help but laugh at the

innocence of her remark. "Just sip it slowly with the meal and I think you'll soon begin to like it."

Though Lyse sincerely doubted that, she thought he knew what he was talking about and was willing to give his advice a try. She wondered if the hotel had champagne, as her mother had once told her it was delicious. It was also very expensive, as she recalled, so Lyse dared not ask Buck to order some. Because she liked the way the chef prepared steak, even though it was still a bit difficult to eat, she ordered one along with her companion.

Lyse seemed so quiet that night, Buck couldn't help but wonder if she were still mad at him about the argument they had had down at the docks. Though he didn't want to start it all over again, he didn't want to sit through supper without speaking either. "You're awfully quiet tonight, Lyse. Is there anything bothering you that I ought to know about?"

Actually, Lyse hadn't been able to stop wondering about the ease with which he told lies and because he had asked outright what was on her mind, she told him in a discreet whisper. "I know you made up that tale about a carriage accident as an excuse for my clothes. But no matter what our problem, you always seem to have a story ready so you can get people to help us. Have you really met Marc Aragon, or was what you told Randolph just another pack of convenient lies?"

With her hair swept atop her head Lyse looked absolutely adorable, but her question was so insulting it was all Buck could do to keep his temper in check. "Yes, I do know Marc. He was captain of the ship that took my company to Vera Cruz during the war. He's a likable fellow and we became good friends. I'll make it a point to look him up when we reach California if you need to hear that same story from his lips to believe it."

Lyse was far too perceptive not to realize she had insulted him, even though it hadn't been deliberate. "I wasn't calling you a liar, Buck."

"Oh, no?" Disgusted, Buck refilled his wineglass then added a few drops to hers. "I told you at the beginning I didn't want you involved in what I'm trying to do, but it ought to be obvious I can't go around announcing I've set out to kill a man. If I have to steer clear of the truth for the time being, it's only to protect myself and you as well. I may have several bad habits, but being a liar isn't one of them."

Because Lyse hadn't wanted to believe that he was, she decided to take his word for it. Then she realized that if he truly was a man who preferred lies to the truth, he would have simply told her another of his imaginative tales in response to her question. Hoping to change the subject, she chose the most obvious one.

"What sort of bad habits do you have?"

"I'll not admit them if you aren't already aware of them, Lyse." Buck chuckled to himself, amazed to again find her so delightfully innocent despite the elegance of her attire. She was like a painting come to life, her beauty and sweetness very real, but her store of worldly experience a complete blank. "Do you have any faults you'd like to share with me?"

Though Buck hadn't been serious, Lyse didn't realize it. She frowned thoughtfully, then took another sip of her wine. "Well, that fool who called himself my pa always said I was lazy, but that isn't true. I suppose my biggest fault is in not knowing how to act like a lady except for what I can remember of my mother. I should have been born knowing how to do that, shouldn't I?"

Buck was touched by the naïveté of her question and hastened to reassure her that just wasn't so. "Most little girls I've seen like to play with dolls and have tea parties. At least my sisters did, but my mother had to teach them proper manners and how to behave. It didn't come any more naturally to them than it does to you."

Encouraged by that news, Lyse grew curious. "Tell me about your sisters. How old are they and what are their names?"

"My mother lost two babies between my birth and the girls', so they are quite a bit younger than I. Elena just turned twenty-two. She got married last year. Patricia is nineteen and has so many suitors I doubt she'll ever be able to choose one."

Because she had never had even one male caller, Lyse felt

a sudden pang of envy at such popularity. She tried to picture the girls and thought they must surely be attractive because Buck was so handsome. They would be pretty and pampered as she assumed all well-to-do young women must be, but she tried not to be jealous of them.

"I used to wish I had a brother or a sister, but now I'm glad that I don't."

Dumbfounded by that remark, Buck pressed her to explain. "Why? I think you would have enjoyed the company."

"'Misery loves company,' you mean?" Lyse shook her head. "No, I wouldn't wish what I had to put up with on anyone else."

The waiter arrived to begin serving their meal then and Buck had to wait until they were again alone to respond. He couldn't bear to think of Lyse growing up with that jackass of a parent he had met. A beating had been too good for him after the way he had mistreated Lyse. "Your life is going to be much better from now on. You can count on it," he assured her confidently as he replenished her wine.

"Lordy, it couldn't have gotten much worse," Lyse replied flippantly, then afraid that sounded ungrateful, she continued. "I do appreciate all you've done for me, Buck, not just buying me the new clothes, but everything. It would have taken me months to earn enough to pay for my passage to Panama and you just arranged it with a snap of your fingers."

"That I did, but the fact that I had the gold to pay Randolph was every bit as important as the 'pack of lies' I told him." Buck couldn't resist making that taunt, but he regretted it instantly when he saw Lyse recoil slightly as though he had swung at her. "I'm sorry, that was a stupid thing to say."

"Yes, it was. I expect better of you, Mr. Warren," Lyse replied coldly, and with dainty sips she began to eat her soup in as ladylike a fashion as she could display.

Buck was afraid every time he opened his mouth he placed his foot in it where she was concerned and kept quiet for the moment, but he took care to see Lyse's wineglass never grew empty. What are your faults? she had asked. According to his father, it was a passion for danger and wild women and from where he sat, Lyse struck him as having a wildness that was totally unique and therefore tremendously exciting.

"I told you you'd like the wine if you just gave it a chance," he remarked with an engaging smile, hoping the potent beverage would lull her senses to the point where she would admit his feelings for her were returned. He didn't want her drunk, just rather pleasantly tipsy so she wouldn't think a good night kiss an outrageous request. He still thought her a young woman who would have to be courted with care, but damn it all, if she didn't give him some encouragement soon, he'd be at his wit's end for a way to impress her.

As they consumed another delicious meal Buck smiled often, but Lyse couldn't help but note that the undercurrent of tension that had flowed between them earlier in the day hadn't abated. Outwardly he appeared as always to be in complete control, but she wondered as she sat thinking of him what sort of thoughts filled his mind. Had she known, her blush would have been a far deeper shade of rose than her gown.

With Buck's constant urging, Lyse consumed several goblets of wine before she realized how deeply they would affect her, and by then it was far too late. As they left the dining room, she felt a strange tingling sensation all over, combined with a marvelous warmth that blurred her vision and left her clinging languidly to his arm.

As they reached her door, she thanked him for the wonderful meal. "I enjoyed your company too," Lyse added graciously, but when her voice rang with a curious echo in her ears, she hoped she did not sound strange to him too.

Not waiting for an invitation, Buck followed Lyse into her room. He had provided a large leather satchel for her belongings. A trunk would have been better for her clothing on board the ship, but since they would have to pack their things over the mountains in Panama by burro, such a cumbersome piece of luggage was out of the question. "I'm glad to see you're already packed."

"I beg your pardon?" Lyse had crossed the room to turn up the lamp, then turned toward him as she began to pluck the pins from her hair. She swayed slightly and had to lean back against the dresser to keep her balance.

A sly smile lifted the corner of Buck's mouth as he went to her side. He had overdone it a bit—Lyse was well past being tipsy—but he felt a nice warm glow himself and didn't really mind. "I said I'm glad you're packed. It will save us time in the morning. Now tell me good night."

As she looked up at him, Lyse wondered how a lady would cope with the terrible longing that filled her heart. The very last thing she wanted to do was tell Buck good night. It seemed as though no matter how hard she tried, their conversations never went in the direction she wished. All too often he got angry, or resorted to teasing as though she had no feelings his words would bruise. Though that night had been no exception, she didn't want it to end that way. She caught a glimpse of herself in the mirror then and for the smallest of instants mistook the image of the lovely blonde for her mother's reflection rather than her own. Her mother would certainly know how to keep a man talking with her all night, but sadly Lyse did not. She stared up at Buck, thinking him far out of her reach, although he was standing mere inches away.

As Buck continued to look down at Lyse he felt the very same reluctance to part as she. Even when they had spent the whole day together on the trail he hadn't grown tired of her company. He simply never got enough of her. Though she might complain frequently of her lack of feminine wiles, it was the very unpredictability of her moods and thoughts that appealed to him. She had grown more precious to him with each new day, but he thought it much too soon to declare it. Instead, he reached out to touch the tip of a bright curl that lay on her shoulder, then coiled it around his fingers.

The problem was not only that Buck was in her room again, but also it seemed to Lyse that he had gained entry to her very soul. She was torn between the conflicting desires to throw her arms around his neck and beg him to stay and the painful awareness that she should demand he leave at once. Unable to choose either option, she continued to do nothing but stare up at him with so wistful an expression it nearly broke his heart.

"You usually tell me good night at your first opportunity. You're never so quiet as this, Lyse. Are you worried about the voyage?" Buck finally drew the breath to ask, but he saw nothing in the brilliant blue of her eyes but his own reflection.

"No," Lyse whispered shyly when she found it impossible to say more, or to tear her gaze from his. His eyes were dark, his thoughts impossible for such an innocent girl to read while a more worldly woman would have recognized the desire that graced his handsome features for the raw hunger it was.

"Good. I don't want you to be worried. You'll come to no harm as long as you're with me." Unable to bear another second of what he considered horrible deprivation, Buck ceased to wait for some tangible sign that Lyse would welcome the affection he was so anxious to give. He leaned down, meaning to kiss her good night as sweetly as he had done on the previous evening, but the thrill provided by the touch of her lips was no longer enough. He wanted more, but even as he slipped his arms around her waist to draw her near he feared he would always want more than she would willingly give.

The pressure of Buck's lips was very light because he was so fearful of hurting her with the enthusiasm of his affection. While Lyse was as enchanted by his tenderness as she had been that morning, her wine-drugged mind could no longer remember why she had been so reluctant to let him see how much she enjoyed it. Now she raised her arms to encircle his neck as she leaned into his embrace. Maybe this was the secret, she thought dreamily: They shouldn't waste their time arguing when it would be ever so much more pleasant to make love.

Buck was no fool. When Lyse did not simply relax in his embrace, but actually returned it, he covered her face with a flurry of sweet kisses. He traced the outline of her lips with the tip of his tongue, then whispered, "Open your mouth, Lyse, let me show you a much better way to kiss."

Whether it was the wine that had warmed her blood, or Buck's charming attentions, Lyse was far too preoccupied to care. All she knew for certain was that if he knew a dozen

ways to kiss she wanted to learn them all. She felt his left
hand move to her nape, his fingers coiled in her hair as he
held her head tilted up to his, but she had not the slightest
desire to try and escape him. When his tongue slid over hers
with a sensuous caress, she clung to him all the more tightly,
wondering as she felt the rhythm of her heartbeat quicken
what else he might want to teach her. It was difficult to draw
a breath with his mouth covering hers so completely, but that
seemed too insignificant a complaint to voice aloud when it
felt so incredibly good. His adoring kisses blurred from one
to the next until Lyse felt so light-headed she could barely
stand. When at last Buck had to draw away a moment to
catch his breath, she couldn't bear to let him go.

Lyse's faint cry of protest as he slackened his hold on her
was all the encouragement Buck needed. He reached for the
tiny buttons that ran down the bodice of her rose silk dress,
forcing himself to undo them carefully rather than to merely
rip the garment to shreds and instantly expose the loveliness
of her body to his view.

"It is the same for you, isn't it?" he mumbled hoarsely. "I
want to please you too, not merely myself."

Not caring whether or not she was being too forward,
Lyse brushed his hands aside. "Here, let me help you."
When he did no more than step back and watch her, she
thought it very odd. "Aren't you supposed to take off your
clothes too?"

Because he had been so worried about rushing her, Buck
needed a second or two to realize her question made perfect
sense. "Of course," he agreed readily, and not caring about
his own clothing as he did about hers, he tore off his coat
and began to struggle with the buttons on his vest.

Lyse raised her hands to try and stifle her giggles but
failed. "I'm sorry, but since the *Spanish Dancer* will not sail
until noon tomorrow, why are you in such a great hurry?
Don't we have plenty of time?" They had already spent more
than the five minutes her father had frequently mentioned,
but Lyse was certain Buck knew far more about making love
than Frank Selby ever had.

Lyse had to be a virgin, Buck was sure of it, but that she
would tease him about his haste as though he were some

gangling youth eager to make love for the first time was almost more than he could bear. Almost, but he didn't want to give some foolish or hostile reply that would only get him thrown out of her room rather than invited into her bed. She had not actually invited him into her bed, but he wasn't about to insist she say it in words when her desire was so plain in her actions.

"I'm not ashamed to admit how badly I want you, Lyse. You shouldn't laugh at me for it," he scolded softly.

"Oh, I'm sorry," Lyse apologized hurriedly. "Was that very rude of me?" Still giggling, she peeled away the tight-fitting bodice of her gown, then stepped out of the skirt. She carried the garment over to the nearby chair and laid it out carefully before returning to face him. When she reached for the ribbon drawstring on her camisole, Buck pulled her back into his arms.

"No, let me undress you. It was only the buttons that were a problem." After removing his vest, he had yanked his shirt off over his head, and tossed both items clear across the room where they lay in a careless heap atop his coat.

Swept back into his arms, Lyse snuggled against his bare chest, taking care not to touch his bandaged shoulder. His skin held an inviting warmth and the spicy sweet scent of the hotel's soap while she feared she simply reeked of roses after spending so much of the day in the Rosebud where the flower's heady perfume touched even the smallest scrap of lace.

Buck kissed Lyse deeply, and savoring the wine-flavored sweetness of her surrender he felt a sudden sharp pang of guilt. She was lucid, he told himself, if a bit giddy, but he knew a woman so strong-willed as Lyse would never do anything she didn't sincerely want to do just because she had had a couple of glasses of wine. Besides, it wasn't his fear that she would suddenly come to her senses that made him so eager to possess her, it was the depth of his own desire.

He wrapped his left arm around her tiny waist to place her on the edge of the bed, then bent down at her feet to remove her satin slippers. She leaned forward to ruffle his hair with her fingers and he reached up to catch her hand and brought it to his lips. "You are a very beautiful woman, Lyse. It doesn't matter to me how you dress, but I'll admit to being partial to pretty gowns like the one you wore tonight."

Lyse was so fascinated by the glow of the lamp upon his dark hair she didn't immediately remember she was supposed to pay him a compliment too. It wasn't until he had pulled off her stockings that she spoke. "You're almost too handsome, Buck. I mean, it's real distracting to try and look at you and talk at the same time."

"Really? I didn't realize my looks posed a problem." Buck's grin was a wide one as he rose to his feet. He wasn't certain how to get Lyse out of her slips gracefully, but she untied the bow at her waist herself, then stood for a moment to let the lace-trimmed petticoats fall to the floor. He grabbed them up and carried them over to the chair where her pink gown lay. Clad only in her chemise and pantaloons now, when he returned to her she raised her hands to put a halt to his efforts.

"You ought to at least take off your boots before you go any further," she advised with another impish giggle.

Since Lyse was so obviously enjoying herself, Buck didn't refuse her request. He sat down beside her and with only a little difficulty pulled off his boots. His right arm still wasn't much use, and he hoped he wouldn't be too clumsy with her. Yet when she leaned over him to kiss him, he pulled her down with him on the bed with a masterful ease. She had learned how to respond to his kisses so quickly, it amazed him to think she had never been with another man. His hand moved to her breast as he continued to kiss her. That delectable swell was exactly as he remembered it. Soft and sweet, he thought her body perfection, and pushing her camisole aside he lowered his head to sample her taste.

Lyse closed her eyes and cuddled against him as she had longed to do that morning. She couldn't seem to hold him close enough, though, and ran her hands over his broad shoulders and down his back before lacing her fingers in his hair. She didn't understand why it was still so difficult to draw a deep breath when his mouth now covered the tip of her breast rather than her lips. Then she realized his breathing was as rapid as hers and with a shy smile decided passion must surely be the cause.

Buck thought Lyse remarkable in all respects. Her every gesture drew him toward a closeness he had never found with another woman and he knew he would long to recapture that magical feeling again and again. He pulled the ribbon free at her waist and slipped his hand beneath the waistband to ease her lace-trimmed pantaloons off her hips. The flesh of her stomach was flat and smooth, and he savored the feel of it before letting his hand slide on down her thigh as he pulled the undergarment lower still. She had marvelous skin, every inch of her slender body was as soft as a rose petal despite the harshness of her life. She was in every way a treasure, but he found it far easier to convey that message with the poetry of a lavish kiss and tender caress than with words.

Whatever fears she might have had dispelled by the lingering effects of the wine, Lyse made no objection as Buck's touch grew increasingly intimate. She felt only the most splendid of sensations that she mistakenly assumed only he knew how to create. When his mouth left her breasts and returned to her lips, his fingertips continued to slide through the triangle of fair curls between her thighs, their path smoothed by the fluids her body had so thoughtfully created to welcome his. The resulting feeling was so exquisitely beautiful it was nearly pain and when he drew away to cast aside the remainder of his clothes, she didn't think she could possibly survive even those few seconds without him.

Buck grabbed a towel off the washstand then put out the lamp before he reached for his belt. He knew Lyse might think him handsome, but he thought it unlikely she had ever seen a man nude and he didn't want to frighten her unnecessarily. The mere sight of her aroused him, but he wanted the pleasure he would feel when he buried himself in the sweetness of her inner warmth to be a gift freely given, not one merely taken. With her help he peeled back the covers, then spread the towel upon the bed so there would be no traces of their passionate encounter to embarrass her in the morning. He then joined her in the bed, and pulled her into his arms.

Lyse again snuggled against him, delighting in the feel of the hard muscular planes of his body as she pressed close. Her hands moved down his back, then over the smooth swell of his hips before returning to his shoulders. She found his endless kisses every bit as intoxicating as the French wine and, drunk with his affection, she hoped the night would never end. When he moved his hand over her stomach and down between her legs this time she knew what to expect. As he shifted slightly to spread her legs with his knee she moved readily to follow his unspoken command, welcoming his touch with complete and utter abandon. Thinking what felt good to her would also be pleasurable to him, Lyse lowered a hand to the taut muscles of his stomach. She felt him shiver as if in grateful anticipation and slid her hand lower still.

As Lyse's fingers closed around him, Buck let out a low moan. She drew her hand away quickly then but he grabbed her wrist. "No, don't stop," he begged hoarsely, but he could scarcely keep his mind on giving her pleasure when at the same time her touch was drawing him to the very brink of madness. He could feel her body's craving for release as deeply as his own and with a patience born of love he led her on until with a shudder of splendor that joy overtook her.

Buck moved swiftly then, his intentions clear, but there was no hesitation on Lyse's part as she welcomed him into her arms. He deepened his kiss as his first thrust tore through the last barrier remaining between them, making them truly one in both heart and body. Lost in the glory of that ecstasy he swore to himself that he would never let her go. He would make her love him. No matter what it cost him, he knew she would be worth twice the price.

Awash in the rapture he had given her, Lyse barely felt the pain of their first union. In its place there was a blissful warmth that flooded her loins then slowly diffused to a radiant glow filling her whole body with the delicious feeling of perfect peace. Buck lay in her arms, his face buried in her tangled curls and she toyed with the curls at his nape, thinking surely he could have nothing left to teach her about making love. It had all been so easy, so perfectly natural, she thought dreamily, and far better than she had been led making love to be. It was obviously her father who had been the liar, not Buck Warren.

Having no clue to her thoughts, and knowing how easily a

fight could erupt between them, Buck decided he would be wise to keep his comments, no matter how adoring, to himself for a while. He raised up slightly to kiss her again, then relieved her of the burden of his weight so she could sleep comfortably. He pulled her into his arms and hugged her tightly. "I'd wish you sweet dreams, but they couldn't possibly be any better than this."

As tired as he, Lyse nodded sleepily, thinking his words made perfect sense. "I hope I dream of you," she offered sweetly, but he was already asleep and in another moment so was she.

XI

March 1849

*F*ully expecting to again awaken nestled in the warmth of Buck's embrace, when Lyse found herself alone in the wide bed her initial disappointment quickly turned to fright. The handsome man's clothing no longer lay where he had thrown them and try as she might, she couldn't shake the horrible suspicion that he had vanished too. To make her situation all the more dire, as she sat up she was greeted by a fiery burst of pain that then became the worst headache imaginable. But mere physical pain was not nearly so agonizing as her panic over being abandoned.

The door between their rooms stood ajar but when Lyse called out Buck's name loudly, there was no reply. Shakily, she got out of bed, and without bothering to put on more than her camisole she hurried into the adjoining room. A cursory glance revealed all of Buck's belongings were gone. Other than the damp towels by the washstand, there was no evidence that the room had recently been occupied. The bed hadn't been slept in, and the wardrobe was empty. As soon as the maid brought clean towels the room would be ready for the next traveler to use.

Lyse tried to be calm, but what had happened was so dreadfully plain even a young woman so unsophisticated as she had no difficulty grasping it: Buck had walked out on her. It was as simple as that. She knew the money he had boasted would be hers should anything happen to him had already been spent to purchase their passage on board the *Spanish Dancer*. Or had it?

Returning to her room in a tear-dimmed daze, Lyse didn't know what to believe anymore. Buck had returned to the ship with the money for their passage while she had been at the Rosebud. Or at least that was one of the places he had said he was going. The only way she would have of finding out whether or not her way was paid to Panama would be to board the *Spanish Dancer* and ask. Even if Captain Randolph said no, however, she knew she couldn't possibly feel any more humiliated than she already did.

What about the hotel bill? she wondered with a mournful sigh. Would James Peters present her with the charges as she tried to leave? Had Buck not only deserted her, but also left a large debt at the hotel it would take her months to work off? Terrified he might have stolen what little money she had as well, Lyse went to the satchel and checked her new boots. It was a relief to find the kerchief hidden in the right one still held her pitifully few coins, but even if by some miracle her passage to Panama was paid, that was only part of the journey to California and she knew the money she had couldn't possibly cover the rest.

She had nothing of value to sell except her new clothes, and knowing what a wonderfully sympathetic person Rose Reynoso was, Lyse decided she would see if she couldn't return them all. They were beautiful garments, several not worn even once and the others no more than a few hours. Rose was her only hope and brushing away her tears, Lyse pulled out an old pair of pants and a shirt from the bottom of the satchel.

The water in the pitcher on the washstand was cool, but Lyse had no time to waste in ordering a bath and did the best she could to wash herself clean. Buck's heady masculine scent still remained on her fair skin but with a vengeance she scrubbed off every last trace of him. Her hands shook and her tears mixed with the soapy water, but she was in too great a hurry to throw herself across the bed and weep when her whole future was at stake. Once dressed in her old clothes, she braided her hair in a single plait, then donned her battered hat.

After carefully folding the lovely pink gown and the lacy lingerie she had worn the night before, she placed them in the satchel, buckled it up, and half carried, half dragged the heavy bag out the door. She couldn't call a porter for help because she couldn't spare the change for a tip, nor could she risk going by the front desk when she was uncertain whether or not the bill for their rooms had been paid.

Conveniently, there was a back stairwell for the help, but as she slung the satchel around the corner to start down the stairs, Lyse ran smack into Buck who had just come up from the kitchen balancing a silver tray holding their breakfast. With a startled shriek she tried to dodge out of his way, but already thrown off balance by the heavy bag, she tripped over it and went sprawling.

"Lyse!" Buck didn't know what was more shocking, her choice of attire or the fact he had caught her trying to sneak out of the hotel. He set the heavily laden tray aside on the table at the end of the hallway and reached down to help her to her feet. Seeing her face wet with tears, he mistakenly thought she had hurt herself and slipped his arm around her waist.

"I can't carry you with only one good arm. Can you make it back to your room?"

Overwhelmed with both guilt and shame, Lyse pulled free of his grasp. "I don't need your help to walk."

Not about to have it out with her in the hall, Buck gestured toward the tray. "Good, you bring our breakfast then, I'll take your bag." He picked it up before she could argue and carried it back to her room. He had time to count to ten before she arrived with the steaming hot food, but that didn't help him maintain the tenuous hold he had on his temper.

"Just where in the hell were you going, Lyse? I thought I'd let you sleep and surprise you with your breakfast, but you obviously had a far different surprise planned for me."

It was the rosebud in the crystal vase that broke what was left of her heart. Lyse set the tray down on her dresser and went to the window rather than respond. It was still early, a few people were out, but she couldn't see their faces through her tears.

Buck closed her door, his heart heavy with the realization

Lyse had tried to run away rather than face him that morning. The last thing he felt like doing was having something to eat, but anything would be better than listening to her halfhearted attempts to muffle her tears. There was a table in the corner of her room just as there was in his and he carried the tray over to it.

"Come sit down with me. Maybe you'll feel better after you've had something to eat." When she didn't move, he rephrased his request. "You'll sit down with me, Lyse, or I'll make you do it. Now come here before I get any more angry with you than I already am!"

Lyse could not even imagine a more impossible situation, but reluctantly she followed his command and sat down opposite him. Buck poured her a cup of tea, but her hand was shaking so badly she couldn't raise it from the saucer without fear of spilling it all over herself. He had provided the most scrumptious breakfast she had ever seen: hot biscuits, fresh-churned butter, orange marmalade, scrambled eggs, thick slices of ham, and fried potatoes. She gazed longingly at the food, fearing it would be much too difficult to eat with Buck staring at her with such a dark and accusing glance.

"It's not what you think," she finally gathered the courage to mumble.

"What isn't?" Buck prompted sharply. "Do you expect me to believe you were just going out for a stroll rather than running away? Hell, I've given you everything you wanted. If you needed something more, all you had to do is ask. If this is because of last night, well, what's done is done and I'm not sorry about it even if you are."

Even seated across from him, Lyse still felt deserted as though a mile-wide chasm separated them rather than a few feet. Her headache was nearly blinding and when she took a bite of the eggs he had piled on her plate, her stomach lurched in rebellion and daring to eat no more she lay her fork aside.

"I don't feel well. I think I better lie down."

"There's no time for that now," Buck pointed out crossly. "We've got too much to discuss. All I've heard from you is how much you want to go to California. Have you changed your mind? Or have you just decided you don't want to go with me?"

Lyse sat back in her chair, and knowing no matter what she said he would be hurt as well as angry, she chose to tell the truth no matter how difficult it was to reveal. "I've never spent the night with a man before," she began with obvious difficulty. "When I woke up and found you gone, well, I didn't think you'd be coming back. I was taking my clothes to the Rosebud where I hoped Rose would buy them back since I need the money."

Lyse looked so thoroughly miserable as she made her halting confession, Buck knew she hadn't made up that outlandish story. It was still difficult to believe, however, since it was so damn insulting. "You thought I'd run out on you, is that what you're saying?" he asked without making any attempt to hide his disgust at the preposterous assumption.

Unable to find the words to beg his forgiveness for her mistake, the distraught blonde merely nodded.

"I realize we've only known each other a couple of weeks, Lyse, but I sure as hell thought you knew me better than that. If you don't trust me now, well, I'm afraid you never will." Buck continued to regard her with a critical glance, and finally seeing the frightened child she was rather than the lady he had tried to create with a fancy wardrobe, he wondered if the fact that she hadn't had anyone to trust for so long had made it impossible for her to trust him. What about love? Was she simply incapable of that too? It certainly hadn't seemed so the previous night, but now he feared the wine had affected her emotions more strongly than he had believed. That realization caused another painful blow to his already badly battered pride.

"I'm sure you're not feeling well because of the wine, Lyse. You've just got a hangover and that's entirely my fault. The next time a man offers you wine, refuse it," he advised in an offhand manner, as though he were an older brother rather than her lover.

Lyse had heard her father complain of hangovers often enough, but she couldn't bear the thought that she was anything like him. "Buck?" she called softly, not daring to hope his mood would grow any less hostile.

"Yes?" He shifted in his chair, wondering what crazy thing she would say now.

"The next time you leave me like that, would you write me a note so I'll know where you've gone?"

Buck nodded, thinking he ought to promise to stay as far away from her as he could get, but knowing such a vow would be impossible to keep, he reluctantly agreed. He had never thought it necessary to provide any woman with an explanation of his whereabouts, but Lyse was like no other woman he had ever met.

"Sure, but if you can't find me on board the ship, better tell Randolph you think I've fallen overboard."

Lyse thought his expression an outright smirk rather than a smile, and was insulted by it. "It's cruel of you to tease me, just plain cruel. It isn't in the least bit funny I got so frightened." Infuriated by his high-handed attitude, she brushed away the last trace of moisture from her lashes and grabbed a biscuit she quickly spread with butter and marmalade. "You have no manners at all, Buck Warren. You're nothing but a—"

When she hesitated, obviously searching for an insult vile enough to use, he supplied one. "Lying snake?"

Startled by that colorful description, Lyse sat with the delectable biscuit halfway to her mouth. She could hardly accuse him of lying to her. He hadn't lured her into bed with promises of love and marriage. He had just made love to her so sweetly she had had no desire to resist. It was a jolt to realize she was as much like her mother as her pa had always accused her of being. Easy was the word, and her cheeks grew bright with shame as she realized how aptly that description fit.

"Let's don't start calling names. I don't want to fight with you. I'm just not up to it today."

"I'd rather not fight either, and I am sorry you don't feel well." Buck made no further attempt at conversation, and when he finished his breakfast, he stood for a moment to yank the bellpull. "I want you to take a long, hot bath so you'll feel better. Then put on one of your new dresses and we'll leave for the ship. I've already taken my things downstairs and told Peters to prepare our bill and find us a carriage. We'll be ready to go as soon as you're dressed."

"Can't I just go like this?" Lyse knew he would refuse that request even as she made it, but she didn't argue when he shook his head. She tried another few bites of eggs, then was able to lift the delicate china teacup to her lips without spilling a drop. By the time the porter arrived with the tub and hot water, she had finished eating and expected Buck to leave. When he didn't, she rose and got out the clothes she wanted to wear. Still he didn't move.

"Well?" she finally prompted him.

"Well, what?" Buck replied with feigned innocence.

"Aren't you going to leave the room while I bathe?"

"No, I don't dare leave you alone again, Lyse. There's too great a danger you might have some kind of terrible scare so I'm going to sit right here and keep you company."

While she thought him insufferably rude, Lyse decided to simply ignore what she was certain was his sarcastic attempt to get back at her for not trusting him. Dimly, she recalled the fun they had had undressing each other the previous evening, but the delightful closeness they had shared then was gone. Now each was too wary of the other to be in a playful mood. While Lyse knew that was her fault, she wished he could have been more understanding about it. If only she had slept later, she would have awakened to find Buck had thoughtfully ordered a marvelous breakfast. Maybe he would even have mentioned love if she hadn't jumped to the awful conclusion he had run out on her.

Because she would never know now, she decided he was right in thinking what was done was done and there was no use crying over it. There was no point in being shy around him either after what they had shared, but Lyse was. Hoping he actually liked skinny women, she tried simply to pretend he wasn't there. She figured once she was seated in the tub there would be damn little for him to see anyway and hurriedly got into the water.

Had Lyse thrown a screaming fit, Buck still would not have left her, but when she didn't offer any objection to his remaining with her, he was puzzled. He watched her peel off her old clothes and step into the tub with a careless nonchalance that amazed him. The tub was placed so her back was toward him, but that made the bath no less an erotic event. Even though he couldn't see the soap bubbles caressing the pale pink tips of her breasts, his imagination painted that picture so vividly his body couldn't help but respond. When it became impossible to ignore the familiar fullness in his loins he left his chair and went to her side. Kneeling down, he reached for the washcloth she was using to lazily scrub her left knee.

"Let me help you," he offered in an enticing tone.

"I know how to take a bath, Buck. I'm not all that dumb," Lyse replied, coolly thinking it was men in general and him in particular she didn't know nearly enough about. She had already scrubbed herself clean once that morning, and knew he wouldn't find a speck of dirt left to wash away.

Though that wasn't the invitation he longed to hear, Buck took the soapy cloth from her hands anyway. "You have very beautiful skin, soft, smooth, and such a luscious shade of creamy peach."

"Like peaches and cream, you mean?" Lyse had heard such a complexion was highly prized, but had never dreamed she possessed such an asset herself.

"Yes, that pretty term was meant for lovely blondes like you."

Lyse held her breath as Buck began to brush her nipples with the soft edge of the folded cloth. Unable to meet his gaze, she watched the smooth buds grow firm then shivered as he dropped the cloth and began to caress the slippery wet fullness of her breasts with his hand. "I thought you were in a hurry to leave," she whispered softly, amazed by how easily her body had betrayed her mind's command to ignore his presence.

"It's not even nine. The ship doesn't sail for three hours." Buck unbuttoned his sleeve, then rolled it up past his elbow before he slipped his hand beneath the water to continue his exploration of her slender body's many charms.

Lyse closed her eyes as her breath caught in her throat. Clearly, she was the most wanton creature ever born but since Buck hadn't criticized her for it, she decided to keep that opinion to herself. His magical caress flooded her body with pleasure, replacing the tension caused by his mistaken betrayal with a warmth far more delicious than that provided by the bathwater. It was an exquisite sensation, and one she was certain ought to be shared. "This tub really is big enough for us both," she reminded him when at last she could draw the breath to speak.

"I can't get my shoulder wet," Buck remarked sadly, thinking it a shame he had to pass up her invitation.

Lyse peeked up at him through a lacy fringe of tear-dampened lashes and noting he again seemed no more able to draw a deep breath than she, she paraphrased a promise he had made to her. "You'll come to no harm with me."

Delighted to find her mood so greatly improved, Buck decided to take her up on that promise. He dried off his arm and began to unbutton his shirt, but he didn't take his eyes from hers. He had always thought she had gorgeous eyes, so big and bright a blue he found her glance irresistibly appealing.

"You would make a marvelous mermaid," he remarked with a ready grin.

"No I wouldn't," Lyse replied, her lilting giggle a further delight. "I can't swim very well, so let's hope the ship doesn't sink."

Buck couldn't help but laugh too since he considered her fears completely unfounded. "I meant that you have the fair beauty of a mermaid, not that I expected you to be able to swim like a fish." When she did no more than shrug, he leaned down to give her a kiss then nuzzled the damp curve of her shoulder.

"Actually, it's a damn good thing you're not a mermaid since I don't know how to make love to them." He watched a slight frown cross her brow and knew without asking that she was trying to imagine that trick herself. He had to sit down to pull off his boots, then hurriedly cast off the rest of his clothes. He gave her a nudge to push her forward slightly then climbed into the tub behind her and wrapped her in an enthusiastic embrace. Her back was all wet, slippery, and warm, and as he whispered in her ear, he pulled her against his chest.

"I would have turned Galveston upside down if you

hadn't been here to have breakfast with me, and I would have found you too."

Lyse rested her chin upon his arm, delighted again by his abundant affection. She hadn't been held since her mother had left home, but she hadn't realized until that very moment how much she had missed being touched. "You must think I'm real stupid," she commented shyly.

Buck licked a drop of water off her earlobe. "No, you're not in the least bit stupid, just young is all."

"Not much I can do about that." She slipped her arms around his knees, thinking they each had such long legs the tub wasn't really large enough for them both after all. She didn't complain about being cramped, though, because she liked being surrounded by his warmth too much. "This is kinda fun," she said instead.

"I think it's a lot better than just fun." Buck thought Lyse an absolute treasure. He liked the luscious smoothness of her skin and the way their bodies fit together so easily. His mood was playful at first, but when she continued to find his touch as thrilling as he found hers, his mood became far more passionate. Because she was so agile a young woman, he was certain they could make love in the tub. He asked her to stand up and turn around so she would be facing him, then gently guided her down upon his thighs.

At first Lyse was too intrigued to question his directions, then when she readily understood what he wanted to do she had no wish to speak. She wrapped her arms around his neck as he began to kiss her, her mood as abandoned as his. Their bodies were slippery with soap, but each was blessed with unusual grace and found that no hindrance to the pursuit of love.

Again Buck marveled at how readily Lyse responded to his loving. He had to do no more than hint at what it was he wanted her to do and she would not merely follow his suggestion but make it seem like her own, heightening his excitement all the more with her own special uniqueness. That she was so new to such erotic play seemed impossible, for she was the most exciting partner he had ever known. He had planned to go slow with her, but now he was overjoyed their relationship had become intimate with such astonishing speed.

As she continued to return his eager kisses, Lyse's hands slid through the soapy curls covering Buck's chest but she took care not to stray near his bandaged shoulder. Even without several glasses of wine, her senses were reeling and she simply could not get enough of the delicious taste and feel of him. When at last his hands gripped her waist, gently lifting her toward him, she grasped his manhood without a trace of shyness, guiding the swollen shaft so he might bury himself more quickly within her. That action seemed so natural to her she welcomed the deep moan that escaped his lips as with a shudder of joy he brought their bodies together as one.

The feelings Buck aroused within her were almost indescribably sweet, filling her with a desperate longing for the stunning release she now knew they would share. Her impatience for that glorious pleasure was equal to his, yet when at last it burst forth within her the rapture was even more profound than she had hoped. Flooded with splendor, she felt her body clinging to his, a throbbing deep within that matched her wildly beating heart then gradually subsided to become a wondrous glow of remembered ecstasy. She thought him the best of lovers, and knew she would never want another man to know her as he did.

"Buck?" Lyse whispered dreamily, aware that he was holding her cradled tenderly in his arms and knowing his mood would be as relaxed as her own.

"Hmm?" He was leaning back in the tub, thinking bathing would never be the same.

"Does making love get better every time?"

"If it did I don't think I'd survive more than a week with you, but it can't get much better than this, Lyse, it just can't."

Lyse wanted nothing more than to fall asleep in his embrace, but the sunlight streaming in the windows was growing brighter and she knew they had to be going soon. "Do you suppose the *Spanish Dancer* has such nice bathtubs?"

"I doubt it." Buck hesitated a moment, undecided about whether or not he ought to warn her they would have to be far more discreet on board ship than they had been there in the hotel. Deciding there was too great a danger she would misinterpret such a comment, he kept it to himself. The last thing he wanted to risk was upsetting her again. Finally noticing the water had grown cold, he gave her one last hug.

"Now stand up very carefully, I don't want you to fall again and hurt yourself."

Lyse was embarrassed by her earlier clumsiness and with a last kiss withdrew from him now with all the grace she possessed. She stepped out of the tub and wrapped herself in a towel, then had to go into his room to find one for him. She stood aside as he hauled himself out of the tub, then wrapped it around his waist.

"My headache's gone!" she exclaimed suddenly and glancing toward the food left on their breakfast tray, she realized she was ravenously hungry too. "There's time for me to eat a little something more, isn't there?"

"Sure, but I'm afraid it's gotten cold." That Lyse seemed not to care amused him. She had gone from seductive enchantress to carefree child in less than a minute's time. As she sat down, her towel dipped low across her breasts, and covered only the top of her trim thighs, but he wasn't about to tell her she should be more modest. He dressed quickly then sat down opposite her again.

"I'm going to take you and our things to the ship, then I'll have to pay the sheriff a call before we sail."

"Oh, do you really think you should?" Lyse asked apprehensively. "Wouldn't Hobart have told him that Jack's death was an accident?"

Buck shrugged slightly. "I sure hope he did, but I want to make certain the sheriff doesn't think I've left town to avoid seeing him. I'm sure to come back through Galveston someday and I don't want to find I'm wanted for murder."

"No, of course not," Lyse agreed, yet his mention of returning to Texas provided a shock coming so soon after they had made love. That they would not be together forever was an excruciatingly painful thought, but she knew he would have to be the one to suggest their partnership become a permanent one. Maybe after he had found Arvin and she had struck it rich the idea would occur to him. She certainly hoped so. Because he was already wealthy, she knew he wouldn't be marrying her for her money.

"Why are you grinning so happily?" Buck asked with a lazy chuckle. "You want to see my face on a wanted poster?"

"Oh, no," Lyse assured him. "I was just thinking about California and how much fun it will be to be rich."

"Well it won't be much fun if you're all alone, but I doubt a rich woman ever lacks for company." Badly disappointed money was all that was on Lyse's mind, Buck excused himself and went to see if their carriage had arrived.

When Timothy MacCormac saw Buck and Lyse coming up the gangplank, he rushed forward to greet them. "I had no idea you were sailing on the *Spanish Dancer*. Why didn't you tell me when I told you good-bye?" Though his question was addressed to Buck, the delighted young man's eyes never left Lyse's pretty smile. She was dressed in a gown of pale green muslin he thought ravishing, but he waited for Buck to reply before he began to pay her compliments.

"We had a sudden change in plan," Buck informed him brusquely. Tim's rapt fascination with Lyse reminded him of his sister Patricia's adoring callers. That wasn't a comparison that pleased him either. "If you'll excuse us, I want to get Miss Selby settled in her cabin as I have a quick errand to run."

Tim watched them as they hurried away, so grateful to learn he would have plenty of opportunities to see the charming blonde again he could barely contain his joy. When the man having the cabin opposite his came to his side, he scarcely noticed him.

Colin O'Roarke had bright red hair, green eyes, and countless freckles, but despite his boyish appearance he was a twenty-five-year-old man, fiercely independent and obnoxiously cynical. "Who was that?" he demanded with a hostile gaze in the newcomers' direction.

"Friends of mine," Tim replied proudly. "I'll introduce you later."

"Wherever did you make friends like those?" Colin asked snidely.

Tim moved a step away, not pleased by Colin's belligerent attitude. Although he had seen no real evidence of it as yet, he thought him a bully and wished he would spend his time elsewhere. They were about the same height, but Colin had a wiry toughness about him Tim knew he lacked. "Right here in Galveston, not that it's any business of yours."

Amazed by the rudeness of that comment, Colin raised his brows in mock horror. "Let's just say I'm making it my business. Is the blonde that man's wife, or just his mistress?"

Tim could not even imagine such a thing of Alyssa Selby and quickly came to her defense, forgetting he had gotten himself punched in the face the last time he had lost his temper over her. "She is his business partner and you better be careful what you say about her. If you insult her, Buck Warren will ram his fist right down your throat, and if he doesn't, I will!"

"That was Buck Warren?" Now Colin was really impressed. "I read about him in the paper. Seems he was involved in a real suspicious accident in one of the saloons. Sounds like he would just as soon kill a man as look at him."

Though Tim thought that an exaggeration, he gained a curious sense of importance from the new look of respect in Colin's eyes. "I was with him that day," he boasted again. "As I said, Buck's a friend of mine."

Colin did no more than nod, but he couldn't wait to get another look at the attractive pair. From what he had seen of the other passengers, women were going to be very scarce, but he didn't relish the thought of taking on Buck Warren to get to the only one on board.

Buck told Lyse to stay in her cabin until he returned, but she considered that request preposterous. In the first place, there was barely enough room to turn around. She dared not leave the door open, but the cabin was stuffy and much too warm. She debated with herself, wanting to please him, and at the same time not wanting to miss any of the excitement of the ship's departure. Finally, she decided to tell him it had been a choice of either leaving her cabin or of suffocating inside it, and went up on deck.

As soon as she appeared, Tim MacCormac hastened to

her side. Lyse then found herself surrounded by more than two dozen young men who were all as eager to make her acquaintance as he. Ignoring their openly admiring stares, she managed to work her way over to the rail. Despite the buzz of conversation going on around her, she kept her eyes on the dock, hoping Buck would soon return. When he hadn't appeared by the time she heard Captain Randolph give the order to take up the gangplank, she waved the men who had surrounded her out of her way and rushed to the captain's side.

"You've got to wait for Buck!" she insisted as she took his arm. "I'm sure he'll be here in just a minute and we can't sail without him."

Gregory Randolph knew it had been a mistake to allow her on board the minute he looked into Lyse's eyes. Gone was the poorly dressed waif he had met the day before and in her place stood an elegant beauty who could cajole a man into becoming her slave. He knew he would have the most miserable of voyages if he began giving in to her whims before they had even left the dock.

"I'll hold the gangplank just five minutes more, Miss Selby. If he isn't here, then we'll sail without him," he informed her coldly.

"Then you will sail without me as well," Lyse responded as she backed away.

Obviously unmoved by that threat, Randolph inclined his head in a mock bow. "As you wish, miss."

When Lyse turned around she found Tim so close she was certain he had been standing on her hem. Grabbing his arm, she hurried him back over to the rail. "If Buck doesn't show up in a minute or two, do you think you can create some sort of a diversion so Randolph will be too busy to set sail before he gets here?"

"What kind of a diversion?" Tim asked skeptically, praying he wouldn't have to refuse her request.

Lowering her voice, Lyse raised up on her tiptoes to whisper in his ear. "A fight would be good. With so many men on deck, it should be easy to start a brawl."

"A brawl?" Tim cried out in dismay. His nose was still so

badly bruised and swollen he didn't know how she could suggest such a thing.

Thinking she would have to take the first swing at one of the men standing close by herself, Lyse turned away, but in that instant she saw Buck running across the dock toward the gangplank and waved to him as she called over her shoulder to the captain. "You see, I told you Buck would be here!"

The captain's returning smile was more of a grimace and he made certain the gangplank was brought up as soon as Buck's feet hit the deck. He was too busy then shouting orders for his first mate to relay to notice the conversation that then took place between the tardy passenger and his lovely lady.

Buck jammed his left hand in his pocket so Lyse wouldn't see his bloody knuckles. "I'm sorry, I had a difficult time getting away from the sheriff."

That he would apologize rather than criticize her for being out of her cabin delighted Lyse. It wasn't until the ship had drawn away from the docks and set out for the open waters of the Gulf of Mexico that she noticed that Buck was clearly furious and she hastened to find out why.

XII

March 1849

"*T*ell me exactly what happened," Lyse insisted as she pressed close to Buck's side.

There were too many men standing nearby to talk freely and Buck sent her a dark glance to warn her to keep her questions to herself for the time being. His desire for discretion was twofold, however, since he could feel the blood oozing through the bandage on his shoulder. Fearing it would soon soak through his shirt and coat as well, he leaned down to whisper.

"Let's go to my cabin." Certain he could count on Lyse's curiosity to compel her to follow, he turned away from the rail and started across the crowded deck.

When Lyse bid Tim a hasty farewell and trailed in Buck's wake, Colin O'Roarke stepped to the disappointed young man's side to gloat. "You see how quick she is to do his bidding? She's his mistress all right and you haven't a chance with her."

That taunt so outraged Tim he completely forgot his earlier worries about his battered nose. He swung at the red-haired man, but Colin saw it coming and lunged out of the way so Tim's fist struck a glancing blow off the ear of the man standing directly behind his intended target. Startled by that unexpected and totally undeserved burst of pain, the injured man responded by tackling Tim with a flying leap.

Like a cresting wave, that sudden outbreak of violence

rolled through the gold-hungry travelers gathered along the rail. As one, they began shoving and pushing first in one direction and then in the other. The more aggressive of the group then grew openly hostile and began throwing wild punches, not caring whom they hurt. Others stooped to biting, kicking, and screaming insults as they fell on one another.

The brawl Lyse had foolishly considered a brilliant ploy spread across the deck with astonishing speed. Nearly engulfed by it, she was utterly terrified. Had Buck not reached out to grab her hand and pull her down with him into the companionway, she was certain she would have been caught up in the wild melee, thrown to the deck, and undoubtedly badly injured if not trampled to death.

Familiar with the havoc an unruly mob could create, when they reached his cabin Buck shoved Lyse inside and hurriedly locked the door behind them. "Now do you understand why I don't want you up on deck without me?" he shouted angrily, for the surprising fierceness of what he saw as totally unprovoked mayhem had appalled him. If tempers were so short at the beginning of the voyage, he didn't want to imagine what they would be like two weeks later when it reached its end. Even in the safety of his cabin they could still hear shouting up on deck, then several shots being fired. After what seemed like far too long an interval, calm returned to the graceful *Spanish Dancer* and was broken only by the fluttering of the wind in the sails as the sleek ship continued on its way.

Lyse clung to Buck, her arms wrapped tightly around his waist, so frightened she didn't care how loudly he yelled at her. Badly shaken, she kept telling herself she had had nothing to do with the ghastly fight. Still, she felt horribly guilty as though the fruits of her lively imagination and the harshness of reality were one and the same. At least she had learned quite rapidly that what she had considered a good idea was a very bad one.

"Do you think anyone was killed?" she finally gathered the courage to ask.

"I hope not." With Lyse cuddled so close, Buck found it not only impossible to stay mad but also difficult to recall why they had started for his cabin in the first place, although he was certainly glad that they had.

Not wanting to make any bigger fool of herself than she had already, Lyse stepped back and smoothed out the folds of her skirt. "I'm sorry to be so silly. I shouldn't have been so scared, not when I was with you."

Though that was an extremely flattering thought, Buck doubted he would have been much help and didn't want to take any undeserved credit for protecting her from harm. On the other hand, he was wise enough not to argue with her either.

"You were right about the sheriff, Lyse," he readily confessed. "I never should have gone to see him. It just gave him the opportunity to tell me I wasn't to leave town until he was satisfied in his own mind that I hadn't already planned to kill Jack when I sat down to play poker at his table."

"But you're here," Lyse said with a puzzled frown. "How did you change his mind?"

Feeling very tired, Buck sank down on the side of his bunk. "I didn't. When I started for the door he made the mistake of grabbing my shoulder. That hurt so much I didn't stop to think about the consequences. I just hit him as hard as I could, shoved him into an empty cell, and turned the key in the lock. Luckily Hobart wasn't there too because I never could have gotten away from the both of them." He looked up at her then, his expression decidedly sheepish. "Well, you know the rest. I made it back to the ship on time."

Lyse shook her head sadly, thinking the pattern of their lives was continuing to go from bad to worse despite their best efforts to do what was right. "Do you think he'll come after us?"

"Us?" That word made Buck laugh. "It's me he'd be after, Lyse, not you. I told him I was heading back to Dallas, so even if he tries to find me, he won't."

"What about the list of passengers Captain Randolph gave the harbor master? Won't our names be on it?"

Buck gave her a sly smile before he answered. "No, I told him to list us as David Bailey and Constance Thorn."

"You were expecting trouble yesterday?"

"Weren't you?"

"I guess you're right." Lyse sat down beside him and laced her fingers in his. "You're all right then, you weren't seriously hurt?"

"Well, now that you mention it," Buck admitted reluctantly. "I need your help. My shoulder's bleeding again."

"What? Well why in the hell didn't you say so?" Lyse immediately got to her feet and carefully pulled off his coat so as not to hurt him again. She quickly unbuttoned his shirt, then peeled it away with equal care. Dr. Glover's neat bandage was marred by a bright red stain, but it wasn't until she had removed it that she began to feel ill.

The first time she had taken care of Buck he had been a stranger whose pain she couldn't feel. Now he was the dearest person in the world to her. He hadn't told her the doctor had used stitches to close his wounds and the sight of his torn flesh where the neat black sutures had been pulled away was more than she could bear. Buck's features began to swim before her eyes, but when she raised her hand to her forehead in hopes of clearing her vision the last thing she saw was his blood dripping from her fingers.

Buck swore as Lyse fell across his lap. She was the last woman he would ever expect to faint at the sight of a little blood, but he guessed his shoulder must look as bad as it felt. He gave her fanny a playful swat, hoping to wake her, but she was out cold. Before he could think of some more effective way to awake her, there was a knock at his door. Hoping it would be someone with a stronger stomach than his beautiful but unconscious companion, he leaned over and swung open the door.

Captain Randolph's dark blue uniform was resplendent with brass buttons and gold braid, but it was medical attention Buck needed, not an impressively dressed visitor. "Is there a surgeon on board," he asked quickly.

The Captain stared first at Lyse's limp form enticingly across Buck's lap, and then at the blood slowly trickling down the young man's bare chest. "Just what in the hell is going on in here, Warren? Using assumed names is a harmless deception, attempting to kill each other is a crime, even at sea."

"Hell, we aren't trying to kill each other." Buck couldn't understand why everyone he met lately suspected his motives and assumed the worst. "I got shot a couple of weeks ago. When I started bleeding again just now, Lyse offered to help, then passed out before she could do anything. Now is there a surgeon on board or not? I don't want to bleed to death while I'm waiting for the answer."

"Yes, there is a surgeon. With so many passengers I refused to sail without one. He's busy setting a broken arm, but I'll see he comes down here as soon as he's finished."

"An arm can wait, this can't." Buck feared it would be difficult to demand much when he was too weak to stand, but he gave the bluff his best try.

Randolph leaned out the door to shout an order to a cabin steward passing by, then gave his full attention to Lyse. "The doctor will be here in a minute. Now let me take Miss Selby off your hands." He bent down to pluck the lovely blonde from Buck's embrace, but found him reluctant to give her up. "I'm only taking her next door to her own cabin. She can't be comfortable where she is."

Buck released his hold on the slender blonde then, but he felt curiously empty as he watched her being carried out the door. She had become like a part of him, and he not only needed her but also he missed her.

When Lyse awakened to find a brawny sailor peering down at her, she sat up so quickly they nearly bumped heads. "Where's Buck?" she asked anxiously as she swung her legs over the side of her bunk. Their cabins were identical and she mistakenly thought she was still in his.

"He's in his cabin," the startled man replied. "The doctor gave him something to make him sleep. The captain told me to bring you to him as soon as you were awake." He spoke very slowly and distinctly, as though she were a small child who might question his order or refuse to obey it.

Having never fainted before, Lyse didn't understand what had happened to her. All she knew was that she had been with Buck, and now she wasn't. That was so upsetting a circumstance she couldn't be bothered with the captain's problems. "Why does Randolph want to see me?"

"Well, ma'am, I don't rightly know but when he tells me to do something, I do it," the sailor again explained with exaggerated care.

"I have no choice about it? Is that what you're saying?"

That query stumped the sailor. He didn't know how to give a polite reply to such an impertinent question. "You better just come with me, ma'am. I'm sure the captain has his reasons."

Knowing the captain had been promised she was a lady, Lyse took a deep breath and tried to summon the poise such a ruse would require. Unfortunately, she was far too worried about Buck to give the appearance of calm she didn't feel. "Just a minute. What's your name?" she asked with a disarming smile as she moved to the satchel containing her belongings. She had had no time to unpack, but knew where she had hidden her knife and quickly took it out and slipped it into her pocket. Standing up with a hastily grabbed handkerchief in her hand, she knew he would believe she had been searching for it. She raised the lace-trimmed square of linen to her eyes to wipe away an nonexistent tear.

"My name is John Charles, ma'am."

Lyse waited a moment, but the man offered no further explanation of why he had been sent to fetch her. She couldn't help but look at his massive shoulders and arms and wonder if he had been told to pick her up and carry her to the captain's cabin if she refused to go quietly. Being slung over his shoulder like a bag of laundry was an indignity she planned to avoid.

"Well John, I'd rather you called me Lyse than ma'am. I want to check on Buck, then I'll come with you." She spoke as she moved toward her partially open door and then slipped through it before he could stop her. Buck's door wasn't locked, but just as John had reported, he was in his bunk sound asleep. He still looked too pale, and Lyse reached out to touch his hair with a fond caress before she closed the door and turned back to face her insistent escort.

"Lead the way, John," she encouraged brightly. She had no idea why the captain wanted to see her but doubted he would have anything to say that she wanted to hear.

Gregory Randolph had had only a brief opportunity to

observe Lyse while they had argued about delaying the ship's departure. Then standing on deck, he had seen the fight erupt as she and Buck Warren had left the rail to go below. When he had quelled the disturbance he had immediately confirmed his suspicion she was somehow the cause. That had prompted him to again berate himself for not having known better than to allow a woman on board. He would not turn back to put her off, but he had no intention of suffering any more disruption in his ship's routine because of her. In his view, a beautiful woman needed a firm hand and he would not hesitate to use one on her fanny if she proved unreasonable.

Yet as she moved across his cabin toward him, he saw only the remarkable blue of her eyes and enchanted by her angelic beauty, he tried to phrase his demands in the most diplomatic terms possible. "Please sit down, my dear." When she had taken a place at his table he took the one at her right.

"I had no idea Mr. Warren was so seriously injured when I accepted you as passengers."

Alarmed that Buck's health was to be the subject of their conversation, Lyse leaned forward. "He's going to be all right, isn't he? I hated to leave him all alone. If you think he's in any danger, then I'll go back to his cabin right now."

The young woman's concern was so obviously genuine, Randolph reached out to give her hand a reassuring pat then continued to hold her fingers lightly in his. "I didn't mean to upset you, Miss Selby. Robert Ash is our ship's surgeon and he's certain Mr. Warren will recover his health with a few days' rest." He paused then, choosing his words with care. "I'd thought Mr. Warren would be able to look out for you himself, but since he can't—"

The weight of her knife resting comfortably upon her thigh, Lyse was quick to interrupt. "I can take care of myself, thank you. Buck is my partner, not my older brother. I'll be happy to take care of him as long as he needs it, but you needn't worry you'll have to find someone else to watch out for me."

The gray-haired captain pursed his lips thoughtfully. "Your presence on board has already created one riot and

I've warned the other passengers I'll not tolerate another such outbreak of violence. It is difficult enough to keep my crew well disciplined without having to worry about the passengers' unruly behavior as well."

Insulted, Lyse pulled her hand from his. "I had nothing to do with that fight. How dare you try and blame it on me?"

"On the contrary, I have proof it was your fault." The captain looked down at the notes he had taken in preparation for making an entry in the ship's log. "You have a friend on board, a Mr. Timothy MacCormac. He took another man's chance comment about you as a personal affront and chose to defend your honor with his fists. You know what happened after that. So you see, you were definitely the cause of the fight."

Lyse thought the captain's logic twisted at best, but she wasn't at all pleased to hear Tim had been so foolish. "Just who is this other man? Tell me what he said, and I'll take care of him myself."

Captain Randolph stared at Lyse, shocked by her surprisingly confident boast. Then he realized that despite her delightfully feminine attire and sweet features, she had the same self-assured manner he had admired in Buck Warren. She was young, and extremely pretty, but unless he missed his guess she also possessed the inner toughness it took to meet life's most trying challenges. It was a remarkable combination in a woman and he was sorry it hadn't been nearly so readily apparent the first time he had met her or he would have kept her off his ship for certain.

"MacCormac refused to repeat what was said, but it was clearly a comment about your virtue and I'll not reveal the source. Since I'll not allow you, or anyone else, to stage a duel on the *Spanish Dancer*, I must insist you ignore the incident."

Lyse was astonished by the captain's remark. Whatever could this unnamed man have said about her virtue? Then with a sudden burst of intuition she knew, and a deep blush flooded her cheeks. "I'm no whore!" she denied hotly.

Taken aback by that brazen retort, the captain attempted to minimize her obvious embarrassment. "I didn't say that you were, my dear." He hadn't planned to reveal so much and was as upset as she by the shocking turn their conversation had taken. "Regardless of what the purpose of your, well, your partnership with Mr. Warren might be, my responsibility is to see this ship sails to Panama without further mishap. I intend to do just that."

Lyse leapt to her feet, livid over the way the man had haltingly described her relationship with Buck as though they were carrying on some sort of sordid affair. "You needn't worry about duels. Buck's not well or he'd find out who insulted me and slit his throat for saying such a vile thing."

"Miss Selby!" Appalled, the captain rose to face her. "I can't allow you to talk that way, not to me or anyone else on board. If Buck Warren is as prone to violence as you seem to think, then he'll soon find himself in my brig. For the time being, you give me no choice but to restrict you both to your cabins."

Lyse protested that order instantly. "I'll have to take care of Buck so you can't keep me in my cabin when I'll need to be in his."

Gregory Randolph raised his hands in a conciliatory gesture that proved to be another futile attempt to cool her temper. "All right, that's fine. Just stay below deck in your cabin or his. John will bring you your meals and see you have whatever you need."

Still not satisfied, Lyse continued to glare at the man. "Some fool insults me, and I'm the one who gets punished? That makes no sense at all, Captain Randolph. Are you sure you know how to get this ship to Panama?"

Able to take no more of the volatile young woman's exceedingly unpleasant company, the captain walked to his door and drew John inside. "Escort Miss Selby to her cabin and see she visits no one but Mr. Warren. If I catch her on deck, I'll give you a whipping you won't soon forget so don't let the wench get past you."

As they left the captain's cabin, Lyse could tell from John's stricken expression that that had been no idle threat. "Don't look so terrified, you won't get whipped on account of me. Now let's hurry. I've left Buck alone too long already."

John watched the seductive sway of Lyse's hips as she preceded him and licked his lips nervously. It wasn't right having one woman on board with so many men and despite her assurance, he feared he would get whipped for sure before the voyage reached its end.

Once in Buck's cabin, Lyse had nothing to do but watch him sleep. She sat down in the one chair, propped her feet on the end of his bunk, and crossed her arms beneath her bosom. Comfortably prepared for a long wait, she was glad he was still resting easily but she was anything but calm herself. She didn't feel in the least bit confined, however, because she had no desire to go up on deck now that she knew what the men were saying about her.

She knew the love she felt for Buck was real, and couldn't believe expressing that emotion in the glorious way he had taught her was wrong. She told herself that again and again, but it didn't ease the pain the gossip the captain had reported caused her. She wanted to thank Tim for what he had tried to do even if it had ended badly and hoped he would come to find her because she couldn't look for him. Lost in her own dark thoughts, she waited patiently for Buck to wake but she had no idea what she should tell him when he did.

When Buck finally awoke, he found Lyse's thoughtful expression so wistful he waited several minutes before he spoke to bring her out of her reverie. Though he enjoyed watching her, he liked talking to her even more. "Have you been in here with me all afternoon?" he asked as he stifled a wide yawn.

Startled, Lyse sat up and fluffed out her skirt, hoping he hadn't caught her in too unladylike a pose. "I wanted to stay with you. Do you mind?"

"Not at all." Truly, Buck couldn't think of anyone whose company he enjoyed more. "What have you been doing, just sitting there daydreaming?"

Lyse nodded. "I guess you could call it that." Seeing she had his full attention, she poured out her thoughts in a breathless rush. "I don't care if it takes me five years, Buck, but I'm going to find so much gold no one will dare say a word about the way I live. It really isn't fair, you know? A man can do as he damn well pleases while a woman has to constantly be on her guard to see there's not a whisper of gossip attached to her name. Young men can get away with being wild. Folks just naturally seem to expect that of them while at the same time they are quick to call a young woman who goes her own way a tramp, or worse. That's not fair at all."

Lyse was so obviously upset, Buck eased himself up into a sitting position so they could converse more easily. With his pillow at his back, he was comfortable enough to chat. "Come here and sit beside me while we talk." He patted the bunk, then gestured invitingly. When she was seated at his side, he took her hand and gave it an affectionate squeeze. "What did I miss this afternoon? I'd never describe you as a tramp, but have you decided I'm 'wild'?"

That was a question Lyse hadn't even considered, but she had a ready answer. "I guess you must be with all the trouble you get into, but that doesn't bother me."

"That's nice to know," Buck responded with a teasing grin. "I sure don't have it in me to be wild now, though. I feel like I've been run over by a stampede and not an inch of me wasn't trampled. Do you suppose we can get a steward to bring our food here? I sure as hell don't have the energy to dress up and dine with the captain tonight."

"Our meals will be no problem," Lyse assured him. "The captain doesn't expect us to leave our cabins." That was the truth, or at least part of it, but Lyse couldn't bear to reveal anymore as yet. She couldn't think of any way to tell him how the riot had started that wouldn't sound like she was complaining about the fact that their traveling arrangements encouraged people to think the worst of her. Not that she cared about the other passengers' opinions, she kept telling herself. They'd all be the same once they reached the gold fields. Neither she nor Buck was ready to settle down and get married, Lord no, but that wasn't something they could explain to other people because it would only increase the gossip about them, not stop it.

"Lyse, what's wrong?"

"Nothing," the near frantic blonde insisted, but she could see he didn't believe her. "I was just worried about you is all."

"I'm worried too," Buck admitted. "If I don't feel better than this by the time we reach Panama, I'll just have to wait until I do before we go on. I've heard going up the river and crossing the mountains is a difficult journey for a healthy man; for an invalid it could be suicide."

"Suicide!" Lyse's heart leapt to her throat at so dire a prospect. "I'll not let you take that risk, Buck Warren. So what if Arvin increases his lead, we'll catch up to him soon enough."

She seemed so determined, a slow smile played across Buck's lips. "I thought you were in a big hurry to strike it rich. Wouldn't you consider going on to California without me?"

Lyse didn't understand how he could even ask such an awful question let alone expect her to answer it. "We're partners, and partners stick together," she reminded him. "The gold can wait right along with Arvin. I'd not leave you behind."

Buck reached out to draw her near. Though he didn't have the strength to make love, that didn't mean he didn't want to. He kissed Lyse with a honey-smooth passion that conveyed both his desire and his sorrow that he could not fulfill it. He held her in a relaxed embrace, content for the moment simply to enjoy the fragrance of roses that clung to her clothes and hair and the delightfully soft contours of her lithe body. "I'll see your dreams come true, Lyse, even if you decide you want to be the richest woman in all California."

Lyse giggled softly as she nestled against him. "I just want a little ranch, Buck, you know that."

"Yes, I know." Buck was so tired he was again on the verge of sleep when John Charles brought their supper, but with so lovely a companion he was wide awake by the time they finished eating.

Despite being in the midst of the fight, Tim MacCormac hadn't suffered too badly. He had cuts and bruises aplenty, but he was so proud of himself for not being knocked unconscious as many men had been that he didn't feel but a twinge or two of pain. He was especially pleased he had actually given Colin O'Roarke a couple of good punches when he hadn't used his fists since he had been in grammar school.

He could tell by the fit of his clothes he had lost weight since leaving Cincinnati, and he could see more color in his skin. He was certain he had never made a better decision than the one to go to California. Yes, sir, he told himself, he was becoming a real man and leaving the shy accountant who had been afraid of his own shadow far behind. The glances of the other passengers now held some respect since they had overheard the captain blame the riot on him. He was certain even Colin O'Roarke would think twice about bothering him now that he had shown he would fight for what he believed. Though he knew he was still a long way from being able to handle himself like Buck Warren, he couldn't help but think he would be that confident soon.

When Buck and Lyse did not come out on deck the rest of the day, nor appear at dinner, Tim was badly disappointed. Not that he wanted to brag to them about what he had done, he just wanted to talk with them again. He admired Buck enormously, and adored Lyse. He thought they liked him too. At least he hoped they did. Finally he grew too anxious to see them to wait a moment longer and found out which cabins were theirs.

John Charles stepped out of Tim's way to let him pass, but when the young man knocked at Lyse's door he didn't know what to do. The captain hadn't said anything about the woman having visitors. This man posed no threat, though. "She's in the next one," John pointed out helpfully.

Tim hesitated slightly. He didn't like to dwell on what Colin had said, but it bothered him to hear Lyse was in Buck's cabin. Still, it was early evening so he didn't think they could be doing anything but visiting. Then again, his cabin wasn't large enough to entertain guests, so he didn't understand how Buck's could be.

John couldn't understand why Tim was simply staring at Buck's door so he leaned over to knock on it loudly himself. "They got to be in there," he assured him.

Buck had been attempting to teach Lyse how to play poker and when he reached over to swing open his door, Tim saw the lively young woman seated cross-legged on the foot of the bunk and gasped in surprise. Then he noticed Buck wasn't wearing a shirt. Stunned to think Colin's vile comments about the couple had to be true, he turned away without speaking and fled with tears stinging his eyes.

"What's gotten into Tim?" Lyse asked as she slid off the bunk and went to the door.

"Beats me." Buck gathered up the cards and shuffled them awkwardly with one hand. "The least he could have done was ask how I am."

"Tim!" Lyse called out, but he didn't turn back. Without thinking she started after him, but John Charles reached out to catch her around the waist and swung her right back into Buck's room. He shook his head as he closed the door and she knew it would be pointless to plead with him to allow her to follow her friend up on deck. Both frustrated and disappointed, she sank down on the edge of the bunk. Feeling trapped, she was near tears herself. "I don't think Tim knows you're not well. How could he?"

"Yeah, I guess you're right. Still, that's not like him to run off like that. He usually wants something when he comes looking for us."

Lyse twisted her hands nervously in her lap. "Maybe he just wanted to see us."

"Well he couldn't have seen much."

"Apparently it was enough." Though she wasn't ashamed, the look on Tim's face wasn't one she ever wanted to see again.

Buck knew something was going on, he was sure of it, but he didn't have the energy to get out of bed and find out just what it was. "You want to call it a night?"

Grateful for the opportunity to be alone with her own thoughts, Lyse instantly agreed. "That's probably a good idea, I don't want you to get overtired." She leaned over to give Buck's cheek a sweet kiss and dashed from his cabin before he had a chance to say that even if they didn't make love, he wanted her to stay.

XIII

March 1849

W**hen** Lyse stepped out of her cabin the next morning and didn't see John Charles lurking about, she assumed the sailor must have stepped away for a moment. Delighted she wouldn't be observed, she entered Buck's cabin where she found him fully dressed and stretched out atop his bunk. He wore a rakish grin and his dark eyes were dancing with mischief, but she couldn't imagine why.

"You look mighty pleased with yourself this morning," she remarked as she sat down by his side. "Did you sleep well?" She had had so many troublesome thoughts she doubted she had slept more than ten minutes all night, but clearly he was well rested.

"No, not especially." In spite of his best efforts to control his mirth, Buck burst out laughing. "With only one good arm, how did you expect me to slit any throats, Lyse?"

Mortified by that question, Lyse's cheeks burned with an incriminating blush. She had known all along she would have to tell him about her confrontation with the captain sooner or later, but she hadn't dreamed Randolph would get to him first, or that Buck would see any humor in their argument.

"I guess it was a pretty stupid thing to say since it got us in a whole lot of trouble. I'm sorry, but the captain made me so angry I had to say something to shut him up."

Buck couldn't bear to see the delicate blonde so embarrassed and reached out to pull her into his arms for a comforting hug. "Yeah, you do have quite a temper," he mused with a deep chuckle. "But did you really think I'd be flattered that you think me capable of such a gruesome deed?"

Certain his teasing mood was uncalled for, Lyse placed her hands upon his chest and drew back. "It's not in the least bit funny, Buck. What I've become might be obvious to all the men on board, but that doesn't mean I'm not hurt by what they're saying about me."

Buck's expression lost all hint of amusement then. "Just what did the captain say to you? If he implied you were my mistress, it's simply not true. Is that the rumor?"

Rather than answer his question, Lyse asked one of her own. "Mistress is just a fancy word for whore, isn't it?"

"No, there's a world of difference between the two," Buck assured her. "A mistress is the pampered companion of one man, usually an extremely wealthy one, while a common whore will accommodate any man who has her price. But you're not selling yourself, Lyse. Not to the highest bidder, or anyone else, so neither of those insulting names applies to you. I've never given a damn about gossip, but if any man hurts your feelings with loose talk then he'll beg me to slit his throat before I'm done with him. You were well within your rights to say that to the captain too."

Lyse knew from the evil gleam in his dark eyes and the steely tone of his voice that was no idle threat, and she squared her shoulders proudly, hoping to become more like him. "You're right. I shouldn't give a damn about gossip, and I'll try not to let it bother me from now on. It never has before, but I'm not used to being around so many people as we have been the last few days. Maybe that's why I'm so uneasy."

"You're right, living on an isolated ranch is nothing like visiting a city," Buck agreed. Not wanting her to miss his point, however, he continued in the same serious manner. "But no matter where you are, it's not what other people say, but what you think about yourself that counts. I don't believe we've done anything to disgrace ourselves. I sure hope you don't either, but if you do, well, that's a terrible shame and I'm very sorry."

Unable to speak because of the painful knot in her throat, Lyse merely nodded. She didn't know what she thought of herself anymore. She had been so damn smart, telling herself love was a trap she'd cleverly avoid, but at her first chance for romance she had jumped right smack into the middle of it. Though she thought Buck's advice to ignore gossip was good, she couldn't forget he had thought Constance Thorn worthy of a marriage proposal though he hadn't offered her one. Not that she would have accepted, but it would have been the gentlemanly thing for him to do. Then again, maybe Buck Warren was no gentleman. Tears filled her eyes at that thought and she turned away to hide them.

Buck had no idea what more to say, but it was plain to him Lyse was still suffering from some painful inner torment she wouldn't share. Knowing what a private person she was, he wasn't all that surprised, but it bothered him all the same. "What you need is some fresh air," he insisted as he gave her a nudge to help her to her feet. "Let's go up on deck. We can't even tell what the weather is cooped up in here."

"But the captain said we can't leave our cabins. Didn't he tell you that too?"

Buck rose to his feet and reached for the doorknob. "Have you forgotten that I'm a close personal friend of Marc Aragon? I just told Randolph that if we didn't enjoy ourselves on this voyage, I'd make certain Marc heard about it. I made it clear he'd lose not only his job, but also his captain's papers."

"You didn't!" Lyse was amazed he would threaten to end Randolph's career for such little cause.

"Yes, I did. Now I'm feeling well enough to walk around awhile and I don't want to be alone." When he reached for her hand, Lyse came along willingly and pleased, he leaned down to kiss her lips lightly. She was wearing a pale lavender dress with a deep ruffle at the hem he hadn't seen before, and as they left his cabin he told her how very pretty she looked. When she responded with a shy smile, he was glad to see her mood had improved, and vowed to do his best to see she wouldn't get so depressed ever again.

Though there were at least fifty men lounging around the deck, Buck paid them no mind whatsoever as they strolled along. He couldn't have stood another day in bed and was glad he didn't still feel so weak he had no choice about it. The sunshine was bright, the sparkling gulf water a rich blue green, and the fair beauty on his arm such delightful company he felt extremely well. When Robert Ash came rushing up to them, he introduced Lyse before acknowledging the physician's worried frown.

"It's far too fine a day to spend below deck, Dr. Ash, even if you recommend it. We're staying right here."

Sensing he would be wasting his breath, the doctor didn't argue. "You certainly look well and as long as you don't become overtired, I'll not try and send you below."

Robert Ash looked young enough to have been a classmate of Malcolm Glover, the doctor who had come to the hotel, and Lyse wondered why she had always imagined physicians had gray hair and a paunch. This man was blond and of so slight a build she doubted he would ever be overweight no matter how old a man he became. He smiled at her frequently as he talked with Buck and his glance wasn't in the least bit critical. She was glad to find him such a pleasant individual when the captain had proved to be so disagreeable a man. She leaned against the rail, as delighted as Buck that they could roam about at will that day.

"Miss Selby?" Robert Ash called her name softly. "Don't hesitate to ask for me should you feel ill. I like to keep busy."

"I'm never sick," Lyse insisted, then seeing the young man's disappointment, she feared she had been rude and rephrased her response. "I've never been at sea, though, so if I do fall ill I'll be sure to seek your advice." When he smiled widely before walking away, she waited until he could no longer hear them to speak.

"I'm afraid I insult people every time I open my mouth. I didn't mean to sound ungrateful for his offer, but you know I don't like doctors," she reminded Buck with a petulant frown.

"Your bruises have disappeared, Lyse, and if you're well you have no need of Ash's attentions. Although I think he'll be badly disappointed if he has no excuse to examine you."

Greatly distressed by that thought, Lyse shook her head emphatically. "Oh, no, you aren't talking me into seeing another doctor, one was bad enough."

It was clear to him Ash had been quite taken with her, but that she hadn't noticed didn't surprise him. Lyse had apparently seen only a man whose profession made him a threat to her personal privacy and didn't care to know him. Whatever the reason, he was glad she had no interest in the fellow. "I hope you're not sick a day your entire life, now let's not argue. It's too pretty a day."

Standing close, Lyse was content to enjoy the fine weather and his company for more than two hours. She paid no attention to the other passengers, but when it came time to eat, she began to look for Tim. She had no idea what she wanted to say to him, but because he was the only other person she knew on board, she wouldn't allow him to avoid her indefinitely. It was one thing to ignore the tasteless gossip of strangers, quite another to put up with being snubbed by a friend.

There was a separate dining salon for passengers traveling first class and Buck was not surprised when they were directed to the captain's table. He winked at Lyse as he bent down to confide, "Enjoy yourself, Randolph will be the one who'll find it difficult not to choke on his food."

Following Buck's example, Lyse greeted the captain warmly, as though they had never had words. Robert Ash was seated at their table, along with a pair of good-natured brothers from Austin, Miles and Max Henderson. Though the captain kept his thoughts to himself, the other men didn't and Lyse found she had to do no more than nod occasionally and smile to make them think she was hanging on their every word. That ruse was no great strain, but she wondered how long she would have to pretend to be a lady before she began to truly feel like one.

Though she hadn't seen him, Tim had spent the morning watching Lyse. He studied her expressions as she laughed and talked with Buck, then wondered why the sweetness of her appeal was undimmed by what he had finally had to face about her. When he saw the ease with which they touched, it was more than clear her friendship with the tall Texan was not the superficial one it was with him. Why that had not been obvious to him when they had first met he didn't know, but he felt very foolish for wanting to know her still.

He knew he lacked Buck's charm and wit, to say nothing of his size and strength, so there was no possible way he could compete with the man for her love without making a complete fool of himself. Still, he could not help but think pride had very little value when she was so very lovely and when one of her smiles filled his heart with warmth the whole day through.

As they left their table, Buck took a firm hold on Lyse's hand so she would not be swept along with those returning to the deck. When they reached her cabin, he opened the door then followed her inside. He sat down on her bunk and pulled her down on his lap.

"The only glances I saw directed your way today have been admiring ones, but I still don't think it would be a good idea for you to make your way about the ship alone. Now we ought to rest a bit so neither of us gets too tired, and then we can go up on deck again later if you like." Without waiting for her to agree, he reached for the buttons that ran down the front of her bodice, making the sort of siesta he wished to take very clear.

Lyse watched as his long, slim fingers traveled down the row of pearl buttons. Though his right hand still gave him trouble, he did quite well with his left. "Thank you, but I really don't need help getting undressed," she pointed out softly. "But I'll be happy to help you."

She'd done it again, Buck realized. She had slipped into the pose of a temptress without the slightest hesitation. Having to display the charm of a gracious lady for others seemed to cause her nearly unbearable anxiety, but the ease with which she made love to him was completely natural. It was also a source of endless wonder to him. How could a woman who had grown up with little in the way of love be so incredibly warm and loving while a pampered creature like Constance was lost in the frozen depths of self-pity? Disgusted that thoughts of that heartless young woman had invaded his mind at the worst of times, Buck lowered his mouth to Lyse's, and he was immediately lost in an intoxicating spell of desire.

As Buck's lips caressed hers with a seductive sweetness, Lyse knew only his opinions truly mattered to her, not the jealous ramblings of strangers. Perhaps he would never love her as she loved him, but his affection was so splendid it felt every bit as glorious as she knew love must. She did not simply relax in his embrace, but drew him near as her kiss became far more demanding than his.

Buck was breathless when he at last drew away. "You don't understand. I want to undress you myself. It's like unwrapping a marvelous present." As he said that, he had to stifle the impulse to rip away her new gown as he would tear away brightly colored wrapping paper. He longed to again lose himself in the sheer beauty of her lissome body, enjoying to the fullest the gifts no other man had ever sampled. He slid her gown off her shoulders to expose the lavish swell of her creamy smooth breasts, then bent down to nibble at the pale pink tips. As his tongue flicked over those sensitive nubs, the flesh puckered like lips eagerly responding to his kiss.

He looked up at her then, and found a knowing smile lighting her eyes with laughter as she ran her fingers through his hair. That she knew he couldn't resist her didn't bother him in the least because he had never made any secret of his desire. His lips returned to hers then, but his thumbs continued to draw lazy circles around her nipples. He wanted her to need him as desperately as he craved her. With that goal firmly in mind, he slowed his pace dramatically as he undressed her.

Driven to near madness by that ploy, Lyse leapt to her feet and tossed aside what remained of her lingerie. "You are a terrible tease, Buck Warren, and I thought only women toyed with their lover's affections." Unmindful of how erotic a sight her nude figure presented, Lyse bent down to yank off Buck's boots. "Yes, sir, you promise paradise with your kisses, but it's time you started to deliver."

"Lyse!" Buck howled with laughter as she came close to ripping off his clothing in her haste to undress him. "Hey, I'm a near invalid, you can't push me around like that!"

"You wanna bet?" Laughing with him, Lyse returned to the bunk and snuggled against his chest. She pressed close, entangling her legs in his as she stilled his laughter with a lingering kiss. When he wrapped his arms around her waist to hold her tight, she was delighted to feel the warmth of his amusement become the bright glow of passion. Filled with desire, Lyse longed only to please him as greatly as he had always pleased her. That a true lady often had too rigid an upbringing to enjoy making love with such careful abandon was something she did not even suspect.

That Lyse reveled in making love fulfilled the wildest of Buck's fantasies. Surely no mermaid could ever match her for bestowing lavish pleasure. As he returned her fevered kisses he wondered how he could channel her need for wealth into a craving directed solely toward him. Knowing she had no idea how wonderfully unique her affectionate nature was, he decided he would be smart to keep that a secret and stress only how he valued her as a partner. They made a spectacular team, and hoping to appeal to her mind as well as her body, he vowed to tell her so at his first opportunity, but now he was in no mood for talk, not even flowery praise for her charms.

That she had never been given the slightest hope a man would find her attractive, nor cause to suspect that making love would be such a thrill, provided Lyse with excellent reasons to despise the man who had raised her. She had been little better than a slave who saw to Frank Selby's needs but was allowed to have none of her own. In Buck's arms she had discovered a whole new world: one where she was valued for herself alone, and she knew instinctively it was that unconditional love she should have known all along. Her desire flavored with gratitude, she promised herself never to place any conditions on him. If he never offered marriage, she would try not to feel slighted, when what he did give was so marvelous.

That he could not move with his customary agility began to pain Buck more severely than the wound in his shoulder. There was much he wished to teach Lyse, and he was certain he now possessed all the grace of an overturned turtle. He thought he could manage to make love to her lying on his left side, but when his right arm had such little strength, he was afraid he would be very clumsy. When she was so new to love, he didn't want anything to spoil it, least of all her partner's lack of polish.

Lyse could feel Buck's anxiety fill his kiss and drew back slightly. "What's wrong?" she whispered as she pushed his coal black hair away from his eyes.

"Nothing's wrong, I'm just trying to figure out how to go about this," Buck confessed sheepishly, astonished to find himself admitting such a thing to her.

Lyse didn't readily grasp his problem. "When you know how to make love in a bathtub, a bed can't provide much of a challenge," she responded with an amused giggle.

It was because Buck knew she had seldom had reason to laugh before she had met him that he could accept her giggles without being insulted. Thinking perhaps laughter was the correct approach in his situation, he tried to make light of it. "There might be a hundred ways to make love, Lyse."

"A hundred?" the blonde interrupted to ask, greatly intrigued. "Have you tried them all?"

"Hell no, I haven't even come close, but what I'm trying to say is that I'm not usually so damn clumsy and I don't want you to think that I am."

That what she thought of him was so important to Buck touched Lyse deeply. She moved against him with a seductive purr, caressing his whole body with the supple beauty of her own. "I'm sure you're never clumsy, and you won't be now," she whispered invitingly before her lips captured his in a soul-searing kiss that wiped all concern for technique from his mind.

Buck moaned softly, but not from pain. When he turned on his side and drew Lyse's knee up over his hip, she needed no coaching to bring their bodies together with an ease that amazed him. Even if he could not cling to her, she held tightly to him as he thrust with his hips and the rapture he had hoped to create began to flood through him. He could then feel from deep within her that same sweet ecstasy echoing with the wild rhythm of a heartbeat until the splendor of their union reached its shattering climax and nothing existed but that glorious sensation and the blissful peace that followed.

Cradled in her lover's arms, Lyse slept for more than an hour before Buck's efforts to find a more comfortable pose for himself woke her. As she looked up at him, she was surprised by the scowl he wore. "I didn't think you were awkward at all. Did you think that I did? Or did I do something wrong?"

Buck silenced her doubts with a kiss before forcing her head back down on his left shoulder. "You are a great treasure, Lyse, and you never do anything wrong."

"Except threatening you'll slit throats?"

Buck chuckled at that question. "I was talking about making love, not about life in general."

"Oh, I see. So what's bothering you now if it isn't the way you or I make love?"

Buck waited a long moment, and not certain he could put his thoughts into words she would understand, his scowl returned. "I was just thinking that now there would be no turning back."

Because she liked neither his words nor expression, Lyse pulled the sheet up to cover her breasts as she sat up. "Look, Buck, you don't owe me a thing. There's no cause for you to feel trapped."

Shocked by the bitterness of her tone, Buck was quick to point out her mistake. "I'm not talking about us. I was lying here thinking about Arvin. The man's a walking corpse, that's all he is. I've no hopes of inspiring Randolph to try and overtake the *Catarina* after we've had so much trouble with him, but this is so swift a ship, Arvin can't have more than a day's head start on us once we reach the Chagres River at the isthmus."

Though she was relieved to learn her fears were unjustified, Lyse was still upset. "If it hadn't been for me, then you and the captian would still be friends. You might have beaten Arvin to the Chagres and be waiting for him on the dock. I'm supposed to be helping you, not creating new problems."

Buck used his left hand to catch her right arm and pulled her back down into his embrace. Because she had provided the perfect opportunity for him to say what he had wanted to, he used it. "I think you make one hell of a partner, Lyse. I couldn't have asked for a more loyal friend than you have been to me. We'll get Arvin. There's no doubt about it. You're so pretty, I bet he won't even see me coming."

"Am I to be bait for a trap?" Lyse asked apprehensively, not at all certain she liked the sound of that.

"No, I'd never risk your life so needlessly. All I meant was that it will be difficult for him to concentrate on avoiding me once he's seen you."

Lyse smiled slyly. "If we go about this right, he won't see me."

Buck studied her expression closely, then certain she wasn't at all afraid of what lay ahead, he took a new tack. "I was just lying here thinking that no matter when I meet up with Arvin, since I've come this far, I might as well try my hand at prospecting too. It would be a shame to reach California and not go home with a pocketful of gold nuggets."

"Why Buck, are you catching gold fever too?" Lyse asked with a playful smile that only partly revealed her delight at the hope they would have more time to spend together.

"No, ma'am, the only fever I have is the one burning for you." Buck wound his fingers in her flowing hair to keep her lips pressed to his until he felt her whole body shiver with the anticipation of what they would again share. Fate had given him a remarkable partner, and he planned to take full advantage of that luck. This time he gave no thought to how he wanted to make love; he simply lost himself in the joy of her surrender and kept them amused until so late in the afternoon they nearly missed supper.

Though he disliked thinking of himself as a coward, the *Spanish Dancer* had been at sea for a week before Tim found both a reason and the courage to approach Lyse and Buck again. The couple was out on deck, singing along with a group crowded around Max Henderson who was playing

"Oh Suzanna" on a banjo. Because amusements on board were few, Tim found himself pushed to the front by enthusiastic singers despite his best efforts to remain in the rear. Standing directly across from Lyse then, when she smiled and waved at him, he found himself grinning like a witless fool in return.

When he saw Tim, Buck pulled Lyse closer to his side. He hadn't wanted her so near the others for fear there might again be trouble, but she enjoyed the music so much he couldn't bring himself to forbid her to join in. She had a lovely soprano voice, as delightfully pure as the ring of a crystal bell. But as always, when he had paid her a well-deserved compliment, she had found his praise difficult to accept.

It was the sparkling beauty of Lyse's voice that captivated Tim anew. She not only had the perfect features and fair hair of an angel, but also she could sing like one. It didn't matter to him that they were singing boisterous melodies never heard in church. Caught up in the excitement of the moment, he began to sing too, thinking no woman as lovely as Lyse could possibly be wicked clear through.

When Max had finally played through every song he knew and begged to be excused, the men who had been crowded around him reluctantly began to disperse. Tim plunged forward then, and reached Lyse's side before Buck could walk her below to her cabin where they usually spent a good part of the afternoon.

"You sing beautifully!" he greeted her enthusiastically.

Lyse glanced up at Buck before responding, still not convinced her voice was in the least bit remarkable despite his repeated insistence it was a rare gift. "Thank you, but I think any woman's voice would sound good with so many men. It's just the contrast is all."

Tim took in Buck's knowing smile and decided there was no point in arguing with that mistaken notion. Because he had a reason to speak with him too, he got on with it. "Some of the men are getting up a poker game tonight. You interested?"

Buck shook his head. "That's one game I think I better

avoid for a while. Besides, I don't want to leave Lyse alone for so long."

Not wanting to be considered a burden for any reason, Lyse quickly spoke up. "Look, you're very good, go ahead and play if you like. I can find something else to do."

"That's what I'm afraid of," Buck responded with an amused chuckle, but Lyse's responding glance was so hostile he took her hand and brought it to his lips. "I'm only teasing you, Lyse. Would it please you if I won so much money we were the only people on this voyage who could afford to go on to California?"

The lively blonde thought he was teasing and responded in kind. "I doubt you're that good."

"I don't dare play with him," Tim confided sincerely. "I'm too thankful you recovered my money to risk losing it, but there are others who want to play some serious poker."

Buck debated with himself a moment. He had never had any problem getting his hands on money, but it wouldn't hurt to have a good deal more than he had at present. Deciding he would be wise to have the cash needed to purchase their tickets for the voyage up the California coast before they reached the city of Panama, he agreed. "All right, tell me where and when and I'll be there."

Lyse pulled her hand from Buck's and moved to the rail. At least gambling hadn't been one of her pa's many faults, but she thought that might just have been due to the fact he lacked the money to get into a game in the first place. Buck was an entirely different man, of course. A slow smile graced her lips as she turned back to look at him. His shoulder was healing quickly, he would soon be completely well, but she was positive he couldn't be any more handsome. When he reached for her hand, she went below with a light dancing step, as eager to spend the afternoon with him as she had been the first time.

Despite Buck's purely practical motivation for entering the high stakes poker game, he soon got caught up in the excitement. He was wise enough not to let that show, though. As each hand was dealt, his expression gave away no hint of what it held, nor of his emotions. He played the first few hands conservatively, getting a feel for his opponents' styles, then he pressed the advantage his coolly logical strategy gave him and won more and more frequently until one by one the others went broke and had to drop out of the game.

Colin O'Roarke had been surprised to see Buck appear for the game because he and Lyse kept to themselves so much of the time. He had hoped to win big as he often did and because Buck obviously had money, he was quick to welcome him. Then when he was one of the first to be forced to fold, he waited around until the game was over and in his frustration turned his anger on Buck rather than himself.

"We'll play again tomorrow night," Colin ordered gruffly, speaking for the others, although no one had appointed him spokesman. "We all want a chance to win back what we lost."

"Sure, I'll give you that chance," Buck responded graciously, "but you'll have to risk more money to do it. Have you got any to spare?"

"What I have and haven't got is none of your damn business," Colin fired back aggressively.

As no one had enough room to play cards in his cabin, they had held the game in the salon used for first-class dining. Buck rose from his chair and straightened up to his full height. Nearly half a head taller than the obnoxious Irishman, he returned his insolent stare with a murderous glance of his own. "If you can't stand to lose, you ought not to play," he advised darkly, then turning his back on him he left.

As Tim watched Buck leave, a wide grin crossed his face. When Colin saw it and shouted at him, he made no effort to deny his accusation.

"You brought that bastard here on purpose, didn't you?" Colin shrieked. "You invited him to the game when you didn't have the guts to play with us yourself!"

"It's not a matter of guts," Tim insisted with far more confidence than he felt. "I'm an accountant, I don't risk my capital foolishly." Not wanting to press his luck, he strode out too, feeling very pleased with himself for having had the last word.

When Buck found Lyse's cabin empty, he swore angrily to himself. He had warned her not to go up on deck as they often did in the evening, but even if she had disobeyed him she should have returned long before now. Fearing Tim had used the poker game to lure him away from her so another man might enjoy her company for the evening, he rushed next door to get his Colt. Lyse was his woman and he wasn't about to allow anyone else a minute of her time. When he found her asleep atop his bunk still wearing the pretty blue dress she had worn to supper, he felt very foolish for having reacted to her absence with such a jealous rage.

Sitting down by her side, he patted her back lightly. "Lyse, wake up."

Lyse opened one eye, then delighted to see him she sat up and gave him an enthusiastic hug. "I'm sorry. I meant to wait up for you, but I guess I must have fallen asleep. What time is it?"

"Past midnight. I'm sorry you got bored, but I did spend a profitable evening if that's any consolation."

"How profitable?" Lyse wanted to know.

"Hold out your hands." Buck waited until she had complied with his request, then emptied his pockets of the gold pieces he had won.

"Buck!" Lyse cried excitedly as a bright cascade of gold coins fell through her fingers and slipped into her lap. "This must be a thousand dollars!"

"It's a bit more. The problem will be to keep it."

"You mean we might be robbed?"

"No," Buck scoffed. "I'll have to give the men who lost that money a chance to win it back. That's all."

"You'll be gone again tomorrow night?" Lyse asked with a dejected sigh.

"Let's not worry about tomorrow night while we still have the best part left of tonight."

Lyse smiled widely as she gathered up the coins. "I like the way you think, mister. I really do."

"I like everything about you." Buck pulled off his coat then sat down to remove his boots. When Lyse poured the coins into his left boot the instant he yanked it off, he laughed and pulled her into his arms, still convinced she was worth more than her weight in gold. Though he did not speak that praise out loud, it flavored his kisses with a devotion that was precious in itself.

XIV

April 1849

*T*he *Spanish Dancer* encountered stormy seas during the
night and when the savage winds and high swells continued on into the day, a majority of passengers as well
as many of the crew became seasick. Most of the men found
it impossible to sit in a chair let alone hold a hand of cards,
and the prospect of a cutthroat poker game lost all its appeal.
The chance to win back his money Colin had demanded
from Buck was postponed for several days until good
weather returned.

Though Buck was one of the few not affected by the constant rolling motion of the ship, Lyse most definitely was.
She refused to leave her bunk and each time Buck looked in
on her he found her fair skin far closer to pale green than its
usual shade of creamy peach. Considerably, he stayed only
long enough to ask if he might bring her something before
again leaving her to suffer alone as she insisted she must.

By the time the storm had passed, three days had gone by
and Buck was thoroughly bored with his own company and
readily admitted to Lyse that he had missed her. "Do you
think we had been spending too much time together?" the
slender young woman inquired shyly, hoping he would not
say yes.

That question amused Buck enormously because he
doubted he would ever get tired of her frustratingly independent and yet enchanting company. Slipping his arm around

her waist, he escorted her across the deck to a secluded spot where they could hear themselves talk above the howl of the wind in the sails.

"If we had been spending too much time together, then I would have enjoyed being by myself awhile. I didn't, not at all."

Lyse hadn't felt well enough to miss him, though, and because that seemed like a very impolite comment to make, she kept still. Before her silence could grow awkward, Robert Ash found them to apologize for being as seasick as the rest of them and being unable to provide any comfort to her. With a sweetness that nearly brought a return of the nausea that had plagued her, Lyse quickly forgave him, but she was delighted the man had been too ill to bother her. Tim Mac-Cormac was the next to join them. Then Max Henderson arrived. As usual he had brought his banjo and a crowd quickly gathered around as he began to play one of the songs everyone liked to sing.

Buck decided there must be close parallels between being with Lyse and working in a traveling circus, for there was always something exciting happening around her. They had to do no more than appear on deck to draw a crowd and he couldn't help but wonder how she would be able to pan for gold surrounded by a swarm of adoring admirers. With him standing so near, none of the men dared to be disrespectful, but would the same awe she inspired now protect her when he wasn't nearby? That wasn't a question he cared to ponder.

The crowd clustered around Lyse annoyed Tim too, for he wanted to spend every minute he possibly could with her and he didn't enjoy sharing her attention with Buck or anyone else. Robert Ash took pains to make his conversations with the blonde appear to be no more than part of his assigned duties as the ship's physician. Behind his professional demeanor, however, he was as smitten with her as any of the others and just as perplexed that he had no opportunities to speak with her alone.

Though he hid his desire beneath a smokescreen of contemptuous comments, Colin O'Roarke found it impossible to deny the attraction he felt for Lyse. It was no longer simply the fact that she was the lone woman on board that inspired his desire either. There was something about the young woman he found totally unique and he was disappointed when Buck again failed to bring her along when they met to play poker that night.

"Miss Selby does not enjoy seeing you win? Or is she afraid you might lose heavily tonight?" he asked with a taunting sneer.

Buck's initial dislike of Colin O'Roarke had not lessened in the days since he had last seen him. He found the sarcastic redhead's company objectionable in the extreme and proceeded to play with a brutal flourish that quickly relieved Colin of his money and the rest of the players of the burden of the man's obnoxious company. At the close of the game, Buck was again the big winner and none of the others thought they had a chance at winning back their money. The subject of another game was not even raised.

Resigned to the fact that Buck Warren was simply a man he couldn't beat at poker, Colin was waiting to talk with him when the game ended. "When we reach the Chagres River, there can't be nearly enough guides for all of us who need them. We'll have to form groups. What do you say to you and me joining up to lead some of the others?"

Buck was so astonished by the absurdity of that proposition, he did not even stop to consider the wisdom of Colin's proposal before he refused. "Sorry, Miss Selby and I plan to hire a guide just for ourselves. I don't want the responsibility for anyone else."

Not about to give up so easily, Colin moved along beside Buck as he made his way to his cabin. "Well now, as I see it, you and I could share that responsibility. You shouldn't go alone. From what I hear, the guides aren't all that trustworthy. If something happened to you, Miss Selby would be left with no one to protect her. You can't guarantee your guide wouldn't just run off, or worse yet, stick around and torment her with demands she wouldn't dare refuse."

"The answer was no, Mr. O'Roarke," Buck replied coldly, and by lengthening his stride he quickly reached his cabin and slammed the door behind him before Colin could utter another word.

Lyse had waited up for Buck, but after one look at his disgusted expression she feared he had lost all his winnings. "What happened? Weren't you lucky tonight?"

"Luck has nothing to do with winning at poker, Lyse. That's what I was trying to teach you. It's purely a game of skill." Buck again dumped a sparkling shower of gold coins into her lap and then sat down beside her. "It's that damn Colin O'Roarke. His company is as welcome as a leech's, but he said something to me just now that made sense."

"Oh, really, and what was that?" Lyse looked down at the sea of gold in her lap, knowing it was more money than she had touched in her whole lifetime. It was Buck's money, though, not hers, and when he reached down to scoop it up she didn't object.

"I think we might be smart to take several men with us up the Chagres. That way if there's any trouble, there will be someone to help me handle it."

"Besides me and the guide you mean," Lyse pointed out. "Don't you know we'd help you all we could?"

Lyse had straightened her shoulders proudly before speaking, but he hadn't meant to offend her. "Of course, I'm counting on your help. Didn't I say that?"

"No, you didn't, but you know I'm not nearly so helpless as these gorgeous dresses you bought me make it look."

"No, you're self-reliant to a fault, Lyse, but I still think we better reconsider our plans and choose the people we want to accompany us. If there aren't enough guides to go around, we might get stuck with Lord knows who and I don't want to take the chance one of them will be Colin."

Lyse wasn't certain she knew which man Colin was, but she knew if Buck didn't like him, then she wouldn't either. "Tim will have to go with us. He'd be too hurt if we left him out."

With a weary sigh, Buck agreed. "All right, Tim goes but since he is a city boy through and through, I think we ought to take the Hendersons along for balance. Those two can handle themselves."

"That makes five. Do you want more?"

"You have someone else in mind?" Buck asked with a

slyly arched brow. "I didn't realize you had any favorites besides Tim."

Ignoring his attempt to tease her, Lyse pursed her lips thoughtfully as she tried to decide who else to bring along. "Tim isn't a favorite, he's like a little brother and we can't leave him behind. The Hendersons are good fun and like you said, they're Texans and can handle themselves. I think the five of us will get along fine if Tim can keep up."

Though that comment might have sounded odd coming from another woman, from Lyse it made perfect sense. She was better prepared to meet the dangers of the journey than Tim any day. "That damn storm cost us at least two days, so I want to be among the first ones off the ship when we reach land. Thanks to my skill at cards, I've got the money to hire the best guide available and I don't want to waste any time once we've agreed upon a price."

"I'll be ready and I'm sure the others will too."

"You know what I'm ready for now?"

Lyse saw Buck's sly wink as he poured the coins into the satchel containing his clothes and knew he was ready for exactly the same thing she was: another glorious night of making love. "I've missed you too, Buck," she suddenly blurted out, sorry that confession was so many hours overdue.

Buck saw only the desire that deepened the pretty blue of her eyes rather than the blush in her cheeks and took her words as the compliment she had intended, whether tardy or not. He felt stronger with each new day and with a wicked chuckle began to prove his company had definitely been worth the wait.

As they approached the isthmus, the ruins of the Spanish fortress San Lorenzo immediately captivated Lyse's attention. Perched atop a rocky point, its stark lines softened by the surrounding lush tropical vegetation, it served as a stark reminder of the days when pirates had turned the peaceful blue green waters of the Caribbean bright red with their victims' blood. They had given no mercy and expected none as they attacked ships bound for Spain with holds bulging with treasure from the New World. The thought of pirates alarmed her as greatly as it had when she had entered Galveston, and yet at the same time the horror of their deeds fascinated her as well.

Knowing they would be unlikely to meet any seagoing bandits because they were on the way to find riches rather than returning home loaded down with wealth, she kept her thoughts to herself until the ship docked at a small port whose only buildings were bamboo huts with palm leaf roofs. Then Lyse couldn't believe they were in the right place. Her expression became one of shocked disbelief. "This just can't possibly be the port, Buck, it just can't be."

"Did you expect it to look like Galveston?" Buck was dismayed himself, but he was wise enough not to let Lyse see he was as startled as she by the poverty of the humble village that lay nestled at the ocean's edge. He could feel her fingers trembling as she gripped his arm and thoughtfully covered her hand with his. "We'll not stay here more than an hour, Lyse, so it doesn't really matter how pitiful the place is. The main port, Porto Bello, is farther down the coast. I'm sure it must be impressive, but this is where the Chagres River ends."

Though simple folk, the natives of the area had swiftly learned there was good money to be made from the flood of Americans traveling to California through the Isthmus of Panama. They waved and shouted at the passengers gathered at the rail of the *Spanish Dancer*, eagerly vying for their share of the travelers' gold. Even those who had never strayed farther from their homes than the next village bragged they were excellent guides, knowing before becoming lost they could desert the party they had been hired to lead and return home to greet the next ship arriving.

"What do you think?" Miles Henderson asked. He and his brother had stocky builds and were already sweating profusely in the oppressive heat.

"I think we might have as much difficulty as Diogenes finding an honest man."

"Why, Buck, how come you never told me that you knew someone who had made this trip?" Lyse asked as she poked a stray wisp of hair up under her battered straw hat. She had coiled her hair atop her head as Rose Reynoso had taught her but somehow that softly feminine style refused to stay put that day. Because she knew Buck was in a hurry to get going, she had dressed in her old clothes as soon as land had been sighted, but she felt far different from the way she had felt the last time she had worn them. She had been a neglected runaway then; now she hoped she was well on her way to becoming not only a full grown woman, but also a wealthy one.

Buck tried not to laugh out loud and when Miles started to chuckle, he shot him a disapproving frown to silence him. "Diogenes was a Greek philosopher who lived more than a thousand years ago, Lyse. I merely meant it might prove difficult to find a guide who'll earn his money rather than try and cheat us."

Mortified she must appear woefully ignorant, Lyse nevertheless scolded him crossly rather than accept the blame for not understanding him herself. "I really don't think we ought to waste our time talking about dead Greeks. How about the man over there? He looks honest to me."

Happy to return the subject to their original one, Buck followed her glance to a lanky fellow lounging against a palm tree. His relaxed pose did not make him look nearly so honest as it did merely lazy. "Interesting choice," he mused skeptically.

"Well, he's at least got the brains not to wear himself out screaming and yelling at us."

"He looks mean as hell," Tim volunteered, then recalling Buck hadn't looked any less menacing when he had first met him, he decided the man might not be so bad after all. "Let's go talk with him. That all right with you?" he asked the Henderson brothers.

"An older man might know more," Miles responded.

"Yeah, and he might drop dead while he's paddling the boat too." Without waiting for the men to follow, Lyse started for the gangplank, but Buck caught her elbow to slow her down.

"Let me do the talking, Lyse. Whomever we hire, we don't want him to think we're a bunch of weak-willed sissies who need a woman to run things."

Lyse's eyes widened as she looked up at him. Then she

glanced back at the solidly built Hendersons before her glance swept over Tim's earnest expression. "No one is going to mistake any of you men for sissies. Don't be silly."

Buck did not speak again. Instead, he glared down at her with the evil stare that always brought a shiver of dread shuddering down her spine. His gaze could be as cold as ice at times and though she knew that the harshness of his glance was intentional, she saw no need for it. Letting him have his way, she was more ungracious about it. "Yes, boss, you do all the talking. You just go right ahead."

That sarcastic response only made his mood worse, but Buck had no time to waste now on providing pointers for her behavior. Maybe it was the clothes. He could swear the minute she had donned the worn outfit she was again the feisty kid who had come to his aid out on the prairie rather than the loving woman who had shared his bunk on the voyage. "We'll all question the man if you like, but let's just get on with it!"

"Well wasn't that what I said?" Upset with him, Lyse shook her head, allowing another handful of hair to escape her hat, which she quickly shoved back into place. "While we're standing here arguing, someone else is going to hire him."

Afraid Lyse and Buck might belabor the issue of who was leading their party all morning, Tim took the lively blonde's arm. "Not if I can help it. All we really need to know is how many times he has made the trip up the river, and what he expects to be paid."

Buck gestured graciously to allow the man from Cincinnati to precede him, but the minute they reached the prospective guide Tim found he spoke no English and he had to again rely on Buck. Up close, the wiry man was obviously closer to forty than twenty as he had appeared at first glance. In reply to Buck's politely worded question spoken in flawless Spanish, he shook his head vigorously. *"Los hombres, sí. La mujer, no."*

Lyse spoke enough Spanish to know the man was refusing to act as an escort for a woman. That possibility had not even occurred to her. "Coward, I'm a better man than you are any day!"

Rather than apologize for her temperamental outburst, Buck took the reluctant guide aside and explained Lyse had been made to work like a man for most of her life and needed to be treated no differently from the rest of them. Though his tone was persuasive, he also agreed to pay the man double the price he could expect from any of the other travelers.

Unfortunately, the man was unmoved by the generosity of that offer. *"No mujer, no, nunca,"* he insisted stubbornly as he made an emphatic slicing motion with his hand.

Disgusted he had not been able to change his mind, Buck nodded, not wanting to waste his breath as well as any more of his time. He turned back to the others and shrugged. "This fellow appears to have a sailor's superstition about the danger of women traveling in boats, so we'll simply have to find someone else. Lyse is scarcely the type to go into hysterics at the sight of a snake or a crocodile, so I know we won't have any trouble because she's with us. It looks like the problem will just be one of finding a guide with more common sense than superstition."

"Snakes?" Tim asked apprehensively. "What sort of snakes do they have here?"

Max Henderson swore under his breath. "I'd rather have two women along than a man who's afraid of his own shadow."

"I'm not afraid of my shadow!" Tim protested heatedly.

"Cut it out!" Buck shouted before Max could respond but he had already begun to regret his decision to bring Tim along if he couldn't stop sniveling like a child.

A gray-haired native approached them then to ask if they needed a guide, but when Buck explained there were four men and one woman in their party, he shook his head as quickly as the first man had and rushed away. It was a scene that was repeated half a dozen times until Buck began to doubt they would ever find a responsible man to act as their guide.

Even more depressed than he, Lyse bit down on her lower lip to stem the flow of tears welling up in her eyes. "It never even occurred to me my presence would create a problem. I suppose I should have suspected as much when Captain

Randolph was reluctant to let me travel on the *Spanish Dancer*, but I didn't."

Buck could see she was hurt, but he wasn't. He was just plain mad as hell. When Robert Ash came running up to them carrying a cumbersome pack as well as his black leather doctor's bag he regarded it as the last straw.

"I've decided to go to California too!" the young physician exclaimed excitedly. "There are plenty of doctors in Texas, but there can't be many in California so I figure if I don't strike it rich, I'll practice medicine to become prosperous. Is it all right if I go with you?"

When Buck's only response was a harshly worded curse, Lyse spoke up. "I'm sure we're all flattered that you want to go with us, Dr. Ash, but I'm afraid we might not get any farther than this since none of the guides is willing to travel with a woman."

"They're not?" Robert's enthusiasm dimmed visibly as he noted the woebegone expressions Tim and the Hendersons wore. He shifted his belongings to distribute their weight more evenly, hoping to cover the fact that he had no solution to their dilemma.

Buck watched Lyse fidgeting nervously with her hair, and unable to bear her anxiety as well as his own he took her hand to draw her aside. "Now listen closely without interrupting me if you can. I'm going to tell our friends to join other groups while they have the chance. If I don't find a guide for us today, then I will tomorrow or the day after. With ships arriving often, the majority of the men who can lead people up the river must always be away. The trip lasts only a few days, so some have to be returning soon. I don't want you to worry. If I have to build a boat and follow a map, I'll get us across to the Pacific Ocean. You know you can rely on me to keep my word to see you reach California safely."

Though Buck's words were reassuring, he only increased Lyse's sense of guilt. She felt as though she were a terrible burden to him. "There's no sign of the *Catarina* or any of her passengers, so they must have already come and gone. I hate to see you falling behind Arvin because of me."

"I hadn't given the man a thought," Buck confided truthfully. "Now please don't fret. You and I will get along just fine as we always have. We don't need anyone else."

Grateful the man hadn't lost his usual confidence, Lyse reached up to kiss his cheek. "Thank you. I agree, we ought to tell the others to go on ahead. That way they can't blame us later if everything goes wrong."

"Nothing will go wrong," Buck whispered hoarsely, convinced there was nothing left to go awry. When he heard someone calling his name, he glanced over his shoulder, then wished that he hadn't.

"Hey Warren!" Colin O'Roarke shouted again as he hurried over to them. "I heard you got troubles."

The brim of Buck's hat shaded his eyes, making it impossible for Colin to see the hatred that glowed in their depths. "That's a damn lie," he said in so threatening a tone he was certain the red-haired man would back off, but Colin failed to heed that warning.

Hooking his thumbs in his belt, Colin wore a cocky grin as he looked up at the tall Texan. "I've got a guide who's willing to take a woman along, with certain conditions, of course."

"Get lost, O'Roarke." Buck dropped Lyse's hand and stepped in front of her, hoping to shield her from the insult he was certain was coming.

"Come on now, Warren, don't refuse before you've even heard our terms." Colin then included Tim, the Hendersons, and Dr. Ash in his invitation. "Any of you men want to come with us, you're welcome. Miss Selby's welcome too, even without you, Warren. All the guide wants is for her to be nice to him and the rest of us."

"What the hell do you mean by 'nice'?" Tim shouted in Colin's face.

Grabbing Tim by the scruff of the neck, Buck set him aside and faced Colin squarely. "You ever come near us again, I'm going to take great pleasure in tearing you limb from limb. You understand me, O'Roarke? You dare to inflict your presence on Miss Selby or me ever again and you're a dead man. You're damn lucky you caught me in a good mood today, or the *Spanish Dancer* would be taking your miserable body home in a pine box."

"Naw," Lyse piped up. "They'd just wrap the swine's carcass in canvas and toss him overboard without a prayer."

Possessed of more bravado than brains, it took a moment for Colin to grasp the fact that both Buck and Lyse were dead serious. "I was just trying to help you all out in a friendly fashion. I didn't mean no offense." He turned then and walked off, trying his best not to break into a run to get away from Buck Warren before he changed his mind about letting him go with a warning.

Though Buck stood glaring at the fleeing man, Lyse spoke to the others. "Buck and I are partners and we mean to stick together, but you all needn't stay with us. Why don't you go on and make the best deals you can? There'll be no hard feelings. We'll probably see you again in California if not before."

Tim was seething over the way Buck had set him aside like a bothersome kid. Too furious to speak, he just shook his head. The Hendersons hemmed and hawed a bit, then obviously relieved they would not be insulting the couple, they shook hands with Buck, planted awkward kisses on Lyse's cheeks, and wandered off. That left only Robert Ash with a decision to make. Though Tim had firsthand experience with Buck's threats, the physician didn't. He had heard the rumors circulating on the ship about the man being involved in a killing, but he hadn't really believed them. Now he began to wonder.

"You kill a man in Galveston?" he asked abruptly.

Not having expected that question, Buck sighed wearily. "What has that got to do with anything?"

Ash shrugged, again shifting the pack he hadn't taken off his back. "I'd just like to know what happened."

"A man died, but it was an accident."

"It really was," Lyse insisted. "You can ask Tim, he was there."

"Oh, so now my opinion suddenly counts, is that it?" Once he had gotten that much off his chest, Tim couldn't stop. "I've gotten the best of Colin before. You didn't need to shove me out of the way. I could have handled him."

Despite realizing their tempers were all growing short, Buck didn't mince words with Tim. "O'Roarke was talking to me since Lyse is my woman, not yours. Now stop sulking, there's no cause for it. You're welcome to come with us, but not if you're too jealous to pull your own weight."

"It's not a matter of jealousy," Tim protested unconvincingly. "Colin is a pest and I could have told him to get lost just as well as you did."

Lyse didn't know what was more embarrassing, Tim's unwanted devotion, Robert Ash's shocked silence, or Buck's brazen announcement she was his woman. Not caring what Tim or the doctor decided to do she turned away, looking for a shady spot to sit down and rest. As she glanced back at the ship, she saw Captain Randolph leaning against the rail. He was watching her with an amused smile, clearly gloating over the difficulty she and Buck had encountered finding a guide.

She lifted her chin proudly, removed her hat, and shook out her hair as she walked over to the closest palm tree. Sitting down, she propped her elbows on her knees and used her battered sombrero for a fan. She felt sick to her stomach again and was afraid it wasn't simply due to the oppressive heat. Since the summer she had turned fourteen her body had maintained a predictable rhythm. Her cycles were as regular as those of the moon. This was the first month she had ever been late, and though it was only a couple of days, she couldn't shake the frightening suspicion she had become pregnant the first time she and Buck had made love.

His back was turned toward her as he continued to argue with Tim, but his words still rang in her ears. "His woman!" she scoffed under her breath. He had made it sound as though she were no more than a possession, one highly prized perhaps, but a possession all the same. She had no intention of taking that from him either. It would have been pointless to object when he had made the offensive remark, for she knew in front of the others he would have only glowered at her. She would have to wait until later when they were alone to remind him that as his partner she deserved more respect. She wasn't a piece of baggage to be claimed in a rude shout.

Resting her head back against the tree, Lyse closed her eyes and wondered how long it would take before her belly got so big she couldn't reach around it to pan for gold. She was so thin it might be several months before that happened. Was she merely borrowing trouble? she asked herself crossly. Maybe being so seasick had upset her whole body and not just her stomach. Maybe she was being a silly fool for worrying she might be pregnant when she had only a faint suspicion and no real proof. But as she glanced over at Buck again, she knew she was kidding herself. He had gotten her pregnant with astonishing ease. The way her luck was running, she was probably carrying twins and would get so big she'd be swept off by the river and drown before she could find enough gold to take care of herself let alone two children.

As those troubling thoughts filled Lyse's mind, her delicate features mirrored her distress. She was completely unaware of the presence of an old man seated in the doorway of a nearby hut, but he had been watching her closely for some time, fascinated by the play of emotions that were so easy to read on her pretty face. He had never seen a white woman, but now that he had seen this one, he wanted to hear her speak. Rising slowly so as not to cause his aging joints any undo bursts of pain, he got to his feet and approached her at a leisurely shuffle.

When the old gentleman was within three feet of her, Lyse noticed him out of the corner of her eye. Though he did not appear menacing, she leapt to her feet and jammed her hat on the back of her head, ready to rush back to Buck's side should he give her cause.

"I speak some English," the old man called out in a high, thin voice.

When he took another step forward, Lyse stepped back slightly, but she greeted him politely. "Good morning. Is it always so hot here?"

Though his posture was still proud, the man was no more than five feet in height. Wiry in his youth, he was now painfully thin. Sensing Lyse's apprehensions, he thought them ridiculous because what harm could he possibly do her? "*Sí*, and soon the rains will come."

"Rain?" Lyse looked up at the clear blue sky, hoping it wouldn't rain that day.

The old fellow frowned, thinking their conversation was going poorly. "We will have much rain, but not yet. Your trip will be easy."

"What trip? Your men have all refused to take me."

The man looked toward Buck then, studied him for a long moment, then turned back to Lyse. "The tall one, he is your *esposo*?"

Esposo was a word she knew. It meant husband. When she found it difficult to reply to what was surely the most embarrassing question she had ever been asked, Lyse jammed her hands in her back pockets, scuffed the toe of her boot in the sandy soil, then again looked up at the sky before finally finding her voice. "No, we're just partners."

An inquisitive look lit the aged man's small dark eyes, but he was wise enough to see by her troubled expression that his question had been the wrong one. "I am Chavez," he volunteered with a dry chuckle that quickly turned into a rasping cough which took him a full minute to bring under control. He held up one bony hand, begging her patience while he gathered the energy to speak. "I will take you and your man up the river, but my price is high."

"Señor Chavez." Lyse was so shocked he considered himself well enough for such an arduous task, she didn't know what to say. She couldn't just laugh in his face, but she dared not accept his offer either when he looked as though he might not live to see the sun set that day.

Buck turned around then to see where Lyse had gone and no longer caring what Tim and the doctor did either, he bid them a hasty farewell and walked over to her side. When she explained the elderly man's offer, he couldn't believe it either.

"That's very kind of you, Señor Chavez, but won't we need several men to paddle the boat upriver?"

Chavez nodded. "*Sí*, but I have grandsons."

"Where are they?" Buck asked, unconvinced.

The old man turned and upon his signal, two strapping youths appeared at the doorway of his hut. They grinned and waved, clearly strong enough for any work he might give them. "I am an old man, but my boat is new so my price is high. If you can pay it, we will go now. We can travel all night and beat the others to Las Cruces."

Lyse turned away to hide her smile, but Buck understood her mood well. Chavez might be an old coot, but he was a sharp one. He probably always waited around to charge the last people needing a guide and boat twice what the other travelers had paid.

"Just what is your price?" Buck inquired as he slipped his arm around Lyse's waist.

"For two, I must have fifty dollars," Chavez replied with what appeared to be genuine regret. "If there were others, then twenty dollars each."

From what he had heard, fifteen was the going rate, but Buck didn't feel like arguing. He looked over his shoulder and found Tim and Robert Ash hadn't moved since he had left them. They were simply staring at him, although he doubted they could have overheard any of Chavez's conversation. "You coming with us or not?" he called to them.

"I'm coming," Tim shouted, his anger forgotten as he saw Lyse begin to smile.

That left Robert alone and still torn by indecision. Lyse looked very different that day from the way she had on board ship. Still, even her well-worn attire didn't make her look common in the young physician's view. To him, she seemed better prepared for the adventure that lay ahead than he. Knowing he would be a fool to let her get away when he barely knew her, he took a firm grip on his doctor's bag and yelled for them to wait.

Buck was smiling at her now, his mood so good he didn't seem to care their companions might need help looking after themselves. That smile warmed Lyse clear through and she decided to think only of the excitement of the trip, and the fun of being with him rather than what she hoped would soon prove to be unfounded fears that she would become a mother.

As they started toward the river where Chavez's boat was tied, she took Buck's hand. There was something she had meant to say to him, something important too, but for the moment she couldn't remember what it was. "I hope you don't mind the fact that I spoke with Chavez first. It wasn't really my fault seeing as how he came up to me."

"No, I don't mind," Buck confided with a teasing wink, but when he had seen the boat and found it as new as promised, he was sorry they had asked to travel all night because that would give him no time to be alone with Lyse. He bent down to whisper that regret in her ear, then laughed when he saw by her appreciative smile that she agreed they had been foolish to be in such a rush.

XV

April 1849

Chavez's boat was like the others lining the muddy banks of the Chagres. Called a bungo and used for the transport of bananas before the rush began to California, it was an elaborate canoe hollowed out of a single guayacan log. Twenty-five feet long and three feet wide, at both bow and stern flat platforms had been fashioned to provide a place for a boatman to stand with a long pole and guide the boat.

Another of the old man's grandsons appeared as they loaded their luggage. A mixture of Indian, Spanish, and African blood, as were most of the natives living in the villages along the Chagres, his skin was dark, his hair thick and curly, and his manner as open and friendly as his cousins'. He introduced himself as Memo and the others as Juan and Lalo. Gesturing with his paddle he took charge and quickly got his grandfather and their passengers into the boat before he and his cousins pushed it away from the bank. When they had the rustic craft out into the swiftly flowing river, they hopped in and began paddling with a brisk rhythm, battling the current to make their way upstream.

Chavez grabbed a pole and took the perch at the back of the bungo while his grandsons did the more strenuous work. On land he appeared frail, but he had worked on the river all his life and savored each hour he spent there still. That enthusiasm provided a vitality that surprised both Buck and

Lyse, but they were far too polite to comment on the man's sudden burst of vigor when they doubted it would last.

Buck was seated in the stern of the bungo, with Lyse directly in front of him. As there were no seats, they made themselves as comfortable as possible, sitting cross-legged on the smooth bottom of the boat. Next came Juan, then a heap of luggage, Lalo, more baggage, then Tim and Robert followed by Memo, who was paddling furiously in the bow.

When he turned back, Buck was amazed to find that though several bungos were being loaded, none was yet ready to depart. Despite their difficulty hiring a guide, they were the first to leave after all. "I told you things would go well from now on," he confided in Lyse's ear. Her hair was now loose, spilling over her shoulders in a shiny mass that reached past her waist and he gathered the silken strands into his hands.

"Let me braid your hair," he asked in an enticing whisper, and before she could refuse his offer he had begun.

Lyse thought it highly amusing Buck would choose to attend to such a personal task when they weren't alone, but thinking none would see him but Chavez, whom she assumed was busy watching the river, she didn't think he would be teased. She loved his touch as his fingers brushed her back, but all too soon he was finished. She pulled the leather thong she used to secure the end of her braid from her pocket and handed it to him.

"Thanks," she murmured thoughtfully, knowing he would think she meant for the braid, rather than the pleasure his attention had given her.

"You're welcome." Buck thought having Lyse practically in his lap an enchanting way to travel. That Tim and the doctor were at the far end of the boat pleased him even more.

Even with Buck so near, Lyse found the beauty of the Chagres so totally absorbing that more than an hour went by before she turned to speak to him. "Is this what a jungle is like?" she asked excitedly. "You can't even see the land for all the plants and the leaves are a thousand different shades of green. The forest is so thick it must have been here since the dawn of time."

"At the very least," Buck agreed, delighted she was enjoying the journey. The river was broad, winding between walls of dense foliage that seemed to sprout up from the water itself. There were tall coconut palms, thick strands of sugarcane, enormous lilies, and a profusion of vegetation with vibrant blossoms of crimson and lavender he couldn't name. It was also so hot and insect-infested a place he couldn't appreciate its beauty nearly as much as Lyse obviously was. He felt like an ant, struggling through tall grass and feeling suffocated, and he longed for the open prairies of Texas where a man's vision was uncluttered for miles.

"Oh, look!" Lyse squealed as half a dozen brightly colored parrots swooped low over the water then landed in the trees at the river's edge. "Are those parrots like the ones pirates had?"

Buck couldn't help but laugh at her question. "Yes, those are parrots, but I think honest sailors must have kept them for pets too."

In too happy a mood to care, Lyse merely shrugged. "Whatever." She thought the birds magnificent and longed to own one, even knowing she could not pan for gold with one perched on her shoulder. They were overtaken then by a swarm of butterflies that brushed by them like vivid flower petals blowing in the wind. She tried to dodge them, but succeeded only in ending up sprawled in Buck's lap. He leaned down to kiss her soundly before helping her back up.

Lyse turned to give Buck a dazzling smile, but when she saw Chavez watching them, her joy vanished as she recalled their conversation. His woman! How could she have forgotten she had wanted to give Buck a piece of her mind for calling her that? Appalled by her own weakness for the handsome man, she faced forward again quickly. There had been nothing malicious about Buck's boast, but the shame of his words pained her still.

Buck had seen the sudden change in Lyse's expression and was too curious not to pursue the cause. Knowing how reticent she was to answer questions, he put his hands on her waist and pulled her back on his lap so he could whisper in her ear. "If it embarrassed you to have Chavez see us kiss, I'm sorry, but you're too pretty to resist."

Lyse squirmed to break free of his confining hold, but succeeded only in becoming more firmly wrapped in his arms. "I don't care about him!" she denied hotly.

"Parrots bother you, or perhaps butterflies?" Buck asked with a teasing chuckle. When she didn't reply, he turned her face toward him with his fingertips. "Tell me what's wrong," he insisted.

Lyse felt utterly ridiculous complaining about his comment now. It had upset her badly, but she found it impossible to put her feelings into words. She didn't like him calling her his woman, but she didn't want to hear him say that she wasn't his woman either. "I just think we ought to be more, well, more discreet," she finally murmured softly.

"Oh yeah, as I recall you're real good at being discreet." Insulted by her request because he saw nothing wrong in showing her affection, Buck moved her off his lap so rapidly he set her down too hard. "Sorry," he mumbled, but she had confused him completely, again, and that was not a good feeling.

Just ahead stood a gnarled tree with low-hanging limbs that hung way out over the water. It was a spot they should have avoided entirely and would have had Chavez been paying close attention to steering his boat rather than to the amorous couple seated in front of him. He ducked down low, but his pole whacked against a branch and he was suddenly awakened to find a tasty bit of prey within his reach: A seven-foot boa constrictor dropped down on the old man.

With a horrified shriek, Chavez flung off the snake before it could coil around him, but the momentum of his action toppled him over backward into the river. Buck's upraised arms hit the boa a glancing blow, but failed to knock it into the water. Landing draped over Lyse's right shoulder, still bent on filling its stomach, in an instant the infuriated reptile entwined itself around her neck and began to squeeze with deadly force.

Disaster had struck with lightning speed but with Lyse's screams cut short by the boa's strangling grip, Buck cared nothing about Chavez's fate. He tried first to grab hold of the creature and pry it loose, but it had muscles of steel and responded by coiling its tail around his right arm to capture him as neatly as it had caught Lyse.

Because there was no possible way he could shoot it, Buck drew his knife then dared not strike the boa a fatal blow for fear of cutting Lyse's throat. Chavez's grandsons had all gone into the water to save him, but Tim scrambled over the piles of luggage that separated them to reach Lyse who no longer had the breath to struggle and could do no more than plead with him with a terrified gaze to set her free.

"Can you pull the head away?" Buck shouted. "Get it away from her so I can use my knife."

The boat was rocking dangerously as they struggled to subdue the boa and Tim couldn't get a grip on the head for several seconds. He had been terrified of snakes all his life, but his fears vanished with the need to save Lyse so acute. Her skin was drenched with sweat and taking on a sickly blue cast by the time he got his hands locked behind the snake's jaws. With a mighty yank, he pulled up as hard as he could and Buck drove his blade clear through the muscular reptile's brain. To their horror, it did not go slack immediately, but instead continued to hold Lyse in its bone-crushing grip.

Keeping a firm hold on the knife, Buck used it to force the boa's head away from Lyse's cheek as Tim fought to free her. She was limp now and he prayed she had passed out rather than died of a broken neck. Robert Ash reached them then, his knife drawn, and as Buck and Tim wrenched the convulsing snake away from Lyse, the doctor hacked it into chunks he rapidly tossed overboard. When that action brought a score of crocodiles swimming their way, Buck looked around to find no sign of Chavez and his three grandsons. Without anyone to row or steer, the boat had begun drifting with the current and moving back in the direction they had come.

They were all splattered with the snake's blood, but that gore escaped Buck's notice as he watched the doctor toss aside the last of the carcass and begin to examine Lyse's neck for injuries. The horrible vision of Jack trying to draw a breath through a crushed throat made him tremble with terror and when Robert pulled Lyse from his arms so he could lay her facedown across the baggage, he screamed at the man. "Were we too late? Is she dead?"

Robert pressed down on Lyse's back with the same firm motion he would use to revive a drowning victim. "No, she's just got all the wind squeezed out of her. She should come around in a minute. I'll worry about her, you just try not to rock the boat or we'll be up to our necks in crocodiles."

"And whose fault is that?" Tim shouted angrily, then ashamed of himself, he apologized. Picking up the paddle Juan had dropped, he handed it to Buck before reaching for the one Lalo had used. "Come on, let's see if we can't get back to the others."

With his eyes never leaving Lyse's small limp figure, Buck paddled first on one side of the bungo and then the other. Neither he nor Tim were used to paddling a boat and their motions were awkward, but by the time Lyse began to cough and wheeze, the tree where all their troubles had begun was in sight. In the lower branches sat Señor Chavez and his grandsons while a lone crocodile swam in lazy circles beneath them.

"God help us," Tim prayed aloud. "We should have taken a ship around the Horn."

"Well, since we didn't, we'll just have to get along as best we can." Buck turned back to see if any of the crocodiles had followed in their wake and shuddered when he found at least a dozen had. Then realizing all in the boat must reek of the boa's blood, he wasn't surprised. Drawing his Colt, he fired several rounds in the beasts' direction and frightened by the noise of the shots the bloodthirsty animals turned in a lazy circle and swam away in search of easier prey. Another shot placed near the lone crocodile that had kept the Chavez family treed sent that animal away hungry as well.

As the bungo slid beneath them, Memo leapt in first, then holding on to a limb he kept the boat steady while his cousins helped his grandfather in. Unlike the old man, he had not bothered to learn English, but when he asked in Spanish how they had subdued the boa, Buck gave a prompt and colorful reply, sharing equally with Tim and Robert the credit for killing the snake.

Still collapsed across the luggage, Lyse was so weak she could barely hold up her head, but she was smiling widely as she uttered a hoarse "Thank you," again focusing everyone's attention on her.

Chavez was crouched in the bottom of the bungo, his expression impossible to read as he contemplated the near tragedy that could have easily claimed all their lives. "We will have to stop in Gatún for the night. We cannot go farther."

Buck looked at Tim and Robert and saw they now had as little interest in traveling all night as he. "We could all do with a rest."

Chavez nodded, but he did not return to his place on the stern. Instead, Juan took up the pole to guide the boat. Memo and Lalo returned to their places, Tim and Robert got settled near the bow, and with Buck cuddling her tenderly, Lyse fell asleep in his arms.

It was late afternoon by the time they arrived in Gatún, which proved to be an even more humble village than the one at the mouth of the Chagres. When Chavez explained they could buy food from the residents and rent hammocks for the night in one of the one-room huts used by travelers, Buck politely refused to accept such rude accommodations.

"I realize ladies do not pass through this place every day, but there must be some way to insure Miss Selby's privacy. If these people are used to sleeping in hammocks, please find a family who's willing to hang theirs elsewhere for the night so we can have their home to ourselves." Buck handed Chavez a generous amount to insure someone would be eager to comply with his request, but as they waited for his return, Lyse was quick to object to his plan.

"I don't mind sleeping in a hammock in the same hut with the men. It's almost impossible to fall out of one, isn't it?"

The comfort provided by a hammock was not the issue, and Buck couldn't understand why Lyse didn't see that. Even in the pale sunlight, the deep purple bruises that ringed her neck like a gruesome necklace were still visible as were the dark blotches of the boa's blood on her shirt. "You could have died today, Lyse. Now I intend to find us some water for baths, and something good to eat. Then I plan to spend the rest of the night celebrating the fact that you're still very much alive."

Tim and Robert had followed Memo into the hut where they could rent hammocks and though they couldn't have overheard him, she looked around to make certain no one else had either. "Don't be so melodramatic. I'm sure you were as scared as I was, but I knew you wouldn't let me die. I don't want to ask for special treatment here since it will only make things harder for any women who come this way after me."

Buck hadn't released her hand since they had left the boat and he drew her close as he whispered, "Your faith in me is very flattering, but I want to make love to you. I'd rather not do it in a hammock with half a dozen men looking on, but if that's your choice, I will."

Certain he was teasing, Lyse ignored that threat. "Is it even possible to make love in a hammock?"

"It must be, look at all the children running around here."

Along with dogs and pigs that seemed to have free run of the village, Lyse had also noticed the children. Accustomed to the presence of strangers, they were laughing happily, playing tag between the huts, and were all as naked as the day they were born. Thinking the heat the reason for such a custom, Lyse didn't give their lack of attire a second thought when Buck's attitude was so troublesome.

The incident with the boa had been mercifully brief. It had left her exhausted and badly bruised, but she sensed Buck had been affected even more deeply. He had always been protective, or perhaps possessive was what she should call it, but now he couldn't seem to stop touching her. That he wanted to make love so badly worried her too, for it wasn't desire that shown in his eyes, but an emotion far more intense. Because she knew no way to tactfully refuse him, she hoped they would be forced to sleep with the others, but Chavez soon returned with a tiny woman he introduced as Señora Montez who was delighted to not only rent them her home but also prepare supper for them.

When Buck caught her eye, his satisfied smirk was

enough to make Lyse want to scream, but she kept still and thanked their hostess as graciously as he did for the use of her home. Like the other structures in the village, the small house had a high-pitched roof covered with palm leaves. The high ceiling provided the single room with a space for a loft whose cane flooring was covered with hides. Reached by climbing a notched pole, Buck thought it would make a far better place to sleep than a hammock and Lyse readily agreed despite her reservations about not staying with the others.

Señora Montez had a pot of rice steaming over the fire and hurriedly added slices of pork to cook while she led her guests around to the back of her home where a wooden tub used for both laundry and bathing sat shielded from her neighbors' view by a stand of cane. Full of crystal clear water from the river, it had been warmed by the heat of the sun. The little woman had only one towel, but it was clean and she handed it to Lyse before bidding them a good evening and hurrying away.

"We'll both need clean clothes," Buck said suddenly. "Why don't you clean up first while I get them?"

Used to doing the laundry, Lyse reached out to catch his arm before he could turn away. "It's only our shirts that are filthy, so that's all that needs to be unpacked. I can wash out these and our underwear when you finish bathing."

"I'll find a woman to do the laundry, Lyse. You needn't scrub shirts after the day you've had." Buck thought her offer ridiculous, and to silence the protest he knew she'd make, he leaned down to give her a lingering kiss before he went on his errand.

Lyse was too tired to argue, but she wouldn't have minded washing their clothes. She sat down on the small stool beside the tub to pull off her boots and when she heard footsteps, she thought Buck had forgotten something. She looked up, expecting him to reappear, but he did not. Alarmed now, she sat with one boot in her hand, listening for another sign of someone's presence. Shrill calls of exotic birds rent the air, but whoever had walked by had either gone, or was now standing still, perhaps watching her through the cane as she prepared to bathe. There was no wind, but she was certain she had also heard the rustling of leaves. It was a frightening sensation to be watched, and not about to remove her clothes in front of a stranger, Lyse yanked off her other boot but remained seated on the low stool until Buck returned with an armload of clothes.

"I remembered your hairbrush. Is there anything else you want?"

Lyse raised a finger to her lips, then signaled for him to look behind the small enclosure. Without speaking, Buck set their clean garments aside, drew his Colt, and went to investigate. He was gone only briefly, then came back wearing a teasing grin.

"There's no one around. Not even a pig. Why did you think there was?"

"I heard something, like the crunch of a boot on gravel," Lyse insisted as she rose and began to unbutton her shirt. "Stay here, will you? I don't mind bathing in front of you, but I won't put on a show for the entire village."

When he had found the area behind Señora Montez's hut deserted, Buck had thought Lyse had just been imagining things; now he wasn't so certain. "The crunch of a boot? Then it wasn't an animal. The kids are all barefoot and most of the adults seem to be too. It won't be much of a challenge to find the man who was here."

"No, don't go!" Lyse begged this time, instantly ashamed of herself for sounding so desperate.

"All right," Buck agreed, every bit as anxious to stay as she was to have his company. He dipped his fingers into the tub of water, then flicked them at her, splattering her face with warm droplets.

"Hey!" Lyse squealed. "I expect you to behave yourself!"

"What fun is that?" Buck asked as he leaned back against the hut and crossed his arms over his chest.

"It's not fun I'm after. I just want to clean up. Let me have my way for once, will you?"

When she turned away and undressed as though he weren't even there, Buck didn't argue. Once she had peeled off her clothes, he saw the ugly bruises on her throat extended over her shoulders and down her back. He and Tim had undoubtedly done that to her in their frantic efforts to kill the boa and he shuddered with the memory of their ordeal. How in God's name was he going to be able to watch her go off to work in the gold fields when he couldn't protect her when she was no more than an arm's length away?

He watched her unbraid her hair, then step into the tub. There was a bar of soap within easy reach, but when it slipped from her hand he bent down to pick it up for her. "Here you are, ma'am."

"Thanks, I'm glad you're making yourself useful."

"I'd like to be a lot more useful, but that tub is too damn small." Her hair filled with soap bubbles, her badly bruised skin all wet and slippery, Buck thought her wonderfully alluring. "You are one beautiful woman, Lyse, even dripping wet you are."

He had told her she was attractive so often Lyse had begun to believe he actually meant it. She had slowly grown used to the way the other men had practically devoured her with their eyes when she wore her fancy dresses, but Buck seemed to find her pretty no matter how much, or how little, she wore. "You're going to make me awful conceited if you don't stop talking like that."

"Well I guess I'll just have to put up with your conceit then, because there's no way I can ignore your looks, Lyse."

Unable to come up with any kind of a reply when his sweetness brought tears to her eyes, Lyse bent over to rinse out her hair. Her bath complete, she stood up and reached for the towel. When Buck stepped to her side, lifted her out of the tub, and placed her on her feet she realized he had had no difficulty using his right arm.

"You're all right now, aren't you? Really well?"

Buck nodded as he wrapped the towel around her tightly. "Almost good as new, thanks to you."

Those unexpected words of gratitude caught Lyse off guard. It was love she wanted, not undying gratitude for what she had done for him. "As I see it, we're even now," she remarked with forced calm. "I saved your life, today you saved mine. We don't owe each other anything anymore."

That was so coldhearted a remark, Buck couldn't abide it. He dropped his hands and stepped back. "Sit down and keep me company," he ordered gruffly before turning to kick the stool away from the tub. "You owe me that much at least."

"What's the matter with you?" Lyse asked in dismay, for truly she had no idea her comment had upset him as it obviously had.

"I'm afraid it would take more years than either of us has left to live to explain!" Buck plunked his hat down on her wet hair, then yanked off his boots. Time and again he had been forced to accept the possibility that though Lyse clearly enjoyed the immense physical pleasure they shared making love, her feelings for him weren't nearly so intense as his for her. She would remember him because he was her first lover, but he would be damned if he would let that be the only reason.

Lyse sat down as directed, but because her company obviously wasn't all that enjoyable, she kept quiet. She thought as always that Buck had a marvelous body, perfectly proportioned, magnificently muscled, and handsomely tanned. He kept his back to her, and didn't speak either, but that didn't spoil her pleasure in being near him. After removing his hat, she leaned her head back against the hut and closed her eyes for what she thought was only a second but when Buck called her name, he had had the time not only to finish bathing, but also to shave and dress.

"Oh, I'm sorry, I must have fallen asleep," she said. Deeply embarrassed that she had provided no company at all, she leapt to her feet, then had to grab for the towel to keep it from falling.

That she would be so flustered amused Buck, and the darkness of his mood lightened several shades. "I'll have another look around while you dress. Whatever Señora Montez tossed in her stew pot must be ready to eat by now." He circled the cane enclosure once again, but the ground was too rocky for footprints to be visible and he still had no proof someone had been lurking about undoubtedly hoping to catch a glimpse of Lyse in the nude. Not that he could blame any man for wanting such a thrill, but he would break him into a thousand pieces if he found out who it had been.

When Lyse got ready to leave the bathing area, she found their dirty clothes already gone. Buck had certainly been busy while she had slept. There seemed to be nothing he couldn't arrange, but she knew even if he didn't have the money to insure his requests were granted, he would get his way just the same. He always knew exactly what he wanted and how to go about getting it. Well, she had her dreams too. Surely determination and hard work would make them true and she was no stranger to either.

When Lyse entered the small house, she found Buck ready to dish up the rice and pork. "That smells delicious, but I swear I'm so hungry I could eat just about anything tonight except maybe a snake."

Buck laughed at that thought. "You're in luck, snake isn't on the menu." The neatly kept home contained a table and two rickety chairs, and as soon as he had served the plates he saw Lyse was comfortably seated. It was nearly dark outside, but the fire from the hearth and a candle on the table gave the small dwelling a homey glow.

"This has to have been the worst day of the trip, Lyse. Another couple of days by boat, then we'll pack our things over the mountains and we'll be on the coast. It will be clear sailing after that."

"I hope I never have a day worse than this my entire life!" Lyse said before taking her first bite. She had seldom eaten rice but thought it wonderfully tasty now, and the pork was tender and flavorful. There were bananas too and Buck showed her how easy they were to peel and eat. It was a delicious meal and though she hoped Tim and Robert had been given nice dinners too, she was certain their food could not have been any better.

After having slept most of the afternoon Lyse was wide awake, but she hadn't forgotten why Buck wanted them to have separate quarters. She glanced up at the loft, wanting to make love to him every chance she got and at the same time longing for a deeper closeness that would remain with them after they left their bed. That was a hopeless wish she knew, for though he had never said she wasn't good enough for him to her face, his lack of interest in making her his wife clearly showed that was how he felt.

The sadness that had suddenly filled Lyse's sweet features mystified Buck, but he suspected his thoughtlessness was the cause. "I shouldn't have yelled at you this afternoon. I'm sorry. Most women would still be in a dead faint after what you suffered and you're not only your usual self, you even volunteered to do our laundry."

"I'm used to keeping busy, not to being pampered," Lyse replied, shrugging off his compliment with her usual nonchalance.

"Well, I'm trying my best to pamper you," Buck insisted with a sly grin, still hoping to lift her spirits.

Lyse looked down at her empty plate rather than returning his smile. "Yes, you're very good to me, Buck. Maybe I don't say thank you often enough."

Buck found her gratitude no more satisfying than she had found his but he failed to make that connection. She looked very young with her hair falling free and he reminded himself that indeed she was. Though her behavior wasn't in the least bit seductive, her effect upon him was still that of an enchantress and he simply could not get enough of her. That was a weakness, however, he would not confess.

"We have to get an early start. Come on, let's go to bed." He rose then, and took her hands to pull her to her feet.

"You don't think we're too heavy for the loft, do you? Señora Montez is just a little bit of a thing, but you and me, well," Lyse wondered aloud.

"It looks sturdy enough to me," Buck assured her. "But if you'd rather sleep on the floor, I'll just pull down some of the hides."

"No, don't go to that trouble. You want to go up first, or shall I?"

"It will be much easier to undress down here, don't you think?" Buck reached for the top button on her worn cotton shirt then leaned down to nuzzle the enticing curve of her slender throat. He had never had the pleasure of removing these clothes from her, and looked forward to it.

Lyse relaxed against him, and as always the thrill of his embrace swept away the doubts created by the fleeting nature of their romance. He called her his woman, and though her mind still rebelled at that boast, her body gloried in it.

With nightfall, the temperature had fallen no more than a couple of degrees. The small house had a window in each wall, but the night air, heavy with the abundant perfumes of the jungle, was still. The fragrant heat that surrounded the lovers was slight, however, compared to the flame of desire that burned within their hearts.

Buck had begun to undress Lyse with a seductive caress, but unable to control the need for more than the mere sight of her lovely body, he soon lost all hope of restraint and rapidly stripped her bare. Rather than leave him to struggle out of his clothing alone, Lyse remained to help him cast his aside.

"What must everyone think of us?" she asked between hurried kisses.

"They must think." Buck hesitated then, unwilling to attribute their passion for each other to love when he thought it hopelessly one-sided. "They must envy us," he finally said instead. He stood close to help Lyse up to the loft, but with her usual agility she climbed the pole easily.

Though his right shoulder ached after the day's exertions, Buck's grip was strong enough to unable him to also reach the loft without strain. "I have never made love on a mattress of furs, but these make a wonderful bed."

Lyse cared only about her handsome companion and not at all about the uniqueness of their bed. He had put out the candle and the cooking fire was now no more than a heap of gray coals. Warm and dark, the loft promised to hold as many secrets as her heart.

With his fingertips resting on the throbbing pulse in Lyse's throat, Buck could not forget how close he had come to losing her. She was so precious to him, he wanted to give her pleasure in every way possible. Her lashes tickled his lips as they brushed her eyelids sweetly. He nuzzled her ears, nibbled the lobes, then savored the incomparable sweetness of her mouth until she was again as breathless as he.

Cradling her in his arms he moved down beside her, his tongue sought the tender tips of her breasts, teasing the soft pink nubs until she could stand no more of that erotic torture and pushed his face away. His affectionate exploration of her slender body not nearly complete, he chuckled slyly, and moved on. He then trailed kisses down the moist, smooth flatness of her stomach, his tongue tarrying at her navel for a teasing invasion that coaxed a throaty giggle from her lips.

He drew his hands slowly over her legs, thinking they were the most shapely he had ever had the pleasure to touch. The loft was spacious enough for him to stretch out fully, so he was comfortable as he tickled her toes with playful nibbles. Certain he had succeeded in making her mood a lighthearted one, he began at her ankles with a succession of adoring kisses, lingering upon the tender flesh of her inner thighs.

She had been born to be his woman and he prayed he could somehow find the patience to wait until that truth filled her heart with joy as it did his. He wanted her to treasure the beauty they so easily created together, to love him not only with her body, but also with her heart and soul. There was so much he wanted them to share, but his thoughts were conveyed only in the passion of his kisses, and not once with words.

Buck's lavish affection made Lyse's whole body tingle with anticipation. His knowing touch brought a delicious excitement as wild as any she had ever felt in his arms. Bathed in sweet kisses, she savored each one, marveling as always that so strong a man could also be so incredibly tender. His lips were as soft as the wings of the butterflies that had brushed by her cheeks on the river, his caresses so light, they left her longing for more.

"Don't tell me to stop," Buck suddenly ceased his affectionate attentions to whisper.

"Why would I want you to?" Lyse asked innocently, and in the next instant she knew.

There was not an inch of her lithe body he had not touched, but she had never expected kisses as intimate as the ones he now gave. He held her so she was completely open to him. Had she wanted to escape him, his warning had come too late, but once he had begun the last thing she wanted was for him to stop. The sensations he created were too exquisitely beautiful to end as he lured her with the velvet smooth motions of his tongue to surrender more of herself than she had known she possessed.

Her whole body trembled as she reached out to him. She

wanted to beg, to plead, to scream for still more of this irresistible new kind of loving, but the only sound that escaped her lips was a low moan of desire. Fortunately, Buck knew exactly what she meant.

Again and again he felt the delicate beauty's supple body flood with rapture until he could no longer delay taking his own. He turned her on her stomach then, and kneeling behind her he wrapped his left arm around her waist to lift her hips so he could bury himself in her hot, pulsating core. He was then the one overwhelmed with the most glorious of sensations and as the ecstasy of their union shuddered through him he called her name and tenderly cupped her breasts. When his passion was finally spent, he lowered her gently to the plush mound of furs so they could lay cuddled together on their right sides. Fully satisfied, and yet knowing he would soon want more, he continued to hold her in a loving embrace.

When Lyse at last caught her breath, she brought Buck's left hand to her lips and tenderly kissed each of his fingertips. He had made love to her many times, but never as beautifully or as creatively as he had that night. She thought she ought to say something about his surprising change of style, but she didn't know exactly what. Would it be rude to make such a remark, or was it what he expected?

"Buck?" she gathered the courage to whisper.

"Hmm?" Buck pulled her closer still so there was not an inch of space between her back and his chest.

"What do women usually say when you do that?"

Buck started to laugh, then feeling Lyse stiffen, he caught himself. "I'd like to say they're eager to thank me, but I've never done any of that with anyone but you."

"Really?" Lyse asked with so pretty a smile it was a pity he could not see it.

"Really." That was not something he would have admitted to another woman, but her curiosity was so delightfully sincere he did not feel as though he was sacrificing his pride to satisfy it. "I told you I wanted to celebrate the fact you survived the day."

"Well you certainly did!" Lyse responded with an impertinent burst of giggles. "It almost makes me hope something dreadful happens to me again tomorrow."

When Buck could not help but laugh then, Lyse laughed along with him, loving him so dearly she didn't care how many close escapes she had from death when his loving made life so unbearably sweet.

XVI

April 1849

*T*hough Lyse found the luxurious bed of furs wonderfully comfortable, it was far too warm for such a sultry climate. Sated by pleasure, she lay wide awake in Buck's arms while he slept soundly, oblivious to the heat and tiny insects that buzzed around their heads.

"I love you," Lyse whispered as she snuggled against him. Certain he would not hear the confession, she had no qualms about making it aloud for love him she did, and desperately. She ran her fingertips along his arm, over his ribs, then down his thigh, memorizing the muscular contours of his powerful body so that she would never forget how handsome he had been. She could not bear to think they would not always be together, but she refused to fool herself into believing he would someday declare his love for her. He was fond of her, grateful to her, but that was all and it was not nearly enough to appease the hunger for love that raged in her heart.

He might have been ecstatic that a boa constrictor had not succeeded in squeezing the life out of her, but even that harrowing ordeal had not wrenched any words of love from his lips. The man clearly wanted to love and marry a real lady, not merely a girl who could sometimes pull off that ruse. Though she would gladly die for him, Lyse knew she couldn't live each day of her life pretending to be something she wasn't and despite how she looked in her lovely new gowns, she was no lady. Her situation utterly hopeless, she lay awake all night, exhausted by the rigors of their journey but too hot and restless to sleep.

Buck was up before dawn, rousing the rest of their party while Lyse again slipped around behind their hut to wash hurriedly and dress. It was still dark when she made her way down to the river, but as she stood by watching the bungo being loaded with the bottles of fresh water, biscuits, and fruit they would consume that day, she felt the very same eerie sensation that she was being watched that she had experienced the previous afternoon. She shivered in spite of the heat, thinking it a bad omen, but when she turned to see who was standing in the doorways of the nearby huts she saw only shadows rather than faces she could recognize.

Eager to be on their way, she leapt into the boat the second they were ready to depart and again riding in front of Buck, she eagerly awaited the dawn so she could see the jungle that surrounded them clearly. Only now instead of appreciating the primordial beauty, she was anxious to keep a close eye out for the dangers that lay hidden behind the deceptively innocent screen of dense foliage.

Were those tangled vines in the trees ahead, or coiled snakes sunning themselves in the first rays of dawn? Were those fallen trees by the river's edge, or crocodiles sleeping until a tender morsel came their way? Tormenting herself with a succession of imagined perils, she moved back so she could relax against Buck's knees. As always she drew comfort from his presence but her dread was only partially lessened by his nearness, and did not entirely subside.

Unaware of Lyse's apprehensions, Buck had his own worries that morning. From brief conversations with the other travelers as they had prepared to depart, he had been amazed to discover that during the night the tale of their encounter with the boa had been told and retold until it had grown to an astonishing epic with all the drama of a Greek tragedy. Rather than a mere six or seven feet, the snake had been described as a monster measuring well over twenty feet in length with the girth of a man's waist. That a reptile of such grandiose proportions would have instantly overturned their bungo hadn't occurred to the men who delighted in spinning fanciful tales. Having no time to waste in what he was certain would be a futile attempt to provide the truth, because it was not nearly so exciting as the imaginative rumor, he merely shrugged off the admiring comments directed his way and tended his own business.

As their bungo continued on its way up the Chagres River, Buck couldn't help but wonder why people were so prone to exaggeration where he was concerned. He had set out to punish Arvin without drawing any attention to himself, but the way things were going he would soon have a reputation for violence that would prevent him from speaking so much as a harsh word without gaining more notoriety than any man could successfully live down. First he had had the misfortune of killing a man by overturning a table, causing everyone who heard about the wretched accident to regard him with awe. Now he had supposedly slain a monster of a snake with a single stroke of his blade while Tim and Dr. Ash had been assigned decidedly minor roles. He shuddered to imagine what ridiculous feat would be credited to him next.

In his preoccupied mood, Buck didn't sense Lyse's tension and he couldn't understand why Tim and Robert Ash turned back frequently to wave at her. He did notice the boatmen were more subdued, however, and indeed all of them were more alert to danger that day. Chavez was again holding the pole at the stern and he kept them to a course well out in the river, so no perils lurking near the shore could again endanger their lives. Though sorely tempted to berate him for that tardy show of caution, Buck held his tongue for he considered them lucky that the man and his grandsons hadn't bolted during the night and left them stranded in Gatún.

When they arrived at the village of Buena Vista late that afternoon, they were all yawning with fatigue and Buck doubted they would want to continue traveling all night, but he gave Tim and Robert that choice. "By taking turns with the paddles, we could make better time than the others and perhaps reach Cruces by tomorrow morning. If mules are in as short supply as boats, we might be wise to try and get there first. Is anyone game to try?"

Though they had done none of the work that day, the sweltering heat had left Tim with no energy at all. His clothes drenched with sweat, he shook his head sadly. "I'd like to go on, I really would, but if you have to depend on me to paddle, we'll be going so slow we'd make better time sleeping tonight and starting out early again in the morning."

Buck had asked him not to disclose the fact that he had been injured, and though the Texan now looked fit, Robert Ash had to insist he be cautious. "I think we should wait until the morning too. Even if we did reach Cruces, which of us would have the energy to sit a mule after having been up all night? Malaria and yellow fever take the greatest toll of travelers making their way to Panama. They've had cholera here too. We get too tired, and before you know it we'll start falling ill. A slow trip would be better than a fast one which led no-where."

Buck glanced down at Lyse. "You voting with them?" he asked.

"Whatever you want to do will be fine with me," she responded sweetly, so glad to get off the river she wanted to shout for joy, but too afraid she'd look like a coward to actually do it.

Buck broke into a wide grin as he teased her. "Well, that's certainly a first!"

"It is not," Lyse countered sharply. After a sleepless night and a long day of constantly expecting the worst to overtake them at every turn, her nerves were flayed raw. Shocked by the fervor of her outburst, the four boatmen were staring at her wide eyed, along with Tim and Robert who appeared to be on the verge of collapse from the merciless heat.

"Look, we're all worn out," she offered apologetically, afraid she had sounded like a shrew. "If we try and go on, one of us will probably fall asleep, topple into the river, and make a tasty meal for a crocodile. The rest of us won't even miss him until dawn. I sure don't want it to be me."

"I don't want it to be any of us," Buck shot right back at her, disappointed by her abrupt change in attitude. He knew he had only himself to blame because he had long been aware she had no tolerance for teasing, but she hadn't been that obstreperous in a long while and he had hoped he had seen the last of it. Clearly he hadn't. "We'll stay here then," he announced, sorry he had not made that decision without taking a poll in the first place.

He motioned for Chavez to come with him as he took several paces away from the others. "Can you arrange for a place for Miss Selby to stay here too? Señora Montez's home was perfect. Have you another such hospitable friend in Buena Vista?"

Chavez glanced back at the striking blonde who stood with her arms folded across her chest, glowering at the tall man by his side. She still looked peeved with Buck and he could not help but comment. "Will she want your company?"

"That's not important," Buck insisted, his temper now as short as the lovely young woman in question. "I want separate quarters for her whether or not she shares them."

"I will need five dollars."

"Hell, that ought to buy half the town." Yet without further protest Buck flipped a five-dollar gold piece into the man's callused palm.

As he waited for the elderly gentleman to return from the village, Buck remained standing apart from the others, hoping a few minutes alone would improve Lyse's mood. When he saw Colin O'Roarke's bungo nearing the riverbank he glared at the redhead, hoping he would have sense enough to move on, but he didn't. It had been a long while since Buck had taken such an intense dislike to anyone as he had this man, and he hoped Colin would keep his distance.

The trouble was, Colin found it impossible to distance himself from Buck when Lyse was always by his side. He just couldn't bring himself to ignore her. Her ill-fitting shirt and pants certainly weren't provocative, nor was her pose. It was the fact that her lips were drawn up in an enchanting pout that gave him a nearly overwhelming urge to kiss her. Certain he would eventually have the good fortune to find her alone, he climbed out of his boat with his friends and started toward the village to seek lodgings, content to bide his time.

When Buck returned to the hut Chavez had rented for them with clean clothes, he found Lyse not preparing to bathe, but instead sound asleep in the loft. The cane was padded with straw rather than furs, but she had been too tired to notice it wasn't nearly as comfortable as the accommodations they had shared the previous night. Clad only in her chemise, lying on her side with her knees drawn up, she wore the endearing expression of an exhausted child.

Thoughtfully deciding to let her sleep until their supper was ready, Buck cleaned up, changed his clothes, and went for a stroll, eager to get some exercise after spending the day seated in the close confines of a hard wooden bungo. There were paths leading in several directions, going to the rivers that flowed into the Chagres and to the neighboring villages. Staying on a well-worn trail, he walked perhaps half an hour, then missing Lyse terribly, he turned back toward Buena Vista.

He circled around behind their hut, meaning to empty the tub and bring fresh water for Lyse, but he came to an abrupt halt when he spotted Colin O'Roarke peering in the south window. Unable to believe the man would be either so stupid, or so bold, he walked silently up behind him. He tapped him lightly on the shoulder and when Colin turned his way as he jumped with fright, Buck belted him squarely on the chin. He caught Colin as he fell, heaved him up over his left shoulder, and with only a slight effort carried him down to the river. He then called to the travelers just arriving to leave their boats to come and enjoy the fun. He dropped Colin in the mud, took the scruff of his neck in a firm grasp, and held the struggling man's head underwater for nearly a full minute before he let him up to catch his breath.

Coughing and choking, Colin took in great gulps of air, terrified Buck was going to drown him while the men he had called friends howled and laughed at his plight. "Help me!" he shrieked, but no one came forward.

Pushing Colin's face under the surface of the water once again, Buck shouted over his shoulder, "I caught him peeking in one of our windows so he deserves to be taught a good lesson."

That statement met with general agreement with the men who had gathered around. "Ain't nobody likes a Peeping Tom!" one fellow called out with a booming laugh. "That's right!" shouted another. "Let him feast his eyes on the fishes for a while."

Though Buck heartily disliked Colin, he had no intention of drowning him. He took care to let him up each time his struggles to break free grew feeble. He would wait then, regarding him closely, his dark eyes aglow with an evil stare as the redhead sputtered and wheezed, but the minute he was able to breathe deeply Buck forced his face back down into the river. He was enjoying himself thoroughly until he heard Lyse call his name. Releasing Colin with a disgusted shove, he rose and turned around to face her.

Awakened by the rude shouts coming from the river, Lyse had yanked on her pants, buttoned only one button on her shirt, and run barefooted to see what was happening. Expecting from the raucous noise to find a man wrestling a crocodile, or some other equally exciting spectacle, she could only gape in horror at the brutal scene that greeted her. Would Buck have killed Colin if she hadn't arrived to stop him? "What in God's name are you doing?" she gasped incredulously.

Buck tipped his hat before he explained, "I'm merely teaching this fool some manners, my dear. What would you have done had you caught him looking in your window while you were trying to sleep?"

Suddenly aware more than two dozen men were staring at her with rapt interest as they awaited her reply, Lyse took a step backward and tried with a frantic clutch to hold her partially open blouse closed. In her haste she had forgotten to bring her knife, but she wished she had it now. "He's the one who's been spying on me?"

"No!" Colin denied in a hoarse croak. "I wasn't spying on you yesterday!"

"Who said anything about yesterday?" Buck inquired with an amused chuckle. "You're as guilty as sin, O'Roarke."

Colin tried to get up, to stand and run, but he was so weak from fright he sank to his knees. Water dripped from his hair and ran down over his face, making his miserable expression all the more pitiful. "I haven't done anything all of you didn't want to do! Every last one of you wants her too!" he shouted accusingly at the jeering crowd.

A quick survey of the sly grins directed her way made the truth of Colin's words excruciatingly plain. Only Tim and Dr. Ash wore sympathetic frowns and they were so badly outnumbered Lyse was terrified. "I don't care what you do to him," she assured Buck in an anguished cry. She forced her way through the circle of leering men surrounding her, then sprinted back to their hut and climbed up into the loft. She moved into the corner and sat hugging her knees tightly, but still she didn't feel safe.

Without giving Colin a backward glance, Buck followed the distraught blonde. "Lyse," he called softly as he ducked to enter the small dwelling. "I just wanted to humiliate Colin in front of the others so he'll leave us alone. I wouldn't have done him any permanent harm."

Lyse was so frightened she was trembling all over. She couldn't help but imagine how ghastly the trip would have been for her had she tried to make it all alone. Embarrassed to have Buck see her in such an awful state, she brushed away her tears on the back of her hand. "What do you mean by 'permanent harm'? Is that killing him?"

"Yes." Buck climbed up the notched pole and sat down on the edge of the loft with his legs dangling over the side. "I'm sorry we woke you up. Why don't you try and go back to sleep? I think you could use the rest."

"I'll never be able to sleep now." Lyse yanked the thong from the end of her braid and began to comb her fingers through her hair, but she was shaking so badly she soon gave up the effort. "Is there some water for a bath?"

"I'll bring some." Buck watched her troubled expression for a long moment, then reached out to give her knee a reassuring pat. "No one is going to hurt you with me around. Not snakes or two-legged vermin. Now let me see you smile."

Lyse tried, but her lips trembled so badly she didn't succeed. "I was a fool to make this trip with you, wasn't I? A stupid fool."

"As I recall, I'm the one who came along with you," Buck reminded her. "Most of the men out there are honest, decent folk, Lyse. They'd not let anything happen to a girl as sweet and pretty as you."

That compliment finally brought a smile to the blonde's tear-streaked face. "You cut that out, Buck Warren. I know how I must look and it sure isn't pretty."

"You're a ravishing beauty, sweetheart, and a smudge or two of dirt or a few tears doesn't change that. I'll go get the water for your bath. That's bound to make you feel better."

As Buck left on that errand, Lyse wasn't surprised to find

that as always, his confident charm had made her feel better. He was quite a man and when she recalled how bedraggled Colin had looked, she began to laugh. Her spirits greatly improved, it wasn't long before she began to look forward to the night too.

The next day, the landscape along the river changed as the banks grew steep and areas where the forest had been cleared for crops came into view. They passed fields planted in maize, plantain, and rice, but there were still long stretches where the wilderness was untouched and the tropical plants spilled over into the river in lush profusion.

Her eyes focused on the exotic scenery, Lyse was jolted rudely when, without warning, their bungo ran up over a sunken log. Because it was heavily loaded, it remained stuck fast until Memo and Juan bravely got into the river to attach ropes to the front of the boat, but they had to struggle a long while before they finally succeeded in pulling it free.

Though Buck had stood watch with his Colt in hand, there had been no crocodiles in sight as the natives worked, but by the time they again had the boat under way the lumbering reptiles were swimming into view. Seeing no point in shooting at the beasts when no one was in danger, the Texan had returned his pistol to his holster and relaxed, but the muscles along Lyse's shoulders remained knotted with tension.

Soon not only the scenery, but also the character of the river changed as the current became increasingly strong. Memo had to grab the pole and take the position in the stern when the work of guiding the boat upstream became too strenuous for his elderly grandfather to manage. Breathless from his labors, he still shouted to Buck to explain to the others when they passed by the peak of Monte Carabali, a hill that provided a view of both the Caribbean Sea and the Pacific Ocean.

"Do you suppose that's really true?" Lyse turned to ask. The pitch and sway of the small boat was beginning to make her feel ill and she would have been happy to debate any issue as a distraction.

"Rather than stop and climb to the top of the hill to make certain, I'll take his word for it." When Lyse merely shrugged, Buck touched her shoulder. "Are you feeling all right? The water's getting awfully rough. I hope you don't get seasick again."

Determined not to give in to her queasy stomach, Lyse shook her head. "I'm fine," she insisted stubbornly. As long as Tim and Dr. Ash weren't ill, she didn't intend to let anyone think she was a weakling.

The delay caused by the fallen log made reaching Las Cruces before nightfall impossible. Tying up instead in Gorgona, the largest settlement they had yet visited, the travelers found preparations for a fandango under way. The Spanish residents of the nearby haciendas had come into town for the dance and Señor Chavez had no sooner succeeded in finding them lodgings for the night than Lyse and Buck were invited to join in the festivities.

"A dance?" Lyse asked, her apprehension well founded. "I don't know how you can possibly expect me to dance."

Buck wondered if Lyse had always been so skittish, but they had been through so much together he wouldn't criticize her over something so minor as a dance. On the other hand, he wasn't about to give in to her either. "Nonsense," he proclaimed loudly. "Your legs must be as cramped as mine from sitting in a bungo the last three days. I think some dancing would do us both good."

Lyse looked down as she made a sweeping gesture to direct his attention to her rumpled attire. "I'm not dressed for a party."

"I doubt they have many celebrations here so they'll probably dance until dawn. We'll have plenty of time to bathe and change our clothes. I'll unpack your green dress. It's sheer enough for this climate, or would you rather have one of the others?"

Lyse jammed her hands in her hip pockets and dug her toe into the sandy soil as she tried to come up with a compelling excuse that would get her off the hook. Once she had left the boat for dry land, she didn't feel nearly so bad as she had on the river. Besides, she didn't dare let Buck suspect there was anything the matter with her health. In desperation, she finally blurted out the truth. "I don't know how to dance."

Buck shook his head sadly, sorry that hadn't even occurred to him. Why he had thought a girl who didn't even
own a dress when he had met her would have been to parties, he didn't know, but he was angry at himself for not
realizing the cause of her shyness.

"Then it's high time you learned, don't you think?" he
asked with an enticing grin.

Her eyes firmly focused on her dusty boots, Lyse continued to argue. "You know I'll never be able to learn how to
dance in one night. I'd just make a fool of myself is all."

"Look at it this way. There will probably be so few pretty
women there tonight that the men will notice only your fair
hair and pretty smile. They won't care whether you can dance
well or not. In fact, I'll bet you any sum you want that you
don't hear a single complaint from any of your partners."

Alarmed by that thought, Lyse risked looking up at him,
but her glance was bright with confusion. "You mean I'd
have to dance with other men? Not just you?"

"Sure, but it would be fun. Why don't we go for a little
while and then if you aren't having a good time, we'll leave.
You could stand dancing with Tim and the doctor, couldn't
you? I know both of them would be thrilled."

"And just who will you be dancing with if I'm with them?"
Lyse asked, straightening her slumped posture proudly.

That Lyse would be jealous pleased Buck enormously, but
he was wise enough not to gloat out loud about it. "I told
you there can't be enough women to go around. I'll probably
just have to wait my turn to dance with you."

The problem was, Lyse really did want to learn how to
dance. She had always longed to be invited to what she
imagined were fabulous parties at the big ranches near her
home, but none of the wealthy owners had been her father's
friends and they had never been included among the guests.
Now here was Buck Warren, the nicest man she could ever
hope to meet, asking her to go to a party with him and she
was trying to talk him out of it! An angelic smile brought out
the dimples in her cheeks as she realized she would be a fool
to miss such a wonderful chance to have fun.

"My green dress will be fine. You just shake out the wrin-
kles, and I'll be happy to wear it."

Buck leaned down to give Lyse an enthusiastic kiss. "This won't be the last party we attend. I promise you that."

As she watched him walk back to the boat, Lyse wondered what he had meant. Then deciding they might have dances in the gold fields, she dismissed that thought and got ready to take her bath.

A level area covered with grass served as the dance floor for the fandango and wooden drums, violins, and guitars provided the music. By the time they arrived the party was already a boisterous one, and Lyse was pleased to find there were at least two dozen ladies present. They were dressed in full-skirted gowns of white or pink with bright blossoms wound in their glossy, dark hair. The men wore loose-fitting white shirts and pants that were not only perfect for the warm climate, but also seemed to her as handsome as formal dress that night.

The musicians were playing a waltz and couples were dancing over the grass with the same fluid grace displayed in the most elegant ballroom. Enjoying the sweet fragrance of the night-blooming flowers, and the beauty of the music and dancers, Lyse would have been content to stay on the sidelines all evening, but Buck took her hand, eager to take an active part in the festivities.

"Buck!" she pleaded in a frantic whisper as she tried to pull free, but with a devilish laugh he drew her into the midst of the swirling couples.

The waltz was a dance he knew well, and he held her so close she had no choice but to follow his lead. She stepped on his toes in the first couple of minutes, but then gradually found the step such a simple one she could do it with ease. She smiled at him then, quite pleased with herself.

"It's easy to dance with you," she complimented him sincerely when the music ended. "But I don't think I could ever get the hang of it with anyone else."

Though she had arranged her hair atop her head, tiny tendrils had escaped her combs and tickled her nape as she looked up at him. Despite the many hours they had spent making love, her eyes were aglow with a charming innocence. "If you could see how pretty you look, you'd know I won't be able to keep you to myself for long."

Lyse moved close and stood on her tiptoes to answer. "Looking good is one thing, dancing well is quite another." Before Buck could reply, the musicians struck up another waltz and Tim dashed to her side. His grin was so eager she didn't have the heart to refuse him and she soon found herself with a succession of men all so anxious to dance with her, she dared not say no to a single one. That Colin O'Roarke had not come to the party pleased her greatly because she would not under any circumstances have danced with him.

When the musicians began the Spanish folkdances popular with the crowd, Buck found himself the partner of a lovely widow who was introduced to him as Señora Catalina. She danced with a lively charm, holding aloft the fringed ends of a crimson scarf. The dance was not unlike others he had learned in Texas and he did his best to portray the same enthusiasm as the pretty dark-eyed woman. When the number finished, several men placed their sombreros atop her head as a gesture of appreciation and Buck quickly backed away to allow another man to claim her.

Though she had swiftly learned how to waltz, the intricate moves and maze of patterns the folk dances required left Lyse begging to be allowed a chance to catch her breath. She watched in fascinated silence as Buck danced with Señora Catalina, wondering all the while if Constance were also dark and petite because they danced so well together. She knew without asking that there probably wasn't a dance Constance didn't know, though she had grown up without ever learning one. When Buck came to ask her for the next dance, she covered a wide yawn before she replied.

"I'd love to dance with you again, but isn't it getting awfully late?"

"Aren't you having a good time?" Buck inquired considerately. "We needn't stay if you're not."

"I'm having a wonderful time, but we got up before dawn and will again tomorrow. Maybe you've forgotten that, but I haven't."

Buck looked down at her, amazed as always by how easily a pretty dress transformed her appearance though the uniqueness of her personality remained unaffected unless she chose to become someone new; someone she continually protested she was not. "I'll be happy to see you get to bed, Lyse, but if you think I'll let you go to sleep, you've got another think coming."

A playful smile spread slowly across Lyse's lips as she considered the full import of his words. "Thank you. I thought you were going to make me suggest that, but you did it ever so much better," she confided as she slipped her arm through his.

Buck patted her hand lightly as they started toward the hut they would share that night. "With but a few notable exceptions, this has been a remarkably good trip, Lyse. I know what I'll remember."

"The way that little señorita dances?" Lyse suggested slyly.

"Who?" Buck asked with feigned innocence, as though he did not know exactly who she meant.

"Never mind, I see you have forgotten her already."

Buck did not reply until he had pulled her through the doorway of their hut. Then assured of their privacy his words spilled out in a torrent of desire. "I swear I have forgotten every woman I ever knew since meeting you, Lyse. You are all I need."

Lyse pressed against him, returning his fevered kisses with a wild abandon all her own. To be needed was not nearly enough, but her heart was too full of him to complain she felt slighted when the passion he showed her always brought them a delectable bliss.

XVII

April 1849

Señor Chavez awakened Buck the next morning with disturbing news. "Memo has a fever. We cannot reach Las Cruces without him, but I have found horses and pack animals for you. The Gorgona trail will take you to Panama by nightfall."

Buck knew they were fortunate to have arrived at the isthmus before the torrential spring rains made the mountain trails impassable, and didn't argue with the old man. Though he was sorry Memo was ill, he wouldn't mind leaving the river, and woke Lyse to tell her their travel plans would have to be changed.

"Just how sick is he?" Lyse wanted to know, genuinely concerned about the friendly young man.

"I've no idea, but apparently he's too sick to manage his share of the work. It will mean a longer ride, but frankly, I'll be grateful to get out of the bungo a few hours early."

"So will I," the still sleepy blonde agreed through a wide yawn. How Buck got by on so few hours' sleep she didn't understand, but because he was obviously eager to get going she forced herself to rise and dressed hurriedly while he went to wake Tim and Dr. Ash.

Chavez introduced the guide as Carlos Mendoza and insisted his prices were fair. The travelers paid the man ten dollars each for the privilege of riding his horses and six dollars for each hundred pounds of freight. Because none of them had much baggage, that expense wasn't excessive. Their mounts were mustangs, tough little horses a man as tall as Buck could nearly step right over, but he just laughed at their diminutive size and made the best of the situation by taking the largest.

Provided with a generous tip for the extra services he had rendered, Chavez and his two healthy grandsons stood by the trail to bid them good-bye. Lyse turned back to wave, doubting the elderly gentleman would volunteer to escort another woman up the river after the near tragic mishap they had had. Well, at least no one had been killed, she thought gratefully, knowing her presence would undoubtedly have been blamed for such bad luck even if she had been the one to die.

A man as at home in the rugged mountains as his horses, Mendoza maintained a steady pace as he led the way along the well-worn trail. It was not a level path even at the edge of Gorgona, but as the surrounding forest grew more dense and dark, the primitive road descended into a narrow gully. Dry now, in another month it would be filled with enough mud to tickle the horses' bellies.

The terrain soon became so steep the horses lost their footing and slid to the bottom of passes, then had to scramble like goats up the sheer opposite walls. Jostled rudely this way and that, their riders could only marvel at the hardy animals' stamina. Stepping in each other's tracks, the mustangs had worn the path not smooth, but into a treacherous succession of holes. It was quite the roughest ride Lyse had ever been on, but whenever she glanced back at Tim and Robert Ash she was so amused by their panic-filled expressions and frantic grips on their saddle horns, her spirits remained high.

To pass the time she studied the treetops that formed a canopy of bright green overhead. The leaves shut out most of the sunlight, but none of the merciless humidity, stifling heat, or relentless swarms of insects. Though she was certain there were snakes aplenty lurking nearby, she was relieved when none slithered into view.

Monkeys chattered constantly, as though complaining loudly that the strangers traveling through their midst were trespassing in their jungle. Constantly flying from tree to tree, the brightly colored parrots Lyse had admired along the river kept up a steady screeching assault on her ears. Observing remarkable sights at every turn, the curious blonde concentrated on the vivid hues and colorful inhabitants of the tropical forest rather than on how hot she was or how badly her back and weary seat ached.

When they had reached the point where those who had continued on to Las Cruces by boat joined the trail, they encountered long trains of luggage packed on oxen and horses as well as mules. Lyse was amazed that with such heavy traffic on the narrow trail, no one had made any effort to widen or otherwise improve it. In the steepest ravines, they passed the bodies of mules who, unable to complete their journey, had died in their tracks. When Lyse spotted bald vultures perched in low branches nearby, waiting to pluck their bones clean, she shuddered at how close Buck had come to suffering the same fate.

At Mendoza's suggestion, they stopped to rest at a rancho whose owner graciously gave everyone cups of black coffee so thick it made Lyse gag. Grateful for the few minutes' respite from the tedious trail, she left the strong brew untouched and sat back against a palm to relax while her companions talked among themselves. When the Henderson brothers appeared among a group making its way toward Panama, she spotted them first and waved.

Their expressions stern, the two young men left their mounts to graze for a moment as they came over to talk. "You hear about Colin?" Miles called out as he approached them.

"What's there to hear?" Tim finally asked when he realized neither Buck nor Lyse cared enough about what the story might be to inquire.

Though Max remained standing, Miles squatted down in the dust, removed his hat, and used his sleeve to wipe the sweat from his forehead before he explained. "He's come down with yellow fever and had to stay back in Cruces. He's not only sick as a dog, but also his skin was turning yellow as a lemon."

12

"Do you think he'll live?" Tim looked over at Robert Ash, hoping he would offer an expert medical opinion.

"I can't say. All I know for certain is that yellow fever has killed thousands in these jungles, so the sooner we get out of here the safer we'll be."

Taking that advice to heart, Lyse leapt to her feet and brushed off the seat of her pants. "That's enough of a rest for me. What about you?"

Buck rose quickly and offered a hand to both Tim and the doctor to get them on their feet while Carlos Mendoza had no trouble rising on his own. "Yeah, time's a-wasting. Let's get going. See you boys in Panama," the Texan called to the Hendersons, and he swiftly escorted his small party back to their horses. "I swear, if anyone says I'm responsible for Colin getting sick, I'll see that's the last lie they ever spread."

"How could anyone blame you?" Lyse asked with a befuddled frown.

"Stranger things have happened," Buck assured her.

"Wait a minute," Lyse requested dramatically as she turned back to the Hendersons. "Did anyone else get sick too?"

"Yeah, maybe five or six others," Miles shouted in reply.

"Thanks!" Lyse waved good-bye then whispered to Buck, "You see, it wasn't just Colin who's ill so there's no way you can be blamed."

Not convinced, Buck shot her a skeptical glance, then swung himself up on his mustang's back and fell in behind their guide, ready to get under way.

The narrow trail continued steadily upward, then briefly leveled off at a broad mesa covered with palms. All too soon that pleasant respite ended and the weary travelers were again confronted with a path that made its way through gullies and clefts looking all but impassable even as they made their way through them. Constantly on the alert, Mendoza called out warnings as he led them around swamps and through thickets where the underbrush grew higher than their heads. Behind every ridge there appeared another incline and still another until as the sun set they all despaired of ever sighting the Pacific Ocean. It wasn't until the scent of the salty sea air grew strong that they realized they were almost there.

The path gradually became lined with the now familiar high-roofed huts, then larger stone houses, and occasionaly a once impressive building now deserted and overgrown with shrubs and vines. When they entered the city of Panama itself, they crossed a plaza in front of a Catholic church with an ornate stone facade, rode down an open corridor along the bay, passed beneath a stone gateway, crossed another plaza, went down a succession of narrow streets, and finally came to a halt in front of the Hotel Americano.

Lyse was the first to dismount. Thrilled the seemingly interminable trek had come to an end, she jumped up and down, nearly dancing around Tim and Robert who, fearing they lacked the strength to stand, had wisely remained in their saddles. Equally excited, Buck slid the short distance to the ground and catching the lively young woman around the waist, he lifted her high into the air.

"Look out, California, there'll be no stopping us now!" he shouted as he swung her around.

Tim couldn't believe his eyes. He had never been so tired, and here were Buck and Lyse looking like they were ready to go dancing again. "I have never thought of myself as old until this very minute," he confided in the physician at his side.

Robert shook his head, readily understanding his companion's awe. "They are used to riding, where you and I are not."

"There's got to be more to it than that," Tim insisted. Vaguely aware of what was happening, he allowed Mendoza to help him from his horse, then staggered into the hotel. He paid for a small room, and without waiting for his luggage went upstairs to bed. Robert Ash thought his example so sensible he followed it, while Buck and Lyse remained outside chatting with Mendoza as he unloaded their baggage from his pack animals.

The men passing by in the street were all speaking English. Some paused to ask from which ship they had come, then moved on after hearing it was the *Spanish Dancer*. The city was enjoying unparalleled prosperity, for it was crowded with Americans on their way to the gold fields. From the sound of their raucous laughter as they strolled by, it appeared they spent most of their time in the saloons while waiting for a ship to take them up the coast to California.

Though the grime on her trail-worn attire attracted curious stares, Lyse was too proud of what she had survived to take offense. She walked into the hotel as unwilling to make excuses for her appearance as she had been on her first day in Galveston and she was relieved when Buck did not make them either.

"I don't think we need two rooms, do you?" she whispered discreetly as the desk clerk checked what accommodations he had available.

Buck tried to stifle a wicked grin but failed. "The extra expense to safeguard your reputation is slight, Miss Selby, and I'm happy to see to it."

Failing to appreciate his teasing, Lyse recoiled as though he had struck her. Of course! She silently cursed her own stupidity in not foreseeing his answer. In order to share a room they would have to register as man and wife and clearly he was not about to agree to that. That he would not even let her pretend they were married hurt her so badly she had to turn away. Four more days had gone by and each new sunrise strengthened her conviction that she was carrying his child. Why she wasn't terrified by that possibility she didn't know, but Buck was the only one concerned about her reputation. She knew it was far too late for that now. What the hell, she mused dejectedly. As Frank Selby's daughter, she had had no reputation to sully in the first place.

"Lyse?" Buck called softly, perplexed by her sudden silence. "I've plenty of money. You know that. Providing your lodgings is no burden to me."

"It isn't a matter of money!" Lyse hissed at him through tightly clenched teeth. How could the dolt imagine she was thinking about the expense rather than what they were to each other? Unable to read her thoughts, Buck continued to regard her with a puzzled frown. His expression was totally innocent, sympathetic; he seemed truly concerned about her feelings even though he had completely misunderstood them.

"Rent fifteen rooms if you like. I don't care," Lyse told him flippantly. She signed her name in the register then directed her attention to the clerk. "Is Arvin Corbett a guest here?"

"No, señorita, he is not, but Panama has a dozen hotels."

Buck was startled by Lyse's question because he had completely forgotten the man he'd come to find. Taking their room keys, he grasped Lyse's elbow and started toward the stairs while two porters followed carrying their luggage. "He might still be calling himself Smith. I'll check the other hotels tomorrow and try both names."

Lyse remained silent until they reached her room, but when the porter carrying her satchel had placed it on the bed and left the room, she bid Buck a terse good night. Hoping the coolness of her mood had been for show, he didn't complain. He walked next door to his own room, but as soon as he had tipped and dismissed the porters he went to the connecting door between their rooms. Finding it locked from her side, he called to her.

"You'll have to open the door, Lyse, it's locked." When he heard no reply, he knocked loudly. Knowing she had to be in the room, he took her silence as a gross insult. Having no further patience with her ridiculously high-handed attitude, he took careful aim at the doorknob and with a well-placed kick sent the door flying open.

Lyse had been hanging her gowns in the wardrobe, and turned to give him a highly disapproving glance. "I wish you'd make up your mind. I thought if you'd wanted to share my room, you would have said so downstairs."

"Is that what's gotten you in such an impossible mood? Did you think I meant to ignore you just because I asked for two rooms?" Buck walked right up to her, bent on settling the matter immediately.

Lyse took a step backward, not wanting him standing that close when his mood was so hostile. She hadn't been in the least bit concerned he would leave her to sleep alone because she was well acquainted with his passions. That he could even accuse her of so silly a thought made her want to burst out laughing, but she controlled that impulse and continued to regard his fierce expression with a malevolent frown.

"I'm good enough to share a hut in the jungle, but the minute we reach a town it's a separate room for sweet, little Miss Selby. Is it my reputation you're worried about protecting, or your own?" she asked with a defiant flip of her long braid.

Buck was so astonished by that question, he needed a full minute to formulate a coherent reply. "Where in God's name did you ever get such an outrageous idea? You're a very beautiful woman and you could never do anything to my reputation but enhance it. I wanted you to have a room of your own not only to protect your name, but also to give you the privacy to bathe and dress, but I still expected us to spend most of our time together. There's absolutely no reason for you to mistake my consideration for your reputation and comfort as an insult."

When Lyse didn't apologize immediately as Buck thought she should, but merely continued to look up at him with a disdainfully suspicious gaze, he lost his temper completely. "That's your pa talking, and you know that, don't you? Frank Selby wanted you to think you were worthless so you'd never leave him, but I've never once treated you that way. I've shown you the courtesy a gentleman should to a lady and you act as though you've been abused! Well, you can just stop that act right now. With your looks you could have any man you want, Lyse, but as long as I'm alive it damn well better be me. You might as well get used to that fact right now and stop pouting about it!"

As if to emphasize that boast, Buck reached out to grab her arms and pulled her close. He was sorely tempted to shake some sense into her, but he stopped short of being that foolish because it would scarcely serve to prove his point that he treated her well. "Do you understand me, Lyse? I don't want you sulking over imagined insults or starting petty arguments with me over nothing. What we have together is too good for me to let anyone, and least of all you, ruin it!"

What Lyse longed to hear was a beautifully worded proposal rather than a loudly shouted harangue demanding she learn her place. She tried to break free of Buck's confining embrace, but he responded by holding her all the more tightly. His passions as well as his temper inflamed, his mouth bruised hers with a rapid series of savage kisses, leaving her so breathless she had to cling to him to remain on her feet. Unable to recall why they were arguing so violently, she begged him to stop.

"Buck, don't be so rough, you'll hurt me!"

"Never!" the tall Texan swore as he scooped her up into his arms. He took a step toward the bed but halted in midstride when someone knocked on her door. "What is it?" he shouted rudely, clearly annoyed by the interruption.

"*El agua, señor,*" replied the porter, "*por la señorita.*"

Lyse took in Buck's startled expression and couldn't resist teasing him. "Oh, my, here's the innocent Señorita Selby with a man in her room," she cooed in a syrupy Southern accent. "I fear, sir, my reputation will surely suffer."

Not even remotely amused, Buck put Lyse down on her feet so quickly she nearly slipped and fell, but he caught her hand to steady her. Then wearing a disgusted sneer, he turned on his heel, marched into his own room, and slammed the door soundly behind him.

Hoping Buck's foul mood would not last long when she was again in high spirits, Lyse was disappointed to find the tub the porter had brought too small to be shared. Knowing Buck would have already tipped the man, she hurried him out of her room and while she bathed and washed her hair she tried to think of some way to restore a smile to her beloved's face.

His words still rang in her ears. Did the miserable way Frank Selby had treated her cause her to misjudge Buck's motives? she pondered. Sadly, she came to the conclusion that it did not, for if Buck truly regarded her as an equal, he would have asked her to marry him by now. Instead, he continued to claim her as a possession while warning her not to question his ownership. The momentary warmth his fiery kisses had brought to her lissome body then cooled faster than the bathwater. When Lyse left the tub, she wrapped herself in a towel and despite the length of her day, she began to pace distractedly at the foot of the bed.

This hotel had none of the elegance of the one in Galveston. The whitewashed walls were bare, the plank floors without coverings, the furnishings plain. The room was clean, though, and the bed linens fresh. The last thing Lyse wanted to do, however, was to go to bed. She wanted to see Buck again, for though she didn't think their argument was entirely Frank Selby's fault, she knew the extreme difference in their backgrounds was bound to cause them problems often. Maybe she had expected too much from him. Perhaps that was their real problem. She had one set of expectations and he had quite another. Because acknowledging that possibility offered a way to apologize without having to admit she was wrong, she decided to use it. Hoping she would be successful and not have to sleep alone, she donned one of the lace-trimmed nightgowns she had gotten at the Rosebud.

Wanting to be as considerate as Buck, she knocked lightly at the connecting door but there was no response. "Oh, come on, Buck," she whispered persuasively. "Don't you be the one to sulk." When the silence in the adjoining room remained unbroken, she tried the knob and slowly pulled the door open.

Buck's room was identical to hers, even down to the small bathtub placed in the center. There were damp towels thrown across the washstand, lather still on his razor, but no sign of Buck Warren. Discouraged to the point of humiliation, Lyse returned to her own room and crawled into bed, but it was nearly dawn before she fell asleep and Buck's room was still empty.

Too disgusted both with himself and Lyse to sleep, Buck made the rounds of the saloons. He wasn't looking for high stakes poker games, strong whiskey, or obliging women as the other patrons were, however. He was looking for Arvin, hoping to find the man and get their inevitable confrontation over quickly so he could concentrate his energies on taming Lyse.

She tried his patience sorely at times, but he couldn't help but feel he had learned a valuable lesson that night. He had discovered she viewed his actions in the same light she had seen her father's and though that was a shame, it was important to know. It took so little to insult the feisty young woman, but considering the abuse she had lived with all her life he thought it was remarkable she had so much personal courage. What she needed was confidence in herself as a woman, though. Try as he might, he couldn't think of any way to give her that if what he had already done had had no effect.

She knew he thought she was pretty. She had to know he considered her wildly exciting in bed. She was bright too, and he'd told her so. What hadn't he told her? What more was there to say or do? Each bawdy hangout he visited revealed no sign of Arvin, but he grew all the more determined that by the time they reached California he would have Lyse figured out, even if he hadn't caught the two-legged snake he was after.

When Buck returned to the hotel, the night clerk was still on duty and called to him. "Señor Warren, the man Señorita Selby asked about, his name is in the paper."

"What?" Buck reached the desk in two long strides and after assuring the clerk he read Spanish fluently, he scanned the article in question. "Do they always list such deaths in the paper?" he asked suspiciously.

"*Sí.* Many Americans have died from yellow fever. There is a record of them all."

"May I keep this?"

"Of course. I am sorry to be the one to give you such bad news," the clerk replied with sincere regret.

"Bad news?" Buck repeated with a deep chuckle. "This is the best news I've received in years!" After giving the helpful clerk a hefty tip, Buck took the stairs two at a time. He sprinted down the hall, dashed through his room, then nearly flew into Lyse's.

"Lyse! Wake up, wait until you see this!" he shouted as he flopped down on the edge of her bed.

Lyse opened one eye, certain she had slept no more than five minutes. "Isn't it awfully early?"

"So what? Look at this!" Buck slapped the paper with the back of his hand as he pushed it toward her. "Arvin's dead. He got yellow fever and died the day before yesterday. Do you believe it? What luck!"

Now fully awake, Lyse sat up and took the paper from him. She pronounced each of the Spanish words softly as she read the headline on the obituary column. Scanning the list of the dead, she found Arvin Corbitt's name near the top. "Arvin Corbitt, Austin, Texas. That sounds like him all right. Now where do we go to see the body?"

"Who cares about his body?" Buck rolled over on his back and making himself comfortable on the extra pillow, propped his hands behind his head. "The bastard's dead, Lyse. Fate caught up with him before I could."

Taking care to roll the newspaper first, Lyse gave her handsome companion a harsh swat on the elbow. "Don't be so quick to gloat. The swine knows you're after him. This could just be a clever trick to throw you off his trail."

That he had considered, then dismissed the possibility so hastily, embarrassed Buck deeply. He wanted Lyse to think him the clever one, not Arvin. Struck by the truth of her words, he sat up slowly, then took the newspaper from her hand and smoothed it out. "You're right. I've been up all night combing the town for him or I'd have been more suspicious of the truth of this announcement too. I'll go right now and find out where the body is."

Lyse licked her lower lip suggestively as she presented what she considered a far better alternative. "It can't even be six o'clock yet, Buck. How are you going to get that information this early? Why don't we wait a couple of hours? Maybe sleep some, have breakfast, then go check up on Arvin. Either the body will be his or it won't, we've no need to rush."

A slow smile lifted the corner of Buck's mouth as he realized she didn't consider him a fool after all. She still wanted him, but he doubted it was as badly as he wanted her. "I'm sorry about last night. You've told me more than once to tell you what I plan to do before I do it and last night's misunderstanding was just another example of what a mess we get into when I forget to confide in you. Will you forgive me? Between my failing to tell you things, and that lively imagination of yours, I can't win."

Though she was delighted he had apologized, Lyse didn't think he should take all the blame. "We were both tired. If you've been up all night, you must be even more tired now, aren't you?"

Buck shook his head slowly. "Whenever I'm with you, the last thing I feel is tired." He reached out to slip his hand around her throat and drew her lips to his for a gentle kiss he deepened when her acceptance of his affection was immediate. This was the problem he realized as he felt her hands moving down the buttons on his shirt. It was times like these, when he felt so close to her, that they ought to talk, but he wanted to savor the taste and feel of her enchanting body far too much to waste time in conversation. If that was a mistake, he didn't see how he could ever avoid it.

A woman with children had to think of the future, Lyse's conscience chided her sternly, but as she relaxed in Buck's arms, the delicate blonde argued that she had no children as yet. What she did have was the undivided attention of the man she adored. His touch was light as he caressed her breast and his teasing kisses tickled as they slid down her throat. She wrapped her arms around him, so lost in the beautiful dreams he created with his affection she didn't want reality to intrude upon them. Not yet, but later, she promised herself to make plans for the future. Not now when the pleasure of the moment was so intense.

Buck made love to Lyse slowly, deliberately delighting her senses, arousing her with lavish kisses that strayed over her creamy, smooth skin in devoted homage to her beauty before he began to delve into the forbidden recesses of her superbly shaped body. He probed the tender passageway to her heart, his tongue playing havoc with her reason until her surrender was complete. Exhalting in that triumph, he brought their bodies together as one, as always tempering his strength with the love that overflowed his heart. He fell asleep snuggled in her arms, never suspecting their passion for each other had created something far more precious than an invisible, emotional bond.

It was nearly noon when Lyse and Buck awakened and they were eager to begin their detective work. They bathed again, dressed, had something to eat, then made their way to the newspaper office. Their inquiries as to the whereabouts of the bodies of yellow fever victims brought astonished stares and an informative reply.

"Fatalities are often buried within the hour, señor. I am afraid your friend's grave might not even be marked."

Not pleased by that news, Buck persisted with his questions. "Where do you get the names you print? Do people just bring them in?"

"Oh, no. Each death must be reported to the *alcalde*, our mayor. The city keeps records of births, deaths, taxes, of everything."

"That's where you get your list of deaths, from the *alcalde*?" Buck asked, recalling the desk clerk had said something about records.

"*Sí*, it is official."

After getting the directions to both city hall and the cemetery, Buck took Lyse's hand, and led her from the newspaper office out onto the street. "We could go searching through the *alcalde*'s records, or we could go on out to the cemetery. Which do you want to do?"

Always practical, Lyse didn't need much time to choose. "I'm not going to be satisfied until I see Arvin's body with my own eyes. Or at least, not until you tell me the body is Arvin's. Let's go out to the cemetery. It's a nice day for a ride."

Because it was so much cooler by the ocean than it had been in the interior, Buck saw no reason not to agree. They found a carriage for hire and in less than an hour were standing at the foot of a fresh grave that bore Arvin's name on a small white cross. The dirt covering the mound had been patted down neatly, but Buck was still unconvinced it held the man he was after.

"I have been meaning to buy you some tools, Lyse. Picks, shovels, all the things you'll need for prospecting. Why don't we take care of that today?"

Lyse looked around to be certain no one stood close enough to overhear her words. Nearby half a dozen men were lowering a coffin into the ground, but she was certain they were too involved in their work to pay them any mind. "When do you plan to do it?" she asked in a hushed whisper.

"Do what?"

"Dig up the coffin! That's why you want the shovel, isn't it?"

"Yes," Buck admitted with a sly wink. "I'll have to wait until dark. Luckily this grave wasn't difficult to find."

"It might not be luck," Lyse warned him as they turned back toward the path. "If some men are dumped in unmarked graves, why did Arvin get such considerate care? He would have been a stranger here. Who could have seen to his funeral arrangements?"

Disturbed by her question, Buck came to an abrupt halt. "The man didn't make friends easily. He was about as likable as Colin O'Roarke. Who do you suppose would have buried him if he died?"

Lyse shrugged. "I've no idea. If travelers frequently die here of fevers, then someone must have that job. I'll tell you what. Why don't you get the tools, and I'll see what I can find out about Arvin's death? Then if we have to, we can come back tonight and see who's buried in this grave."

"No," Buck warned her, his mood now completely serious. "If Arvin did arrange his own burial, or that of some convenient corpse, then we don't dare arouse his suspicions by asking questions. Let's see what's in the coffin before we do any more snooping."

"Good plan," Lyse readily agreed.

"I wish you were always so quick to agree with me."

"Is it my fault that not all of your ideas are that good?"

Buck chuckled, delighted to find her mood so playful. "What do you think of this one?" he asked before whispering an enticing suggestion of how they might spend the time between buying the tools and sunset.

Pretending a modesty she didn't truly possess, Lyse appeared to be shocked, but for only a few seconds before she burst into lighthearted peals of laughter. "Two good ideas in a row! Would you like to try for three?"

"I'll give it my best," Buck promised, thinking their mood totally inappropriate for a cemetery and not caring one bit.

It took some effort to elude Tim and Dr. Ash, but by nine o'clock, Buck and Lyse had returned to the cemetery and retraced their steps to the grave bearing Arvin's name. Finding no guard on duty, Buck had removed his coat and immediately begun to dig. "Stand well back, I don't want to fling any of this dirt on you."

"I'll stay out of your way," Lyse promised. She was holding a lantern aloft, taking care to keep its narrow beam of light focused on the grave. The breeze was coming in off the ocean and though she hadn't thought she would ever feel cold again, she was growing chilled. Buck worked with a steady rhythm, his right shoulder apparently not causing him any pain but it seemed to her as though he was working much too slowly.

"Can't you hurry it up a bit?" she asked as her teeth began to chatter.

"Hang on, I've hit the lid of the coffin. I just need to clear the way of dirt so I can pry open the lid with the pick. Hold the light steady. You make a very poor grave robber, Lyse, your nerves are showing."

"I'm not nervous," the fragile blonde argued, "I'm just cold. Hurry up!"

"Cold? You can't be serious." Sweat was pouring from Buck's brow, but he was working and she wasn't. In another five minutes he had the lid off the pine box he had uncovered, but as he looked inside, he was disappointed to find the body securely enfolded in a white linen shroud.

"Come closer with the light, Lyse. I'm going to have to unwrap the body."

As she stepped closer, Lyse suddenly felt so faint she feared she might topple into the open coffin if she wasn't careful. The lantern was just too heavy to hold any longer and she bent down to set it at Buck's side. He swore as the knots securing the shroud refused to come undone. "Use your knife! The body's not going anywhere!" she advised hoarsely.

Because he couldn't argue with that, Buck pulled his knife from his belt and taking a firm hold on the top of the white linen garment, he hurriedly slit it open. "Oh my God!" he swore as the fabric fell away to reveal the face of a young woman whose badly smeared cosmetics hadn't been removed before her hasty preparation for burial. Clearly she had been attractive, but her long black hair was now matted with the blood that had poured from the deep gash which nearly encircled her throat.

"I'm sorry, I'm going to be sick," Lyse whispered as she turned away.

"Don't apologize, honey, so am I," Buck answered, but when Lyse fainted in a heap at his side, he had no more time to fret over their gruesome discovery. As he drew her into his arms, he found her fair skin hotter than the flame in their lantern. Fearing she had fallen victim to the fever that had claimed so many lives, he let out a horrified shriek that would have terrified even a ghost had there been one hovering nearby.

XVIII

April 1849

W hen Lyse awakened in her bed at the Hotel Americano, Buck was seated by her side. That he had several days' growth of beard amazed her, for she could recall nothing after losing consciousness in the cemetery. "What did you do with the body?" she asked anxiously.

"She is still delirious," Robert Ash announced with a weary sigh, badly disappointed. "She's suffered neither chills nor fever since last night. She ought to be lucid by now. I simply don't know what more to do for her."

"Don't fret so, she is lucid," Buck assured the agitated physician as he took Lyse's hands in his. He leaned close, frowning slightly, his expression earnest as he spoke to her. "You've been very sick. Why you came down with malaria while the rest of us didn't I'll never understand, but you're going to be fine now."

Lyse had been unaware of Robert's presence until she had heard his voice. Looking up, she found Tim peering over the doctor's shoulder. All three men looked exhausted and, sorry to have been such a bother, she hastened to apologize. "Besides getting seasick, I'm never ill. I'm so sorry if you've been worried about me."

"The word 'worried' is a gross understatement, Lyse," Buck replied with a good-natured chuckle. "Agony more closely describes what you've put us through this past week. You were either burning up with fever or shaking with chills.

We had our hands full trying to bring your temperature down, or keep you warm enough. The only hope we had was in knowing that you'd gotten malaria rather than yellow fever. As if malaria weren't bad enough, Robert's afraid you've had a miscarriage. I knew there hadn't been time for you to conceive, but he needs to hear you say it before he'll allow you to get out of that bed."

Stunned by that casual summary of the days she could not recall, Lyse could do no more than stare at Buck in shocked silence. She was not only deeply hurt but also horribly embarrassed that he would discuss such personal details of her health so matter-of-factly in front of the others. He sounded as though he and Robert had been arguing over some trivial question they now expected her to decide. Unable to bear being talked about in such a humiliating fashion, she was overcome with sorrow. Her eyes burning with the threat of tears, she shut them tightly in the vain hope of defeating such a display of weakness.

Despite Buck's tragic news, in her mind's eye Lyse could still see the twins. They looked exactly like him, and each time she had allowed herself to think about the possibility of a child, they had immediately come to life in her imagination. As she thought of them now, the handsome pair were taking turns hiding behind her skirt while they played a hilarious game of tag. They were all having a wonderful time and laughing happily. One of the twins was named David, she knew that now. But what had they called the other boy? At that instant, Buck spoke her name, and at the sound of his voice the vision vanished. How strange, she thought, that the twins were still so real. Would they now be born to another woman rather than her?

"Lyse!" Buck called her name more insistently this time. "You've got to stay awake for a while. You need to eat something to get your strength back and I want you to answer Robert's question."

"Please, I want to talk only with you," Lyse begged as the huge tears she could no longer contain welled up in her eyes and spilled over her lashes. "I need to talk to you, no one else."

Buck frowned impatiently. "I know you're not fond of

doctors, but you're being totally unreasonable now. All I could do was count the days we've been together, but that same count might have meant something far more significant to you. I don't see how you could have been certain, but if you had even the slightest suspicion you were pregnant you would have told me, wouldn't you?"

Had he beaten her with his fists, Buck could not have abused her more cruelly. She had wanted those dear babies and surely this was no way for him to tell her they were dead. Unable to cope with his obstinate refusal to spare her feelings and cease discussing their private lives in front of others, she lost her tenuous hold on her self-control and screamed at him. "Get them out of here!"

Horrified that their presence upset her so badly, Tim grabbed Robert's arm and pulled him toward the door. "My God, Buck, can't you see the answer in her face? Don't you know what you're doing to her?"

Because the three of them had worked together to save her life, Buck's only thought was that Lyse was being incredibly rude to show her gratitude by insisting he throw Robert and Tim out of her room. Such a selfish demand far exceeded his concept of a rational desire for privacy and he wanted no part of it. "Wait a minute, I'll go with you. There's obviously no reason for me to be here either."

When Tim turned back then, wanting to remain with the distraught young woman if he didn't, Buck shoved him out the door. Lyse could hear them arguing out in the hall and was surprised Tim would stand up to Buck when he had to know there was no way he could beat him if their difference of opinion came to blows. Gradually the sound of their angry voices receded as the three men moved toward the stairs, but the despair that engulfed her was unrelenting. Heartbroken that Buck had deserted her when she needed him most, she muffled the sounds of her sobs with her pillow and cried herself to sleep.

That evening Lyse was awakened by a plump woman she dimly recalled as being the hotel's laundress. She found it impossible to focus her eyes on the tray balanced on the edge of the bed. She couldn't tell what the woman had brought, but it didn't matter for the aroma of the hot meal was making her nauseated. The very last thing she wanted to do was eat. She was too weak to chew, let alone swallow. "No, thank you," she murmured softly. "I'm not hungry."

"But Señor Warren said you must eat," the woman scolded crossly as though she were speaking to a naughty child.

Lyse attempted to turn away, but she was so tired her whole body felt as though it were encased in lead and her position shifted only slightly. "Please, go."

"He told me I had to make you eat."

With a great deal of effort, Lyse finally recalled the woman's name; it was Lorena. She had given her some clothes to wash the day after they had arrived. "Did you finish my laundry, Lorena?"

"Sí, but Señor Warren threw it all away. He does not want to see you in such old things."

"Where is he?" Lyse inquired politely, but she was so furious with the man for discarding her garments without her permission she could barely draw the breath to speak.

Lorena shrugged. "I do not know."

"Please go and look for him. Tell him if he wants me to eat, he'll have to come here and feed me himself."

"I do not think Señor Warren will like that, señorita."

Lyse didn't reply. Her mind made up, she stubbornly ignored Lorena until the woman realized she had no choice but to go and fetch Buck Warren. Afraid to go on such an errand herself, she sent one of the porters to find him, but the man had no success and returned to the hotel alone.

After leaving the hotel, Buck wandered down to the bay. The offices of the Pacific Mail were always crowded with men trying to book passage on the company's steamers to San Francisco. He skirted that noisy throng and kept on walking. He had forgotten all about the need to make further travel arrangements when Lyse had fallen ill. Now he knew he should check into them, but he was in no mood that afternoon to battle a hostile crowd for the few places the Pacific Mail would have available.

Both emotionally and physically exhausted, he walked down by the ocean until he came to a deserted bluff that provided not only a magnificent view, but also a quiet place to stretch out for a much needed nap. When he did not awaken until after dawn, he was disgusted with himself for being away so long and hurried back to the Hotel Americano hoping to find Lyse in a far better mood than he had left her.

Seated on the front porch, Tim recognized Buck from his distinctive height when he was still a block away and ran to meet him. "Where in God's name have you been? We've had people combing the town for you since last night. Lyse won't eat. She won't allow anyone in her room. She just keeps asking for you."

"Charming creature, isn't she?" Buck wasn't at all pleased to hear the high-strung young woman had continued being so uncooperative. "It's early yet. Give me a chance to clean up and then I'll take her some breakfast."

Tim fell in beside Buck as they returned to the hotel, but they reached the porch before he had gathered the courage to speak his mind. "The shameful way you've treated Lyse simply can't continue. I would be proud to have her as my wife. If you've no intention of asking her to marry you, then I will."

Tim's startling announcement was so touchingly sincere, Buck dared not laugh although he was sorely tempted to do just that. "Lyse takes a great deal of pride in being her own woman. There's no point in your proposing to her because she'd just turn you down flat. Save yourself that embarrassment because I know from my own experience that it's a real blow to a man's pride."

"You mean she's refused to marry you? It's not the other way around?"

"Why would I refuse to marry her?" Buck asked, rather than give him a straight answer to his question.

Tim gestured helplessly. "Well, I just thought, that, well, that if you wanted her you two would already be married."

Discussing Lyse and marriage in the same breath was not something Buck was willing to do. As politely as possible, he excused himself from the befuddled Tim and went upstairs to his room. He bathed and dressed quickly, then decided not to shave off his beard. He liked it, even if he doubted Lyse did. He went downstairs to the kitchen and when the cooks had prepared a breakfast he thought the lovely invalid would enjoy, he carried it up to her room.

After one look at the delicate blonde's swollen eyes, Buck was filled with remorse for having neglected her. He'd be damned if he'd apologize, though, because he still thought she was the one lacking manners. "I had no idea you'd be so miserable without me, Lyse, but it's plain that you were. Now let's have something to eat, and then we can spend the whole day talking if you like."

The man looked well rested, his smile was warm, but his teasing tone failed to lift Lyse's spirits. "I still don't feel like eating," she whispered softly.

"I was afraid of that so I brought tea rather than hot chocolate, and if fruit doesn't sound appetizing, just try one of the rolls. They're quite good, not so wonderfully light and flaky as your biscuits, but passable." Buck sat down on the edge of the bed and placed the tray between them. He smiled at her again, but she didn't make an effort to return the gesture. She looked so utterly forlorn she suddenly reminded him of Constance and he was appalled by that unexpected similarity.

"Look, let's just start over as though yesterday never happened. You weren't feeling well and I was so tired I wasn't thinking clearly." He paused to pour her a cup of tea and stirred in two teaspoons of sugar. As soon as she had taken a few tentative sips, he continued. "You asked about the body. Tim and Ash don't know anything about Arvin, so I couldn't answer your question in front of them.

"I left that poor woman right where we'd found her. Cemetery workers discovered the open grave the next morning and the authorities immediately began a murder investigation. The victim was a prostitute by the name of Dolores Rojas. It's fairly obvious how she met Arvin, but no one has any clues as to why he killed her, or to his whereabouts. The man apparently forged his own death certificate, had Dolores buried in his place, then disappeared. My guess is that he was on a steamer bound for San Francisco before we reached Panama, but I can't prove it. After the problems I had with the sheriff in Galveston, I'm not about to go to the authorities here with what I know."

Lyse nodded thoughtfully. "Yes, I think that's wise." After replacing her teacup on the tray, she took one of the rolls and broke off a small piece. "If only I hadn't gotten sick. Now Arvin's gotten another head start."

"So what? His plan didn't work. Not only do I know he's alive, but also I know he's wanted for Dolores's murder. The cards are all in my hands."

Though she didn't share that optimistic view, Lyse didn't want to argue. She washed down a small lump of roll with tea, then broke off another. "Have you made plans to leave here yet?" she asked without looking up.

"No. I want to make certain you're completely well before we leave. There's a danger of a relapse with malaria, and if you did lose a child, then you'll need an even more extended rest. I know you're in a hurry to reach California, but I'll not risk your life to get you there."

When Lyse appeared to be more interested in plucking apart her roll than the subject of their conversation, Buck knew something was very wrong. She had always been quiet, but today she was unnaturally so. "We're alone now, Lyse. What did you want to say to me yesterday?"

"May I have more tea, please?" Lyse asked in a feeble effort to stall for time. "I don't think I can lift the pot."

"Of course." Buck refilled her cup, added sugar, then replenished his own. "Tell me, Lyse," he coaxed, his deep voice filled with sympathetic concern. "What did you want to say?"

Lyse felt the very same near paralyzing embarrassment that had plagued her at their last meeting. Why was he determined to wrench a confidence from her lips that she couldn't possibly reveal? Barely able to catch her breath, she finally found the courage to voice one of her concerns, even if not the major one. "I don't want you sharing our secrets with Tim and Dr. Ash. It's none of their business."

Though he could readily tell from her consistently averted glance that he was upsetting her again, Buck couldn't understand why. "Talking about your health with a doctor is scarcely inappropriate, Lyse. As for Tim, the man's madly in love with you. When it comes to secrets, I don't think we have any those two aren't perfectly aware of without my putting them into words."

Because that was not the answer she wanted to hear, Lyse sighed unhappily. She took several sips of tea, then wiped her mouth on her napkin. "I can't eat anything more. I don't feel well."

Lyse was too pale for Buck to doubt her word and he got up and moved the tray to the dresser. When he returned to the bed, he sat down close and after gently slipping his arms around her waist he drew her into a tender embrace. Cradling her head on his shoulder, he patted her back with a soothing rhythm. "You can't possibly know how badly I've missed you. I can't wait for you to be well again. I want to see that pretty smile of yours, and hear your laugh. I want things to be the way they were between us."

As she relaxed against him, Lyse could not help but think things would never really be the same. She loved him as much as ever, but her heart now held a heavy burden of grief for the children she would never have. Content to be held forever, she was nearly asleep when he spoke again.

Convinced he would never get the answer he was seeking from her, Buck took a new tack. "We'll just take no chances and keep you in bed until you've got so much energy you can't stand another minute of rest. You've got to promise me something, though."

Though his tone was still warmly reassuring, Lyse's apprehension returned instantly, making her suspicious of his motives. "What's that?"

"Don't leave me out the next time you think we're going to be parents, Lyse. I have every right to know about it just as soon as you do."

Puzzled, because she could see no good reason why, Lyse leaned back against her pillows so she could face him as they talked. "Why? What possible difference would it make?"

"What difference?" he asked incredulously. Her glance was not without its former sorrow, but he also recognized a sparkle of curiosity he considered a good sign even if her question had been preposterous. She was finally facing him squarely too, and he was encouraged by that. "You're actually serious, aren't you?" Though that sorry fact was difficult to grasp, Buck gave it a try. "All right, you tell me. What do you think I'd do if you told me I was going to be a father? Do you think I'd be angry, or that I'd beat you? Or maybe you think I'd just walk out on you since you jumped to that conclusion so quickly in Galveston. Come on, out with it. Just what was is it you think you can expect from me?"

Lyse began to twist her hands nervously, but Buck reached out to take them in a firm clasp. He had backed her into a corner and she didn't like the uncomfortable sensation of being trapped one bit. "I know you'd never hurt me, Buck. You're not mean, or cruel. I know you would provide for your children," she admitted hesitantly, obviously choosing her words with care so as not to insult him.

She was only seventeen. Buck reminded himself of that fact repeatedly and it actually helped him maintain a slim hold on his temper. She was so incredibly beautiful, but she was a dear waif who had raised herself. She had so little idea of what a home should be it was no wonder she hadn't realized he would want to give her one. He leaned forward to kiss her, and when he felt her lips tremble under the pressure of his it broke his heart.

"I think we ought to get married, Lyse. Just as soon as you feel up to it."

Hardly able to believe she had heard him correctly, Lyse held her breath, waiting for the words of love she had longed to hear, but Buck seemed to think his suggestion a practical one that required no sweet words of flattery to gain her consent. Deeply disappointed, she gave him the only answer her pride allowed. "If you really wanted me to be your wife you would have asked me a long time ago. There's no reason for you to be so generous now."

"Generosity has nothing to do with it!" Buck exclaimed as he released her hands, then getting a firm hold on himself, he rose to his feet and apologized. "I'm sorry. I didn't mean to yell at you, but I've always planned to ask you to marry me. I was just waiting until you'd gotten that fool notion of prospecting for gold out of your head so you wouldn't turn me down."

"What?" Lyse knew she couldn't believe her ears now. How could he have wanted her for his wife and never once mentioned it to her? What kind of poppycock was that? "How many times did you sleep with Constance before you proposed to her?"

Astonished Lyse would bring up Constance's name, Buck answered her question without realizing the effect his words would have. "I never slept with her. Not once. But so what, she's got nothing to do with us."

"She's got everything to do with us, you dolt!" Lyse sat forward, wishing he were still seated close enough to slap. "You asked her to marry you and you never asked me!"

Now Buck readily grasped her point and though her accusation was correct, he had to try and defend himself. He hadn't stolen her innocence to take advantage of her affection for him. He had never used her. He adored her, but he could also understand how his actions could appear near criminal to her. He was happy to talk about Constance then, overjoyed in fact. "Look, I told you David and I both liked her. Courting her was sort of a game to us. I was far more interested in winning that competition with him than I was in actually marrying her."

"Oh, really? What would you have done if she had accepted your proposal? Would you have backed out of the engagement, or would you have gone ahead and married her?"

Buck put his hands on his hips, his pose conveying the frustrated rage of his mood as readily as his deep scowl. "She was in love with David, Lyse. She would never have said yes to me, so there's no point in my answering that question."

Lyse was stymied for only a moment, then she leaned back and folded her arms across her chest. "You would have gone through with it, wouldn't you? Constance would have been a trophy rather than a wife. Did David feel the same way too, or did he actually love her?"

"How should I know? That's not the kind of thing one man would admit to another."

"What isn't? That he loved her, or that he didn't?" Lyse shot right back at him.

"Stop it right now!" Buck shouted, no longer able to tolerate her insightful inquisition. "This argument is stupid and it's not getting us anywhere I want to go." He turned away from the bed, took several paces in an attempt to clear his head, then came back to her side. "Constance is a dead issue. I don't want you to mention her name to me ever again. I wish to hell I had never told you about her in the first place, since she's caused nothing but trouble between us. All we need to talk about is you and me."

"All right," Lyse agreed, but her temper was no more under control than his and she couldn't leave her bed to walk it off. "How dare you call my interest in prospecting for gold a 'foolish notion'? I have the same right to live my life the way I choose as you do. I've never once called you daft for trying to track down Arvin. Why is what you want to do fine, and what I want to do a 'foolish notion'?"

That was another question Buck saw no way to answer tactfully and he cursed his own bad luck that she had asked it. "All right, I'm sorry. I shouldn't have put it that way. What I meant was, I wanted you to be more interested in marrying me than in prospecting for gold. If that sounds selfish, well maybe I am. I'd like to have a wife who'd rather be with me than standing out in some river panning for gold."

"Well you certainly have a peculiar way of going about creating that kind of devotion," Lyse pointed out snidely.

Buck opened his mouth to reply, but before he could speak they were interrupted by a loud knock at the door. "Wait, this is my room," Lyse warned him in a frantic whisper. "Yes, what is it?" she called out sweetly.

"La policía, señorita. I need to ask you about the murder of Dolores Rojas."

Lyse pointed to the window as she mouthed the words, "Get out of here!"

Buck stared at her for a moment, then considering the way his luck was running, he leaned down and kissed her soundly. "I'll keep in touch," he promised, and with a sly wink he was out the window and gone.

"Come in please," Lyse invited when she was certain Buck had had sufficient time to scramble down off the roof overhanging the porch and reach the street. She lay back upon her pillows and knowing she must look ghastly, she decided to play the part of an invalid to the hilt.

Salvador Lopez stepped across the threshold, and finding Lyse alone and in bed, he left the door wide open. "Señorita Selby, forgive this intrusion. I was sorry to learn you have been ill."

"Oh, I have been much worse than ill and even now my physician fears I may suffer a relapse, señor. I don't believe you told me your name," she added weakly.

"I am Salvador Lopez, chief of police."

"How do you do?" Lyse extended her hand limply and tried to hide her astonishment when the man placed a sloppy kiss upon her wrist. When he released her hand, she wiped away the last traces of his overly affectionate greeting on her blanket. He was a heavyset man, not unattractive, but old enough to be her father so she did not think his gesture appropriate.

"I could not possibly have heard you correctly. Did you say something about a murder?" Lyse appeared to listen with rapt interest as Lopez related the few clues they had in the Rojas case. "Forgive me, but I simply do not understand why you have come to see me."

"An attractive couple was seen visiting the grave where her body was found. Could it have been you and Señor Warren?"

"We didn't know the woman. Why would we have visited her grave?" Lyse replied, accenting her response with a loud sigh, hoping she looked even more pathetic than she felt.

"The name on the grave was Arvin Corbett. Did you know him?" Lopez continued, not realizing Lyse had not answered his first question.

"I've never met the man," Lyse responded with a faint smile. "But I thought you just told me a woman had been murdered."

Lopez began again, struggling to explain the baffling case in English but each time he paused, he found Alyssa Selby more confused until finally he was convinced she had no information on the case whatsoever. "Forgive me for bothering you, señorita. I hope you will be better soon. I do not want you to have unpleasant memories of Panama."

"Thank you." Lyse covered a wide yawn with her hand. "I'm sorry I couldn't be of some help."

"I will keep looking, but it is plain you and Señor Warren were not the couple I am seeking."

"Good luck," Lyse wished him as he left, but she didn't take a deep breath until she was certain he wouldn't return, for his visit had frightened her badly. "Damn it all!" she swore to herself. They were going to have to leave Panama immediately, and when Buck came back to her room she told him so.

"I can keep the police at bay, Lyse. Don't worry about them. My only concern is seeing that you get well."

"I can rest in a cabin on a ship just as easily as I can rest here."

"That's probably true, but it isn't all that easy to book first-class passage on a ship from here. The Pacific Mail Line runs three steamers up and down the coast, but none is expected in soon. They have been taking on almost twice the number of passengers they were designed to carry and while that might be tolerable accommodations for a man, they won't do for you. The schooners are even worse. I've heard they have put tiers of bunks in their holds so they can wedge nine men in six feet of space."

Raised on the Texas plain, Lyse couldn't even imagine such close quarters. "What about your friend, Marc Aragon? Where is he when we need him?"

Buck couldn't help but smile, for they were plotting again, working as a team without any of the tension that had filled their earlier meeting that day. "That's a good question," he agreed. "If the Aragons are sending ships through the Caribbean to the Chagres River, they must be running others to pick up passengers here on the Pacific coast."

"Do they have a harbor master here? Or perhaps an agent for their company?"

"I'll go and see." Eager to run the errand, Buck was still reluctant to leave her alone again. "I just ducked around the corner, Lyse. If the police had given you any trouble, I would have been back here in a minute."

"I know that."

"Do you?" Buck had taken care to make the suggestion they marry, rather than to offer a proposal she could refuse. She hadn't really refused him either. She'd merely criticized his timing and he had to agree he would have spoken his thoughts aloud a lot sooner.

"I never meant to insult you, sweetheart," he began as he took her hand in his. "Even if I had had the sense to ask you in Galveston, there was no time for us to get married. You didn't like Captain Randolph, so I couldn't have asked him to perform a ceremony for us. We've had no chance to get married here in Panama either."

Though Lyse thought he was being far more practical than romantic, she didn't criticize him for it. "Find us a ship, Buck. Then we can argue about getting married on the way to California." When his grin took on a wicked gleam, she had to laugh. "Go on, get out of here." He leaned down to kiss her and this time she lifted her hand to his nape, her response filled with the love she still dared not confess. Maybe she was being a fool to want Buck to fall in love with her before they got married. Wasn't it possible that he could learn to love her after they became man and wife? That intriguing thought kept a smile on her face the whole time he was gone.

XIX

May 1849

*M*ore than two weeks passed before the afternoon a ship bearing the red and gold flag of the Aragon line docked in Panama, but rather than a steamer it was a splendid China Clipper. Christened the *Angelique*, it was a sister ship to the *Spanish Dancer*. Her captain was Marc Aragon and when he saw Buck Warren standing on the dock with his arm around a striking blonde's narrow waist, he waved enthusiastically and welcomed them aboard.

"You are the very last man I would ever expect to find stranded here in Panama. It's indeed fortunate you have so charming a companion with whom to pass the time." As they were introduced, Marc's admiring gaze swept slowly over Lyse's slender figure. He was delighted by the fullness that stretched the bodice of her pale blue silk gown taut, outlining her ample curves nearly as erotically as his imagination did. Though he found something to like about every pretty girl he met, willowy blondes were his favorites. Slender women with lush curves fascinated him completely and his appreciation of Lyse's beauty lit his sky blue eyes with a predatory gleam.

Lyse had thought a man with a Spanish surname would be dark like Buck and she was surprised to find that though Marc Aragon was nearly his equal in height, he resembled him not at all in coloring. He had light brown hair and eyes nearly as bright a blue as her own. His skin was deeply tanned, and his features more ruggedly hewn than Buck's but he was also a remarkably handsome man. Unfortunately, the longer the three of them talked the more convinced she became that he was overly aware of that fact. He wore the same well-tailored and elaborately trimmed navy blue uniform as Gregory Randolph had, but with far more flair. He exuded charm from every pore, but his gracious nature struck her immediately as being pretentious rather than sincere. When Marc took her arm as they started for his cabin, she was disappointed that Buck allowed it for she found his possessive touch no more pleasant than his overly familiar gaze and ingratiating manner.

"Alyssa Selby," the name rolled off the debonair captain's tongue like the refrain of a favorite song. "You must be an English girl. My mother is also an attractive blonde, but she is French. My father loves her so dearly this is the third ship he has named the *Angelique* in her honor. Would you like to have a ship named after you? I can arrange it," he promised as his glance focused on the inviting rose sheen of Lyse's immensely kissable lips.

Astonished by such a grandiose offer when they had just met, Lyse glanced over her shoulder at Buck, and found him struggling valiantly against the impulse to laugh out loud at his friend's outrageous flattery. She frowned angrily, certain he could see she was annoyed, but apparently he considered the discomfort Marc was causing her amusing. She was thoroughly disgusted Marc Aragon would flirt with her so openly. Why hadn't Buck told him to stop? Wasn't he in the least bit jealous of his friend's intentions where she was concerned? Turning back to Marc, Lyse eyed him coldly, primed to put him in his place herself because Buck hadn't handled that chore.

"I think you would be smart to save such flattering tributes for women you have some compelling need to impress. All Buck and I are interested in is getting to the gold fields as quickly as possible. Now how soon can you set sail?"

Buck did laugh then, and he was still chuckling when Marc ushered them into his cabin. "I'm sorry, Marc. Maybe I should have warned you, but Lyse is determined to make herself a fortune so she's got no time to waste trading com-

pliments. Since I'm as eager to leave Panama as she is, we'd
regard more than a few days' delay as a real hardship."

Shocked that the superlative technique he had perfected
on scores of beautiful women had had absolutely no effect
on Lyse, other than to offend her, Marc sat back in his chair
and regarded his guests with a skeptically raised brow. Deciding a change of tactic was definitely needed, he grew
serious. "I owe my crew a few days' shore leave, but leaving Panama in a timely fashion is no trick at all. It's leaving
San Francisco that's become the problem. The harbor is so
jammed with abandoned ships there's scarcely room for us
to dock. The only way I could get a crew for this voyage
was to affix a zero to the amount of each man's pay so the
lure of quick riches wasn't irresistible. But a woman? Can't
say I've heard of many women going out to the diggings
unless they planned to earn their fortune in another way." He
winked at Buck then, as though they were sharing a hilarious
private joke.

"I don't plan to work the gold fields on my back, Captain," Lyse was quick to deny, deeply insulted he obviously
thought her too dense to understand his meaning. As far as
she was concerned, he and Buck could talk all night if they
wished, but she wanted to take care of the business that had
brought them there and return to the hotel. "Your agent here
said there were always a few cabins you didn't allow him to
book in advance. Can you let us have two? We've the money
to purchase them with us."

Marc was taken aback not only by Lyse's crudely worded
response to his suggestive innuendo but also by her high-
handed demand for cabins. Because he was a man who relished a challenge, he tried another dazzling smile on her in
hopes of melting the arctic chill from her piercing glance.
"Forgive me if I offended you, Miss Selby, it was completely unintentional. I spend my time almost exclusively
with male companions and I failed to consider your feelings
just now. That was very thoughtless of me. I'm honored that
you want to travel on the *Angelique*. I can promise you and
Buck two of the finest first-class cabins."

"Good," Lyse responded without accepting his apology or
showing a trace of the smile he'd hoped to see. "Buck and I

will share one, the other is for the doctor and accountant who are traveling with us."

His mouth agape, Marc looked to Buck for an explanation. He'd been surprised to find his friend traveling with a lovely young woman, but that she would flaunt the intimacy of their relationship stunned him. And who were these other men? "Forgive me if I seem too curious, but it's one thing to hope to strike it rich, quite another to already have a personal physician and accountant on your payroll. Aren't you being overly ambitious?"

Buck glanced at Lyse, thinking the proud set of her chin delightful. She was far too levelheaded a young woman to be impressed by Marc Aragon's wealth and flamboyant charm and he was tempted to reach out and clap her on the back for having such good sense. "They're our friends, not employees. They've proven their worth several times over, so we won't sail without them."

Though he had yet to recover from the shocking fact that Lyse had quite proudly admitted to being Buck's mistress, Marc nodded agreeably, but he was bent on paying back the haughty blonde for her rudeness. "Fine, I'll put two double cabins at your disposal. Utilize them in any way you like. There will be no charge, but I'll expect ten percent of your winnings at cards." His smile was mocking them, lighting his eyes with a mirthless sparkle as he waited for Buck to respond to that stipulation.

A keenly observant man, Buck had never expected Lyse and Marc to hit it off so poorly. His friend was a proud man, and clearly he felt he had been insulted, though Lyse's reaction to Marc's abundant charm had been the violently negative one he cursed himself for not having been smart enough to foresee. In such an unfortunate situation, retreat seemed the wisest course, and he tried to effect one immediately.

"The Pacific Mail is getting two hundred dollars for first-class passage. You can't ask for more than that since you can't guarantee the wind the way they can the steam. On a good night I can win two thousand dollars easy. You'd have your fare in two nights, and I'd be handing money over to you for another month. Keep your free cabins, they're much too expensive."

Marc shrugged. "If that's the way you feel, then you should book passage on a steamer."

"Maybe we will." Buck rose to his feet, and reached out to take Lyse's hand. He would come back later and talk with Marc, when Lyse wasn't there to complicate the situation unnecessarily.

"Of course, we might be able to make another deal," Marc offered in a tone sly enough to pique Buck's interest.

Just as Marc had anticipated, Buck hesitated beside Lyse's chair. "Such as?" he asked with a casual disregard for the unfortunate direction their conversation had taken.

"Let's say you have something I want," Marc began as he traced Lyse's delicate features with a slow, smoldering glance. Alyssa Selby obviously regarded him with contempt, so he decided to give her a dose of her own medicine. "You said you could pay the fares with two nights' winnings. Two nights sounds fair enough to me, but it's not money I want now."

Before Buck could reply, Lyse leapt from her chair. "Give me your knife," she demanded boldly as she reached out her hand.

"Surely you don't need my knife," Buck chided her softly, knowing Marc's injured pride had goaded him into offering a very foolish bargain.

"Oh yes I do!" the feisty blonde insisted. "I'm going to slit this obnoxious dandy's throat myself rather than threaten to have you do it this time!"

Though Buck thought that outburst highly amusing, Marc saw no humor in it whatsoever. "Have you actually slit someone's throat over this, this—" he was so shaken he could not think of a suitably insulting term to describe her.

Incensed that Buck had not defended her honor himself, Lyse moved toward the door rather than bear another second of Marc's disgusting company. "You, sir, are one of the most vile individuals it has ever been my misfortune to meet. I will swim to California before I will sail in your ship. God help your poor mother if your father is anything like you!"

Buck paused long enough to give his friend a comforting pat on the shoulder before he followed the irate blonde up on deck. "Isn't she adorable? I'll come back alone so we can talk."

Marc stared after Buck, certain now he had never really known him if he could have misjudged his taste in women so completely. Alyssa Selby had an enchanting beauty, but she had the manners of a trollop and he didn't care what Buck said when he returned, he didn't want her on his ship any more than she wanted to be there.

Buck caught up with Lyse before she reached the gangplank and took her elbow in a protective grasp. "I had no idea Marc could be such an overbearing ass. I'll take you back to the Americano, then I'll talk some sense into him."

Lyse yanked her arm from Buck's, every bit as furious with him as she was with Marc Aragon. "How dare you let that swine fawn all over me like that? You might have thought it was funny, but I sure didn't. Then he had the audacity to suggest I sleep with him! And you, you just stood there!"

Before he replied, Buck slipped his arm around her waist and pressed her close to his side so she couldn't escape him as they walked along. "When I met Marc, we were in the middle of a war. I had no idea he'd nearly drool on you the way he did. If it struck me as amusing, it was only because I knew you'd despise him for it. As for my reaction, had this been the first time I'd met Marc too, I would have been twice as offended as you. I might very well have killed him."

They had crossed the dock and reached a street crowded with passersby, but Lyse came to an abrupt halt and turned toward Buck. If he had worn a self-satisfied smirk she would have slapped him clear into the middle of next week. What she saw, however, was so serious and determined an expression she didn't doubt the truth of his words for an instant.

"You really would kill a man for insulting me, wouldn't you?" she inquired in an awestruck whisper.

"Yes, ma'am, I would and I thought you knew it too. I forgave Marc for overstepping his bounds because I know him and I can straighten him out in a matter of minutes. I wouldn't be nearly so understanding with a stranger."

Ashamed she hadn't understood the reason for his relaxed

attitude, Lyse looked out over the calm waters of the Pacific as she wondered aloud, "Which of us made the bigger fool of himself, Buck? Marc or me?"

Unmindful of the people walking by, Buck pulled Lyse into a comforting hug. "If Marc had looked at you any closer, he could have taken your measurements more accurately than Rose Reynoso did. I can't blame him for admiring you, but he went much too far and I'll see that it doesn't happen again. There's no reason for you to be embarrassed. You're a high-spirited young woman and I wouldn't have had you act in any other way. I'm sorry if I let you down by not speaking up before you did."

Conscious of the many curious stares they were receiving, Lyse quickly stepped out of Buck's arms. "I can find the hotel alone. Why don't you go back and talk to Marc before he gives someone else our cabins?"

Taking her hand, Buck continued on their way. "No, I will give you a proper escort. I can't have you cutting throats willy-nilly every time you go out for a stroll."

"I wouldn't really have cut Marc's throat," Lyse argued persuasively. "I just wanted to discourage him a little and I couldn't think of anything else to say."

"You could have pointed out you were engaged to me and so his advances were most improper." Buck was disappointed by the frown that furrowed Lyse's brow at that suggestion. Though he had gone out to play poker in the evenings, he had spent each day of her convalescence with her. Although he knew it was much too soon to resume making love, he had slept in her bed every night. He had still wanted to be near her, to hold her in his arms while she slept. He had enjoyed the closeness they had shared the last two weeks, but Lyse hadn't once brought up the subject of marriage and now that he had, her negative reaction had made him instantly regret it.

Depressed by her sullen expression, he was relieved when they reached the front steps of their hotel. "Go on up to your room, I won't be long."

"Wait a minute," Lyse called to him as he turned away. "I shouldn't have lost my temper with you, or Marc, and I hope you'll tell him I'm sorry. I'm just not used to men flirting with me and I guess I took it the wrong way. Stay and have supper with him if you like. I won't get lonely. I'm awfully tired and I think I better go to bed early."

Alarmed, Buck again took her hand. "If you aren't well I won't leave, Lyse. I can send a note to Marc with Tim. His opinion of us isn't nearly so important as your health." She had been up and about for just a few days, and Buck was certain if she had become overtired it was his fault.

Lyse reached up to kiss his cheek lightly. "I'm just tired, Buck, not at death's door. Now go on, have a good time with your friend, and I'll talk with you in the morning."

"You're sure?"

"Very sure." Lyse hesitated a moment, then made a far more serious request. "I want you to have a good time, but please don't tell Marc anything about me."

Buck found her fearful expression deeply troubling because it was such clear evidence of how little she trusted him. "I would not try and amuse him at your expense, Lyse. Your secrets, our secrets, will stay with me."

The stern set of his jaw made his mood so plain Lyse cringed unhappily. "I've offended you again, haven't I?"

After considerable effort, Buck found a reply that wouldn't offend her. "No, I want you to tell me when something's bothering you. Now you know I won't reveal anything that would embarrass you so you won't be worrying the whole time I'm gone. You'll be happy and that will make me happy too."

"Thank you," Lyse said shyly, hoping it would be enough. As Buck walked away, she stayed on the porch and waved each time he turned back to wave at her. It was a good thing one of them had such a cool head, she thought, scolding herself for having behaved so badly on board the *Angelique*. She was definitely going to have to ask Buck to teach her how a lady rebuffs a man's unwanted advances short of slitting his throat. The thought of making that request made her laugh. Despite the fatigue the trying afternoon had caused, she had to take herself firmly in hand in order to walk up the stairs at a sedate pace rather than leaping them two at a time.

* * *

When Buck returned to the *Angelique*, he found Marc on deck in his shirtsleeves. He was conferring with his first mate and when he finished their exchange he motioned Buck to come forward.

Eager to make amends for the scene for which he felt at least partly to blame, Buck shook his friend's hand with a hardy grip. "Had I known you fancied yourself a ladies' man, I would have come alone earlier today and saved us both a great deal of embarrassment."

Still in a black mood, Marc returned Buck's friendly greeting with a derisive snort. "Where did you find that golden-haired witch? She has the face of a Madonna and the tongue of a demon!"

Taking no offense because he considered that description quite apt, Buck followed Marc over to the rail, leaned back against it, and folded his arms across his chest. "How we met is actually an exciting story, but Lyse just made me promise not to talk about her, so I won't. Let me just say that she has good reason to be distrustful of men and ask you to be more patient with her. Since I hope to marry her soon, I would appreciate it if you treated her respectfully, as though she were already my wife rather than as a woman you hoped to win for yourself."

"You can't be serious about marrying her," Marc scoffed. "She'll make your life hell if what I saw was a fair sample of her moods."

"It wasn't, but I didn't come here to debate my choice of bride. I want to pay you the going rate for two first-class cabins and then buy you supper. What Lyse creates of my life is our business, not yours. You needn't concern yourself about us because, while I know you will find it difficult to believe, we are remarkably well suited to each other."

Marc frowned impatiently, unable to accept Buck's words as true. They had been good friends once, and he considered himself a friend still. "If I saw you walking off a cliff I'd try and stop you. A hot-tempered mistress might be exciting as hell, but a wife who's so high-strung will only make your life miserable."

"What you don't understand," Buck revealed confidently, "is that I know how to handle Lyse, and you don't. That's why she'll make the perfect bride for me and no more than a passing acquaintance for you." Buck began to chuckle then as he recalled how violently the two had clashed. "Just what do you do when young women say they would love to have a ship named after them?"

Embarrassed by how poorly that offer had been received, Marc needed a full minute to compose himself before he replied. "That was no more than the effusive flattery a man usually gives a beautiful woman. I never dreamed she would take me seriously."

"Well, since Lyse has never been courted with such abundant, if complimentary lies, if you're incapable of speaking anything else, then the less you two see of each other the better. She's just gotten over a bout of malaria. Dr. Ash will probably insist she spend most of her time in our cabin, so your paths will seldom cross."

"While I'm sorry to hear she's been ill, I still don't think she has any excuse for being so hostile or defensive."

"You'll have to trust me when I say she most definitely has good reasons for being the way she is," Buck insisted forcefully. "I'll keep her out of your way, though. She won't spoil the voyage."

"You two won't expect to share my table at night?"

"Only if we are invited."

Deciding to trust in his friend's word, if not his judgment in women, Marc reluctantly agreed. "All right. She is a beauty, so I know I'll enjoy looking at her, but you can't expect me to converse with her with any wit when she slings barbs with such deadly aim."

"I don't want you to even try. She's my woman, Marc, and if you forget that fact and start flirting with her again as you did today, I won't hesitate to remind you."

Buck's intentions were so clear, Marc couldn't miss the deadly gleam in his eyes. "With the tip of your blade at my throat, no doubt?"

"Precisely."

As the two men regarded each other silently, Marc swiftly came to the conclusion they would be an even match in any contest. Both were strong, quick, and bright. A fight between them could easily leave one or both of them maimed, if not dead. He hoped neither of them was fool enough to take such a risk. Straightening up, he broke into a wide grin. "I'm sorry. I thought Lyse would enjoy a little lighthearted flirting since most pretty women do. Since it's so plain that she doesn't, I'll be the perfect gentleman with her from now on. Just as I do in most ports, I have a woman here who keeps me more than amused, so you needn't worry I'll try and steal the affections of your intended."

"Good. I'm glad to see you've come to your senses so quickly. If you'd rather skip supper to be with your lady friend—"

"No," Marc interrupted. "Dolores won't expect to see me before midnight. There's plenty of time for us to get something to eat and drink and maybe play a few hands of cards."

"Dolores?" Buck asked with the sinking suspicion he knew the woman, although the name was a common one. "You don't mean Dolores Rojas, do you?"

Completely forgetting why he had come to the conclusion that he didn't want an argument between them to ever come to blows, Marc gave Buck's shoulder a hostile shove. "So help me God, Buck, if you're sleeping with Dolores and your little blonde too, it's coming to an end tonight!"

With the speed of a striking rattler, Buck grabbed Marc's wrist and twisted his arm up behind his back. "Now who's the one with the hot temper?" he asked caustically. Because this was Marc's ship, and he could expect the men working on deck to come to their captain's rescue, Buck released him almost immediately, but his point was already made. He was ready to back up everything he said with his fists and Marc had to know that for certain now.

"Just listen to me for a minute," Buck demanded in a threatening whisper. "Dolores Rojas is dead. It seems you and I have a lot more to talk over at supper than I thought. Now come on, let's go get something to drink and I'll tell you what happened."

Stunned by the news of the death of the vibrant brunette who had always made Panama one of his favorite ports, Marc took a moment to grab his coat and hat from the heap of rope where he had tossed them, but then he dashed after Buck, eager to hear his tale. He steered him into the closest cantina and bought a bottle of whiskey for himself while Buck ordered ale. The place was crowded not only with American and South American sailors, but also with men from Europe and Asia. A dozen different languages floated on the smoky air, but Marc was paying such close attention he would have heard Buck easily even if he had continued to speak in a whisper.

Thoroughly sickened to learn he and Lyse had been tracking Arvin only to discover Dolores's body, Marc shuddered at what the murdered prostitute must have suffered. He downed three shots of whiskey in rapid succession before he began to talk about her. "She was such an innocent girl. Oh, I know that must sound absurd, but she really did have a childlike sweetness about her which never wavered.

"It made no difference how much money I gave her. She'd spend it all the very next day. She'd buy a new dress for herself, then gifts for her friends, or toys for the little children in the neighborhood. If she saw a beggar on the street, she'd give him whatever money she had left. I thought perhaps she would become more practical in time, but now she'll not have that chance."

"That she was so unselfish a person makes her death all the more senseless," Buck offered sympathetically.

"Yes, it does." Marc caught the barmaid's eye to get another tankard of ale for Buck before he poured himself another whiskey. "Why would he have killed her? That's what I can't understand. They can't have had an argument because she would have done anything he asked. It's no wonder the chief of police wants to solve her murder. I'll wager he knew Dolores well too. I'm sure every man in Panama did."

"I knew you wouldn't remember Arvin, although he traveled down to Mexico on your ship with the rest of us. He's a difficult man to describe since his looks are so damn ordinary, but it's his personality that makes him remarkable. He has absolutely no character; that he let my whole company walk into an ambush in the hopes I'd be killed proves that. Rather than face me like a man, when he discovered I intended to make him pay for his treachery, he shot me in the back. In Galveston, he might have killed another man had

John Smith not been smart enough to trade tickets with him for the voyage to the Chagres."

"Arvin knows I'm coming after him and he's running for his life. That can't have put him in a good mood. I think he might have killed Dolores just for the thrill of it since death has to be weighing very heavily on his mind."

"Then he'll probably kill again," Marc predicted with obvious disgust.

"Not if I overtake him first," Buck vowed darkly. "He knows I have a score to settle with him, but I'll make a point of telling him I'm avenging Dolores Rojas's murder as well."

Buck's tone was so coldly calculating, Marc couldn't mistake his sincerity and he was convinced Arvin Corbett didn't have long to live. "You sound like you're hunting down a mad dog rather than a man."

"No, I have more respect for a mad dog that I do Arvin and I'd kill him quickly. I haven't decided how I'll do it as yet, but after the grief he's caused me, I'll make the bastard suffer until he begs me to put him out of his misery."

"I wish I could be there."

"Did Dolores mean that much to you?"

Marc shook his head regretfully. "Not really. I cared about what happened to her, sure, but I wasn't in love with her. I just think you and I would make a great team. Hell, we could call ourselves bounty hunters. After Dolores's murder, there's got to be a price on Arvin's head."

"There probably is, but you have a ship to sail and I already have a partner. Now come on, let's get out of here and get something to eat before we get so stinking drunk we can't chew." Buck grabbed Marc's bottle and slammed on the lid before he could argue. He offered his hand to help his friend rise to his feet, and arm in arm they went out the door looking like two old buddies who had nothing more important on their minds that night than having a rip-roaring good time.

When he reached her hotel room, Buck tried to shut the door quietly, but Lyse was sleeping so lightly she was awake in an instant. "What did Marc say?" she called out as she sat up and swept her hair out of her eyes. When she had had to stay in bed, Buck had bought her half a dozen sheer cotton nightgowns and she had on one now. Nearly transparent, it hid little of her lush bosom from his view.

"About what?" Buck asked as he began to undress. Despite his best intentions to stay sober, he had had one brandy too many and swayed slightly as he yanked off his coat.

"About letting us have two cabins, of course."

"Oh, that." Buck continued to pull off his clothes until he had removed them all. Leaving them scattered about the room, he climbed into his side of the bed. "I managed to convince him you'd give him no trouble and we'll sail day after tomorrow."

"I'd give him no trouble?" Lyse asked with an incredulous gasp. "What are you talking about? It was the other way around."

"What difference does it make? We've got the cabins. Marc and I spent most of our time talking about Dolores, not you. It seems he knew her rather well."

"Just how do you mean that?"

Buck gave his pillow a savage punch in a vain attempt to make it conform to the shape of his head. "Don't play dumb, Lyse. You know exactly what I mean."

"Are you saying that a man who absolutely drips with charm has to pay a woman to make love to him?" That thought was so hilariously funny, Lyse had to cover her mouth with her hands to muffle the sound of her laughter so she would not awaken the hotel's other guests. "I'm sorry, I know he's your friend," she apologized when she at last regained her composure. "But don't you realize how ridiculous that makes him look?"

Alarmed that the two of them would never get along, Buck propped himself up on his elbow. "I think you better keep that opinion to yourself. Sailors are seldom in one place long enough to meet respectable women. That Marc spent his free time here with Dolores isn't so odd. He seems to know the same sort of women all up and down the coast."

One whore was bad enough, but dozens of them quite another thing, and that bit of information made Lyse curious. "He's older than you, isn't he?"

"A couple of years, why?"

"Don't you think it's time he married and started a family? Even if he continued to travel he would have the memory of his wife's love to warm his heart while he was away from home."

It wasn't the brandy that brought the blood racing to Buck's head now, but the sheer stupidity of Lyse's remark. "What if the woman he has asked to be his wife doesn't want to be married, Lyse? What sort of advice would you give him then?"

Lyse was far too bright to misinterpret the intent of those two questions. Knowing she had brought them on herself by thoughtlessly suggesting something for Marc she couldn't recommend to Buck, she felt very foolish indeed. "That would be a problem," she admitted breathlessly.

"It certainly would. So being such an understanding woman, what would you advise him to do?" Buck's stare turned increasingly defiant as he dared her to come up with a rational reply.

Lyse licked her lips nervously before she found her voice. "Well, I know he would never come to me for advice, but if he did, I would ask him if the woman had a good reason for not wanting to be married. If she did, then I would tell him to try and be more patient with her."

"And if his patience is at an end? What then?" Buck challenged hoarsely.

Lyse knew she had gotten herself in many a difficult situation, but never one so important to get out of as this. "I would ask him if he loved her with all his heart and soul. If he did, then he would have to be patient because no other woman could ever take her place and it would be very foolish of him to leave her."

He had been careful never to mention the word love and now that Lyse had, Buck didn't know how to react. Both his voice and expression softened as he said, "It's real difficult for a man to keep on loving a woman who doesn't love him in return, Lyse. Did you ever think of that?"

"No, but I suppose that's true. I think women are more loyal. A woman would stay with a man forever on the slim hope he might someday come to love her. I don't think a man would do that."

"You're wrong. There are plenty of men who are just that stupid." Buck leaned across Lyse to turn down the lamp and after plunging the room into darkness he moved away from her. He gave his pillow another hearty thump before stretching out with his back toward her, but he knew it would be several hours before he fell asleep.

Lyse attempted to make herself comfortable too, but as she lay staring up into the darkness, she was certain she had given Buck the wrong answers but she didn't know what else she could have said. It pained her so greatly to think he thought love was stupid, she finally had to speak up. "It's not stupid to love someone, Buck, it can't be. If no one ever fell in love, no one would get married. There would be no children and before long all the people would get old and die. I think the world would be a very sad place without love."

"That's a real sweet way to look at things, Lyse, but you're wrong. People don't have to be in love to make love and have children. The human race isn't in any danger of dying out, not when making love is so damn much fun."

Such a cynical view of love was more than Lyse could bear. "Just get the hell out of my bed, Buck Warren. I don't want you here! Now go on, git!"

Buck was in no mood to sleep by himself now. As Lyse tried to shove him off the side of her bed, he grabbed her wrists and moved across her to keep her pinned beneath him as he silenced her protests with a soul-searing kiss he didn't end until he felt all resistance melt from her body. "You see, making love is far too pleasurable an experience for people to ever give it up. There will never be any shortage of children in the world."

Lyse had never admitted she had been pregnant, if only briefly. She had simply refused to discuss the matter with Robert Ash or Buck until the men had finally stopped asking her about it. Now she wished she had told the truth, for she could not believe Buck would deliberately be so cruel as to taunt her about children when she had so recently lost his.

Since she could not point that out, she revealed something just as important.

"The pleasure is in being with you, Buck. I can't think of any worse torture than having to make love with a stranger. Sailors and whores probably aren't the only ones who sleep with people they have just met and will never see again, but I could never do it. If I didn't slit my own throat first, I'm sure I'd feel so ashamed that I would right after."

Buck was sorry he had turned out the lamp now, but even without the light he knew Lyse's eyes would be brimming with tears. How she could speak of love, and have no interest in marrying him he didn't understand, but he knew despite the gruffness of his questions, he was nowhere near the end of his patience with her. He leaned down to kiss her lips very gently before he spoke. "If you really want me to leave, I'll go."

Nestled in his arms, with his brandy-scented breath warm against her cheek, Lyse couldn't bring herself to repeat that demand. Instead, she wrapped her arms around his neck and with a lingering kiss, convinced him he had to stay.

XX

May 1849

With a deep sigh of regret, Buck ended Lyse's luscious kiss and rolled over on his back. "You mustn't tempt me like that. It's much too soon for us to make love."

Because she couldn't agree, Lyse refused to behave. "Don't you think I'm the one who ought to know if I'm ready or not?" she purred seductively as she drew her nightgown off over her head. Before he could argue, she tossed the cotton garment aside and moved over him, bringing their bare bodies together in perfect alignment. She rolled her hips against his, arousing him so easily she knew he would not be able to refuse her for long.

"It was more than three weeks ago that I got sick. I'm fine now," she murmured softly as she began to nibble playfully at his ears. Her fingertips slid down his neatly trimmed beard to his throat, then came to rest on his shoulders as she ground her hips more insistently against his.

"My God, woman, I'm not made of stone!"

"Really? It sure feels like you are to me," the wily blonde teased as she rubbed against him to bring the tip of his manhood into contact with her body's most sensitive bud of flesh. When that brought the first tremors of rapture's most delicious excitement, she saw no reason to stop her suggestive motions despite his protests.

Buck tried to grab her, to hold her still, or push her away

but each place he touched his hands lingered over the creamy smoothness of her fair skin, instantly betraying his efforts to end the torment she was putting him through. He could still speak, although hoarsely. "Lyse, it's much too soon!"

"Can't be too soon for me," the lithe minx whispered as she raised up slightly before sliding down the length of him with a deeply erotic caress. Leaning forward again, she propped herself up with her hands to let the tips of her breasts brush over his chest where the coarse black hairs tickled her, so she began to giggle. "I feel so good. Don't I feel good to you too?"

Buck could no longer remember why he had thought they shouldn't make love when it now sounded to him like the best idea he had ever heard. A slow smile of surrender played across his lips, but he knew it was too dark for Lyse to see she had already won this latest argument and he seized that advantage because he had no other. "No, I won't do it," he lied.

"Oh yes you will," Lyse leaned down to whisper in his ear. Her left thumb strayed across the scar which marred the hollow of his right shoulder and she shifted her position slightly to kiss him there. She could feel the same quivers of excitement that had heightened her senses coursing through him, making every muscle in his superb body tense. Delighted he was so very weak when it came to resisting her, she continued to spread adoring kisses across his chest then slowly down the smooth, flatness of his stomach. Her tongue traced the trail of dark hair as it narrowed to a thin line at his navel before gradually flaring out again into the dense curls that framed his manhood.

Buck soon realized he had been too clever for his own good as Lyse's hungry kisses began devouring not only his all too willing flesh, but also his mind and soul. She had never been shy with him, but she had suddenly become so uninhibited he was certain he had to be dreaming. It was the brandy that was playing havoc with his senses, his alcohol-clouded brain surmised, making Lyse's playful affection seem like the most relentless seduction he had ever enjoyed. then as the ends of her long hair spilled over his hips in a silken cascade he knew this was no dream, but reality of the most splendid sort.

Her lisp were soft, her mouth warn, her breath hot and when he could stand no more of the incredible pleasure she was giving so generously, he pulled her back into his arms. With an agile move he captured her in a loving embrace, and entered her while he still had the self-control to give rapture as well as take it. Her body's response was immediate, surrounding him with rhythmic vibrations that lured him ever deeper until the joy he could no long contain spilled forth in a blinding rush, leaving him only too glad to admit she had gotten the better of him.

Several minutes passed before he had the strength to make that confession out loud. "You won," he whispered between tender kisses.

"No, we both did." Lyse could not recall ever feeling so content. As usual Buck had promised nothing, not that he loved her, or that he would be patient with her, but as always, when he made love to her nothing else mattered but the stunning beauty of the ecstasy they always shared. It was the lingering warmth of that memory, rather than the uncertainty of their future, that filled her dreams.

The first few days she was on board his ship, Marc Aragon managed to avoid Lyse until the dinner hour. Her behavior then was so reserved he began to wonder if he had only imagined her to be a spitfire. She seemed to have a small wardrobe, but her gowns, though few, were perfection— pastel silks and fine muslins that complemented her fair coloring and slender figure beautifully. She had his mother's grace when she moved and he found himself thinking frequently that she must look very much as Angelique had in her teens.

He had promised Buck he would behave as a gentleman rather than a rake, but he was so intrigued by his sole female passenger that he found it an extremely difficult promise to keep. When he found her on deck one morning with Timothy MacCormac, rather than Buck, he hurried over to join them.

"If this brisk wind holds, we'll make San Francisco in

record time," he promised confidently, certain the weather would be a safe topic for discussion.

Though Lyse found sailing an agreeable way to travel, she was terribly impatient to arrive at their destination. "I hope you're right. Since every day there must be less gold to be found, we haven't a moment to lose."

While Buck had convinced him Lyse was sincere in wanting to become financially independent, he had not revealed enough of her past for Marc to be able to comprehend the reason why. In hopes that she would be more willing to discuss her motives than his friend had been, he attempted to strike up a conversation that would be revealing as well as entertaining.

"When my mother and grandmother fled France at the time of the Revolution, they sought out relatives in Spain. They were both lovely blondes, and chanced to meet and marry into the same family, a man and his son."

"Really?" Lyse asked in dismay. "Didn't that cause something of a scandal when your father married his stepsister?"

Marc had to laugh at that question, because it was an obvious one he had overlooked. "No, he and my mother were married first and left Barcelona for the New World. Then his father and her mother married several months later. That wasn't the point of my story, however."

"Oh, I'm sorry. Did I interrupt you?" Lyse asked contritely, hoping she had not insulted the man again. She had done her best simply to avoid him, and barring that, had said as little as common courtesy allowed.

"No, not at all. What I was about to say was that my mother had hoped to earn her own living, but she married before she had that opportunity. I'm impressed that you are equally ambitious. Mining for gold will be a difficult challenge, but I think you have the determination to succeed."

Lyse was astonished to find that Marc actually seemed sincere. Her glance swept his expression more than once, searching for some telltale sign that his words were no more than empty flattery, but this time she saw only a friendly smile and an earnest gaze. "Thank you. I'm not hoping to make a fortune; just enough to buy a small ranch where I can raise a few fine horses."

Marc frowned slightly as he tried to figure out where Buck fit into her plans. "I thought Buck's family had an enormous ranch with that land grant his mother's family received from the Spanish crown. Isn't he willing to give you a few acres for horses as a wedding present?"

Sorry she had confided in the man when it had immediately brought such an embarrassing question, Lyse straightened her shoulders proudly as she replied. "This is something I want to do on my own, Captain." Then, hoping to divert the conversation away from herself, she hastened to distract him. "Buck refers to his family often, but he never mentioned he had Spanish blood."

"Well, he most certainly does," Marc exclaimed. "He and I are both half Spanish, except in his case it's on his mother's side rather than his father's."

Tim had been enjoying a few minutes alone with Lyse. Though he thought Marc Aragon an agreeable sort, he wished he would go about his duties so he could again command Lyse's undivided attention. "My relatives are all from Scotland," he remarked loudly, hoping he would no longer be ignored.

Marc had forgotten Tim completely, and smiled as he included him in the conversation now. "Have you had the opportunity to visit there, Mr. MacCormac?"

Suddenly realizing how little he had to say on the subject, Tim wished he had thought of a better one. "Well, no, I haven't," he admitted with an embarrassed shrug. "Not yet."

"You must consider it once your fortune is made," Marc advised with only a light inflection of sarcasm deepening his voice. "It's a fascinating country. I think Edinburgh is one of the most beautiful cities in Europe."

"You've been there?" Lyse asked, her blue eyes alight with an appreciative curiosity.

Marc's smile spread into a wide grin as he realized he had finally found a way to impress Alyssa Selby. "There are only a few places in the world that I haven't had the good fortune to see, Miss Selby. Would you like me to tell you a little something about Scotland since that's Mr. MacCormac's interest?"

"Oh yes, would you please?" Lyse encouraged him readily, delighted to talk about any subject other than herself. Scotland would suit her just fine.

Half an hour later when Buck came up on deck he wasn't at all pleased to find Lyse hanging on Marc's every word. His friend was laughing, telling some tale with elaborate gestures and she appeared to be enjoying it immensely while Tim looked only mildly amused. Not understanding why Marc would dare flirt with her, or why she would respond, he started toward them with an aggressive stride.

When Lyse caught sight of Buck she turned away from Marc to wave. Her welcoming smile was so radiantly beautiful, the Texan's angry scowl instantly dissolved into a charming grin. She looked delighted to see him and he didn't want to do anything that would spoil the heady wave of joy that had flowed between them the moment their eyes had met. She had to love him, she had to! It was written all over her wonderfully expressive face. Reminding himself that with Lyse nothing could be reduced to simple terms, the instant he reached her side Buck slipped his arm around her waist and hugged her tightly.

"Marc has been describing Scotland so vividly I swear we could almost smell the heather, couldn't we, Tim?" Lyse gave Buck's waist a squeeze, hoping he would not feel left out.

"If it were not for the scent of the ocean breeze, I'm sure that we could," Tim responded, trying to make the best of the situation. He had lost twenty pounds, and a handsome tan had replaced the pallor his former occupation had given him. He was now as trim and fit as he had been in his teens. He knew he was far better looking than when they had first met, but though Lyse had commented on his newly slim build, he was painfully aware that both Buck and Marc were still far more handsome than he. His only consolation was that he was a damn sight better looking than Robert Ash, but Lyse seemed to enjoy his company no more than that of the physician. She was always considerate and sweet, but Tim knew he would never win her for his wife and that tragedy was almost more than he could bear.

Marc had also seen the lovely smile Lyse gave Buck and fell silent in mid-sentence, certain she wouldn't care what he had to say now. When she turned back to him, he knew better than to try and capture her attention again with Buck standing so close. "Thank you, I'll be happy to talk about Scotland or anywhere else that interests you whenever I have the time. Now I must beg you to excuse me." He gave her a slight bow and left to find his first mate who always listened when he spoke even if a particularly beautiful blonde wouldn't.

Buck raised his hand to Lyse's cheek, brushing back a stray wisp of hair that had escaped her combs. He'd just come from talking with Dr. Ash, who had scolded him crossly for allowing Lyse to spend so much of her time up on deck rather than in their cabin resting as he had insisted she do. Buck hadn't dared admit how Lyse spent her nights when the physician was so concerned about her days. He chuckled to himself as he noted the bloom of health that filled her cheeks. She was so well she nearly glowed and he knew the evenings they spent in amorous adventures were as good for her as they were for him.

"Why have you never told me you have Spanish blood?" Lyse inquired as she reached out to catch Buck's hand in a loving clasp.

"Did Marc tell you that I did?"

"Do you or don't you?" the fetching blonde asked more insistently.

Buck hesitated a moment, then deciding he had nothing to lose by confiding in her, he told the truth. "Yes, I do, but that's not always considered an asset in Texas. Some people have the mistaken notion our loyalties are divided."

Lyse frowned slightly. "That must have been more of a problem when Texas separated from Mexico than during the Mexican War, wasn't it?"

That Lyse had so serious a nature never ceased to amaze Buck. He caught Tim's eye and saw that he was also surprised she had such an analytical mind. "In 1836 I was only fifteen, and while my father refused to let me fight, he supported independence so vigorously no one ever doubted his sincerity despite the fact he had a Spanish wife. Her family considered themselves Texans anyway since they had been among the original families to settle along the Trinity River.

It's just people who don't know us well who question our right to own what we do."

At that thought, an evil chill of foreboding shot down Lyse's spine, making her shiver with dread. "You said Arvin was jealous because you were an officer and he wasn't. It's more than that, though, isn't it? Wasn't he jealous of everything you stood for? The wealth, and power, the pride he couldn't hope to match?"

Buck nodded. "That's one way to put it, but he was from Austin so I doubt he knew anything about my family."

"David would have known and some of the others in your company," Lyse pointed out. "Arvin might have overheard all kinds of revealing comments made about you."

"It's possible, I suppose, and every confidence would have fed his hatred," Buck agreed.

Feeling very left out, Tim asked plaintively, "Who's this Arvin person?"

Buck looked first at Lyse and when she nodded, he broke into a wide grin. "Yeah, maybe it is time I told you about Arvin. That way if I have to be away, you can look after Lyse for me. This afternoon while Lyse is taking a nap I'll tell you and Ash all about him."

"I don't need a nap," Lyse protested immediately.

"Take one anyway," Buck countered forcefully. When she merely shrugged, acknowledging defeat, he leaned down to kiss her lips lightly, hoping he was making some progress with her after all, even if it was almost too slight to measure.

Rather than jeopardize his authority, Marc didn't gamble with his passengers, but he knew that Buck did. He paused at the doorway of the first-class salon to make certain his friend was involved in a game of cards before he made his way to Lyse's cabin.

"Miss Selby," he called softly. "It's Marc. I found a book you might enjoy. I hope it's not too late to give it to you."

He had been so nice to her that day, and because she was still dressed in her blue gown, Lyse did not hesitate to open the door. "A book? How thoughtful of you," she said as she took the slender volume from his hand. Her mother had taught her to read simple nursery rhymes and she had swiftly graduated to the advertisements in the *Telegraph and Texas Register* and then to the text. Books had been a rare commodity in her home, however, and she had read only a few. No one had ever given her one as a present, and she was touched.

"Are you just loaning this to me, or am I to keep it?" she asked shyly.

That request caught Marc by surprise, for he had never expected her to think the book anything other than a passing amusement while she was on board his ship. "Why don't you read it first," he offered graciously, "then if you like it, keep it. It's something I picked up in Scotland, and I hope you'll find it entertaining."

"Thank you, I'm sure that I will." They were still standing at the cabin door because Lyse did not think it would be proper to invite him to come inside.

Reluctant to leave now that he had completed his errand, Marc quickly came up with an excuse to remain with her awhile longer. "I think we'll reach San Francisco in just under three weeks' time. There should be plenty of gold left for you to find; whole mountains of it."

Lyse responded to Marc's engaging grin with only a slight smile. "I don't want you to think me the mercenary type, Captain, but I do need money desperately and prospecting seems like a good way to get it."

"Whatever sum you require, Miss Selby, I would feel honored if you would allow me to make you a gift of it," Marc offered smoothly. "You're far too beautiful to be desperate for anything a man can provide."

His expression was now too serious for Lyse to accuse him of flirting, but she thought his offer absurd nonetheless. "Men always expect something in return for their generosity, Captain. That's why I intend to earn the money on my own."

"You have every right to be cautious, but I would be content if you merely called me a friend." Marc was enormously intrigued by the game they were playing. He wanted Lyse, and he was certain she had to know it, but she remained maddeningly distant. When she did no more than stare at him with a puzzled frown, rather than refuse his offer of friendship in a hostile fashion, he considered the evening a success.

"If you enjoy that book, I'm certain that I have others that will interest you. Good night." He turned away, confident he had left her anxious for more of his company. He would invite her to his cabin the next night so she could select another book or two, and then who could say what might transpire? If only this voyage weren't so damn brief! he swore to himself, but he vowed to make every minute of it count.

Lyse had found Marc's visit unsettling because she could not believe he routinely made gifts of money to women in exchange for nothing but friendship. Glad he was gone, she opened the book he had brought and found it to be a volume of Robert Burns's poetry. Making herself comfortable atop the bunk she and Buck shared, she began to read softly to herself and was soon engrossed in the enchanting verses.

When Buck returned to their cabin and found Lyse reading poetry, he was delighted she had found a new way to pass the time until she told him who had given her the book. "Marc just stopped by to bring it to you?" he asked, forcing himself to hide his displeasure at the audacity of the man's underhanded tactics.

"Yes," Lyse replied. "What's wrong with that? He probably knows you play cards at night and that I'm alone."

Buck sat down beside her as he attempted to put the blame on Marc rather than her. "Yes, I'm sure that he does. I'll speak to him tomorrow and see that he doesn't pay you another call when I'm not here."

"Don't bother," Lyse scolded playfully. "I wouldn't take anything more from him than the loan of a book. You've got no reason to be jealous."

"I am not jealous," Buck insisted through clenched teeth.

"Yes, you are!" Lyse was greatly amused to find him so angry with his friend until she realized he was probably just regarding her as his property again. She had no reason to gloat then. "I've tried to be nice to Marc since he's your friend, but I'm not interested in him and I never will be. There's no need for you to punch him in the nose just 'cause he loaned me a book."

"It's not the book, Lyse. That was just an excuse to come see you." Buck got up and started to remove his clothes. "Let's not argue about it. I'll set him straight in the morning."

"And if I don't want him 'set straight'?"

"I've already said I don't want to argue about this." Buck folded his coat neatly and set it aside before sitting down to remove his boots.

He looked so calm and cool, but Lyse knew he was seething. "You don't own me, Buck. Don't treat me as though you did," she warned. "That's just going to make both of us miserable."

Lyse had moved off the bunk, but she was pacing restlessly rather than getting ready for bed. Buck watched her for a moment, thinking her agitated stride conveyed far more than she realized. He then asked the question he could no longer put off. "Are you ever going to marry me, Lyse? I want a simple yes or no, and if it's yes, I want to know when. You don't have to give me an exact date, just come within a week or two."

Shocked by that demand, Lyse had to force herself to turn and face him. "I want the chance to make some money first, you know that."

"Why?" Buck asked as he rose to his feet, cleverly stepping in front of her so she had no way to avoid him. He had to brace himself slightly to make up for the rolling motion of the ship, but he blocked the way to the door so solidly she had not way to escape the confrontation he was determined to have.

"If you're mad at Marc, you should take it out on him, not on me," the clever blonde pointed out in a futile effort to divert his anger.

"To hell with Marc. I told you I'd take care of him in the morning. Now what's your answer, Lyse? Is it yes or no?"

"Why are you doing this?" Lyse asked with a perplexed frown, her panic growing to near suffocating proportions. "Everything was going so well between us. Why are you trying to start a fight with me?"

"As I recall, you were the one who suggested we fight about getting married on the voyage to California, so I'm just letting you have your way. Why should we put this discussion off any longer? I want an answer. If you don't know me well enough by now to know if you want to be married to me, then you never will."

Lyse could feel the heat of a bright blush as it flooded her cheeks, but she couldn't find any way to put her feelings into words that he would understand. "Please, Buck, don't do this. I want to have some money of my own before I get married. Can't you just accept that? I need to have my own money first."

Disappointed she was being so stubborn, Buck's scowl deepened. "Was that a yes? Is that what you're saying? That you'll marry me just as soon as you've found enough gold dust to make you happy?"

Unable to meet his accusing gaze, Lyse looked down as she nodded. She refused to believe that he would never love her. Someday she knew he would, he just had to because she loved him so much. She could marry him first, and wait for the affection he showed her to deepen into love. She was strong enough to endure living with hope rather than love, she was sure of it. "Yes, I'll marry you."

Convinced that winning a consent from her lips was a tremendous victory, Buck pushed on for another. "Just how much money are we talking about, Lyse? Is it five hundred dollars you want, a thousand, a hundred thousand? I'd like some idea of how long I'm going to have to wait."

"I don't know," Lyse confessed hesitantly. "I've never had enough money to feel secure, so I'm not sure how much I'll need."

When she looked up at him her glance was so full of pain Buck began to feel ashamed of himself, but he wasn't about to quit now when he felt he was actually getting to the heart of her problem. "Secure, Lyse? When a woman marries, her husband provides for her security. Haven't I already shown you how easily I can provide for you?"

"Yes, you're very generous, but—"

"But it's not enough?" he pressured her to admit.

"I must have some money of my own," Lyse insisted again.

Buck sighed in frustration, concerned their argument was

so ridiculous they might spend the entire night going around in circles without ever reaching any satisfactory conclusion. "Just tell me how much you want, Lyse, and when we reach San Francisco, I'll see that amount is deposited in a reputable bank in your name. You don't have to waste your time panning for gold when I'll be happy to give you all the money you need to feel secure."

"You can help me track down Arvin, then we'll head for home. I don't care what you want to raise—horses, mules, buffalo if you like. We've plenty of land and you can do whatever you please. We've got more money than you could spend in one lifetime, so you don't need to worry that you'll ever find yourself poor again."

Despite the obvious sincerity of his promises, the sadness in Lyse's expression didn't lessen as she replied. "I've got to earn the money myself, Buck. It can't be a gift from you. I don't want your family to think I'm no better than some stray puppy who's followed you home. I've got too much pride for that. I'm certain your folks are nice, and your sisters too, but they can't help but think you could have done a lot better than to marry me if I go home with nothing."

The more she talked, the crazier Buck feared Lyse was, but when she mentioned his family, he was certain she had lost her mind. "All my family will ever think is that I'm damned lucky to have married such a fine woman. I can't put up with your fears another minute when they are as groundless as that, Lyse. We're going to do things my way from now on."

"I'm going to talk with Marc right now. He has the authority to marry couples at sea and tomorrow is as good a day as any for us to become man and wife. You name whatever figure you like and I'll write you a note for it that Marc can witness. You'll have your money, and no one need ever know it didn't come from the gold fields. Meanwhile, I'll have a wife and after all the trouble I've had talking you into getting married, I am going to be ecstatically happy!"

Lyse watched in awestruck silence as Buck sat down to yank on his boots. When he grabbed his coat and left the cabin without kissing her good-bye, she sank down on the bunk and tried to think of some way to postpone their wedding that wouldn't cost her all hope of winning his love. Finally an absolutely brilliant idea occurred to her and she dashed from the cabin, eager to put it into action.

When Buck returned to their cabin fifteen minutes later, he found Lyse in bed with the covers pulled up to her chin. Tears were pouring down her cheeks and Robert Ash was seated by her side holding her hand.

"I warned you only this morning that Lyse needed more rest," the physician informed him in a sharply critical tone. "She's complaining of dizziness and nausea and I've forbidden her to leave her bed before we dock in San Francisco."

Buck stared down at Lyse, amazed at the pitiful sight she had made of herself in the few minutes they had been apart. "This doesn't change a damn thing, Lyse. Marc can perform the ceremony in here tomorrow just as easily as he can in his cabin. As for you not leaving that bed, that's fine with me. Since we'll be starting our honeymoon in the morning, I didn't plan to let you out of it anyway."

Lyse would have cringed even if Buck hadn't slammed the door on his way out. Wiping away her tears, she quickly apologized to Dr. Ash. "I'm so sorry; I shouldn't have dragged you into this mess, only Buck is always so concerned over my health it seemed like the best excuse to give."

"You're not sick?" Robert asked in dismay, astonished she had fooled him so completely.

"Oh, I'm sick all right. Sick with disappointment, but that won't kill me. I'm sorry I bothered you. I hope you'll forgive me."

Robert picked up his black leather bag and went to the door. "I really don't know what to say, but if you don't want to marry Buck, then don't."

"You don't understand," Lyse admitted reluctantly. "I do want to marry him, but just not yet."

"I'm afraid this is all too much for me," Robert offered apologetically. "Good night."

Lyse waited until he had left to get up and put on a nightgown, but she didn't feel like sleeping. Instead, she stretched out on the bunk and began to read Robert Burns's pretty poems again, wishing with all her heart she had as much talent with words. Then she might be able to make Buck understand why it was so important for her to make something of herself first, before she became his wife.

XXI

June 1849

"*T*his is the worst mistake you could ever make," Marc predicted harshly.

Buck's dark eyes narrowed to menacing slits as he turned toward his friend. He couldn't help but think that to a great extent that dire opinion was motivated by Marc's selfish desire to see Lyse remain single. They had argued half the night, but regardless of what Marc wanted, as far as Buck was concerned the wedding would take place as planned.

"I will not explain again," he hissed through tightly clenched teeth. "I know what is best for Lyse while clearly she doesn't and neither do you!"

Before Marc could reply, the door to his spacious cabin swung open, bringing their conversation to an abrupt end. Robert Ash had volunteered to provide Lyse with an escort, and Tim had asked to be Buck's best man and stood at his side. That there was no woman on board to serve as Lyse's maid of honor struck all four of them as unfortunate, but of little consequence since it could not be helped.

As Buck turned toward her, Lyse gathered up the skirt of her pink gown to ease her way through the narrow door. She had never looked more ravishingly beautiful, but as she came forward to take her place at his side, she did not look up at him, nor in any way acknowledge his presence. There was no trace of the radiant smile she had given him the previous morning when he had come up on deck and he missed that unabashed show of affection more than he had thought possible.

Lyse had obviously taken care to look her best, as had he, but her mood was so subdued Buck felt a sharp pang of regret that she was not looking forward to their marriage with the same enthusiastic optimism as he. He would not have been surprised if Ash had returned to tell him she had refused to leave her cabin. He had been prepared for that and would have gone to get her himself and carried her over his shoulder if need be to start their wedding on time. That was an eventuality he had readily foreseen, but not this calm acceptance of defeat. It was so unlike her he was puzzled, but not sufficiently so to inquire as to its cause until after the ceremony had been performed.

Trying to make the best of what he saw as a difficult, if not outright disastrous, situation, Marc attempted to smile as he opened the book of services he conducted at sea to the section on marriage, but Lyse's attention was focused firmly on the highly polished toes of his boots rather than his face. He sent a pleading glance to Buck, hoping he would at last come to his senses, but the Texan only glared at him, and with a nod encouraged him to begin.

Buck held Lyse's trembling hand in a determined grip as Marc read the introduction to the exchange of vows, but when a large tear fell on his wrist with a loud plop he could no longer ignore the fact that he was causing the woman he adored untold anguish. She had had so little happiness in her life, he could not bear to think her memories of their wedding day would be forever veiled in a mist of tears.

"Just a minute please, Marc," he requested with a forced calm. Including Tim and Robert Ash in his glance, he looked toward the door. "Would you give us a few minutes alone, please?"

Delighed by that request, Marc opened his mouth to congratulate his friend on finally coming to his senses, but catching sight of Buck's warning stare he thought better of speaking his mind out loud. Herding Tim and the doctor ahead of him, he saw that the bridal couple had the privacy he was certain they needed to iron out their differences.

When Lyse still did not look at him after she had brushed

away another tear, Buck reached out to catch her hand and drew her into his arms. He gave her a comforting hug, then led her to the chair at Marc's desk, sat down, and pulled her down on his lap. Her hair was coiled atop her head in a flattering upswept style, but as always a few tendrils had escaped her combs to brush against her nape, providing a sweetly feminine reminder of her lack of guile. She was wearing his favorite among her gowns, for he thought the pale rose shade enhanced not only her fair beauty but also the innocence of her charm. Her lovely skin held the faint but delectable scent of roses, but her expression was one of such profound sorrow it broke his heart.

"I wanted this to be the happiest day of our lives. Why won't you let it be?" he asked as his lips brushed her pretty curls in an affectionate attempt to draw the truth from her.

For a moment, Lyse didn't know which was worse, being forced to marry Buck, or having him stop the ceremony as soon as it had begun. He had stayed away from their cabin all night and although she had gotten little sleep, she had thought of no new way to impress him with how desperately she needed to become a success. That didn't mean she wouldn't give it another try, however. She was no quitter.

After drying the last of her tears on the back of her hand, she spoke with deliberate care. "You're proud of your family. Marc likes to talk about his folks. Tim told us how his father had helped him out by giving him the money to come to California. But what have I got to brag about, Buck? I don't like having to admit to people that my mother ran off with another man or that I don't think the husband she left was really my father. All I'll ever have to be proud of is myself, but I haven't done anything worthwhile yet, not one thing."

"You saved my life," Buck reminded her. "I'm real proud of you for that, even if you don't consider it much of an accomplishment."

Distressed that she had insulted him unintentionally, Lyse lay her head on his shoulder and snuggled close. "You're the best thing that ever happened to me, Buck. I just want you to be able to say the same thing about me."

That was something he was more than willing to do, but as always, he knew Lyse would find it almost impossible to accept such a compliment as sincere so he did not waste his breath in paying it. "Do you remember the first time I said you were pretty, and you called me a liar and went home?"

"Yes," the tearful blonde admitted shyly. She recalled that day all too well.

"Do you believe me now?"

"Well, the fancy clothes you bought me help, and knowing how to fix my hair."

"Don't quibble. You believe you're a beauty now, don't you? Even if you don't trust your reflection in a mirror, can't you see that truth in the admiring glance of every man you meet?"

Lyse frowned slightly, not understanding where his questions were leading. "Since I'm the only woman around most of the time, I think maybe it's just that they're desperate to see anything female."

For a moment, Buck thought his task was utterly hopeless, but with so much at stake he refused to give up. "You're not only beautiful, but bright as well, far too bright to continue thinking the worst of yourself just because Frank Selby wanted you to be so shy you'd never have the courage to leave home. It's my opinion that counts now, not his. Can't you believe that?"

When Buck put his fingertips beneath her chin to force her gaze to meet his, Lyse finally noticed he had shaved off his beard. That she had not even looked at the man before then embarrassed her deeply. "Why didn't you keep your beard?"

That question was so totally irrelevant, Buck couldn't help but chuckle before he answered. "It's not every day that we get married. I wanted you to think I looked handsome."

Lyse peered at him closely, certain he must be teasing her, but he seemed completely serious. "You always look handsome. Even half-dead, you were the best-looking man I'd ever seen."

"That's only because you hadn't seen all that many men," Buck reminded her with a teasing wink. When her smile grew wide enough for her dimples to show, he couldn't resist the impulse to kiss her and he was delighted when she returned that gesture without hesitation. He loved her so dearly, he didn't want to see her in tears ever again.

"I'm going to make a bargain with you," he began with a sudden burst of ingenuity.

"What sort of bargain?" Lyse asked, and immediately suspicious, she drew away slightly.

"I'm willing to postpone our wedding awhile, let's say for sixty days. By that time, you will have had the opportunity to earn some money prospecting. I don't care whether it's a little or a lot, that will be your chance. At the end of sixty days, you are either going to marry me, and willingly without the slightest hint of tears, or we are going our separate ways. Do you understand me? I'll give you some time to work in the gold fields, but in return, you have to promise either to marry me or to tell me good-bye. I can't wait forever for you to find out what it takes to make you happy when I'm sure we can be happy together."

Lyse took a deep breath, then held it a long moment before she replied. "Is that sixty days from today, or from the day we reach the gold fields?"

That she would at least consider his proposition inspired Buck to be generous. "From the time we reach the gold fields."

"What if I don't agree?" the clever blonde had the presence of mind to ask.

Buck was very good at bluffing at poker, and he hoped he would sound equally convincing now. "Then you'll have to give me your answer today. Either I call Marc back in here and we continue the wedding, or we part company forever. It's as simple as that. I'm not going to get down on my knees and beg you to be my wife, Lyse. That's got to be something you want to do. I won't force you to marry me. You have a choice." He paused a moment, then felt like an idiot for expecting her to say that her fondest hope was to marry him. "Well, make up your mind, what's it to be? Do you want the sixty days, to become Mrs. Warren this morning, or to tell me *adiós*?"

Lyse's initial reaction was one of blood-chilling dread, for she would never willingly tell Buck good-bye. That was no option at all when she loved him so much. The only choice she had was either to marry him now, or after she had had two months to try and strike it rich. Was two months enough time for that? she wondered. She had heard of men who had spent their whole lives searching for gold only to die broke. She didn't want to make that mistake, so perhaps it was a good idea to accept Buck's time limit even though it was a short one.

"What about you?" she asked suddenly. "How long am I going to have to put up with you chasing Arvin?"

Though he had not thought of that, Buck realized she had a good point. "You're right. If you're going to have a time limit, then I should too. I'll give it the same sixty days. If I can't find him by then, I'll leave him to fate to punish."

Lyse held out her hand, ready to shake on their bargain. "All right, we'll each have sixty days. Is it a deal?"

It was an option that allowed them both to keep their pride, and though Buck would have much preferred to marry her then and there, he shook her hand. "It's a deal, Miss Selby. You have your sixty days."

Relieved beyond words, Lyse threw her arms around his neck and covered his face with enthusiastic kisses. "Thank you, thank you. I'll make us both rich, you just wait and see."

Growing bored outside, Marc opened his door a crack and peeked in. Finding Buck and Lyse in an amorous pose, he called to them. "You want to go on with the wedding, I take it?"

"No!" Lyse responded brightly. "We've decided to wait a couple of months, but we'll be sure to invite you."

Thinking he would never understand women, Marc pulled his door closed. "Well gentlemen," he said as he turned to face Tim and Robert Ash, "I hate to disappoint you, but it looks like there won't be a wedding today."

"What a shame," Tim replied, but as he broke into a wide grin, he knew neither the doctor nor the captain was any more disappointed than he.

To Buck's everlasting amazement, he found Lyse responding to their bargain with a newly found sense of calm he never could have anticipated. She had always been a delight in bed, but the playfulness she displayed at such intimate times now lingered to brighten her mood for the remainder of the hours they spent together. The heady undercurrent of tension that had always seemed to be seething within her no longer flared up to show itself in caustic words or belligerent attitudes.

She had told him herself that if a man truly loved a woman with all his heart and soul, he would be patient with her. Desperate for some way to make her his wife willingly, he had tried such an unlikely approach but the success of that ploy still struck him as remarkable in all respects. He had never meant to break her spirit the way a brutal man would tame a lively mare, but that she would respond to a promise of two months of freedom with such lavish gratitude was a constant thrill. Best of all, he was certain that at the end of their bargain, that same gratitude would make her the most devoted of wives. He had simply stopped arguing with her, yet rather than feeling as though he had lost by giving in, he knew he had won something far more important than a mere battle of wills.

He looked forward to each new day, for Lyse filled his hours with her unique brand of charm and as always, she made a sensual paradise of the night. As far as he was concerned, they had already begun their honeymoon and he intended to see it last forever. He couldn't fail to gloat over the fact that Marc's ceaseless attempts to impress her met with no more than an occasional smile. Not only was Lyse unschooled in the appreciation of the fine art of flirting, but also she had no idea how to participate in the teasing banter that barely masked Marc's desire, and that was one thing he had no intention of teaching her.

The three-week voyage up the coast sped by so rapidly, Lyse lost none of her eagerness to reach the gold fields, though Tim and Robert Ash grew increasingly interested in helping Buck track down Arvin Corbett. Other than accepting their promise to look after Lyse in his absence, however, he would allow them no further involvement. Neither could shoot well, nor fight with any skill, and Buck wouldn't take any chances with their lives while at the same time he didn't feel he would be risking his own. Even with a two-month time limitation, he was determined to put Arvin Corbett where he belonged: in his grave.

When the *Angelique* entered San Francisco Bay, Lyse could at last appreciate the accuracy of Marc's description of the place, for it was a veritable forest of masts because there were nearly five hundred abandoned ships laying at anchor. "Will you be able to keep your crew?" she asked him considerately, genuinely concerned, because despite her natural reserve, which had made her rebel at his overly attentive manner, she had come to think of him as a nice man who was truly fond of her.

"Most of them," Marc assured her. Thinking he would be unlikely to ever see the rays of the afternoon sun bless her fair tresses with a lush copper sheen ever again, he sighed regretfully. "I wish I had met you first," he whispered too softly for Buck to overhear. Despite his carefully laid plans, he had never succeeded in luring her to his cabin to peruse his small library, nor had he been able to spend any time alone with her anywhere else. That he had had no such opportunity to enjoy her company frustrated him no end.

Startled, because Marc's behavior had been respectful and friendly after the mutual antagonism of their first meeting, Lyse drew away slightly. Then she realized that the sadness that filled his eyes conveyed a very real emotion. "You must forgive me," she replied in a hushed voice. "I don't know what to say."

"Just tell me that you're sorry too," Marc suggested with only a hint of the rakish grin he was in no mood to flash.

Lyse was wearing her blue dress and as she glanced down at the elegantly ruffled garment, she wondered what Marc would say if he saw her dressed as she had been when she had first met Buck. Practical as always, she gave him a sensible rather than flattering reply. "Since a sea captain like you would never find himself lying unconscious on the Texas plain, I don't think there is any way we could have met first."

"You'll give me no hope at all?" Marc pleaded with a low moan, for he could not believe he would have lost out to Buck had their chances to win her heart been equal.

"What are you two whispering about?" Buck asked sharply. He'd been so fascinated by the view of the harbor, he had been completely unaware of his companions for a moment. Now his attention was focused squarely on Marc and he didn't like what he saw. Though he had not accused him of flirting with Lyse since the morning they had postponed their wedding, he knew damn well the man was far too friendly.

Covering up for an indiscretion she was certain existed only in his mind, Lyse gave Buck an enchanting smile. "We were just talking about the loyalty of the crew and did not want any of the men to overhear us. You can see for yourself there are hundreds of ships stranded here for want of sailors to man them."

Suddenly ashamed that he had given no thought to the problems Marc was likely to face, Buck apologized immediately. "Forgive me for being so thoughtless. I hope you don't have to raise your pay again to keep a full crew."

"So do I," Marc was quick to agree. "A man who can find twenty dollars in gold dust a day isn't likely to go to sea, but the men I have with me now are more fond of adventure than of a life of ease."

"Twenty dollars a day?" Lyse voiced her amazement aloud as she calculated how much she would make in sixty days. Deciding twelve hundred dollars was a tidy sum, her smile grew wide.

"That's nothing compared to what some of the gamblers are winning from the miners day in and day out. If you'll pardon my saying so, there are ladies here in San Francisco who charge a man four hundred dollars for a night's entertainment. So you see, there are plenty of people getting rich a lot faster than the miners."

Though she blushed at the scandalous nature of that revelation, Lyse could scarcely believe a woman could earn four hundred dollars so quickly. "They must be incredibly beautiful," she whispered in awe.

"No, none of them are half as pretty as you," Marc assured her.

Because he knew there was no way Lyse would ever consider that profession, Buck wasn't alarmed that she had found out how well it paid. Slipping his arm around her waist, he drew her close. "You'll have to take Marc's word for that, sweetheart, because you and I aren't going to meet any of those women."

"Nor do I want to!" Lyse exclaimed, then seeing Buck had been teasing her, she laughed with him. "Do you suppose they are worth that much?"

It was Marc's turn to laugh now. "Most of the miners have

never had so much money as they do now, and to them it is. They like living the way rich men do, if only for a few days each month before they have to return to their claims."

Leaning on the rail, Lyse looked out over the city, thinking it must be a wonderfully exciting place. What she saw, however, was a town made up mostly of tents. Nestled among nearly two dozen hills, she knew it had to be teeming with men bent on making their fortunes and she was anxious to join them.

"When can we go ashore?"

"You won't be able to find a hotel room this late in the day, so I think you better plan to stay on board tonight," Marc was quick to advise. "Tomorrow I'll see to it that you get on the first steamer headed up the Sacramento River."

"Does your family own steamers too?" Lyse thought it highly amusing he had not mentioned the Aragons were undoubtedly making a fortune supplying transportation for the miners.

"Yes, of course," Marc readily admitted. "I much prefer sailing ships myself since on a steamer you can only go as far as the coal you can carry will take you. We run a whole fleet of small steamers on the rivers to ferry miners up to the diggings and back, and I'll be happy to book passage for you."

"Thank you." Lyse turned to Buck, still not wanting to leave without seeing more of San Francisco than what she could glimpse from the docks. "Couldn't we go ashore for a walk at least? Maybe find someplace to have supper?"

"I wouldn't risk it," Marc warned. "Last year before gold was discovered, there were about nine hundred people living here and they were as pleasant a group as any you'd find anywhere. Now there are closer to five thousand here and not even ten percent of them are women. It's just too wild a town for a decent woman to think she can go out for a stroll without being molested."

Buck noted Marc's worried frown, but thinking his reasons for keeping Lyse on board were undoubtedly selfish, he ignored him. "Lyse will be safe with me, and since I'd like to see something of San Francisco too, I'll be happy to take her on a brief tour."

"Then I'll send an escort with you," Marc insisted firmly.

"That won't be necessary," Buck declined even more emphatically.

"Oh yes it will." Determined to get the last word on the matter, Marc summoned four of his strongest men and told them they were to see Buck and Miss Selby enjoyed themselves without getting into trouble.

Even knowing trouble dogged their every step, Buck wasn't alarmed and after going to their cabin to strap on his Colt, he considered Lyse in the best of hands. She was wearing her one bonnet, the blue ribboned straw she had gotten at the Rosebud, and as they made their way down the gangplank the streamers flew out behind her like the plumes of an exotic bird. Buck took care to walk with a carefully measured stride so she could keep up, but Lyse still skipped along beside him, her excitement the unbridled joy of a happy child.

As they made their way to Portsmouth Square, they did not pass another woman on the street, but they saw men of every type and description. There were Californios dressed in short jackets and flaring pants elaborately decorated with silver and braid, clearly flaunting their Spanish ancestry. There were prosperous merchants from the East clad in stylish suits and tall hats interspersed with Chinese wearing their traditional silk coats. Their long queues reached nearly to their waists and swung back and forth in rhythm with their steps.

Most numerous of all, however, were the miners. Dressed in red or blue flannel shirts with bright bandannas, denim pants, and clay still clinging to their boots, they appeared to have just stepped away from their claims for an evening in town. Most were bearded, but their eyes shown brightly as they traded stories about who was the latest among them to strike it rich. With pokes containing gold dust tied at their belts, they wore their newfound wealth proudly.

Lyse was enjoying herself so thoroughly she took scant note of the curious glances and loudly voiced compliments directed her way. Wind off the bay sent dust from the unpaved streets swirling up all around her and she wished she had a fan to sweep it away, but that bother struck her as a slight inconvenience. She had never thought she would ever get used to the noise and crowds of a city, let alone like them, but the energy created by gold fever was a tangible force that filled the atmosphere with an excitement she found wonderfully exhilarating rather than distasteful.

When they passed a print shop, Buck drew Lyse to a halt. "I have an idea. Let's go inside a minute." Cocking his hat on the back of his head, he leaned on the counter and introduced himself to the proprietor as a Texas Ranger.

"I've used the last of my 'wanted' posters and I'll need you to print up five hundred more for me by tomorrow morning. I'm sure that will be no problem," he predicted confidently as he slapped two twenty-dollar gold pieces down on the counter.

Because the print shop had not experienced the same tremendous increase in business the saloons and sporting houses had, the owner was only too happy to fill that request. Taken in by Buck's confident manner and noting he wore his Colt strapped to his thigh as all the gunfighters did, he didn't think to ask him for his credentials. "You have a photograph of the man?" he asked instead.

"No, but I can make you a sketch real fast." When the printer handed him a piece of blank paper and a pencil, Buck pursed his lips thoughtfully, and in a matter of minutes drew Arvin Corbett's likeness so well the man would be easily recognized. "That's him, don't you think, darlin'?" he stepped aside to let Lyse judge for herself as though she had actually met the man.

That Buck had come up with a fanciful but plausible tale to get what he wanted didn't surprise Lyse any longer, but she couldn't resist teasing him a bit. "Don't you think his mustache is just a touch more full?" she asked as she indicated the necessary change on his drawing.

Delighted that she would go along with his ruse so playfully, Buck agreed. "Yes, now that you mention it, I do." He added a few strokes, and then wrote down the information to be included on the poster. "He's wanted for the murder of Dolores Rojas. I want the ten thousand dollar reward printed in large letters, along with the name Arvin Corbett. I want any leads on the man's whereabouts to be sent to the office of the Aragon Line here in San Francisco."

"You want him dead or alive?" the printer asked as he made his notes.

"Alive. He's not worth a plug nickle to me dead."

"Sure thing. I'll get started on this now. Ten o'clock early enough for you?"

"Make it nine," Buck insisted with a tip of his hat. Taking Lyse's arm, he escorted her back outside and whispered softly. "Just keep still until we get past the shop then you can laugh all you want."

"Do you really expect someone to turn Arvin in? Where are you going to get the reward money if anyone does?" the curious blonde demanded, completely disregarding his wishes that she be quiet for a moment.

"I doubt any of the miners will take their noses out of their claims long enough to recognize him, but I want Arvin to see the posters and keep running scared. With any luck, he'll run right into my arms. If anyone earns the reward, I'll pay it out of what I've won playing cards."

"I thought you told me there wasn't any such thing as luck."

"I was talking about poker when I said that. Life is different. Look how we met; wasn't that pure luck?"

Lyse gave that question a moment's contemplation before she replied. "Well, I guess it was lucky for you."

"And not for you?" Buck inquired with a skeptically raised brow, encouraging her to admit the truth.

"It's really too soon to tell," Lyse remarked with a saucy toss of her head that sent the long streamers on her bonnet sailing again.

That her mood was so conducive to teasing gave Buck the answer he was seeking. Her smile was delightful, showing off her dimples and he would have swept her into his arms and kissed her soundly had the street not been so crowded. Before he could take another step, he heard someone calling their names and turned to find Tim and Robert Ash hurrying to catch up with them.

Lyse couldn't help but note Buck's scowl, but laced her arm through his as she pleaded. "Don't be too hard on them. They just want to see San Francisco too."

Though Buck didn't argue, he knew Lyse was the main reason they had come into town. The two men were like puppies who followed her everywhere she went. "Well, gentlemen," he greeted them warmly. "Don't feel you have to stay with us. I imagine you two would like to visit any number of places it wouldn't be proper for me to escort a lady."

Lyse understood exactly what sort of establishment he was talking about, but it took a moment for Tim's and Robert's blank stares to be replaced by bright blushes. "Would you like to join us for supper, at least, if we can find a nice place to eat?"

"Yes, we would," they both answered as one.

"Come on then, let's go find one." Lyse smiled at Buck. "The food was good on the *Angelique*, but I'd like something different for a change, wouldn't you?"

"Why no, I find the same thing delectable every day," Buck confided with a glance that swept her spectacular figure with clear longing.

"Stop it!" Lyse hissed between lilting giggles.

Buck's grin revealed all that needed to be said, but as he glanced back over his shoulder, he found not only Tim and Robert and the four sailors close behind, but also a growing crowd of miners who were anxious to discover just where Lyse was bound. Not wanting to lead that sort of parade, he turned into the first restaurant they reached and requested two tables for four as far from the front windows as possible.

Lyse had scarcely been seated before the restaurant was filled to capacity and she was the lone female. Though she had been able to ignore curious onlookers on the street, it was difficult to do so when she was surrounded by them. "It is no wonder a woman can demand four hundred dollars for her favors if the entire city is filled with men who are as starved as these fellows for the mere sight of a feminine figure."

"Don't sell yourself short, sweetheart. Your face is also perfection," Buck was quick to point out.

"Four hundred dollars?" Tim asked incredulously, obviously pained to learn women were so far out of his reach.

Buck couldn't help but laugh. "Ask one of the sailors who came along with us. They'll know where more reasonable priced entertainment can be found."

That he would discuss such a delicate subject in front of Lyse amazed Robert Ash, but he thought better of saying so to the man's face. "I understand canvasback duck is one of San Francisco's specialties. Do you suppose they serve that here?"

Lyse forced herself to look down at her menu to hide the smile she couldn't contain and when Buck reached beneath the table to pat her knee, she gave his hand an affectionate squeeze. She still couldn't imagine how a woman could make love to men for money, but she thought it unlikely either Tim or Robert Ash had ever been with a woman and she hoped they would think the experience worthwhile regardless of the cost.

Before they had had time to place their orders, a widely smiling gentleman in a gray suit and brightly striped vest came rushing over to their table. Nearly as round as he was tall, his hair and neatly trimmed beard were a snowy white, his cheeks were pink, and his eyes were a sparkling blue.

"Forgive me for intruding," he began with a slight bow, addressing his greeting to Lyse. "I am Horatio Slipsager. I own a small theatrical company, and the young woman who starred in most of our productions has eloped with a gambler. I have no hope of ever seeing her again and I'm at my wits' end trying to replace her before we begin our next tour of the mining camps. I wonder, are you by any chance an actress?"

"No, I'm sorry, I'm not," Lyse answered with an emphatic shake of her head.

Undaunted, Slipsager tried again. "Well then, would you like to be?"

Lyse stared up at the man, astonished he had not understood her lack of interest. "No," she told him in a slightly louder tone.

Slipsager sighed dejectedly. "What a pity. If you should change your mind—"

"I won't," Lyse interrupted quickly, hoping to impress him with her sincerity.

"Miss Selby has no more time to speak with you," Buck informed the promoter with an icy stare. "Please don't disturb her any further or you and I will have to take a little walk outside."

"Selby? I've heard that name," Slipsager murmured as he began to back away. "Can't place it, though." He needed no more than a glance in Buck's direction to know he didn't want to risk tangling with him, but he foolishly tarried a minute longer. "Good-bye, my dear. If you should ever wish to see one of our plays, I will be delighted to furnish complimentary tickets." As Buck began to rise from his chair, Slipsager wisely came to the realization he had overstayed his welcome and bolted toward the door.

Though Lyse was curious to know why Slipsager recognized the name Selby, she had thought his offer ridiculous. They had barely begun their meal, however, when Buck suggested she give the man's offer serious consideration. "What? I came here to make whatever I can in the gold fields, not to begin a theatrical career."

"Why couldn't you do both? They must be in each town a couple of days. You could work in the gold fields during the day and star in plays at night."

"You're not serious." Dismissing the idea as absurd, Lyse took another bite of duck. It was as succulent as promised and she preferred to enjoy her meal rather than talk nonsense.

"Believe me, I'm dead serious," Buck exclaimed. "A traveling theatrical company would draw huge crowds. You might easily make more than you could prospecting and I'll bet Arvin would turn up sooner or later right in the front row."

Lyse lay her fork aside and took a long sip of wine before she replied. "You're the one who's after Arvin, not me. Why didn't you ask Mr. Slipsager if he needed another actor?"

"Maybe I will. I was just trying to think of some way for us to spend the next two months together rather than apart, but if it makes no difference to you, I won't bother."

That retort stung Lyse as badly as Buck had intended. she couldn't bear the thought of their being separated, but becoming an actress was so farfetched a prospect she simply couldn't accept it. As she glanced at their two supper companions, however, she realized they were following her argument with Buck so intently she might as well be onstage. She straightened her shoulders proudly, but as she gazed about the restaurant while trying to think of some clever way to put Buck in his place, she found all eyes focused on her. She had been so involved in her own table's conversation, she hadn't felt the eerie sensation of being watched, but she did now in full force and she didn't like it one bit.

"I will never become an actress, never. Do you hear me?"

Buck regarded Lyse closely, his smile a taunting grin as he disagreed, "Sweetheart, I think you're extremely talented. You were born for the stage, but you just don't realize it yet."

Lyse glared at Buck, thinking him absolutely daft. They were going to have a long talk about this, but not while Tim, Robert Ash, and Lord knew who else was looking on, straining to hear their every word. "We'll talk about this later," she informed him coolly.

"No we won't, I have something entirely different planned for tonight."

Buck's sly wink made his intentions clear, but Lyse wasn't about to give in. "We will talk first!"

"Whatever you like, sweetheart. I just want to make you happy."

Lyse knew that was so far from the truth she was tempted to toss the rest of her wine in his face. Forcing herself to get a firm grip on her temper, she smiled at him sweetly, but her rebellious spirit was seething inside. He might dress her as a lady and encourage her to act like one, but if he thought he could turn her into an actress just so he could catch Arvin, he had another think coming!

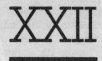

XXII

June 1849

*L*yse sat perched primly on the edge of the bunk in their cabin, slowly rolling up the ribbons on her bonnet so they would not get wrinkled when she packed it away. "I wish you hadn't thrown away my clothes," she blurted out suddenly.

Startled by so unlikely a complaint, Buck looked up from his own packing. "I bought pants and shirts to replace them, which were long overdue, but I did save your old hat and boots. I don't mind your wearing pants while we travel or work in the gold fields, but I don't want you looking like some pitiful orphan."

"Why not? That's all I am," Lyse contradicted stubbornly.

She had been in such high spirits that afternoon, Buck was sorry to find she had slipped back into her old cynicism. Certain he knew the cause of her downcast mood, he sat down by her side and put his arm around her shoulders.

"I won't be offended if you don't want to be an actress. I just thought the chance to stay together might make it worth the bother to you. I think it would be fun myself, but since you obviously don't, we'll say no more about it. I'm not ever going to force you to do something you don't want to do. It's just not worth it to me when it makes you so unhappy."

"Really?" Lyse licked her lips slowly as she studied his expression. She was so relieved to find it sincere, she was prompted to confide in him. "How can I call myself an actress, Buck? I've never even seen a play. I've no idea how to memorize lines, much less speak them so they sound right. I'd be laughed off the stage and I couldn't bear that."

Buck nodded, thinking her worries justified now that she had voiced them. At the same time he silently berated himself for not remembering how limited her experiences were. "What about school? Didn't you put on little plays or memorize poems as a child?"

Grateful she had the elaborately trimmed bonnet in her lap to hide how badly her hands were trembling, Lyse replied truthfully. "I never went to school. My mother taught me how to read and I figured out how to do arithmetic all by myself. Until Marc gave me that book of poetry, the only poems I'd read were the ones they sometimes printed in the *Telegraph and Texas Register*. I never thought to try and learn them by heart." After sighing unhappily, she continued. "You see, there's just no way Mr. Slipsager would want to hire me."

Though turning Lyse into an actress was going to be a damn sight more difficult than he had first thought, Buck knew it wasn't impossible. "Nonsense, the man was absolutely captivated by you, as most men are. We'll have to find out what sort of plays he puts on, though, before we give any more time to worrying about your theatrical career. If he does original melodramas, I'll wager you could learn your part and be polished enough to perform it in a week. If he does Shakespeare's plays, or classical Greek drama, then it would take you much too long to prepare. After all, we only have two months to get rich and find Arvin."

Buck's engaging grin coaxed a shy smile from Lyse and he reached for her bonnet and carefully set it aside. "I don't want you to spend another minute worrying about becoming an actress when there are other far more amusing ways for us to spend the night."

As Lyse leaned forward to kiss him, she wasn't certain what had been decided but as long as she had Buck's word that she wouldn't have to do anything she didn't want to do, she saw no point in pouting. She raised her hand to ruffle the hair at his nape as their lips met, instantly eager for more of his touch and taste. She snuggled against him as he spread adoring kisses down her throat, then across her bare shoulder as he peeled away her gown.

Buck knew the men in the mining camps had to be so eager for entertainment they would think Lyse remarkably talented even if she forgot her lines each and every night. But she had to be led very gently to something new, he reminded himself. She could be neither pulled nor pushed, but she could be lovingly coaxed and he set his mind on that. "You are as pretty as a rose, Lyse, a creamy, white bloom with a long graceful stem."

Lyse drew back a moment, wondering where he had ever gotten such a silly thought. "Just because my clothes still have the scent of rosebuds, doesn't make me one."

Pretending his compliment had drawn the polite response it deserved, Buck continued to nuzzle her throat, nibble her earlobes, and ease her apparel aside to allow him to fondle the enticing fullness of her breasts. She could utter whatever protest she desired, but he had no intention of getting into an argument with her now, not when his whole body ached to possess her.

Buck had come to believe there was something positively magical about Lyse. The lyrical beauty of her face and figure combined with a melancholy soul to create a uniquely fascinating woman. He could not help but long to flood her body with the enduring happiness of his love.

How he wished he could speak of love, but when she did not even think herself pretty, Buck knew she would never believe how desperately he had come to love her. He knew exactly what she would do if he were ever to make such a foolish confession and could picture that scene in his mind clearly. She would scoff as she just had when he compared her to a rose. Or she might question his motives, or worse yet, refuse to listen to him repeat the words of love that overflowed his heart. With the result so uncertain, he dared put none of his emotions into words. Not yet, at least, but he hoped the day would soon come when she would accept his delcaration of undying love as her right. Until then, he would pleasure her in a thousand ways, so his would be the name she whispered in her dreams.

Buck moved slowly, his touch tender, adoring, but Lyse was in a far more passionate mood as she hurriedly undressed him. She returned the warmth of his kisses with lips of fire, searing his very soul with the rapture of her touch. Her every motion seductive, she was so incredibly alluring that her sense of urgency swiftly became his. Once nude, he peeled away the last layer of her lingerie then enfolded her in his arms, seeking to wrap her in an embrace she would never wish to escape

Inspired by the abandon of her desire, he brought them together with an eager thrust, plunging deeply, his strokes rapid until neither could hold back the brilliant flames of ecstasy that burned within them. Engulfed in passion's fire, the thrill of their union even surpassed the perfection they had previously known. They were born to be mates, Buck would stake his life on it. Lyse was the blood in his veins, the beat of his heart, the life force that made his soul immortal. For a few precious seconds he felt not only their bodies, but also their spirits fuse with an overwhelming joy that enveloped him in a cloud of warmth that bore the delightful fragrance of rosebuds.

Lyse held Buck so tightly she felt that warm peace following his climax ripple through his powerful frame bestowing a sensation of perfect calm she shared in full measure. She was most definitely his woman, but she longed for the day Buck would be proud to be her man. A sassy smile played across her lips as she thought how marvelous it was that there were so few women in California. She had always had Buck all to herself, though, and with that blissful thought she drifted off to sleep, still cradled in his arms.

It was Buck's low chuckle that awakened her late the next morning. He was comfortably seated in the cabin's one chair, the heels of his boots propped up on the end of the bunk. He was reading what looked to her like a thick pamphlet.

"What do you find so amusing at this hour?" she called out before giving into a lazy yawn.

"It's nearly noon, sleepyhead, and this is a copy of Slipsager's play. I got up at a reasonable hour, found out where he's staying, and had a chat with him."

Lyse sat up slowly, and keeping the covers pulled close to her bare breasts, she regarded her early rising companion with a suspicious glance. "Just what did you two decide?"

Buck stood up to move the chair closer, then leaned down to give her cheek a light kiss before he made himself comfortable again. "I wouldn't have presumed to decide anything without your being there. I told him you wanted to read the play and he was so thrilled by that show of interest he immediately handed over a copy. Fortunately, it's a romantic comedy and from what I've read so far, it's very good." When Lyse did no more than raise a brow to register her skepticism, Buck hastened to convince her his opinion was correct.

"The heroine is a pretty young woman named Willamae, who sets her cap for her city's most eligible bachelor. While the hero, Tom, is something of a rake, she's willing to overlook it. Willamae is from a modest home, but she takes elaborate care to appear wealthy to catch his eye. The problem is, that while everyone assumes Tom is rich, his recently deceased father made such poor investments that he has inherited so little money he will soon be forced to sell the family estate."

When Buck paused to take a breath, Lyse was certain she knew what was coming. "So he decides to marry Willamae for her money?"

"Exactly. You've got it. Each endeavors to impress the other with wealth which is totally nonexistent. That's where the humor comes in. Tom proposes, Willamae accepts, but she has fallen in love with him and her conscience bothers her so badly she confesses the truth about her finances."

Genuinely intrigued because she could readily identify with Willamae's desire to better her life as well as to marry the man she loved, Lyse leaned forward, anxious to hear how the play ends. "Well, go on, what happens then?"

"That's where you woke up, I don't know how it ends yet."

"Damn it all, Buck! Just read it out loud so we'll both know!"

Delighted he'd been able to pique her interest with a brief summary of the plot, Buck was far too clever for that. He simply swung his chair around alongside of the bunk so Lyse could read Willamae's lines while he read Tom's. "You read everywhere Willamae's name is printed in the margin. That's her part. Now I'll begin here, where Tom says, 'My God, how could you have played such an underhanded trick on me?' Buck paused, and Lyse spoke her lines with so touching a combination of affection and shame he knew he had been correct to think her a born actress.

Absorbed in the lively exchange between Tom and Willamae, Lyse had no idea she was doing anything in the least bit extraordinary. She was near tears herself when Tom stormed off, swearing he never wanted to see Willamae ever again and the emotion that choked her voice as she spoke the heartbroken heroine's lines was quite real. To her immense relief, however, Tom soon realized he could not in good conscience accuse Willamae of being a fortune hunter when he was guilty of the very same crime. After explaining the sorry state of his finances, he repeated his proposal swearing his sole motive was love.

Buck found Tom's part wonderfully easy to play. "So you see, my darling Willamae, I am as guilty of deceit as you. I think anyone who marries for money must pay dearly and neither of us deserves to live such a loveless life."

As Buck recited the proposal Slipsager had written, Lyse thought it much too flowery, but she enjoyed hearing him ask the question anyway and waited patiently until it was her turn to reply. "Oh, Tom," she cooed sweetly, "of course I still want to marry you. You are the only man I have ever loved." When she looked up from the script and found Buck grinning widely, Lyse gave him a savage poke in the ribs. "This is only a play."

"Hey, cut that out! I know that. I'm just trying to make Tom look glad Willamae's agreed to become his wife is all. I know it isn't all that easy to get a woman to say yes and I'm real happy for him."

Lyse gave Buck a withering glance and ignored his chuckles as they read the last couple of pages of dialogue. Slipsager had given the play a completely happy ending, for moments after Willamae had agreed to become his bride Tom received word a generous loan his father had made to a friend many years before had been repaid with interest. Their financial problems solved, the play ends with Tom and Willamae tenderly whispering words of love.

As Buck closed the script, he paid Lyse a sincere compliment. "That was superb. With you playing Willamae, Slipsager is sure to make a fortune. He offered to pay you two hundred dollars each for five performances a week. That's for Friday, Saturday and Sunday nights and matinees on Saturday and Sunday afternoons.

"Last year miners were earning two hundred dollars a day. This year they're lucky to find one ounce, or sixteen dollars worth. It's your choice. You can make a thousand a week playing Willamae, or you can try your luck panning for gold and hope to clear a hundred dollars for six days of back-breaking labor. It doesn't sound like much of a choice to me, but like I said, you're the one who'll have to decide."

Lyse nodded thoughtfully, as though her decision would be an extremely difficult one. Because none of Willamae's speeches were long, and the dialogue seemed genuine, she didn't think the part would be too difficult for her to learn. "Who's playing Tom?"

"Slipsager's son, Harold. I met him, he's a nice enough fellow. Not as good looking as me, but he'll do."

With the mention of appearance, Lyse raised her hands to her hair, embarrassed to realize she must look far from her best. "You'd help me learn my lines, wouldn't you, so I won't make a fool of myself?"

"I'll give you all the help you need," Buck promised generously. "With the exception of donning your costume and acting the part for you, that is."

Buck's teasing didn't bother Lyse at all that morning and she laughed along with him. "If I only have to work on the weekends, I could still look for what gold I could find during the week, couldn't I?"

"Sure. There's always the chance you'll stub your toe on a ten-pound nugget, so I see no reason why you can't put your spare time to good use. In fact, since Slipsager said the sets and costumes weren't quite finished, we can go on ahead and get in some prospecting before he's ready to begin the tour."

What Buck wanted her to do was very plain, and Lyse had to admit the play was one she truly liked. That she might humiliate herself was still a risk, but she thought she would be a great fool to pass up the chance to make money so easily. "Give me some time to bathe and dress, and I'll go back with you to tell Mr. Slipsager I'll give it a try."

Buck wound his fingers in her tangled hair to draw her close for a kiss. "You'll be marvelous. The play's entertaining, and I'm sure the half dozen others in the cast will be as nice as the Slipsagers. I told Horatio that you had only two months to devote to being an actress and he was sure that would be long enough for him to complete the tour he has planned." Buck rose to his feet, and replaced the chair at the small desk built into the end of the bunk.

"I think the next two months are going to be real productive, and we might have some good fun too."

"You were right, Buck, it will be worth the bother of becoming an actress if I can stay with you," Lyse admitted shyly.

"You're as bright as you are beautiful, Lyse. I just hope you don't have so many adoring fans you won't have time for me."

Immediately wary, Lyse waved him away. "Now you're fishing for compliments. Go on, get out of here and let me get dressed."

Buck stole another hasty kiss, then left their cabin with a confident stride. He'd given Slipsager some "wanted" posters, and told him to see that the man who was going to do publicity for the tour put one up beside every advertisement for the play. He hoped the title *A Costly Deceit* would not prove coincidental, however.

As promised, Marc had made reservations for Buck and Lyse on a steamer bound for Sacramento. The sidewheeler, *Antelope*, was the pride of the river fleet and their stateroom was spacious, though Tim and Robert Ash thought themselves fortunate to have narrow bunks rather than having to sleep on deck like many of their fellow travelers.

Sorry to see them go, Marc regarded Lyse with a wistful smile as he gave Buck what he considered some valuable last-minute advice. "Even though I have a Spanish name, since I'm fair haired I haven't encountered any of the prejudice the miners have toward Mexicans, but I want to warn you their hatred is completely unreasonable at times. American citizens are the only ones with any right to gold as far as they're concerned and there are plenty of men who do all they can to run off every foreigner they see. With your dark coloring, you might find yourself a target for those bigots' hatred. Be careful.

"California might belong to the United States now, but it's not a state yet. There's no one to enforce the old Mexican laws, nor make any new ones. Towns spring up wherever there's news of a big strike, but there's nothing even remotely resembling law and order. I wish you were waiting for Slipsager. You'll be far safer when you're traveling with his troupe."

Buck brushed Marc's warning aside as unnecessary. "I've been taking care of myself too long to worry about whether or not some fool mistakes me for a Mexican. What the hell, I spent the first fifteen years of my life as a Mexican citizen when Texas was part of Mexico, so I won't be insulted."

Disappointed he'd not made more of an impression on his friend, Marc asked Lyse to excuse them for a moment and drew him aside. "Two women were brutally murdered during the time it's likely Arvin was in San Francisco. He's proven to be a crafty son of a bitch. If he sees the two of you together he might go after Lyse. If I thought you were just baiting a trap with her, I swear I'd stop this trip right now. If you let anything happen to her—"

Buck interrupted before Marc could complete that threat. Smiling so Lyse would not realize they were exchanging insults, he spoke in a hoarse whisper. "All I asked you to do was to see I'm notified should anyone actually send you any information on Arvin's whereabouts. You have the play's itinerary so the clerks at your office will know where we'll be. You don't need to sit up nights worrying about us. I have no intention of allowing Lyse to come to any harm. I'll not allow Arvin, or any other man to get close to her. I'm all the protection she'll ever need and don't you forget that. Spend your time looking for your own woman rather than worrying about mine." He turned away then and returned to Lyse's side at the rail.

Marc refused to believe he'd never see Lyse again, but he was also smart enough to realize if Buck got his way, he wouldn't. With the *Antelope*'s whistle giving loud notice that it was time for visitors to go ashore, he wanted to wish Lyse one last good-bye.

Marc's expression was so heartbreakingly sincere, nor even someone so unused to displays of emotion as Lyse could misunderstand his sorrow at their parting. He shook hands briefly with Buck, then pulled her into his arms for a kiss that was far too lengthy for a mere friendly farewell. Startled, she didn't respond and was simply relieved when he released her and turned away. When Buck took a step after him, she reached out to grab his arm.

"Let him go. He's just being a flirt like he always is."

"I know, but it's high time he learned to flirt with some-body else!"

Finding Buck's dark scowl highly amusing, Lyse took his hand to pull him back to the rail. "Did it ever occur to you Marc might just be showing an interest in me to see if he could get the better of you?"

"Good Lord, Lyse, where did you ever get such an absurd idea? Marc's done his best to impress you since the hour you two met."

"Well, I can't help but think of what you said about you and David. About how the excitement was in the rivalry between you two, rather than in being with Constance."

Buck looked away for a moment, certain he had told Lyse never to mention Constance's name to him ever again. Deciding he would be wise not to remind her of that, he broke into a mischievous grin. "Come on, let's go to our cabin."

"Couldn't we stay out here for a while? I really don't feel like unpacking yet." Lyse had worn her green muslin dress that day and looked delightfully comfortable and relaxed as she leaned against the rail.

"Who said anything about unpacking," Buck reponded with a sly wink. "I thought maybe you'd be interested in creating some excitement of our own."

"You are a devil, Buck Warren," Lyse teased in a sweet

Southern drawl, but she took his arm and with a charming smile, whispered just how exciting she would like things to be.

Buck patted her hand lightly, assuring her she would not be disappointed. Her love would provide the most welcome of all distractions and he was eager to lose himself in the bliss of her affection for a few hours.

It was not until Lyse lay cuddled beside him in a passion-sated sleep that Buck admitted to himself that Marc's accusation had been uncomfortably close to the truth. He was hoping the publicity for the play combined with the "wanted" posters would lure Arvin out into the open. But he was counting on the man's hatred for him bringing that about, not using Lyse as irresistibly lovely bait. Marc hadn't been able to see that distinction, but he certainly did.

Lazily combing a strand of her hair through his fingers, Buck vowed Arvin would get no closer to Lyse than a seat in the audience. With a sardonic smile, the determined Texan hoped the man enjoyed *A Costly Deceit* because he had no intention of giving Arvin the luxury of a last meal before he sent him to hell for his crimes.

XXIII

July 1849

*L*yse used her sleeve to wipe the perspiration from her brow then replaced her frayed hat over the braid she had coiled atop her head. The day was a hot one, and although she was standing knee deep in the frigid waters of a creek that fed into the south fork of the American River, the chill that enveloped her feet and legs failed miserably in keeping the rest of her body cool.

After a pleasant rip to Sacramento on the *Antelope*, they had continued by boat up the American River to Mormon Island where they had bought horses for the ride into the gold fields. That summer the diggings on the Stanislaus and Toulumne Rivers farther south had yielded such a bonanza miners were heading there in droves. Because the tour of *A Costly Deceit* would take them in that direction, Lyse considered panning in streams already worked by others merely practice for the more profitable prospecting she hoped to do later on.

Her back ached from bending over to fill her pan with the gravel-filled silt from the streambed. Once upright, she had to struggle against the brisk current to keep her balance on the slippery rocks beneath her worn boots. To make matters worse, continuously swirling water in the broad tin pan in order to separate the heavier flakes of gold and precious dust from the worthless sand was exceedingly tedious work. They had heard a miner could wash fifty pans of gravel and sand a day, but she knew she would not even come close to doing that many.

About a dozen yards upstream, just out of sight around a bend, Tim and Robert Ash were at work building a contraption known as a cradle out of a barrel they had cut in half lengthwise. They had nailed a box with an iron bottom pierced with holes across one end to serve as a hopper that would sift the gravel. The other end of the barrel was left open and they had lain narrow wooden bars, called riffles, crosswise to catch the gold-laden sand as the mixture that had been strained through the hopper poured across them. They had put rockers on the bottom of the barrel and a handle on the side so the cradle could be continuously kept in motion.

The two men hoped to learn how to operate the device with a steady rhythm. One would fill the hopper with gravel and pour water over it while the other kept it rocking from side to side. When the water washing through the cradle had left enough sand gathered behind the riffle bars, both novice miners would stop to pan the mixture, hoping their efforts to strain the placer gold from the streambed would provide more of the precious metal than simply panning would in far less time.

Because neither man was used to working with wood, they had taken their cradle apart and rebuilt it several times but were still dissatisfied with the result. Though they had invited Lyse to join them when they got it operating as efficiently as they hoped it soon would, she hadn't wanted to waste a minute waiting for that to happen and had been panning all afternoon on her own while Buck had ridden into Coloma for supplies.

He was back now, comfortably seated beside the stream. His shirt off, he was fanning himself with his hat as he quizzed her on her lines. She knew it was an unusual way for an actress to prepare for opening night, but she welcomed the distraction from the drudgery panning for gold had turned out to be.

"That's the end of the second act, isn't it?" Lyse called loudly to be heard over the bubbling hum of the creek.

"Right. Tom says he'll meet you that afternoon. You exit

to the left, and he to the right. You have a costume change during intermission, but you shouldn't have to rush."

Lyse had been so close in size to Slipsager's last female lead that only slight alterations had been required to make the new costumes originally designed for Genevieve fit her. After her initial reservations, she had enjoyed rehearsing with Buck so much she had actually begun to look forward to the play's first performance, which was now less than a week away.

As she glanced up at the man she adored, she couldn't help but wish he would be the one onstage with her rather than Harold Slipsager. She had run through *A Costly Deceit* with Harold in San Francisco, and though he was helpful and polite, she didn't know how she would say the words "I love you" convincingly to him. She couldn't help but smile as she recalled how delightful it was to have the excuse of the play's rehearsal to say them to Buck.

Chiding herself to pay closer attention to the task at had, Lyse peered closely at the silt remaining in her pan. When she caught a glimpse of a shiny lump shouted excitedly, "Hey Buck, is this a nugget?"

"Could be. Bring it over here where I can get a good look at it."

Lyse handed Buck what at first looked like a worthless lump of clay, but when he turned it over he found the other side had a bright yellow gleam. He bent down to wash it thoroughly in the stream, and then broke into a wide grin. "It's gold all right. A couple of ounces, I'd say. That's a pretty good day's work."

When he stood and lay it in her palm, Lyse admired her find, turning the wedge-shaped droplet this way and that. "Doesn't it look sort of like a heart to you?"

The nugget looked like a simple triangle to him, but Buck saw no harm in agreeing with her more imaginative interpretation of its shape. "That it does. Let's have it made into a locket, that way you'll never forget your first day of panning for gold."

Thinking that a remarkably sweet idea, Lyse returned the nugget to her pocket for safekeeping. She stretched then, but that didn't alleviate the dull ache in her lower back. "Panning for gold is miserable work. Why are people still coming up here if they're finding no more than an ounce a day now? From what we've seen, the prices are so high in the camps it takes that much just to live."

"Besides the nugget, I bet you've got another ounce in dust, Lyse. For a lot of men, that's more money than they've ever made in a week, let alone a single day. Gold fever sets in, they're certain the next day, or the next, they'll be the ones to strike it rich. With hopes that high, they can't leave."

Lyse turned to look up at the Sierra Nevada, the mountain range from which the loose placer gold found in the rivers and streams had been washed. "If you hadn't talked me into starring in a play, I'd head for the mountains and look for the source of the gold. There's got to be tons of it for so much to have ended up down here."

A slow smile played across Buck's lips as he followed her gaze to the rocky mountainside. In 1848, there had been plenty of men who had picked veins of gold out of rocks in the canyons—dry diggings, it was called. "I think all the gold that could have been found easily has already been claimed, Lyse. You'd have a lot of territory to cover, and you might have to tunnel all the way through the mountains to make your effort pay off. That could take a lifetime. I think you're far better off becoming an actress."

They often talked about her new career, but never what adventures they might encounter at the end of their two-month stay in California. It wasn't gold fever that clouded her thinking when she tried to see into the future, however, but the prospect of becoming Mrs. Buck Warren. She hoped by then she would have won a small part of her lover's heart, but she longed to have it all. Her fingertips brushed over the heart-shaped nugget in her pocket and she considered it a good sign a far more valuable heart would soon be hers for the asking.

Horatio Slipsager's brightly painted wagons reached Coloma two days prior to the opening of *A Costly Deceit*. Set on the south fork of the American River, the boom town was the site of John Sutter's sawmill where James W. Marshall's discovery of gold had sparked the nation's rush to the West Coast. The mill was now running around the clock to satisfy the demand for lumber created by California's burgeoning population and frequently visited by novice miners who wanted to see where gold had first been discovered. Mill workers and those new arrivals provided the enterprising shopkeepers who had set up business there with a steady stream of customers. Most of the city's buildings had been hastily constructed of wood, but the jail was built of stone with the added security of iron doors and shutters.

Upon their arrival, the Slipsagers had wasted no time in assuring all their performances over the weekend would be sellouts. At five dollars a seat, they stood to make one thousand dollars each time they filled their tent to capacity. With five performances scheduled, they knew many men would come to the play twice, but they did not care how many times the miners wished to attend as long as they paid for their tickets in gold.

Horatio's nephew, Owen, had distributed posters all over town and because amusements were few, a long line formed the minute tickets went on sale Friday afternoon. In addition to family members and the others who completed his troupe of actors, the flamboyant producer usually traveled with half a dozen men whose job it was to set up the tent and benches, sell tickets and refreshments, maintain order and change sets during performances, and then clean up or prepare to move on afterward. With the lure of the gold fields so strong, however, on this tour Horatio had been able to hire only two boys not yet out of their teens for that work and he feared they would soon desert. To his dismay, when he had mentioned being shorthanded, Buck Warren had graciously offered to do all that he could to help out.

While Horatio and Buck were making sure the sets and props were in order, Ernestine Slipsager and Lyse checked the costumes for the last time. Ernestine was as short in stature as her husband, but delicate rather than robust. She wore her snow white hair in a glorious swirl that hovered atop her head with the ethereal beauty of a cloud gracing a mountaintop. The style fascinated Lyse, but because she had so little experience with elaborate hairdos she had made no attempt to duplicate it.

The tiny woman had thought Lyse perfect for Willamae the first time she had heard her read the part, and as the theatrical company's seamstress, in addition to playing a variety of supporting roles, she took care to see that all the blonde's costumes had a flattering fit. "You will be so lovely, every man in the audience will dream of you for months," she purred as she checked the hem on the last of Lyse's gowns. "It's such a pity my son hasn't gotten over his heartbreak at losing Genevieve to that no-account gambler, or I know he would fall in love with you too. Of course, since you'll be with us two months, that might still happen."

Though Lyse had liked Ernestine immediately, she never took her compliment-filled conversation too seriously. "I'm sorry to hear Harold was so unlucky in love, but since I'm engaged to Buck, I've no intention of encouraging his attentions."

Her mouth filled with pins, Ernestine merely nodded until she was certain the skirt of the royal blue gown fell in an attractive sweep rather than drooping sadly. "Forgive me for saying so, but your Mr. Warren reminds me of that scalawag Genevieve couldn't live without."

Amused by that observation, Lyse laughed as she slipped off the stunning gown. "How can you call Buck names after all he's done for you and your husband? He's the one who did most of the work in setting up the tent, and he refused to even discuss being paid. You ought to be grateful he's so willing to help rather than calling him names."

Because Lyse didn't seem offended, Ernestine didn't apologize. "He's a gambler too, isn't he? Isn't that how he plans to earn his fortune while you appear in our play?"

Lyse turned away as she reached for the pale blue suit that would be the first of the seven costumes she would wear that night. Buck might be posing as a gambler, but it was a lust for revenge rather than wealth that had brought him to the gold fields. That wasn't a secret she would reveal to Ernestine, however. "Buck's a rancher, although he's not opposed to earning pocket money playing cards. He wanted to see

California before he settles down. So did I, so we came from Texas together."

"And fell madly in love on the way?" Ernestine surmised correctly. "That is so romantic a story, it would make a good play."

"Yes it would. Maybe your husband would like to write such a story someday," Lyse agreed, not admitting that she was the only one who had fallen in love.

"I'll suggest it." The tiny woman fluttered about the small tent that served as the dressing room for their actresses. She was already wearing the costume for her brief appearance as Willamae's mother in the first act. The only other woman in the play was Owen's wife, Tessie, who played Willamae's best friend and confidant. "I hope you didn't mind trying on that blue gown again; the velvet is so beautiful I wanted to be certain the fit was absolute perfection."

"I didn't mind, in fact, it was nice to have something to do rather than just being nervous." She was still far from calm, but trying on costumes for the tenth time was a welcome distraction. "Harold told me not to look out at the audience, and that I'd forget they're there. Can that possibly be true?"

"Oh yes, it's true. Just pretend you're really Willamae. Say her lines as you did in the rehearsal this afternoon and you'll be wonderful. It's common for actors to have the jitters on opening night, but with two performances tomorrow and two on Sunday, you won't have time to be nervous after tonight. I can promise you that."

"I hope you're right." Lyse hoped Buck would come backstage to wish her luck. He had been out front filling the whale oil lamps that lined the stage the last time she had seen him. She began to pace with a restless stride, but when Tessie joined them to put on her costume, Lyse had to move to a corner and stay put.

At twenty-four, Tessie was too plump to ever play the female lead in a play, but in rehearsal she had been delightful as Willamae's scatterbrained friend. Lyse thought the lively brunette truly talented. Lyse knew she had been lucky to be hired to portray the same type of flirtacious blonde that her mother had actually been. Fidgeting nervously, she fussed with the charming bonnet she was to wear in the play's first scene.

"If I faint, will you please pretend it's part of the play, Tessie?" Lyse requested with a brittle smile that readily conveyed her fright.

"You'll not faint, honey," Tessie assured her. "Don't fret so. This is Coloma, don't forget, not London or Paris where theatergoers are royalty covered in jewels!" She laughed and reached out to give Lyse a comforting hug. "The last time we played the mining camps, I swear the men cheered and whistled so enthusiastically we all got spoiled and thought ourselves destined for fame. I just know the same thing will happen again on this tour. You'll find you like the applause so much, you'll want to be an actress until you're so old the only parts you can play are ghosts."

Though that ridiculous thought brought a faint smile to her lips, Lyse doubted she would find the stage that enjoyable, but she didn't argue. They could hear the buzz of conversation as the tent began to fill and she went to the mirror to put on the beribboned bonnet. She looked pale despite the rouge on her cheeks and she prayed for the hundredth time that she would not forget her lines.

Buck hadn't expected to find Arvin attending opening night, so he wasn't disappointed when he failed to appear. Caught up in the excitement of the evening, he was certain Lyse would do beautifully because every time he had heard her perform Willamae's part she had been superb. Making his way backstage, he waited until Horatio had announced the play would begin in five minutes to speak with her. Her being dressed so prettily made his compliments flow easily.

"Slipsager seems to have spared no expense to make your play a success. The sets are beautifully designed, your costumes exquisite, all the players well rehearsed. From the remarks I've overheard, many in the audience remember their troupe's last play so fondly, *A Costly Deceit* is sure to be another smash hit."

As Lyse looked up at Buck, the lines she had been repeating endlessly in her mind instantly vanished from her thoughts. She couldn't even remember what the play was about, let alone what part she had in it. "Oh, Buck, this was all a terrible mistake and I'll never live through this!" she wailed.

"Of course you will! Just pretend you're going over your lines with me, sweetheart. The men in the audience will be so taken with your looks, I'll bet half don't hear a word you say." He kissed her then, a lingering expression of his affection that served only to make her all the more confused. He stepped back as he heard Horatio begin his brief welcoming speech.

"I'll be right here in the wings the whole time. Just think how much easier this is than standing in a creek all day and I know you'll do fine." With a teasing chuckle, Buck took Lyse by the shoulders and thrust her out on the stage but when the curtain swung open, she and Tessie were greeted with such enthusiastic applause a full five minutes passed before she could speak her first line.

Never in all her life had Lyse experienced such a heady wave of boisterous acceptance. A bright blush graced her cheeks, rendering her rouge unnecessary. She had yet to do anything, to speak even one line and the audience already loved her! Though Buck and everyone else had repeatedly assured her she would win the miner's hearts, she had never believed them until that instant. As the affection they naturally felt for such an attractive young woman swept over her with a luscious warmth that made her whole body tingle, she turned to look at Buck. He was laughing, delighted he had been right that her popularity wouldn't depend on the quality of her performance and she knew being an actress wasn't going to be nearly as difficult as she had feared.

When at last the audience grew quiet, the line that began the play came readily to Lyse's lips. She was every bit as involved in the drama as the audience and as the story unfolded every word she spoke, each gesture she made conveyed the delicious excitement of a real love affair. Just as when she sang, her speaking voice had a marvelous clarity that carried easily and yet sounded soft to the ear. She was so graceful, each of her motions held the audience in awestruck captivation, and she had an innate sense of timing that no amount of coaching could have instilled. By the end of the first act, the audience was completely enthralled with her talent as well as her looks and Buck couldn't help but stare at the young woman he now felt he had never really known.

There was a remarkable depth to Lyse that continually amazed him. Tonight she seemed far removed from the reed-thin kid who had come to his rescue on the Texas prairie, but he knew in many ways she was that innocent child still. For most of her life she had been a stranger to love, but even standing in the wings he could feel the heat of the glow of the love she inspired in the audience. Now he began to wonder if after the adoration of a tentful of fans, the affection of one man would ever again satisfy her. That the radiance of her smile had nothing to do with him as she came offstage only deepened that concern.

"I'm doing all right, aren't I, Buck?" Lyse asked breathlessly as she rushed into his arms. "I mean, I've really got them fooled into thinking I'm an actress, don't I?"

That question was so absurd, it took several seconds for Buck to come up with a rational reply. "You've made them care about what happens to Willamae and Tom. That's what being an actress is all about. I knew it would come easily to you and I'm so glad that it has."

They were interrupted then as Ernestine took Lyse's arm to urge her to hurry with her costume change. The lithe blonde turned back to blow Buck a kiss and that pleased him enormously, but it didn't squelch the uncomfortable feeling that this sudden theatrical success might make marrying him and living on a ranch in Texas sound very dull by comparison.

As she completed the second act and then the third, Lyse was so dizzied by her unexpected success she felt as though she were dancing through a dream. When at last she and Harold took their bows, the applause was thunderous and the gracious young man insisted she take the final curtain calls alone. Thrilled beyond measure, Lyse blew kisses to the men in the audience, and then with a friendly wave bid them all a good night. When she came offstage for the last time, the applause and whistles continued but she refused to step out again and Horatio went out instead to plead for everyone to leave in an orderly fashion so the play might be performed again the following afternoon.

Buck stood at the main exit to insure Horatio's directions were followed and couldn't help but overhear the praise for Lyse that was on every man's lips. Though he was proud of her for giving what was clearly an outstanding performance in her very first effort as an actress, hearing the miners sing her praises was almost more than he could bear. He had always discouraged other men's interest in her, but here there was no individual he could confront and the jealousy that choked his throat nearly suffocated him.

Horatio always hosted a party for the cast after opening night and that night the troupe had to dash to their hotel through the admiring throng waiting around the tent for another glimpse of Lyse. Once gathered in the Slipsagers' room Ernestine produced tins of delicious cookies and cakes while her husband poured wine until everyone was tipsy. They had all known *A Costly Deceit* was a clever and appealing play, but it had experienced such hearty acceptance that Horatio now thought it might be possible to extend their tour longer than two months and then perform it indefinitely in San Francisco. When he tested the idea on Lyse, she seemed surprised he didn't recall their bargain.

"I agreed to play Willamae for two months. I'm sorry, but that's all the time I have to be an actress."

Buck studied Lyse's slight frown closely, wondering at its cause. Was she sorry she would have to give up her newfound popularity so soon, or merely concerned that her refusal to continue would cause Horatio problems? "I think we made ourselves real clear from the beginning that Lyse would appear for a limited time only. If you want to keep touring with the play, then you'll have to replace her."

A hushed silence fell over the crowded room as all eyes focused on the slender blonde and her tall, dark escort. The fact that he was clearly strong enough to lift Horatio off his feet and toss him out the window should he argue wasn't lost on any of them, so none spoke up to try and change Lyse's mind. When she and Buck left a few minutes later, the conversation swiftly turned to them.

"Now don't become upset," Horatio cooed in a soothing tone. "It's possible Genevieve will tire of her gambler and be back with us soon."

Harold winced at that thought because he missed her so terribly, but he spoke what was on everyone's mind, "Rather than wait for that miracle to happen, I think we'd be wiser to do all we can to make certain Lyse tires of her gambler in less than two months' time."

"My darling," Ernestine murmured softly, "how can you have failed to notice how the applause made her glow with happiness? She's one of us now, and she'll never be able to leave."

Approving nods passed around the room, and when Horatio proposed another toast to their star, the whole troupe downed their wine with a contented sigh. They were all convinced Lyse would soon realize she would never want to leave the theater now that she had had a chance to hear the exhilarating sound of applause echoing within her heart.

XXIV

August 1849

*B*uck closed the door to their room, then leaned back
against it. That Coloma had even one hotel had surprised him, but the Meyer House where Slipsager had
booked rooms was one of nearly a dozen. Though the furnishings were probably no older than the new wooden structure, Lyse seemed not to have noticed that their
accommodations were less than grand. She had taken only a
sip or two of wine, but she appeared so excited he doubted
she would sleep a wink that night. Fortunately, he wasn't in
the mood for sleep either.

"I'm glad you didn't want to stay at the party," he confided. She was still wearing her last costume, the striking
blue velvet gown, and he came forward to help her unfasten
the hooks on the bodice.

Lyse slipped her arms around Buck's waist and relaxed
against him. "I know this is one night I'll always remember.
All those people, mostly miners I guess, I never expected
them to like me as much as they did. I thought they'd ap-
plaud just to be polite, but they really and truly loved the
play, didn't they?"

As she looked up at him, her eyes aglow with the memory
of her success, Buck found it difficult to reply. He wanted to
keep her all to himself. Her fair beauty, her lively charm, her
uniquely appealing personality. He wanted this fascinating
young woman to belong solely to him and he could feel her

slipping away even as she hugged him more tightly. That he could be so selfish made him ashamed, but at the same time he had every intention of holding her to their bargain.

"I meant what I told Slipsager, Lyse. You'll give it two months and that's all," he insisted with unmistakable sincerity.

"Buck? What's wrong?" When she was so deliriously happy, Lyse didn't understand why his mood was so black. His frown frightened her, and she stepped back to confront him with the essence of their bargain that he seemed to have forgotten. "As I recall, we each have two months, and then we're either going to get married or part company. You're acting like my decision has already been made."

Buck's first impulse was to turn on his heel and leave her to spend the night alone, but he emphatically discarded that idea. The hotel room would be far more comfortable than the tent they had been sharing, and he knew leaving would only make things worse between them than they already were. He would have to stay, and he would also have to get a firmer grip on his emotions, or he was certain he would say something he would regret.

Forcing himself to be calm, he shrugged off his coat and tossed it over the room's single chair. He knew he should be happy for her, but that night he had come to the harsh realization that Lyse might soon decide to pursue a theatrical career rather than marry him. That possibility wasn't one he had forseen and now he was desperately sorry he had talked her into doing the play. He had thought it the perfect way for her to earn the money she was so desperate to have while he searched for Arvin. Now that plan struck him as being utterly stupid he didn't now how he could have been so naive.

Lyse adored Buck, and when he remained silent she couldn't let him sulk without at least trying to guess what was wrong. The immensely flattering response she had received that evening encouraged her to be bold. "If you don't want me in the play, I wish you'd just say so. Why you'd be jealous of one miner or a tent full of them I'll never know, but if that's all that's bothering you, then you can get over it right now."

Buck peeled off his shirt and vest before turning back to

face her. She was busy removing the velvet gown and he waited for her to hang it up in the wardrobe. They were fighting as all married couples did, he supposed. The problem was, she might never agree to become his wife if he continued to behave like an arrogant ass and he knew it. That she had understood his jealousy so easily amazed him, but then she did that quite often.

"I'm sorry, Lyse. I want you to be happy, I really do, but I can't bear the thought that I might lose you."

Lyse took a step toward him then hesitated, praying he would finally say that he loved her, but he gave her only a sad, sweet smile. Reluctantly she realized that if she didn't want him to spend the next two months moping around like he had already been jilted, she would have to confess the reason why she would never want to leave him.

"I love you," she murmured softly. "Don't you know I'd never leave you unless you told me to go?"

At first Buck was so stunned by that calmly worded declaration of love, he didn't now how to respond. Dumbstruck, he watched Lyse's expression become as confused as his own and knew he had been an even greater fool than he had feared. He reached out to grab her around the waist then, and swung her clear off her feet before wrapping her in a near suffocating embrace. "I have loved you for such a long time, but I never thought you'd ever fall in love with me. Thank God that you finally have!"

When Buck at last slackened his hold sufficiently for her to draw a breath, Lyse scolded him crossly. "Why didn't you tell me you loved me if you did? How long did you plan to make me wait to hear you say those words?"

In no mood to argue when he wanted so badly to make love, Buck lifted the feisty blonde into his arms, carried her over to the bed, and stretched out beside her. "I didn't think you'd believe me. How many times have I told you how pretty you are only to have you question my taste? No man likes to be laughed at, Lyse, and especially not when he's talking to the woman he loves."

Lyse was crushed by that criticism and huge tears welled up in her eyes. "You're no coward, so you should have taken that risk. You should have told me you loved me the first

instant that you did instead of leaving me with so little hope
that you ever would."

Buck had never dreamed that being cautious about speaking his feelings aloud could hurt her as he now knew it had.
"Couldn't you tell how much I loved you by the way I
looked at you, or how often I touched you, or how eager I
was to make love to you every chance I got? Doesn't everything that I do show you how much I care for you?"

Lyse considered that question a moment, not understanding how she was supposed to be able to recognize love when
she had had so little of it. "You've always been nice to me,
Buck, but I thought that was just because you're a nice person, not because you thought I was anything special."

"Well think again, because you are far more than merely
special, Lyse. You're adorable, and precious, and..."
Buck's flood of compliments was muffled as he mixed them
with lingering kisses. That she loved him as dearly as he
loved her inspired him to an enthusiastic abandon in which
he freely expressed how he felt without fear that she would
scoff at his devotion.

As he kissed away her tears, Lyse thought she might simply die of happiness. Though Buck's affection had always
been a delight, she had longed to hear the words of love he
had never spoken. Surely this would be the most perfect
moment she would ever live. When he paused to look down
at her, his smile wide, there was only one thing she wanted
to say. "I do plan to marry you, Buck. I don't want you
worrying for two months that I might not. There's nothing I
want more than to be your wife."

"Nothing?" Buck inquired skeptically. "If that were true,
we'd already be husband and wife."

Lyse reached up to smooth his hair off his forehead, still
overwhelmed by the fact that so handsome a man truly loved
her. "The day that I found you, I asked my pa, well, Frank,
to buy me some buttons but he said they cost too much.
Now I knew they were just a few pennies, but he wouldn't
part with them. I've never had the money to buy what I
wanted, even if it was something so small as a few extra
buttons. I didn't want to be that poor ever again or have to

depend on a man to take care of me. Was that so wrong of me?"

Buck kissed her tenderly before replying. "No, it wasn't wrong. Now I intend to ask Slipsager to pay you after each performance. I don't want to wait to the end of the tour and find he's gambled away the money you've earned. I'll save all of it for you and when we get home we'll put it in the bank and you'll always know it's there. You can spend it however you like or just leave it to earn interest if that's what you want, but you'll never have to worry about having money ever again. You'll have accounts in all the stores and all the cash you need to run the house. You're never going to be poor again, Lyse, never."

Lyse smiled prettily as she snuggled against him. "If I'd known how agreeable you were going to be, I'd have told you I loved you long before this."

"I wish you had." Buck couldn't help but believe the fault was his that she hadn't. If only he hadn't told her about Constance. That had been the worst mistake he had ever made and in the future he would never give her any reason to doubt his love.

"I don't want you keeping secrets from me ever again, Lyse. I can understand why you wouldn't have shared your thoughts with Frank Selby, but I'm nothing like him. You don't need to keep everything to yourself for fear you'll be laughed at. I'd never do that to you."

Lyse knew overcoming her natural reticence to confide in others might take some doing, but she was willing to give it a try because she wanted so badly to please him. "You must make me the same promise, Buck. You can't keep secrets from me either."

Buck nodded, then broke into a wide grin. "It's a deal. Now that you know that I love you, I've no secrets left." Tightening his embrace, he leaned down to spread sweet kisses along the soft curve of her cheek. His lips tickled her throat with teasing nibbles before he loosened the ribbon ties on her camisole to fondle her breasts. She giggled as she pressed his face close to her heart, the sound of her laughter deep in her throat, and he wasn't in the least bit offended by it.

As they continued to exchange tender caresses and lavish kisses, their passion warm and sweet, neither hurried the other. Lyse's fingertips brushed across Buck's shoulders then slid through the thick curls that covered his broad chest. The soft light from the lamp on the dresser made his deeply tanned skin glow like bronze. Despite the scar on his shoulder, she thought his body perfect. He had not only physical strength but also strength of character, and as she lay in his arms she was perfectly content, thinking herself the most fortunate of women to have found a man she could not only love, but also admire.

His vision blurred by the blissful haze of her affection, Buck stripped away her lingerie so he could savor each lush curve and sensuous dip of her lithe figure. Seductively supple, and filled with a natural grace, her sweetly scented body invited the kisses he was so eager to give. He wanted to touch and taste each delectable swell and cleft until he had completely satisfied the gnawing hunger to possess her that had filled him with jealousy earlier that evening. Enchanted, he continued to tell as well as show her how dearly she was loved.

His need for her intense, Buck feared that the next afternoon the sound of the crowd would again drive him to distraction, and probably every performance she gave. But as long as he knew he was the man she loved, he would hide his pain at sharing her with strangers and try to think only of moments like this when they were truly one and allow nothing to ever come between them.

Glorying in the rapturous sensations he had created within her, Lyse found Buck remarkably easy to please. With skillful hands and soft, sweet lips she lured him to the brink of ecstasy, then welcomed him into her arms for the final surrender to the magic of love's ageless spell. Even after the heat of their passion had cooled to a still-luscious warmth, they remained together, their bodies entwined, too content to part as sleep at last stilled their whispered endearments and loving play.

After five performances that were every bit as well and enthusiastically attended as the first, Slipsager's theatrical troupe moved on to the next settlement that bore the charming name of Hangtown. Lyse had earned one thousand dollars in three days' time but that accomplishment, though satisfying, was not nearly so thrilling as hearing Buck's continued promises of love. She was so deliriously happy, she found it difficult to appear saddened by Tim's and Robert Ash's farewells.

Tim had seen *A Costly Deceit* three times and Robert twice. He had not thought it possible to love Lyse more than he had, but there was something so magical about her performance that Tim was certain he would soon make a complete and utter fool of himself if they did not part company now. Robert agreed they should move down to the Toulumne River while there was still gold left there to find, but both men found it difficult to say good-bye.

Buck shook their hands and wished them luck, but he hadn't forgotten the reason he had come to the gold fields. "Thanks for taking some of the 'wanted' posters. If you should happen to cross paths with Arvin don't challenge him. Just send word to me. You have our schedule."

Tim nodded, not trusting himself to speak. When Lyse stepped forward to give him a good-bye kiss, he managed to repond with a brotherly hug, but it tore his heart in two to think he might never see her again. He watched as she planted another affectionate kiss on Robert's cheek, and then with a jaunty wave turned away before they could see the tears in his eyes.

As the two men mounted their horses and headed toward the trail out of town, Lyse slipped her arm around Buck's waist. "I'll miss those two. Do you think they'll be lucky?"

"I hope so, but if they're not, I know they'll have sense enough to quit. Both could probably make a good living with their professions in San Francisco. That's always been Ash's plan even if Tim never mentioned doing accounting again."

"Think they'll last two months?"

"Quite frankly, no. Would you like to make a bet on how soon they'll quit?"

"I know better than to make a bet with you, Mr. Warren." Lyse raised her hand to shade her eyes as she looked toward the large oak tree at the corner of Main and Coloma streets. Slipsager had told them Hangtown had gotten its name after the citizens had meted out a swift dose of justice to three outlaws who had stolen fifty ounces of gold from a Frenchman. Captured the morning after the theft, the culprits had been tried in the street by a hostile crowd and promptly hanged from the massive oak. Just the sight of the tree sent cold chills up Lyse's spine.

"Cold?"

"No." Lyse brightened immediately as Buck hugged her close. As always, his touch was so soothing her dark thoughts faded instantly.

Despite its forbidding name, the audiences of Hangtown proved to be as appreciative as those in Coloma. The weekend's performances were a repeat of the play's initial success and Lyse became convinced she would have only fond memories of her brief career as an actress.

In the following week, the Slipsagers' troupe traveled on to Jackson. The flourishing city was a favorite stopping point on the Carson Pass Emigrant Trail, and roads met there from Sacramento and Stockton. Located on Jackson Creek, teamsters hauling freight to Mokelumne Hill and miners making their way through the Mother Lode country tarried there to enjoy both a rest and entertainment. Main Street was a narrow winding lane bordered by iron-shuttered stone buildings with overhanging balconies. Just as in Hangtown, there was a stately oak that had been the site of more than one hanging and Lyse again cringed when it came into view.

After checking into their hotel on Thursday, Buck joined the men in raising the tent, while Lyse helped Ernestine and Tessie unpack the costumes. Because that chore took far less time than the men's, the other two women prepared to sell tickets, and Lyse started back for the hotel alone, looking forward to having a leisurely bath after several days on the trail.

As Lyse approached the corner occupied by a blacksmith's shop, she raised her skirt and quickened her pace to escape the noise and soot. She was annoyed at having to wait for several wagons to pass before crossing the street, but that delay allowed her to catch sight of a petite blonde who was entering the shop on the opposite corner. The woman was clad in a gown of lavender satin that seemed far too elegant for the dusty streets of Jackson. She had paused to chat with the man who was holding the door open for her. She raised her hand to pat his sleeve, obviously pausing to flirt before she slipped by him, coming so close her full bosom brushed against his chest.

Though Lyse had only a brief glimpse of her, the woman's gestures were so familiar she was certain she knew exactly who she was. What her mother was doing in Jackson, she couldn't begin to imagine, but suddenly that was the very last place she wanted to be. Rather than cross the street, she hurried down the block to the next corner before making a dash for the hotel.

By the time she reached the room she and Buck would share that night, Lyse was sick with fear for surely her mother would come to the play and that could only lead to the worst of confrontations. All thought of a soothing bath was forgotten as she realized she had not merely one terrible problem, but two. She couldn't bear the thought of facing her mother, and the fact that she would have to tell Buck that she had seen her filled her with such horrible dread she didn't think she could possibly do it. When she had promised never to keep another secret from him, she had not dreamed she would ever learn something so difficult to reveal as this.

Slipsager had said the name Selby was familiar; had he met her mother on a previous tour through Jackson? Lyse walked to the window and stood for a long while watching the traffic in the street below. There were miners on mules, freight wagons, shoppers coming and going on foot, but she did not see the woman in lavender again.

There were few women in the towns that had sprung up along the mining camps and from the way she had dressed, it was plain to Lyse that her mother was no struggling miner's wife. Unless she had married a man who had struck it rich. Knowing her mother as she did, however, she thought it far more likely the woman was a madam than a respectable married woman.

"You can't be sure it was her!" she scolded herself. But even as she said those words she knew that woman had to have been Millicent Selby, or her twin. She had moved just like her, constantly touching the man holding the door and turning sideways with the grace of a dancer to lean close as she moved by him. There might be a few other women in the country who flirted that boldly, but how many were petite blondes? She hadn't seen her profile clearly, but she had seen the glorious crown of blond curls that could have belonged to no other woman.

It was her mother all right. Millicent was in Jackson, beautifully dressed and flirting with every male she met just as she always had. Wearing a dejected frown Lyse turned away from the window and began to pace the length of the room. She didn't want to ever see her mother again. The woman had run off, abandoning her without so much as a farewell note and Lyse felt she owed her nothing, less than nothing. Yet at the same time, she knew Millicent would be thrilled by her success as an actress and want to use it to her own advantage. She would undoubtedly introduce her proudly as her daughter now, but where had that pride been five years ago? Or the long lonely years she had spent with Frank?

By the time Buck returned to their room, Lyse was nearly beside herself with anxiety, but he was far too rushed to notice. He bolted through the door then gathered her up in a fervent embrace and swung her around twice.

Excitement lit a dark fire in his eyes as he explained the cause of his high spirits. "Miles Henderson is downstairs. I'd forgotten that he and his brother are from Austin, but thank goodness Tim didn't. He saw them in Mokelumne Hill and showed them one of the 'wanted' posters. They'd known Arvin back home and while they hadn't talked with him, they were certain they had seen him pass by their diggings last week. Since neither of them liked the man, they didn't call out to him but they're positive it was Arvin. Miles left Max, Tim, and Ash to locate Arvin's camp while he came here to get me."

Mistakenly believing Lyse's strained expression was due

to worry for him. Buck pulled her back into his arms. "This is the break I've been hoping for, Lyse. You'll be fine here with the Slipsagers to look after you and with any luck, I'll be back by the first of the week to move on with you."

Lyse was astonished by his news, but because it provided a reason not to tell him she had seen her mother, she kept that revelation to herself. "Can't I go with you?" she asked instead, as desperate to leave town as he was but for an entirely different reason.

"No," Buck insisted emphatically. "I'll not have you in on this, sweetheart, since it can't possibly be anything I'd want you to see. You're going to stay right here and do the play."

Lyse continued to argue with him as he gathered up his belongings, but Buck was adamant. With the Hendersons to back him up, he was confident he could settle his score with Arvin in a few days and rejoin her with the satisfaction that he had finally accomplished the mission that had brought him to California.

"I don't want to fight with you about this, Lyse. You know I'm right. Now kiss me good-bye and I'll be back before you've had time to notice I'm gone."

"That's impossible," Lyse assured him as she reluctantly accepted his decision to leave her behind. Her lips trembled as her mouth met his, for truly she was worried that he would be in danger. "You'll be careful, won't you? You know Arvin would just as soon shoot you in the back as not."

"That's not something I'm likely to forget," Buck teased and with a sly wink he grabbed up his saddlebags and hurried out the door.

The moment he was gone Lyse sank down on the bed, missing Buck terribly already. She doubted she would be able to eat a bite for supper, but knowing the Slipsagers would expect her to join them, she looked forward to their company as a welcome distraction. She bathed and dressed in her pale blue gown and went downstairs at the time they usually gathered in the evening. She found Harold standing at the foot of the stairs talking with a silver-haired stranger.

"There you are, Alyssa," Harold greeted her warmly. "I was just on my way upstairs to provide you with an escort.

Forgive me for being late." He took her hand and drew her close. "I'd like you to meet Justin Kelly. He and his wife will be joining us for supper."

"How do you do, Mr. Kelly." Lyse thought Justin might only be in his late thirties, although his hair was almost completely gray. A blue satin vest added color to his well-tailored black frock coat and matching trousers. Clearly a prosperous and confident man, his eyes were an unusual smoky gray, their pale color contrasting sharply with his dark lashes and brows. Clean shaven and deeply tanned, he was remarkably handsome and yet he was staring at her with so intense a gaze Lyse withdrew her hand from his with what she hoped he wouldn't regard as unseemly haste.

Though Justin found it impossible to take his eyes from the lovely young woman, he had not meant to appear rude, and knowing that he had, he apologized. "Forgive me, Alyssa, but your resemblance to my wife is astonishing. Ah, here she is now. My love, I want you to meet the star of Horatio's latest play."

Entering from the parlor with Ernestine, Horatio, Tessie, and Owen, Millicent smiled prettily as she reached her husband's side. She was dressed in a low-cut satin gown whose deep ruby color flattered her hair coloring almost as beautifully as its style displayed her voluptuous figure. Her cheeks were filled with a charming pink glow until she turned toward Lyse, then her face turned as white as her husband's neatly pressed shirt.

"Hello, Mama," Lyse greeted her softly, but Millicent was too stunned to reply.

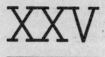

XXV

August 1849

*T*hough Lyse had dreaded a meeting with her mother, the confrontation she had envisioned bore no resemblance to the bitter scene now taking place between Justin and Millicent in the crowded lobby. Justin Kelly was not merely surprised to learn why she and his wife resembled each other so closely, he was outraged to learn Millicent had a grown daughter she had never bothered to mention.

Now in no mood to attend a dinner party, Justin quickly made his apologies to the Slipsagers and before any of their astonished clan had the presence of mind to object, he took a firm grip on both Millicent and Lyse and ushered them out of the hotel. With a purposeful stride he escorted the two striking blondes to his saloon, but rather than parade them through the boisterous Golden Colt, he took them around to the rear entrance where stairs led to the private apartment on the second floor.

That her mother had kept her existence a secret from her husband didn't surprise Lyse and she took a perverse pleasure in watching Millicent take the tongue-lashing she deserved from Justin. Though it was obvious from his comments that he had known she had deserted Frank, he was infuriated that she had not admitted she had abandoned a child as well.

Unable to justify what she had done, Millicent wept, but when her tears had no effect on her husband's anger, she sat down in a dejected heap on the plush velvet settee, her expression one of utter despair.

Justin was far too angry to be moved by Millicent's sorrow and he turned to Lyse instead. "I hope you'll forgive me for providing such a poor welcome to our home, but I had no idea Millicent had ever had a daughter, let alone such a lovely one as you. Even if you have outgrown the need for a stepfather, I hope that you'll allow me to be your friend."

He sounded so sincere that when he held out his arms Lyse had no qualms about stepping into his embrace. She returned his fond hug, then turned away. "Meeting like this has been a shock for us all. Perhaps I should return to the hotel."

"No, stay as long as you wish," Justin insisted. "Even if your mother won't give me any answers, she owes them to you. I'll be downstairs in my office when you're ready to go."

Lyse waited until Justin had left before seeking to satisfy her curiosity. One glance had revealed that the spacious apartment was filled with lovely furnishings. Her mother's gown was as expensive as the one she had seen her wearing that afternoon. Despite her tears, Millicent was still the beautiful woman Lyse had remembered her to be and clearly she was enjoying a pampered life as the wife of a wealthy and passionate man. It was difficult for Lyse to hold her temper as she recalled the miserable years she had spent alone with Frank Selby.

"Is Justin the reason you left Frank?" Lyse asked accusingly.

Millicent wrung her hands, even more distraught than she appeared. "I don't expect you to forgive me for what I did. Lord knows I'll never forgive myself, but I just couldn't take another day on that desolate ranch. Justin had nothing to do with my leaving, though, so you mustn't blame him."

Proud that she had retained her composure, even if her mother had not, Lyse spoke calmly as she sat down in the brocade chair opposite her. "I know Frank Selby isn't my father. Who is?"

Millicent's tear-brightened eyes grew wide as she gasped, "How could you know?"

Lyse shrugged. "I just do."

After a moment's pause, Millicent nodded. "You're so pretty, Lyse. I've missed you terribly, but I always imagined you as the little girl I left behind, not as a young woman." Ashamed of what she was about to admit, the distracted woman twisted the sparkling ruby and diamond ring on her left hand as she spoke.

"My mother died when I was small, so I have no memories of her and my father was a stern man who seldom showed me any affection. He owned a large ranch with lots of hands and the summer I turned sixteen, he hired Charles Larson." Even after nearly twenty years, the joy of that memory brought a smile to Millicent's trembling lips.

"Charlie was handsome, bright, and fun. He could rope and ride even better than our Mexican vaqueros. He wasn't more than twenty and so proud of himself he swaggered rather than walked. I was a good girl, truly I was, but I fell in love with Charlie the first time I saw him and I know he loved me too. Almost immediately my father suspected Charlie was paying me more attention than he should. He gave him his wages and told him if he ever came near me again he'd shoot him dead." Millicent paused then, the fright of that day well remembered. "He meant it too. Neither Charlie nor I doubted that.

"In a few weeks I realized I was in trouble, but Charlie was long gone by then and I knew he hadn't been the marrying kind. I was sick so often my father guessed what was wrong. I don't know why he picked Frank Selby, maybe just to punish me all the more, but when he told me I was getting married I didn't dare refuse. You were born seven months later, but you were so tiny Frank didn't realize you weren't his.

"My father never gave us any help. When he died suddenly we found he had left everything he owned to a brother back East who just sold it all and didn't give us a dime. I was hurt, but Frank was bitterly resentful, as though he'd been promised something and then forgotten. He must have expected that we'd inherit my father's ranch, and when we didn't I got the blame.

"It was just too much for me, baby. It was so hard to put

up with Frank's foul temper, especially when he drank. To make matters worse, I remembered Charlie every time I looked at you. When I got a chance to leave, I took it. I wanted to take you with me. I wasn't the one who insisted you be left behind."

"A man who would make you give up a child couldn't have been much good," Lyse pointed out.

"No, he certainly wasn't, and we weren't together long."

"That's when you met Justin?"

Millicent chose her words carefully, fearful of how her story would sound. "No, that wasn't until later. I'd divorced Frank by then, and I was living in New Orleans with a gambler named Harlan Blake. He was wonderfully generous when he was lucky, but even more abusive than Frank Selby when things weren't going his way. I had put some money aside and planned to leave him as soon as I'd found a place to go. Justin was one of Harlan's friends. He noticed how unhappy I was, and offered to take me away."

Too nervous to remain seated, Millicent rose and began to pace. "Justin was helping me pack when Harlan came home. Naturally they got into a terrible fight. Harlan drew his gun, they fought over it, and he was killed but it could just as easily have been Justin who died. Under the circumstances we didn't think we'd have much chance of convincing the authorities Harlan's death had been an accident, so we didn't report it. We just left town on a ship sailing that night for California. We arrived in San Francisco about the time news of the gold discovery began to spread. Since Justin knew miners would be eager for a place to spend their gold we built The Golden Colt and we've done real well."

Millicent stopped in front of her daughter then, not knowing what to expect from her, and fearing the worst. "I married Justin because I love him dearly. I know I could have told him about you, but I thought it was too late. Too much time had passed, and while I knew leaving you had been the worst mistake of my life, I didn't think I could ever undo it."

When Millicent's eyes again filled with tears, Lyse rose to face her, but her expression was one of calm acceptance rather than disdain. It was clear to her now that her mother had indeed led a very difficult and traumatic life. Millicent had not left her daughter behind because she was ashamed of her. It had been Frank Selby's incessant lies that had given her that impression, and he was the one who deserved her hate, not her mother. Her mother deserved a second chance.

Though Lyse knew her life would have been far different had she left the ranch with Millicent, she couldn't bear to think that had she gone she might never have met Buck. Buck's love had made such a tremendous difference in her life that the pain of her childhood no longer mattered. Lyse was taller than her mother now, and easily enfolded her in a warm embrace.

"There's no point in crying over the past, Mama. I'm glad you're happy with Justin, and when he finds out what a wonderfully happy life I have, he won't still be angry with you."

"You don't hate me?" Millicent whispered anxiously.

"No, of course not," Lyse assured her with a smile.

Eager to believe her daughter, Millicent gave a delighted squeal and reached out to take her hands. "Let's make some supper and then invite Justin to come up and share it. He'll want to hear how you became an actress as much as I do. I'll bet you're very good. Do you remember how we used to read stories and act them out when you were small?"

"Yes, Mama, I remember." Lyse followed her mother into the kitchen, thinking if only Buck were there to join them the evening would be perfect. She hoped he would be back as soon as he had predicted, but she hadn't forgotten for an instant just how dangerous his errand had been.

Friday morning, Arvin saw one of the "wanted" posters as he led his mule over Mokelumne Hill. It wasn't the first one he had seen and just as he did with the others he yanked it off the tree and ripped it to shreds. He knew Buck Warren had to be responsible for putting up the reward for his capture, but he had no intention of allowing anyone to collect. He'd grown a full beard and called himself by a different name each time he reached a new town, so he doubted he would ever be recognized. Still, he was badly disappointed that putting his name on Dolores Rojas's grave in Panama hadn't thrown Buck off his trail.

Despite the darkness of his mood, the colorful poster for *A Costly Deceit* caught Arvin's attention and held it. Thinking it couldn't be a coincidence that the two posters were always displayed together, he read the dates for the play and noting it would be in Jackson that weekend, he quickly made up his mind to go. Buck Warren had to have something to do with the play, and as an added bonus, a theatrical production was sure to have some mighty pretty girls.

It had been too long since he had had a woman, and as Arvin began the trek toward Jackson he couldn't decide what he wanted to do first: slit Buck Warren's throat, or amuse himself with a pretty actress.

Owen was standing at the entrance of the tent that night when Arvin joined those lining up to enter. "Is Buck Warren around?" the bearded man asked as he handed over his ticket.

"I haven't seen him all day," Owen replied. "If it's something important, maybe you'd like to talk with Miss Selby. She's his fiancée."

"No, I won't bother her. I'm a friend from home and I just wanted to say hello." Arvin slipped by Owen, entered the rapidly filling tent, and took one of the few seats left close to the stage. He was pleased to have confirmed his suspicion that Buck did indeed have something to do with the play. That he had a fiancée tickled Arvin enormously. He paid close attention as the players' names were announced and when Alyssa Selby stepped out on stage he couldn't suppress a predatory grin.

Lost in his own devious plans, he heard only a few of the actors' lines. It was going to be almost too easy, he thought with a satisfied smirk. He would take the fetching Miss Selby prisoner, and make Buck plead for her life. It would just be a game though, 'cause he meant to kill them both. After he had had a little fun with the pretty blonde, of course. Maybe he would make Buck watch. That prospect held a great deal of appeal, and Arvin squirmed in his seat, anxious for the play to end so he could get on with killing

Buck Warren, and this time he intended to see the man stayed dead.

Just as Lyse had predicted, Justin couldn't remain angry with his wife when her daughter had forgiven her completely. Lyse spent most of Friday with the charming couple talking about Buck and the adventures they had shared on the way to California. That night she saw they had two of the best seats for the performance, then the three of them joined the Slipsagers for a late supper.

Saturday morning Lyse went shopping with her mother, and although the selection of ladies' apparel carried by the merchants of Jackson was meager, they enjoyed being together immensely. Lyse returned to the hotel before noon to prepare for the matinee, but as she bathed she had the uncomfortable feeling she was being observed. Unable to ignore it, she left the tub to peek through the curtains but found the balcony deserted. Because Buck had caught Colin O'Roarke spying on her, she was certain she wasn't imagining things, for she had felt the very same eerie sensation of being watched that she had experienced in the village along the Chagres River. She didn't mention her suspicions to anyone because she had no proof, but she took the precaution of sliding her knife under her pillow before she went to bed that night.

After the performance of *A Costly Deceit* on Sunday night, Justin and Millicent invited several of their friends to a small party honoring her daughter. Though Lyse was flattered, she was tired after a long day and was relieved when Justin offered to walk her to the hotel.

"I'm sorry your young man wasn't back by tonight. Both your mother and I are anxious to meet him. Do you think we'll approve?"

They had reached the steps of the hotel and Lyse turned to give Justin a light kiss on the cheek. "I'm afraid it's too late for you to offer an opinion. I've already promised to marry Buck, and I wouldn't dream of disappointing him."

Because she had made no secret of her feelings, Justin had a sincere request. "Will you consider having the wedding here? I know it would mean a great deal to your mother, and I'd be honored if you'd let me give you away."

Lyse was touched by his thoughtfulness. "Let me talk it over with Buck before I say yes, but I can't think of any reason why he wouldn't be as delighted as I am by your offer."

Pleased by her response, Justin gave Lyse a loving hug, then after making plans to meet again on Monday, he bid her good night.

Lyse was disappointed to still find no sign of Buck when she reached her room. The prospect of planning a wedding, and a real wedding this time with her mother, Justin, and all her friends from the play pleased her so much she was slow to fall asleep. Then almost as soon as she had closed her eyes, she was awakened by the sound of a boot heel scraping across the wooden floor. Terrified, she reached for her knife and sat up.

"Who's there?" she called out.

Buck lit the lamp on the dresser before he spoke. "I'm sorry. I didn't mean to wake you."

Not about to brandish a weapon now, Lyse replaced her knife beneath the pillow before she slid off the bed and went to him. "How did it go?"

"Arvin's vanished. We couldn't find a trace of him. I'm sure he was in Mokelumne Hill if the Henderson brothers saw him, but he's not there now. We combed every inch of the place, Lyse. The man's gone."

Buck looked so tired and discouraged, Lyse slid her arms around his waist and pulled him close to offer what comfort she could. "I've missed you so much. Let's worry about Arvin tomorrow."

"That's fine with me." Buck tilted her lips up to his and as the enticing warmth of desire melted away his fatigue, he found it difficult to recall why he had been away. He quickly discarded his clothes, turned out the lamp, and followed Lyse over to the bed. "You smell even more delicious than usual, like a dozen rosebuds," he complimented as he pulled her into his arms and buried his face in her silken curls.

"I found some rose-scented soap," Lyse confided softly, knowing there would be time later to tell him she had gone shopping with her mother. Being with Buck was like a glimpse of paradise, and she didn't know how she had managed to survive three nights without him.

Arvin's eyes reflected the moonlight with a feral gleam as he kept a watch on Lyse's room from the roof of the dry goods store across the street. When a man of Buck's unmistakable height was silhouetted against the window, Arvin was able to rejoice that his vigil was finally over. He waited until he was certain his unsuspecting victims had had time to fall asleep, then hurriedly left his hiding place. Staying in the shadows he crossed the street, climbed the tree at the side of the hotel, and swung himself up on the wrought-iron balcony. He crawled soundlessly on his hands and knees to the french doors outside Lyse's room. He had learned to pick locks in his teens, and soon eased the doors open.

He listened for a full minute, and hearing only the soft rhythm of relaxed breathing he rose to his feet and stepped into the room. His eyes were already accustomed to the darkness and he studied the couple cuddled in the bed only a few seconds before discerning on which side Buck lay. He drew his pistol, planning to use the handle as a club, and took the first step toward his prey. He meant to knock Buck out first, and then his sweet little fiancée. After he had them both securely bound and gagged, he would use the water in the pitcher on the washstand to bring them around. That's when the fun would begin. He licked his lips, remembering the salty taste of blood as he moved another step closer to the bed.

Lyse felt rather than heard Arvin's malevolent presence. It was like a bitterly cold wind that filled the room with an evil mist and sent chills of alarm racing up her spine. She sensed Buck was awake too, and with a silent stealth she withdrew the knife from beneath her pillow and slid the weapon into his hand.

For an instant Buck could not decide which was more astonishing, that someone had entered their room, or that Lyse had taken to sleeping with a knife handy, but he didn't stop to consider the question. As he sprang off the bed, he threw his whole weight into a flying tackle that sent Arvin sprawling. The revolver went sailing out of his hand, clattered across the floor, and came to rest well out of his reach.

As Buck wrestled with the intruder, Lyse knelt on the bed, frantically searching the bedclothes until she found the nightgown she had discarded earlier. She yanked it over her head, then slid off the side of the bed nearest the wall and in a few seconds found Arvin's gun. She was confident Buck had to have the upper hand in the fight, but she didn't understand why he didn't just use the knife she had given him and get it over with quickly.

With the wild beat of her heart echoing loudly in her ears, Lyse inched her way along the wall toward the dresser. She meant to light the lamp, for if Buck was getting the worst of it she would waste no time in shooting his assailant, but she had to be certain she didn't wound the man she loved by mistake. The moonlight filtering in the partially open french doors revealed the shadowed fury of the brutal fight and though she recognized Buck's curses, she couldn't place the other man's voice as he uttered a string of filthy insults.

Just as Lyse's fingers touched the base of the lamp, Arvin reached out to grab her ankle and with a desperate yank he pulled her down across his chest. Her scream was drowned out as Horatio began to shout for them to open the door, but she was too busy trying to keep from shooting either herself or Buck to yell that they needed help. A fist struck a glancing blow off her shoulder and she retaliated by striking out with her elbow only to hear Buck groan in pain. Memories of the brawl she had barely escaped on board the *Spanish Dancer* flooded her mind, and shoving and pushing with all her might she broke free of Arvin's grasp. She scrambled to her feet, and this time succeeded in lighting the lamp.

Buck had wanted to be certain who his victim was before he plunged a knife into his heart, but once he saw the terror in Arvin's eyes he didn't hesitate. Blood sprayed up his arm as he drove the blade clear through the hated man's chest and after a convulsive shudder Arvin lay still. Satisfied that the man he had tracked for so long was finally dead, Buck withdrew the knife before rising to his feet.

"Is that Arvin?" Lyse asked in a horrified whisper.

"It was. Are you all right?"

"Yes, I think so." Lyse's eyes swept over Buck's lean frame with an anxious glance, and satisfied that the only blood spilled had been Arvin's, she looked back at the fallen man. "With that beard he looks like most of the miners, doesn't he?"

"Yeah, and I'll bet that's what he was counting on too." Buck reached for a towel to wipe Arvin's blood from the knife and himself, then he yanked on his pants before going to the door. He found most of the Slipsagers gathered in the hall, but before he could explain what had happened, Harold came running up with a silver-haired stranger who forced his way into the room. When the man pulled Lyse into his arms and smoothed her tangled hair away from her face as he began to ask questions, Buck couldn't believe his eyes.

"Christ almighty, Lyse!" he shouted. "I was only gone three days!"

Though Lyse found the warmth of Justin's embrace comforting, she hadn't meant to make Buck jealous and quickly stepped away. She was relieved that when she introduced Justin as her mother's husband, the fury of Buck's hostile expression dissolved into one of wonder.

"You've found your mother?" the Texan asked as he reached out to shake Justin's hand.

Justin glanced toward the rumpled bed, then at Lyse's shapely figure, which was only partially veiled by her sheer nightgown before his eyes came to rest on Buck Warren's bare chest. He had been so impressed by Lyse's spirited sweetness that he had not considered the couple might enjoy the benefits of marriage during their engagement. Taking his newly assumed role as her stepfather seriously, he responded with a sternly voiced demand.

"You'll meet Millicent tomorrow at your wedding. Lyse has already agreed to be married here in Jackson, and I'll not take it kindly if you refuse."

Though dismayed, Buck decided from the firmness of Justin Kelly's jaw that he had the courage to back up that order. Fortunately, there was no need for them to come to blows over it. "I've been trying to marry the woman for months. Tomorrow will be fine as long as there's time for our friends at Mokelumne Hill to get here, but right now we need to take care of Arvin's body before it starts stinking up the place."

Thinking he recognized him, Owen knelt down by the dead man. "This man asked for you at the play Friday night. He said he was an old friend."

A cold wave of terror shot through Buck as he realized why there had been no sign of Arvin in Mokelumne Hill. "My God, you mean the bastard was in Jackson the whole time I was away?"

"Oh, Buck." Lyse rushed to his side, and clung to him as she related her fears that she had been watched. "That's why I had my knife close. I had no idea it was Arvin, I just didn't want to take any chances."

"It was me he wanted, Lyse. He must have been watching you and waiting for me to turn up. He sure didn't waste any time once I got back either."

Without being asked, Owen pulled a blanket off the bed to wrap the body. He took the shoulders, and Harold came forward to lift the feet. "We all heard you fighting with him so clearly it was self-defense. No one can say it was murder."

"This is California," Justin reminded him. "The only law here is the one we make ourselves, and from what Lyse has told us about this fellow, I'd say he deserved exactly what he got. We'll take care of the body. If you'd rather not stay here, there's room at our place."

After Owen paused to wipe up the pool of blood forming beneath the body, only a faint stain remained as evidence of what had transpired there. Buck knew he would never be able to sleep no matter where they went, but he felt sure he would make a much better impression on his future mother-in-law in the morning than he could that night.

"Thank you, but I'd rather stay put." He kept his arm around Lyse as everyone filed out, then hurriedly turned the key in the lock.

"Thank God Arvin turned up tonight," he joked. "It sure would have made a mess of our wedding night if he had waited until tomorrow."

For an instant, Lyse didn't see how Buck could laugh about the tragedy she had witnessed, but then she understood that his deep chuckles provided a healthy release from the tension they had been under.

"It's finally over, isn't it? All these months, the senseless killings, it's over and now we'll be able to go home," she remarked as she returned to bed.

"We could," Buck agreed. Not wanting any of Arvin's dirt or sweat to remain on him, he quickly washed up. Rather than extinguish the lamp, he turned it down low to bathe the room in a seductive glow before tossing his pants aside and joining Lyse.

"I've been giving a lot of thought to going home," he whispered as he drew her into his arms. "We had so much trouble getting to California, it would be a real shame to leave at the end of two months. I think an ambitious man could do well here, and you're such a fine actress I'd hate for you to give up your career so soon."

Lyse snuggled against him, delighted by the fervor of his embrace. "I've no reason to return to Texas when everyone I love is here, so I'll be happy to stay if you want to. As for my career, well, I may have no choice about giving it up."

Buck was too intrigued by Lyse's words not to want to know exactly what she meant. "*A Costly Deceit* has done so well, I'm sure Horatio will beg you to star in his next play. I won't hold you to our bargain if we're going to stay here in California. You can be an actress as long as you please."

Lyse raised her hand to stroke his cheek lightly, and in a halting whisper confessed the reason why she might soon have to retire. "I'm almost certain I'm pregnant again, and this time I don't want anything to go wrong." It was easy now for her to tell him how she had been able to visualize the twins in her imagination. "They were such darling boys. One was named David, but it wasn't until I'd met Marc that I knew we would have named our other son for him."

Buck was touched not only by the sweetness of Lyse's confession, but also by the fact that she finally trusted him enough to make it. "I'll do my best to see we have those twins, if not this time, then the next, or the next." He began to laugh then at the thought of just how many children they were likely to have because they were so passionate a couple.

He raised up on his elbows so he could look down at her and thought as he had the first time he had gazed into her vivid blue eyes that a man could drown in their incredible beauty. "You'll be the best wife any man could hope to have, Lyse, and I'll be proud to father all the children you want to have. I hope we have some little girls who look just like you. Can you imagine them too?"

Lyse licked her lips thoughtfully, surprised at how enthusiastically Buck was taking to the idea of fatherhood, and yet enormously pleased. "Not yet, but like you said, we can always keep trying until we have exactly what we want."

Buck leaned down to kiss her forehead, then her eyelids and the tip of her nose before he reached her lips. "When you first suggested we become partners, I had no idea how close we'd become. I have all that I need to make me happy, Lyse, but what about you? You've quite a bit of money saved. Is it going to be enough to make you content?"

The lovely blonde continued to smile as she lifted her arms to encircle his neck. She felt the wondrous contentment she had always found in Buck's arms, and at last understood that was a treasure worth far more than gold. "I don't know when it happened. I can't name the hour, or even the day, but I've nothing left to prove to myself or anyone else. Having my own money just isn't important to me anymore. I don't need anything but your love to make my life complete."

Buck had always considered winning Lyse's heart a challenge, but as her lips met his he knew from the passion of her lingering kiss that she was truly his. "I love you," he vowed with all the emotion that filled his soul, and her unspoken response was so joyous, he knew the adventure they had been living since the day they had met had only just begun.

NOTE TO READERS

As a native Californian, I have long wanted to write a story about the gold rush. When I began my research for *Hearts of Gold*, I soon discovered the 49er's true adventure lay in surviving the perils of the journey West, rather than in their quest for easy riches in the gold fields.

California was as fascinating a place in 1849 as it is today. The irresistible allure of gold fever increased the population from 20,000 in 1848, to 225,000 by 1852. In 1850 when California became the thirty-first state, only 8 percent of her citizens were women. Is it any wonder then, that the miners followed few of the social conventions of the far more civilized East?

To make this story come alive, I chose characters who are a representative cross section of the immigrants who flooded the newly acquired territory hoping to make their fortunes. Many were young men from fine families who came seeking adventure, but there were also veterans of the Mexican War who weren't ready to resume their former lives, and other men with nothing to recommend them but high hopes that instant wealth would provide the security they had never known. That their personalities and ambitions would clash with the graceful traditions of the Californios was inevitable. A miner could easily make a fortune in 1848, but as competition increased and gold became more difficult to find, prejudice grew rampant. Chinese and Mexican miners suffered almost constant persecution.

Panning for gold was hard work, and miners soon grew starved for entertainment. A dancer who had gained fame in Europe, Lola Montez, was immensely popular, as was her protégée, eight-year-old Lotta Crabtree, who was known as the "darling of the mining camps." Theatrical troupes always had a ready audience and a play like the one I created for Lyse would have been an instant success.

The California gold rush was a time of high drama, and in *Hearts of Gold* it serves as an exciting background for the greatest adventure of all: the quest for a true and lasting love. If you would like to comment on Buck and Lyse's romance, I would be delighted to hear from you. Please write to me in care of Warner Books/Popular Library, 666 Fifth Avenue, New York, New York 10103.